Praise for Lynsay Sands

"It's hard to resist her witty dialogue, off-the-wall scenarios, sexy moments, and tongue-in-cheek sense of humor . . ."

—*Entertainment Weekly*

"You can't help but fall in love with Lynsay Sands!"

—Christina Dodd

"Lush, lively, and romantic—Lynsay Sands hits all the right notes."

—Suzanne Enoch

"A love story as bighearted and exciting as the highlander at its heart."

—*Kirkus Reviews* on *Falling for the Highlander*

"[Sands] definitively answers the question of what is worn—or not worn—under the kilts of her sexy Scot⟨...⟩s."

⟨...⟩s Weekly on ⟨...⟩ Highlander

"Me⟨...⟩ danger-infus⟨...⟩

—*Booklist* on *The Highlander's Promise*

By Lynsay Sands

THE HIGHLANDER'S RETURN
IN HER HIGHLANDER'S BED
HIGHLAND WOLF
HIGHLAND TREASURE
HUNTING FOR A HIGHLANDER
THE WRONG HIGHLANDER
THE HIGHLANDER'S PROMISE
SURRENDER TO THE HIGHLANDER
FALLING FOR THE HIGHLANDER
THE HIGHLANDER TAKES A BRIDE
TO MARRY A SCOTTISH LAIRD
AN ENGLISH BRIDE IN SCOTLAND
THE HUSBAND HUNT
THE HEIRESS • THE COUNTESS
THE HELLION AND THE HIGHLANDER
TAMING THE HIGHLAND BRIDE
DEVIL OF THE HIGHLANDS

WHAT SHE WANTS
LOVE IS BLIND • MY FAVORITE THINGS
A LADY IN DISGUISE
BLISS • LADY PIRATE
ALWAYS • SWEET REVENGE
THE SWITCH • THE KEY
THE DEED

THE LOVING DAYLIGHTS

LYNSAY SANDS

The Highlander's Return

AVON

An Imprint of HarperCollinsPublishers

THE HIGHLANDER'S RETURN. Copyright © 2024 by Lynsay Sands. All rights reserved. Printed in the United States of America. No part of this book may be used or reproduced in any manner whatsoever without written permission except in the case of brief quotations embodied in critical articles and reviews. For information, address HarperCollins Publishers, 195 Broadway, New York, NY 10007.

First Avon Books mass market printing: September 2024
First Avon Books hardcover printing: September 2024

Print Edition ISBN: 978-0-06-313535-2
Digital Edition ISBN: 978-0-06-313536-9

Cover design by Amy Halperin
Cover art by Tony Mauro
Cover images © iStock/Getty Images; © Dreamstime.com

Avon, Avon & logo, and Avon Books & logo are registered trademarks of HarperCollins Publishers in the United States of America and other countries.

HarperCollins is a registered trademark of HarperCollins Publishers in the United States of America and other countries.

FIRST EDITION

24 25 26 27 28 BVGM 10 9 8 7 6 5 4 3 2

The Highlander's Return

Chapter 1

"Is THERE ANYWHERE PRIVATE HERE AT Gunn?"

Graeme paused in reaching for the keep doors and turned to Payton MacKay with surprise. "Private?"

"Aye. Somewhere I can talk to me sister alone to give her the news," he explained and then added, "'Twill be embarrassing for Annella later does she faint or begin in keenin' over the loss in front o' everyone as she's like to do when I tell her. So 'tis best to do it away from all."

"Ah." Graeme nodded with understanding, but his gaze moved to the two men behind MacKay. Symon and Teague. He wasn't surprised to see his friends showing the same discomfort he was feeling at the thought of a weeping woman. The two warriors had been with him for years, the three of them hiring themselves out to anyone with a need and the coin to pay them. They'd battled their way across the better part of Scotland, as well as more far-flung and exotic places. That being the case, none of them were used to dealing with members of the opposite gender. At least not ladies with their delicate sensibilities. They were more used to camp followers and tavern wenches who'd as soon scratch out their own eyes as let tears leak from them. Tough women who had fought to survive and would continue that fight all the days of their lives. Women for whom weeping and wailing would do little to make their lives better, so didn't bother with it as ladies were apparently wont to do.

At least that's what Payton claimed ladies were like. The man had spent a good deal of the past six months regaling their traveling party with how sweet and sensitive his sisters, Kenna and Annella, were, and had made it obvious he worried over how Annella would take the news that she was a widow. He seemed to think it would shatter her delicate sensibilities.

After sharing a grimace with Symon and Teague, Graeme shifted his gaze back to Payton. "There are gardens behind the keep. The vegetable and fruit gardens closer to the kitchens are often crowded, but there is a floral garden beyond that should suit your purpose."

"Good, good," Payton said, but it seemed obvious he wasn't eager to attend to the task ahead of him. Graeme understood that. He himself wasn't eager to impart the news to his parents. His father would no doubt be fine and take it like a man, but his mother . . .

Graeme didn't even want to consider her reaction. William had been her favorite son, her little angel. She would no doubt be fainting and keening right alongside Annella for the next three days.

Shaking his head at the thought, Graeme finally

opened the doors to the keep and led Payton and the other men inside.

"Damn me, Raynard! Ye're making me head ache with yer bellowing. Do you no' stop it, I swear I'll knock ye silly!"

Graeme's footsteps slowed, his gaze searching the great hall for the source of those words. It was a woman's voice, but her accent was an odd combination of Scots and English. Rather like Payton, whose mother was English and father was Scottish, so that his speech was not wholly one or the other, but—

His thoughts died abruptly as his gaze found the gathering of men crowded around the only trestle table presently set up. As a couple of the men shifted, he caught sight of a woman. It was only the back of her that he briefly glimpsed before the men moved again, hiding her from sight. Graeme was left with an impression of a short, shapely female in a dark gown, with long blonde hair cascading down her back. But that image didn't at all match the words he'd just heard, he decided.

"Stop pokin' me with that damned needle, and I'll stop bellowin'!" a deep voice roared back.

"It'd serve you right if I did stop and let you bleed to death, ye big oaf. I've told ye and told ye that you drink too much and need to cut back ere ye kill yourself with one o' your drunken falls. Yet here ye are! On the table again, me having to sew ye up after ye passed out and fell on your own damned knife."

"The hell I did!" The man sounded outraged at the suggestion. "Somebody must ha'e stabbed me, I tell ye!"

A sharp snort of disbelief was followed by the demand, "Where's the knife?"

Curious, Graeme started forward again, toward where the men were gathered. He was vaguely aware that Payton and the others were following him, but his attention was on the blade that was suddenly held aloft by one of the men at the back of the group. It was passed overhead from man to man until it reached the woman who had asked for it. He knew it was her hand that was the last to take it because the men had shifted once more, giving him a clear view of the petite blonde.

His gaze slid over the blade she now held aloft. It was bloodstained with a crushed and equally bloodied apple at its base, he noted, as she held it up for the complaining man to see.

"'Tis your own damned knife, Raynard. Your apple's still on it." The woman's voice was filled with disgust.

"Nay, I—"

"There were three witnesses to your fall," the woman continued impatiently. "Sadly, they were behind ye and did no' ken about your falling on your knife so left ye to sleep off the drink in the path. It was no' until sunrise someone noticed the blood pooling around ye and brought ye in for sewing. Now quit your bellowin' and let me get on with this ere ye *do* bleed to death."

It appeared Raynard did not take direction well. The moment the lady bent to again set to work, he immediately resumed struggling and hollering and making a hell of a racket.

"Should I knock 'im out, Lady Annella?" one of the men helping to hold down the furious Raynard roared to be heard over the noise as he and the others struggled to hold the man still for her to sew up.

Lady Annella shook her head and, in a brief silence as Raynard stopped his bellowing to suck in air, said, "Cook's bringing me something to make him sleep."

"I dinna want to sleep!" Raynard bellowed at once.

"I dinna care!" Lady Annella roared right back, and Graeme had to bite his lip to keep a snort of laughter from slipping out. But his urge to laugh faded quickly as he noted how much trouble the half a dozen men were having holding down Raynard.

Graeme was growing concerned the man might actually break free and strike out at Lady Annella when the kitchen door swung open. Turning his gaze that way, he watched a short, round, gray-haired woman come rushing out with a pot in hand.

"Cook," Graeme murmured under his breath with affection.

"What?" Payton MacKay sounded distracted even as he asked the question.

Graeme's expression changed as he glanced to the man beside him and he arched one eyebrow. "Did I hear one o' the men call that woman Lady Annella?"

"Aye." Payton frowned slightly as he admitted it.

It was Symon, his voice amused, who then asked, "No' yer sister and Graeme's sister by marriage, *Lady Annella Gunn*?"

"Aye," Payton growled, looking a little annoyed now.

"The same lady sister ye've spent the last six

months telling us was sweet, kind and delicate?" Teague asked pointedly.

Payton opened his mouth to answer, but then paused and simply stood there, eyes narrowing as he watched his sister.

Made curious, Graeme turned back to see that Cook had pushed her way through the men surrounding the trestle table to reach the blonde and was holding out the pot.

Graeme would have assumed it held some sort of medicinal to put the man to sleep, except that the pot was handed over at an angle that showed it was empty. He realized the pot itself was what Cook had been bringing to put the man to sleep when Annella turned back to the still complaining Raynard and slammed it over his head. Even as the belligerent man went unconscious and blessedly silent, the lady handed the empty pot back to Cook with a murmured, "Thank ye, Millie," then bent back to sewing up her patient.

Graeme spun on his heel then and hurried past Symon and Teague, headed back the way they'd come. As quickly as he moved, he barely made it out of the keep before the laughter burst from his lips.

ANNELLA SET THE LAST STITCH, AND THEN quickly applied salve before straightening. Pain immediately shot through her lower back, her body's protest at being bent so long. It wasn't unexpected and Annella merely rubbed her back absently as she murmured an order that had several men moving to raise the unconscious Raynard to a sitting position. Once they had him seated upright with his arms held up and out of the way, she stepped forward to begin wrapping clean linen around his upper chest and back to cover the wound. Hers wasn't the only sigh of relief when the task was finally done and Raynard was laid back on the table.

They all then stood and stared at the man with dissatisfaction for a moment. He couldn't be left there, of course. Raynard would definitely be in the way when people began to wake and wanted to break their fast.

"Should we take him to the barracks?" Angus finally asked.

Annella gave up rubbing her back and scowled down at the unconscious man, but nodded. "Aye. Take him to the barracks. But have someone stay with him. He's not to get out of bed until I say so."

When Angus nodded that he understood, she grunted and turned away to begin gathering her tools and medicinals.

"I can do that, m'lady."

Annella glanced around with surprise to see her maid, Florie, slipping past the men now carrying Raynard away. The moment she reached Annella's side, the petite brunette began snatching the various items she'd already gathered out of her hands. Annella was so surprised to see her that she let her.

"What are you doing up?" she asked as the maid quickly began repacking the items in the bag Annella kept them in. Florie had been asleep on a palette in Annella's room when one of the servants had come knocking and let her know that Liddy in the village was "birthin' her bairn." Annella hadn't been concerned that the noise hadn't even made Florie stir.

Aside from being a deep sleeper and hard to wake, the maid had been up with her the evening before last, helping her with the ailing blacksmith all through the night. That being the case, Annella had decided to let her sleep this night. Hence her surprise to see her up and about now.

"'Tis morning," Florie told her dryly and gestured around the great hall.

Annella glanced around to see that nearly every trestle table had already been reassembled. And while some servants and soldiers were still working on setting up the last of them, everyone else was finding a spot to sit. There were even several people milling about waiting for her to leave so that they could claim seats at the table Raynard had been lying on just moments ago.

"Damn," Annella breathed. She hadn't realized it was so late. In fact, she'd been hoping to get at least an hour or so of rest before starting the day. It looked like that wouldn't be happening though.

"Come." Florie closed the bag of medicinals, clasped it in one hand and Annella's arm in the other and began to urge her away from the table. "'Tis to bed with ye now."

"Nay." Annella tried to pull her arm from Florie's grasp. "'Tis morning, and I've much to do today."

Florie scowled at her with exasperation. "Ye've been up all night, and that after being up all through the night before too. Ye must rest, m'lady, or ye'll make yerself ill, and then what will we do?"

Annella hesitated at the words, but finally shook her head. "Today is market day in the village, and there are things Millie needs me to purchase for her to continue making our meals. We also need soaps and candles and—I'll go to bed early tonight to make up fer it," she interrupted herself to say when Florie opened her mouth on what would no doubt have been a protest. When the maid hesitated, obviously not convinced, Annella added, "I promise. I shall go early to bed tonight and rise later on the morrow to make up fer it."

Florie didn't look happy, but didn't protest further either and simply released her arm. "I'll take yer bag up to yer room. Ye go sit yersel' at table. Cook already has food and drink fer ye to break yer fast with. No doubt she's just waitin' fer ye to sit to bring it out."

"Thank you," Annella murmured and headed for the high table. She was almost to the spot where she normally sat when she realized it wasn't empty as she would have expected. The high table was usually for the laird's family, honored guests and the more senior soldiers, but Gaufrid, the old laird, never left his room now, and Eschina, Lady Gunn, never rose early. That left only Annella's youngest brother-in-law, Dauid, who was away at the moment, and the senior soldiers—but they were the men who had carried Raynard away and wouldn't have returned yet.

For one moment she thought perhaps Dauid was back and her mother by marriage must have risen early for a change. Not a happy thought. Annella didn't mind Dauid so much. He could be annoying and tended to follow her around like a pup. But his mother was a nasty old biddy, who liked to make any- and everyone unfortunate enough to encounter her as miserable as she was. Annella had made an art form of avoiding the woman. She'd become quite skilled at the endeavor these last six years. Her mind was even now searching for a way to avoid her. But as she gazed at the high table, Annella realized that her mother-in-law wasn't one of the people there. It was four men she didn't recognize. All were big and strapping with at least a week's worth of dust and dirt coating their long hair, clothes, and even their skin.

Guests then, she thought, and only then recalled Lady Gunn saying something about expecting her cousins at some point. Annella couldn't recall when exactly Lady Gunn had said they would arrive, but had thought she had weeks yet to prepare. It seemed not, however. This must be the cousins, freshly arrived from what she guessed had been a long journey. No doubt weary, hungry and in need of drink, food, a bath and a bed in that order. She approached the table, mentally running through where to house the men even as she offered a welcoming smile.

"Welcome, gentlemen, I'm—"

"Annella," the nearest of the four men said as they all got to their feet.

"Aye," she said with surprise, but supposed she shouldn't be. The cousins would have heard of her marriage to William Gunn six years ago. "And ye're the cousins Lady Gunn mentioned were coming to—"

"Annella," the man said again, his tone this time more than a little exasperated. "'Tis I."

She paused at that, her mouth closing on the words that she hadn't got to say as she peered at the man. Under closer inspection, he did look familiar around the eyes. But between the dirt and dust coating his skin and the bushy beard and moustache covering the better part of his face, she just couldn't—

"It looks like yer sister does no' recognize ye," one of the other men said with amusement. He was the shortest of the four, but only by an inch or two, and as big as the others when it came to wide shoulders and muscled arms. His hair appeared to be darker than the others', although honestly, it might have just been dirtier. She couldn't tell. The only things not dust or dirt covered were his eyes, which were a brown so dark they were almost black.

"And here we've heard nought these last six months, but how close ye and yer sisters were while growin' up, MacKay," another of the men added. This one had his long hair pulled back into a ponytail, and his beard braided. She couldn't tell at all what color his hair was, but his beard appeared to be lighter than the hair on his head and his eyes were blue. That was all Annella noticed before his words made it through her weary mind. *MacKay?* She looked at the man who had first spoken with fresh eyes.

It had been six years since Annella had seen her brother, Payton. He'd been nineteen then, tall, strong and proud, but he was stronger now, his chest and arms nearly twice the size they used to be. In fact, he was as big as their father now. Good heavens!

"Payton!" she squealed, launching herself at her brother. She heard his muttered curse as he stumbled backward under her impact, but he caught her and managed to stay upright. His arms closed around her briefly, before he just as quickly began to urge her away.

"Nay, Nella, I'm filthy from the journey and will get muck and dust all over ye," he protested.

Annella gave a snort of laughter at that as he set her away. "Then 'twill go well with the blood and other muck already on me gown."

Payton wrinkled his nose at her words, his gaze sliding over her gown, which really had very little blood or anything else on it.

"What are ye doing here?" Annella asked finally, pulling his gaze back to her face.

"I—" He paused, frowned and then took her arm and said, "We should go to the gardens and—"

"Nay." Annella tugged her arm from his grasp when he tried to urge her away from the table. Frowning with concern now, she asked, "What's happened?"

Payton glanced around with a scowl, and then muttered, "We really should talk in private, Nella. I have grim tidings and—"

Her eyes widened with dismay. "Grim tidings? What kind of—? No one has died, have they?" she interrupted herself to ask with alarm.

The way Payton's mouth compressed suggested she had guessed right.

"Da?" she asked, her voice weak. Her father was an amazing warrior, strong and skilled, but even the strong and skilled could take an unlucky blow.

"Nay," Payton said quickly, reaching for her arm again. "Come, we—"

"Ma?" she asked with horror, stepping back from him to avoid his hand.

"Nay, Mither is fine," he assured her soothingly, but that merely increased her horror.

"No' wee Kenna," she begged. "She's so young. No' e'en wed yet. She—"

"Our sister is fine," Payton said firmly.

Annella sagged where she stood, relief rolling over her like a warm breeze. Her parents and siblings were the most important people in her life. That they were all alive and well was wondrous. In fact, she couldn't really think of anyone else who— "Cousin Jo!"

"Nay," Payton said, beginning to sound impatient. "Annella, I really must insist ye come outside and—"

"Just tell me who the devil died, Payton," she snapped impatiently. "I've been up all night tending to one person or another, am exhausted and cranky, and ye're just making me—"

"'Tis William," he shot out, his shoulders straightening and chin lifting as if bracing himself for something.

Annella stared at him blankly. "William who?"

"William Gunn," Payton said quietly, sympathy filling his face at first. But when she continued to stare at him blankly, some of that sympathy slipped away and he prompted in a soft, grim voice, "Yer husband."

Annella blinked at those words. Her husband? Her husband, William Gunn, was dead? For a moment, her mind was completely silent, and then a small burble of laughter slipped from her lips and she punched her brother in the arm in the same way she had when they were children. "For heaven's sake, Payton! You scared me silly with yer nonsense about grim tidings and someone dying. Why, this news is no grim at all. Good Lord."

Grabbing him by the ears, she pulled his head down

until it was even with hers and bussed him on the cheek
with a noisy, sloppy kiss. Still holding him by the ears,
she then pulled back and said, "That's because I love
and have missed ye." She gave him another wet one
on his other cheek, and then pulled back to add, "And
that's for bringing me such grand good news."

She added a quick peck to the tip of his nose when
she saw the mingled shock and dismay on his face,
then released him with a chuckle and said, "Thank
ye, brother."

Payton stared at her briefly, his eyes wide with
horror, and then growled, "Annella MacKay Gunn.
How could you say such things about your husband?
What kind o' wife thinks her husband's death is
grand good news?"

Annella's eyes narrowed at the accusation in his
tone. Propping her hands on her hips, she growled
right back, "What kind of husband marries a lass,
dumps her in what is to be their shared chamber, and
then flees the keep in the middle o' the night to go on
a 'pilgrimage' that lasts *six years*?"

Payton looked uncomfortable, but muttered, "Lots
of men go on pilgrimages to the holy lands."

"Since my *husband* took the village lightskirts
with him, I somehow doubt there was anything holy
about his *pilgrimage*," Annella said sarcastically and
then glanced over the three men behind—and apparently with—her brother. The shorter one and the one
with the ponytail were looking shocked and glancing
worriedly from her to the last man, who was staring at
her hard. He was the tallest of the four of them, having perhaps an inch on her brother. He also had just a

touch more muscle than her brother. Not much, barely even noticeable really, but she was noticing. She was also noticing that while he was as dusty and dirt covered as the others from travel, it was doing nothing to hide the fact that he was an incredibly handsome man. Who was starting to frown, she saw, and Annella turned back to her brother, one eyebrow cocked in question.

Payton sighed unhappily. "Sister, meet Graeme Gunn, William's brother."

Annella's eyes widened slightly as those words snapped through her. Damn. The second son, born between William and Dauid. The warrior. She felt a brief bite of regret for speaking so plainly about her husband, this man's brother, but there was really nothing to do about it now. She couldn't, and even wouldn't, take back her words. Each one had been true, so she merely gave him a solemn nod, and murmured, "My condolences, m'laird." She didn't wait to see his reaction, but simply headed for the stairs, saying, "I'll go pack."

"Pack?" Payton sounded surprised. "For what?"

"For the journey home," she said, and then paused and swung back to survey him briefly. "Do no' fret. I ken you have just arrived and no doubt are in need of a bath and good sleep ere you head out again, but that's fine. 'Twill be good to have a day or two to pack and say me goodbyes before we go."

Nodding with satisfaction at that, she turned away again and continued on, saying, "Break your fast. I'll have rooms readied for the four of ye."

"My apologies, Graeme."

Graeme pulled his gaze away from Annella's retreating figure and glanced to her brother at those words.

"My sister should not have—"

Graeme waved him to silence. He wasn't interested in the man's apology for his sister's words. "Did William really leave on their wedding night?"

Payton's eyebrows rose. "You did not know?"

Graeme shook his head slowly as he recalled the wedding of his brother to his pretty young bride. "I left shortly after the feast. Symon and Teague had made camp on the edge o' Gunn land and were waiting fer me. We had taken on a job with the Stewarts and had to ride hard to reach the rendezvous point at the agreed time."

"Oh." Payton frowned slightly, and then sighed and said, "Aye. William was gone when everyone got up the morn after the wedding. He'd left a note that he was heading off on a pilgrimage." Payton paused briefly before adding, "There were rumors whispered around the keep that some lass from the village . . . Maisie, I think the name was, was missing and that someone had seen her riding off with William in the middle o' the night."

"His wedding night," Graeme murmured thoughtfully and then speared Payton with hard eyes. "And he's been gone all this time?"

Payton's eyebrows rose slightly. "You did not ken that either?"

"Nay. I've no' been back at Gunn since the wedding, and ye did no' mention how long he'd been missin' when ye approached me to join the search fer him," Graeme pointed out. "I just assumed he'd left at some point this last year or mayhap the one before." He shook his head. "I find it hard to believe me parents waited six years ere sendin' a search party fer him. Especially me mither. William was her favorite."

"It was no' your mother who arranged for us to search for William," Payton said solemnly. "It was me da."

When Graeme's gaze sharpened on him, Payton nodded firmly.

"The only reason he did not do so sooner was because he assumed your father must already have men out hunting fer him. It's when me da came here to question yers on what news there was, and yer mother told him that no search had been mounted that he sent me to find and invite ye to join me and our men in the search. He thought a member of yer family should be involved, and at first Dauid was unwilling." He paused briefly and then added, "Which is why I was so surprised when we arrived at MacDonald and he was there with you."

Graeme nodded. He, Symon and Teague had just finished a job for the MacDonald and were camping their last night on MacDonald land when his brother had arrived. Dauid had obviously ridden hard to reach them. He'd barely blurted a rather garbled story about William being missing and a need to search for him before falling asleep. Graeme had intended to question him further the next morning, but Payton and his men had ridden into camp just as Graeme and the others were rising to greet the day and he hadn't had the chance.

"When I told you we were heading out to look for yer brother William who was missing and you said ye kenned, Dauid had told ye, I just assumed he'd told you all," Payton said apologetically.

"Nay," Graeme murmured. "He did no' mention how long William had been gone."

When Payton just grunted at that, Graeme smiled faintly. He knew the man didn't like his younger brother. He didn't blame him. Dauid had grown spoiled, arrogant and annoying as hell over the decade since Graeme had left Gunn. He had been nothing but a trial during the last six months, which was why the minute they'd got off the ship that had brought them back to Scotland, Graeme, Symon, Teague and Payton had left Dauid in charge of the men guarding the wagon carrying William's bones and ridden on ahead.

Since the wagon moved slowly, he expected it would be at least four or five days before the traveling party arrived, his younger brother with it, and they could lay William's bones to rest.

A William who had, apparently, abandoned his bride and ridden out to seek adventure with the village lightskirts.

Graeme scowled as the thought went through his mind. It just did not fit with the man he'd known his brother to be. Shaking his head, he moved back to his seat at the table, grabbed up his watered ale and gulped down some of it as he considered what he'd learned.

William had been missing for six years and his parents hadn't bothered to send out anyone to try to find him? Graeme was having serious trouble accepting that. William had been clan chief here. His father had stepped down and passed on the title to him the week before the wedding. Gaufrid Gunn had never enjoyed the work needed to run the castle and its people, and had decided, since William was marrying, he should be laird as well. Which made it even harder for Graeme to accept that no one had gone out to look for William ere this. Hell, if he'd known his brother had been missing all this time, he would have gone in search of him himself years ago. And why the hell had a messenger not been sent to inform him?

"I suppose I should talk to Annella ere she gets too far in her packing."

Pulled from his thoughts, Graeme glanced to the man who had settled in the seat beside him and raised an eyebrow in question.

Payton shrugged and pointed out, "Well, she's a Gunn by marriage. She can't just hie off home to MacKay without the clan chief's permission." He frowned slightly, and then added, "And she can't get permission until the next clan chief is named. I'm assuming that would be you?"

Graeme straightened slightly in his seat. He'd been told from a young age that his older brother would inherit Gunn castle and the title of laird that went with it, while he would gain nothing and would either needs must become a priest or find some other way to make his way in the world. Graeme had never seen himself as a priest. Spending his life on his knees praying the day away . . . nay, that hadn't been for him. He wasn't a very pious man. But he was a hell of a soldier. He could wield a sword with deadly skill.

So, he'd chosen work as a mercenary and had spent more than ten years knee-deep in bodies and blood, battling his way around the world. He'd even enjoyed it. At least for the first several years. The camaraderie of the soldiers as they sat around a fire of a night telling their tales of the fearsome battles they'd fought in. The thrill of winning fight after fight. The coin he'd made with his hard work . . .

But all of that had begun to lose its luster the last couple of years. The camaraderie had been lessened by the growing number of new faces replacing the mercenaries who had been lost over time. The stories had begun to all sound the same. Even the thrill of victory had waned a bit. As for the coin he made . . . Well, all he was doing was storing that away. A man didn't need much coin to sleep on the ground rolled up in his plaid and follow whoever hired him into battle. He now probably had enough to build his own manor, if not a keep. He just didn't have the land to put it on.

Aye. He'd tired of battle. Ten years of killing was long enough. Mayhap he *would* take up the mantle and become laird of Gunn. The only problem with that was that he'd then be expected to marry and produce heirs. Graeme didn't have much interest in that.

It wasn't that Graeme didn't like women. He did. Very much. And he would like a son or two. But a marriage had never been contracted for him or Dauid when they were children as had been done for William. His parents hadn't felt it necessary since neither of them would be laird. So, he'd have to find and woo his own bride . . . which might be a problem. Unfortunately, he'd spent so long in the company of men that he'd quite forgotten how he should act around a lady. He also definitely didn't have the patience to deal with their weaker natures and simpering ways.

An image of Annella slamming a pot over Raynard's head flashed through his mind, followed by her cussing and bellowing at the injured man ere that, and a small smile slid across his lips. Now there was a lady he wouldn't mind dealing with. Despite all Payton had claimed these last six months, his sister was no weak, weeping female. She was strong and no-nonsense, and really quite fetching even with her hair a mess, streaks of blood on her cheek and exhaustion hanging around her like a cloak.

Annella was a woman he might be able to woo.

"Well? Are ye the laird now that William is dead?" Payton asked, sounding impatient.

"We shall see," Graeme said mildly and stood up to head for the stairs. His parents had yet to make an appearance and he would speak with them. He would give them the sad tidings of William's death. Once that was done and they had recovered from the news, he would bring up who was to be the next clan chief. By rights it should be him, but Dauid had avoided talk of home these last six months and he had no idea what had been going on since the wedding.

It was possible his father had reclaimed the title of laird after William's leaving and might not be willing to give it up again. That didn't seem likely since he'd happily abandoned it six years ago, but it was still possible.

If his father had stepped in to take up the job of laird again in William's absence and was ready to be done with it, he would take on the job, Graeme decided. Then he would spend some time getting to know Annella better to see if they would deal well together. He suspected they would. He liked what he'd seen so far. He definitely found her appealing enough that he was sure he would enjoy her in his bed, and he'd liked what he'd seen of her spunk and no-nonsense attitude in dealing with the injured man. If they got on as well as he suspected they would, he'd then try to convince her to remain at Gunn and be his wife. It would save him having to hunt up and woo a bride.

Chapter 2

$\mathcal{A}$NNELLA ROLLED OVER WITH A LITTLE SIGH, opened her eyes, and then sat up abruptly with a small gasp. It was bright daylight, almost midday by her guess. Dammit. She'd fallen asleep while waiting for Florie to bring her fresh water for the washbasin . . . and the woman hadn't woken her.

Muttering impatiently under her breath, she tossed aside the fur that someone—no doubt Florie—had laid across her and slid off the bed. Her feet immediately took her to the washbasin by the window. It had been empty when she'd come up to her room. She'd wanted to wash up and change into a clean gown before starting her packing. Florie had arrived then with food and drink for her to break her fast, spotted the problem and suggested Annella go ahead and eat while she went to fetch fresh water for her.

Annella had thanked her, but instructed her on preparing rooms and baths for the newly arrived men first. She could wait. She'd consumed the food and drink Florie had brought for her, and then paced around the room briefly, before her sore back had made her first sit, then stretch out on the bed. She'd intended only to rest for a minute to allow her strained muscles to ease. She'd known there was a danger of drifting off to sleep, but had counted on Florie's return to wake her. Obviously, that hadn't happened.

Florie had definitely returned; the water pitcher was now full to the brim with room temperature water. However, her maid must have slid in silently and crept about to avoid waking her. Annella wasn't terribly surprised. Her maid was actually a couple of years younger than her, but fussed over her like a mother hen and had done so since she'd been assigned to be her lady's maid. Something that Lady Eschina had arranged a few days after Annella's wedding to William. She suspected it had not been meant as a kindness at the time. From the moment she had learned he was gone, Lady Eschina had made it plain that she held Annella wholly responsible for her precious William's leaving so abruptly on his "pilgrimage" on their wedding night.

Annella obviously hadn't been woman enough to keep her new husband at her side, Lady Eschina had said. Annella had driven William off with her pathetic ways, flat chest and lack of looks, the woman had claimed. So, it had been quite a surprise when Lady Eschina had sent Florie up to her room. It had made more sense once she'd learned that Florie had previously been a scullery maid and had absolutely no idea how to *be* a lady's maid.

Annella suspected Lady Eschina had wanted her to toss the girl from her room and insist on a proper lady's maid—a request Lady Eschina would then have the pleasure of refusing. It was what most ladies would have done in response to such an insult. But Annella hadn't.

At that point she'd felt a complete failure. She'd been sure Lady Eschina was right and she was utterly useless, so unattractive and uninteresting to William that he'd fled his own castle. Annella also hadn't had a clue what to do with herself. She knew no one at Gunn, had no idea how things worked in her new home, and hadn't yet made a place for herself. So when Florie arrived at her door, stammering that she was to be her new maid, Annella had taken one look at the very young and frightened lass, had offered a smile and begun to train her in how to be her lady's maid. Six years later, Florie was the best damned lady's maid Annella could have asked for. She was also her best friend and ally.

But Annella was still going to give the maid hell for letting her sleep. She knew the lass had done it out of love and concern, but Annella had things to do. She ran this whole damned place by herself, fulfilling the roll of both laird and lady in her husband's absence. It often kept her working from sunup to sundown. Throw in the healing skills her mother had taught her over the years and there was rarely a night when she was allowed to sleep in her bed for more than an hour or two. It had been a hard six years, and Annella could almost weep with joy that it was coming to an end. Her husband was dead, she was free and she could return to MacKay and her family and . . .

Well, frankly, she had no idea what would happen

after that. Annella was quite sure that her mother would love and coddle her and ease away all the misery and insecurity caused by the last six years. But then what? She was hoping that her father would arrange another marriage for her. It was what she wanted. Despite how miserable an experience her marriage to William had been, Annella wasn't willing to give up her dreams of having her own loving husband and children. She just hoped her next husband and his family were not like the Gunns. But that should be easily avoided since, surely, she'd get to meet any prospective husband and his family first. Wouldn't she?

Annella was pondering that when the sound of her door opening caught her ear. Turning sharply, she saw Florie entering and scowled. "You should have woken me."

"I did try," Florie said, completely unconcerned by her anger. "Ye did no' e'en stir when I shook ye. Ye were exhausted. As evidenced by the fact that ye slept through the day, the night and most of this morning . . . missing Laird Graeme's taking on the position o' laird, and the whole clan swearin' their fealty."

"What?" Annella squawked with dismay. She didn't really care about missing the ceremonies for Graeme taking over. It wasn't like she would be here long anyway, and once she left, he would not be her laird. It was the length of her sleep when she had so much to do that upset her. "Surely, I did no' sleep *that* long?"

Florie nodded firmly. "Aye. Yer brother and yer husband's brother arrived yester morn, and ye've slept e'er since." She shrugged as she crossed the room to her. "Ye must ha'e needed it."

Annella let out a slow breath and turned to pour the pitcher of cool water into the basin. It wasn't the first time she'd slept overlong. That seemed to happen every few weeks. She'd be up the better part of most nights for two or three weeks, and then just crash and sleep for an extended period. Not this long though. A day and night, yes. A day, night and then the better part of another morning? No. It seemed she had though, and supposed it was just her body claiming what it needed. Still, it was annoying.

"Would ye no' rather ha'e a nice warm bath than just a standin' wash?" Florie asked suddenly.

It was a tempting thought, but she'd slept so long and—

"I think it may be in yer best interest to bathe."

Annella stilled at those soft words. Turning, she eyed Florie warily. "Why?"

"Because yer hair needs washin', ye smell like a charnel, and I'm thinkin' ye'll want to look yer best when ye next meet yer husband's brother."

"Graeme?" she asked with surprise.

Florie nodded and then started to work on her laces to get her out of the gown she'd now not only worn for more than two days but had slept in.

"Why would I want to look me best fer Graeme?" Annella asked with bewilderment.

"Because yer a Gunn, he's Laird Gunn now, and ye need his permission to leave Gunn land," she said succinctly.

Annella sagged back against the table the washbasin and pitcher sat on and then stiffened when cold water sloshed out onto her lower back and the top of her behind through her gown. She didn't straighten at the splash of cold, but stayed slouched against the table, unsure her legs alone would hold her up just then.

Florie's words had shaken her. Mostly, because they were true. She was a Gunn, by marriage, and so was under Gunn rule. She could not go home to MacKay without permission. If she tried, he, by rights, could hunt her down and drag her back.

But surely, he wouldn't do that . . . would he? Really, he shouldn't even care. The man didn't know her. She didn't even think they'd met before the previous morning, although she couldn't be sure. She thought he'd probably attended her wedding to his brother. Annella seemed to recall someone mentioning at the wedding that both of William's brothers were there, so she may have been introduced to him. If she had, she didn't recall. That whole day was just a blur in her mind. Still, she couldn't imagine he'd care if she left or not.

It wouldn't hurt to make herself as presentable as she could in the hopes of earning his favor though, she acknowledged. Especially since she'd made it so plain that she was glad her husband, his brother, was dead. Annella recalled her conversation with Payton in front of the other man, and winced at the memory.

"Oh dear," she breathed with dismay as she realized how insulting he must have found that.

"What is it, m'lady?" Florie asked. Tearing her gaze away from Annella's laces, which appeared to be giving her difficulty, she arched an eyebrow in question.

Annella straightened from the table, sending it

rocking again and making more liquid slosh out of the basin, this time onto the floor.

"I need a bath," she announced grimly. "And my prettiest gown."

Florie smiled at her approvingly. "I'll be right back. I've had Cook keeping warm water on fer ye all morning."

Annella watched her go and then moved to the window to look out over the bailey below as she fretted. There was no reason for her brother-in-law to want her to stay . . . other than as punishment for her reaction to learning her husband, his brother, was dead. The problem was, she didn't know the man and had no idea if he could be that petty.

"Damn," she breathed, leaning against the cool stone of the window frame. She was so close to freedom she could smell it. Only Graeme Gunn stood in her way.

"So?"

Graeme pulled his attention from the men he was watching practice at battle and glanced at Payton MacKay in question.

"Yer laird now," he pointed out, reminding him of the ceremony that had been held that morning once the members of the Gunn clan had all been gathered in the courtyard. It hadn't been fancy and there had been no feast. In fact, it had been as brief as could be by his request, but he was now Laird Gunn.

"Will ye let Annella leave with me, or no'?" Payton continued.

Graeme scowled slightly at the question and turned

back to watch the men of Gunn wield swords, spears and battle axes as he considered how to answer.

As expected, his father had taken the news of William's death stoically, with just a flash of grief that streaked across his face and disappeared. His mother, however, had not fallen apart as he'd believed she would. In fact, she hadn't seemed affected at all. Her only comment had been, "Well then, I guess Dauid is laird now."

"Dauid?" Graeme had repeated the name of his younger brother with surprise, even as his father made a distressed grunt of protest.

"Well, ye always said ye'd no interest in bein' laird," his mother reminded him coldly. "Ye enjoyed battle too much to stop. So, o' course, Dauid will take the position."

"Nay." His father had growled the word with effort, and then had said, "Graeme." Or at least Graeme felt sure that was what his father was trying to say, though his speech was much impeded. That had been another surprise on speaking to his parents. His father was no longer the strong, hale man he'd last seen six years ago. Apparently, he'd taken a tumble down the keep stairs some weeks after the wedding. He'd survived the fall, but was no longer the man he used to be. While Gaufrid Gunn appeared fine from the waist up other than his trouble with speech, his legs were now useless, leaving him confined to his bed.

The biggest surprise though had been that his brother's wee wife had been running the keep, acting as both chatelaine and laird in her husband's absence these last six years. From what he'd seen so far, she'd done a damned fine job of it too. Though he suspected it must have been hard to act as *both* chatelaine and laird for such an extended length of time. As well as healer, he thought, recalling the scene they'd walked in on when they'd arrived. He supposed it was no wonder the woman was eager to leave.

Whatever the case, his father had made it apparent he was to become laird now that his brother was dead. Meanwhile, his mother's expression puckering with displeasure had made it equally apparent she was displeased with this outcome.

It would seem Dauid had become the favored child since William's leaving. Graeme supposed he should have expected as much. He hadn't been here himself. Although, even if he had been, he didn't think his mother would have favored him. She'd always found his size and strength somewhat vulgar. Probably because he looked much like his father, a man she had always made it obvious she hadn't wanted to marry, and wouldn't have, had her father not forced her to uphold the marriage contract he'd arranged when she was just a bairn.

"Well? Will ye let her leave with me?"

Payton's impatient voice drew him from his thoughts and Graeme hesitated, but then said, "That depends."

"On what?" Payton asked at once.

Graeme shrugged. "While I ha'e been away at battle these last six years, yer sister has been runnin' Gunn and its people. She kens them and how the keep works and it wid be helpful did she aid me in settlin' into rulin' here."

Payton heaved out a resigned sigh. "Aye. I can see how that would be helpful."

"Aye," Graeme agreed, marveling at his own ability to come up with such a bullocks excuse so quickly. Honestly, he hadn't known he had it in him. He'd had little need for prevarication as a soldier, but he was definitely showing some skill at it now, because Graeme had no real need or desire for Annella's help in taking up the position she'd filled these last six years. He was quite sure that if a woman could do it, he would have no difficulty managing the task.

"How long do ye think ye'll need her here?" Payton asked now.

Graeme glanced around at Payton, his mouth opening to spit out an answer, but paused as he spotted Annella crossing the bailey toward them.

"What is it?" Payton asked, noting his expression. Then he turned and looked over his shoulder and sighed. "Annella," he murmured and shook his head. "She'll no' be pleased ye want her to stay."

"She'll settle to it," Graeme said softly and hoped he was right, because the sight of her with rosy cheeks, her hair clean and flowing, along with the pretty blue gown she wore made Graeme quite sure he wanted to bed the lass, which meant he'd have to wed her first.

Graeme found the idea of marrying her terribly appealing just then. Aside from being attracted to her, finding an alternate bride would definitely be a pain in his arse. He had no idea how many women were presently available to marry, but suspected the number would be small. It would be made up of lasses whose contracted intendeds had died ere reaching adulthood, or lasses whose parents hadn't bothered with the task of arranging a marriage while they were bairns. Despite the fact that that was exactly what had happened with he and Dauid, Graeme didn't think there would be many lasses in the same position. He found it hard to believe there were a lot of parents out there coldhearted enough to leave their daughters' futures undecided.

Another consideration was that, so far, he actually liked the woman. Contrary to the impression Payton had given them of his sister during the six months they'd traveled together, Annella was smart, strong, capable and a hard worker. The last of which was evidenced by how well Gunn was doing. His people were well dressed, well fed and happy. They'd also been sure to tell him what a fine job Lady Annella had done since his brother's leaving. It was apparent that his people loved the lass. The clan would definitely be pleased if he married her. More important, he was quite sure that she was someone he could respect, and even like.

His gaze slid over her again as she approached. Her stride was confident and quick, her expression relaxed and easy. It would definitely be no trouble for him to fill her belly with bairns and bring about those heirs he would need.

"Well, I best go give her the news," Payton said, dragging Graeme from thoughts of making babies with Annella and back to the man beside him. Payton MacKay's face was filled with a resignation that made it obvious he wasn't looking forward to the task ahead of him.

Graeme would have laughed at the man, but suspected Payton was in for an ordeal. Judging by the eagerness that had been in her voice the morning before when she'd said she'd go pack for the journey home, it seemed obvious Annella was eager to leave and that her time at Gunn had not been happy. Graeme wasn't surprised. His mother had a tendency to make those around her miserable. She always had. Certainly, he hadn't been sorry to leave Gunn when he had. It was also the reason he'd only returned once in the decade since leaving, and that had been to support his brother on his wedding day.

From what Graeme had seen, his mother had not changed from the cold, disapproving old bitch she'd been when he was growing up. Which meant it would no doubt take a lot of convincing to make Annella agree to marry him and live here.

Ah well, he'd always enjoyed a challenge, Graeme thought as he watched Payton rush away to head off his approaching sister.

A crooked smile claimed Annella's lips as her brother hurried toward her. It then quickly turned apologetic before she said, "I'm sorry, brother, I ken me sleeping so long has delayed our journey. I'll pack as quick as I can, I promise, and then we can—"

"There's no rush," Payton interrupted to assure her. "Why do we not go find something for you to break yer fast with and we can discuss the journey home."

Annella didn't fight him when he caught her arm and turned her back toward the keep, but she was frowning. "I already broke me fast. In fact, I'll most like skip the nooning since I ate so late. Besides, what is there to discuss? Other than whether we leave today or tomorrow?"

Her eyes narrowed suspiciously when Payton's expression became pained. "We *are* leaving today or tomorrow, are we no'?"

Her brother's response was to clasp her arm firmly and urge her to move more quickly. "We really should wait until we are somewhere more private to speak. Mayhap the gardens."

Annella immediately dug in her heels and forced them both to a halt. Her expression was accusatory as she turned on him. "The last time you wanted to talk to me in private, it was because you thought ye had bad news to give me."

Payton's mouth tightened with irritation. "You were always a stubborn cuss, sister. Why can you no'—just this once—allow me to take ye somewhere private to discuss matters?"

Annella snorted at the suggestion. "There is nowhere private at Gunn."

"Ye're wrong." Payton sounded smug. "Graeme says there's a flower garden behind the vegetable gardens that would give us privacy."

Annella gave a derisive laugh at the suggestion, and when he began to urge her along again, said, "Oh aye, if ye do no' mind the dozen or so couples indulging themselves under the trees, in the tall grasses and hidden in the bushes." When he glanced at her sharply, she explained, "'Tis a popular spot for young Gunns to get up to houghmagandie."

This time it was Payton who stopped walking. Spinning on her with amazement, he cried, "Nay!"

"Aye," Annella assured him. "Although, sometimes they're actually in the trees rather than under them."

"*In* the trees?" Payton echoed with disbelief.

"That's right." She turned and started to walk again, forcing him to continue as well. "Although, I only know of one couple who's done that," she told him and then pursed her lips and corrected, "At least there's only one couple I caught at it." She shrugged. "And since I spotted the young male of the couple in question at practice in the courtyard just now, I suppose we'd be safe from that. Mayhap," she added with a little uncertainty, and then pointed out, "I mean, just because I only caught one couple at it, that does no' mean there are not others I have no' caught."

"In trees," Payton muttered, his expression a cross between amazement and horror. "How the devil did they do it without falling out o' the tree?"

"They didn't. Or at least they did no' the time I caught them. That's *how* I caught them. They fell out of the tree, and just missed landing on top o' me."

"Good God," Payton muttered.

Annella nudged his arm with her elbow to draw his attention back to her, and then suggested, "Why do ye no' tell me what has your tunic in such a tangle that ye think we should talk in private?"

A series of expressions crossed Payton's face as he apparently had an internal debate. Annella watched as first a scowl, then irritation, then uncertainty, and then a frown slid over his face, one after the other. When it ended in a look of resignation, she knew he was ready to talk.

"We cannot leave right away," Payton said apologetically.

"What exactly do ye mean by right away?" Annella asked suspiciously. "Are ye saying we must wait till tomorrow? Or perhaps the day after that?"

Before Payton could respond, she added, "And why exactly can we no' leave today or tomorrow? Are one o' your men ill? Is your horse lame? What—"

"Because Graeme needs your help takin' over as laird o' Gunn," Payton interrupted.

Annella stopped again and turned to face him. She opened her mouth to speak, closed it, opened it again and then just gaped at him.

Taking advantage of her stunned state, Payton immediately burst into speech. "He's been away at battle for the last decade. He's no idea who does what here or even what all needs doing. He wants ye to help him ease into the position."

"Well, bugger that!" Annella burst out the moment he stopped speaking. "*He's* their laird now. He'll figure it out. I did. Nobody was here to train me to take over the duties of the laird of the clan when his brother abandoned me here. His mother and father left me to sink or swim. I had to sort it out on me own," she said resentfully, and then her chin jutted up and she growled. "He can too. In fact, he'll have to, because I'm going home. With or without ye."

Annella whirled on her heel and headed for the keep at a swift march. She heard her brother's sigh and his footsteps as he hustled to catch up to her. This time when he grabbed her arm, it was to slow her down rather than to steer her anywhere.

"Annella," he said firmly, "Graeme is the clan chieftain now. He is laird over the Gunns."

"I am aware, brother," she said shortly.

"Well, then you are aware that as a Gunn yourself ye cannot leave Gunn land without your laird's permission."

Annella came to an abrupt halt and whirled on her brother. "Are ye sayin' he's refusin' to let me leave?" she asked with disbelief. She had really hoped this would not be the case. In fact, she'd convinced herself of it. After all, Laird and Lady Gunn had despised her these last six years. Lady Eschina had told her outright that she wished that Annella had never come to Gunn. Earlier, while she'd bathed, Annella had assured herself that William's brother would feel the same and be happy to see the back of her.

Payton paused before he responded, obviously choosing his words carefully. "He'd like your aid in takin' up the mantle o' laird so that the transition is as smooth as possible." When her gaze narrowed, he rushed on, "The people of Gunn have just learned his brother, their laird, is dead. They're about to lose yourself, who stepped in and took up that position while he was missing these last six years, and are faced with a man they have seen only once and briefly since he earned his spurs more than a decade ago. He thinks, and probably rightly so, that this could be a tricky situation and that your presence would reassure the clan members and aid in making the transition smoother."

Annella stared at her brother, her thoughts racing as she turned the matter over in her mind. In truth, it might not be a terrible thing for her to help Graeme take up the reins of Gunn. She did know the people better than him at this point. She could tell him who was trustworthy, who wasn't, who had issues that needed dealing with and who didn't. The fact of the matter was she would not mind doing that, because while some people—mostly her mother-in-law and the woman's maid, Agnes—had tried to make her life miserable here, it hadn't been all bad. There were many members of the clan who had been good to her, who had appreciated her efforts and had made her feel welcome . . . if not right away, then after she'd proven herself. Certainly, she hadn't blamed them for being leery of her. At first, she'd been an untried young bride, abandoned by her husband and dropped in the laird's seat. Even she had been positive she would make a muckle mess of it.

However, Annella had spent several years trailing her father and brother around MacKay before her mother had decided it was time she settled down to lessons in running a keep. While she'd been a dutiful student under her mother's tutelage, she'd also apparently paid attention during those years accompanying her father on his tasks as laird, so that while she hadn't been expert at the job, and hadn't known absolutely everything a laird had to do at first, she'd had a basic understanding of it, which had helped her quickly pick up the rest.

Despite her own fears, and the expectations of the others, Annella hadn't actually been a horrible laird. In fact, by the end of the first year, she had become quite efficient at the job and had started to earn the respect of both her soldiers and her servants. Over time that had turned into affection on both sides, and there were some people here she would be sorry to leave. Which was something she hadn't thought of in her eagerness to get home to her mother's comforting embrace and the possibility of her parents arranging a proper marriage for her.

Annella was thinking of it now. She began to drum her fingers on her outer leg through her skirt as she considered the issues. Stay and help Graeme take over as laird here in the hopes that he would treat the people well? Or refuse, and leave, which quite possibly could result in his making some error that ended with their people not having enough food to carry them through the winter, selling their goods at such a low price the coffers were affected, or even saying the wrong thing and landing the Gunns in a war with another clan. Annella wouldn't want to leave the people she'd overseen these last six years to such a fate.

The very thought had the faces of the people of Gunn running through her mind . . . including Florie. Annella's frown deepened. Florie was who she'd miss most. The maid had been her greatest supporter and encouragement these last six years. They'd become dear friends. She couldn't imagine not having her in her life.

Biting her lip, Annella pondered the possibility that Graeme might agree to allow her to take the young maid with her. That was something she hadn't even considered in the first rush of knowing she would be going home. Now she did.

He might, she considered. But Graeme was more likely to agree to give her such a boon if she helped him. Perhaps that was something she could negotiate with him. She would stay and help him if he allowed her to take Florie with her when she left.

"Fine. I'll help," she said abruptly, and her brother had just begun to relax when she added, "But only if he agrees to a boon for me."

For some reason, her words brought worry to her brother's face. "What kind of boon?"

Annella merely shrugged. "That would be between Laird Gunn and myself. There's no need to trouble ye with it."

Leaving her brother staring after her in the court-yard, she made her way back to the keep. She had to speak to Florie. She wanted to take the lass with her, but would only do so if the girl was willing. If the maid would rather stay here at Gunn with her family, Annella would be disappointed, but would understand. She had to talk to her about it before she made the request of Graeme. Then she would go check on Raynard and young Liddy to be sure she was recovering well from having her bairn and no infection had set in. She had a busy day ahead of her despite the fact that Graeme now had the responsibilities of laird in her place. She still had her other duties to attend to.

Chapter 3

"SHE DID NO' SAY WHAT THIS BOON WAS?" Graeme asked, concern drawing his eyebrows together.

Payton's mug of ale made a sharp sound as he slammed it onto the tabletop with exasperation. "As I've already told ye *half a dozen times*, nay, Graeme, she did no' tell me what the boon is."

Graeme grunted at the impatient words and took a drink of his own ale as he worried over what the boon might be. This boon business was completely unexpected. Graeme did not like the unexpected. He didn't like surprises of any sort.

"Doona fash yerself so, Graeme," Symon said, nudging him with one arm. "She's a lass. Most like she just wants a new gown or two fer the journey home."

"Aye," Teague agreed, leaning forward to look at him around Symon. "Or mayhap some bauble or other. Ye ken how women are."

Grunting, Graeme shifted impatiently at the table and glanced toward the stairs to the upper level.

"Where the devil is she? She *is* coming down to eat, is she no'?"

"O' course she is," Payton said irritably.

"Ye needn't act like 'tis a foregone conclusion. She has no' been at table since we arrived yester morn."

"Nay, she hasna," Symon agreed with a frown. "That was full on rude o' her."

"Mayhap she doesna ken we've bathed and thinks we still smell o' the road and sweat," Teague said judiciously.

"She was sleeping," Payton said a little irritably.

"From yester morn to this morn?" Graeme asked with concern. "Is she ill?"

Payton smiled wryly. "Aye. That was my concern as well when she slept so long. Which, I think, is the only reason this was explained to me, but apparently, she had no' spent more than an hour abed o'er the last two or three nights ere our arrival thanks to the need fer her healing skills, yet would no' take to her bed during the day to make up fer it because o' her other responsibilities. Yer people were beginning to worry, so a tonic was slipped into her drink to make her sleep."

"What people?" Graeme growled, his hand tightening on his mug. It was bad enough that every time he'd given an order today someone had felt the need to tell him that Lady Annella did it differently, but he'd be damned if he'd have anyone dosing his or his wife's drinks. Well, future wife's drinks, he corrected himself, and then added a "hopefully" to the thought as well.

"I'm no' sure—oh, there's Annella," Payton said, and Graeme glanced up sharply to see the lass and another woman walking toward them, heads together and chattering. Graeme was just wondering who the other lass was when a man he didn't recognize rushed up to the two women. He seemed a little overexcited, Graeme noted as he watched the man speak quickly, his hands gesticulating about. The fellow hadn't even finished talking when Annella grabbed his arm and started to urge him quickly toward the keep doors as his mouth continued to move.

"I wonder what . . ." Payton began, but that's all Graeme heard; he was already hurrying away from the table, after the pair.

ANNELLA HAD TO BITE HER LIP TO KEEP FROM groaning at the pain that shot through her back when she straightened. It was becoming a common ailment for her. She'd spent entirely too many nights bending over the ill or injured, and her body was not happy with her for it.

"How is he, m'lady? Will he be well?" Mary, the blacksmith's wife, asked anxiously. The petite brunette stood on the other side of the bed, wringing her hands and eyeing her husband with worry.

Annella peered at the man she'd been working on. As tall and burly as his wife was short and slender, the man was out cold, his long dark hair falling away from his face. His cheeks were flushed, but not as badly as they had been when she'd first arrived that night, thank goodness.

Leaning down, she felt his forehead and was sure he felt a little cooler than earlier as well. Perhaps she'd managed to remove all of the infection. Annella hoped so, and also hoped that it didn't return.

"If all goes well, he should recover," she said cautiously as she straightened again. Turning, Annella began gathering the items she'd used to work on the blacksmith as she warned, "But 'twill be a long recovery, Mary, and ye must watch him closely. His fever appears to be goin' down now, but if it starts to rise again, come fetch me right away."

"Aye. Right away." The woman nodded to add to the promise.

"Good." Annella finished putting everything away, then picked up her bag with one hand and patted Mary on the shoulder with the other, before heading out of the small cottage the blacksmith and his wife lived in. She slipped into the cool, dark night and took a deep breath, then stiffened when a figure moved toward her out of the shadows along the walls.

"I thought I'd wait and see ye back to the castle."

Annella stared silently at the black blob before her. She didn't recognize the voice. All it told her was that it was a man. Not a lot of help.

"Will the blacksmith recover?"

Annella blinked as she finally recognized the man before her. Not because of the question, but because he'd stepped closer, and the light coming from the window, a combination of the candles and the glow from the fire inside, revealed his face to her. It was Graeme Gunn.

Relaxing a bit, she turned and started along the path leading through the cottages and back to the keep, before saying, "I'm hopeful he will, but we shall have to wait and see."

"Hmm." Graeme fell into step beside her. "Do ye

often ha'e to spend the better part o' the night tendin'
to someone who's been injured or ailin'?"

"Often enough," Annella said, trying not to sound
as weary as she felt just then. She'd missed dinner and
been in the blacksmith's cottage for hours.

When an apple appeared in front of her face, her
thoughts scattered and she stopped walking to stare
at the sweet fruit lying on Graeme Gunn's large
open hand.

"Ye missed the sup, and I thought ye may be hungry, so stopped a passing lad and sent him to the castle
to fetch us food," Graeme said solemnly.

"Oh. Aye. Thank you." Annella smiled weakly and
accepted the apple, then glanced to the side to see him
lifting one to his own mouth.

They walked in silence as they ate. Annella had
barely finished her apple when a peach was produced
for her pleasure.

"I was no' sure if ye liked apples or peaches better, so brought one o' each," he explained when she
glanced from the fruit to him.

"Oh." Her smile was more natural this time as she
took the peach. "I like both actually. In fact, the only
fruit I do no' care for are pears."

Graeme grunted as he swallowed a bite of peach,
and then said, "Too gritty."

"Aye," she agreed with a smile, glad he understood
and appeared to agree. Pears were a favorite of her
husband's mother. At least, Lady Eschina had insisted
cook serve them at almost every damned meal when
in season after learning Annella didn't like them. *Old
bitch*, she thought grimly, and then shrugged the mat-

ter aside. It was no longer an issue. Once she'd gained confidence and taken over as chatelaine of the castle, Annella was sure she would have handled the matter, but in the end it hadn't been necessary. God had handled it. The pear trees had been hit with a blight the first fall after her arrival, killing off most of them.

Lady Eschina had demanded that fresh pear trees be found and planted to replace the old. But Annella had claimed a concern that these new pear trees might suffer the same fate as the old, and had instead had apple and peach trees planted next to the few pear trees that had survived. She'd also immediately doubled the number of strawberry plants, raspberry bushes and grapevines to fill in until the trees grew large enough to produce, which was only now happening.

"We have meat, cheese and bread too," Graeme announced as they finished their peaches. "Shall we sit here to finish our sup?"

Annella glanced up from taking her last bite of peach to see that they'd reached the keep stairs. He was suggesting they sit on the stone steps to enjoy the meal he was offering. She hesitated, but supposed it was a good idea. By now, the trestle tables would have been disassembled and put aside to make room for people to sleep on the great hall floor as was done every night. She wouldn't intrude and insist on a table being set up again just for them to eat. She still felt bad about displacing several people to have one of the trestle tables set up in the middle of the hall the other night to deal with Raynard's injury. Not that anyone had complained. It had been a cool night but not cold, and most had just moved out to the courtyard to sleep.

More had followed when Raynard had started in bellowing and cussing so that few remained inside at the end but the men helping to hold him down.

Eating out here was really their only option, so she nodded and murmured, "That would be fine, m'laird."

It wasn't until they were seated and he was digging through the bag of food he'd brought that she said, "Thank you for coming to the cottage to walk me back, and supplying the food. 'Tis appreciated."

"As are yer efforts to heal the blacksmith," Graeme countered as he pulled out a chicken leg and offered it to her. Turning back to the bag once she'd taken the meat, he added, "Though, it does sound as though yer kept quite busy with the task o' healin', and I do wonder that ye ne'er trained someone who could help relieve ye o' the burden on occasion."

Annella frowned at the words, feeling the sting of criticism whether he meant his words that way or not. But now that he'd said it, she was also wondering about the matter herself. The truth was, it had never occurred to her. She had at one point tried to teach Florie so that she could help her on trickier occasions. Unfortunately, Florie had fainted the first time she'd accompanied her. When it happened again the next time as well, Annella had realized the lass had an aversion to blood that was so bad that the sight and smell of it had her swooning. It had made her give up on training the maid, although the girl still accompanied Annella on less bloody occasions. That being the case, it hadn't occurred to her to try to train someone else, or if it had, it had only been a fleeting thought, quickly pushed aside by the need to do this or that.

In truth, between her duties as healer, as well as her duties as chatelaine at Castle Gunn, and her having her absent husband's duties as laird foisted upon her too . . . well, she felt she could be forgiven for overlooking something like that.

Unfortunately, forgiven or not, Annella suddenly felt terribly guilty . . . because her lack of forethought in not training someone in healing meant that when she left, there would be no healer at Gunn at all. Bett, the old woman who had originally been healer here, had died in the first year after Annella's arrival. Busy as she already was, Annella had simply added that task to her already long list of duties and rushed about trying to accomplish everything she could in each day. It had resulted in many things being neglected.

Sighing, she lowered the hand holding the chicken leg and said, "My apologies. I've just realized that my departure will leave Gunn without a healer. I should have trained someone in the skill these last years since old Bett's passing."

"Old Bett," he said softly, affection in his voice. "She tended many an illness and injury fer me and me brothers growing up."

"I can imagine," Annella said with a faint smile. Her mother had been the healer at MacKay and she had done the same for Annella, her brother and sister.

"When did she pass?" Graeme asked, his smile fading.

"Oh . . ." Annella had to think for a minute, and then said, "It was just days or near a week after your father's fall down the keep stairs." Nodding as her recollection returned, she added, "Aye. She tended him at first, and then I took over when she passed. Although, by then there was nothing to do but check on him every day." Glancing, at him she explained, "To make sure he's not getting bedsores, or that no other issues have cropped up."

Graeme grunted at that around a mouthful of meat, and Annella turned her own attention to the chicken leg she held. They ate in a companionable silence until the meat, cheese and bread were gone, and then Graeme packed the leavings back into the sac he'd had the food in, set it on the step above them and stood to offer her a hand. "Shall we take a short walk to let our stomachs settle ere finding our beds?"

Annella hesitated. The food had gone a long way to restoring her energy. A short walk might help to expel some of it so that she could sleep, she thought and took the offered hand so that he could help her rise. She was a little surprised though, when he then drew it through the crook of his arm as he led her along the front of the keep. They were turning the corner to start along the side of the keep when he said, "Yer brother told me ye wanted a boon."

Annella glanced quickly to and away from the man beside her. "In exchange for helping you settle in, aye."

"And what would that boon be?"

Annella bit her lip, but then said quietly, "You ken I want to return home to me family at MacKay."

"I ken."

Annella frowned slightly. She would have been happier had he said, "Aye, and o' course ye will," or something else to indicate that it was fine with him, and once she'd helped him, he wouldn't prevent it.

But she left that concern for now, and said instead, "Florie—she's my lady's maid—I'd like to take her with me when I return home to MacKay. If she's willing, of course," Annella added quickly, because she hadn't had the chance to ask the girl yet.

"Hmmm."

Annella peered at him with one eyebrow raised. "Is that an aye, a nay, or a ye-wish-time-to-think-on-it?"

Surprisingly, her dry question brought a chuckle from the man.

"An aye," he assured her. "If ye're happy with her, I've no wish to stop Florie from bein' yer lady's maid."

Annella felt her body relax at his words. She was glad to stop worrying about losing Florie when she finally left. "Then I'd be happy to take a couple o' days to help ye sort things here ere I go."

Graeme nodded, but was frowning to himself. He was pretty sure it would take more than a day or two to woo her into agreeing to marry him. Especially since he had no idea how to go about it. Another woman, one who wasn't a lady, he might lure into the gardens and seduce. But he would never treat her thusly. Tossing up a lady's skirts in the gardens was just not done. He knew that much at least.

"The gardens."

Graeme blinked and glanced to Annella with surprise, thinking it was almost as if she'd read his mind. But then he saw that their walk had somehow taken them to the very place he'd been thinking about. Apparently, his feet had brought him here despite the fact that seducing her was off the table.

Glancing around the gardens, still beautiful even

in moonlight, he sought for something to say and then blurted, "I always liked them when I was growing up. I used to climb the trees and hide in them when me mother was sufferin' from bad humors."

"Hmmm." Annella's voice sounded grim. "She seems to suffer those quite a bit. Every time she sees me, in fact."

Her words surprised a chuckle out of Graeme, but he assured her, "'Tis no' only you. 'Tis pretty much everyone she encounters. Except perhaps William," he added. "She liked him well enough. He was the first born and heir, after all."

Annella nodded, but asked, "What about you? As her son, surely she favored you too?"

"Oh, nay," he assured her with a dry laugh. "William was no' just the heir and future laird, he also took his looks from her. Unfortunately, I meself look more like me father, who she always loathed and felt was beneath her."

"Really?" she asked with surprise. "Then why does she spend most o' her time up in their bedchamber with him?"

"Does she?" he asked with interest.

"Aye. When she's not following me around, trying to make me miserable, she's above stairs in their bedchamber with yer father."

"Probably makin' *him* miserable," he muttered, and then said "I did no' wish to trouble ye with such a question while we were eating, but what happened to me father? Me mither said he fell down the stairs . . ."

Annella sighed and turned to continue walking through the gardens before saying, "That's what I was told, though I was not here to see it. Angus—me husband's first, then me first and now, I suppose, yours," she said with a wry twist to her lips before continuing, "He was showing me around the castle, courtyard and Gunn land that day, explaining how things ran. When I returned, I was told that Gaufrid had slept late, which is apparently unusual, then woke up dizzy and shaky, tried to make his way down to the great hall, lost his footing or fainted and fell."

Plucking a leaf from a bush they were passing, she began to absently tear it into pieces and said, "It was a terrible fall. He was lucky to survive, but did not come out of it unscathed. He broke his back and has no feeling or movement from the waist down. I think he also must have knocked his head hard several times on the way down the stairs, because he has some issues there as well."

"I know his speech is impeded," Graeme murmured.

"Aye. He also remembers nothing from the wedding night on, up to and including his fall a week or so later. 'Tis like those memories were knocked out o' him," she said solemnly. "But his arms and hands work fine and he remembers his letters and can write, so we keep scrolls and ink by him so at least he's able to communicate what he wants or needs."

She saw Graeme's eyebrows rise, and then he murmured, "There were no scrolls or ink by him when I went to tell me parents about William the day I arrived."

Annella's eyes narrowed at this. "'Tis always there when I check on him, which I do every other day."

"Do ye check him at the same time e'ery other day?" Graeme asked.

"Aye."

"Then Mother probably puts it beside him when she kens ye're comin'," he said grimly. "She was no' expectin' me when I went above stairs. Other than you and the men holdin' down yer patient, most o' the castle was sleepin' when we arrived and I did no' trouble to make our presence widely known. And, while I knocked when I went above to speak to them, I also did no' wait after, but opened the door at once because I'd seen one o' the maids enter with a tray o' food as I went up the hall so knew they'd be awake."

"But she would no' have had the chance to put scrolls and ink near him if she normally kept it from him," Annella reasoned.

"Aye."

"Do ye really think she would keep ink and scrolls from him and leave him unable to communicate?" she asked. Annella was pretty sure the woman would. Eschina Gunn really was a bitter, miserable old woman. But Annella was curious to know how Graeme saw his mother. She was not disappointed.

"Oh, aye, she would," he assured her. "In fact, she'd no doubt enjoy doin' it too. I wid be more surprised were she no' torturing him in other small and petty ways as well." Pausing, he met her gaze and said solemnly, "Me mither is no' a good woman."

"Hmm," Annella murmured, opening her hand and letting the pieces of torn leaf flutter to the ground. "You would think he would write that to me on one of my checks on him, rather than suffer in silence."

"Nay. He's too proud," Graeme said with certainty.

"He'd no' wish anyone to ken if he's sufferin' under her hand. He'd fear lookin' less a man."

Annella nodded in understanding. Her father was a proud man, so she wasn't surprised to hear that the old laird might be as well. He'd seemed a lot like her father before his accident. Pushing the thought aside, she said, "I've suggested more than once that we could have a couple men carry him outside and set him on a blanket to enjoy some sunlight and fresh air of an afternoon, but yer mother keeps saying no, that he might catch a chill and die."

Graeme snorted. "I doubt she cares fer his health. 'Tis more like she fears he might enjoy himself by escapin' her fer a bit."

"Aye," Annella agreed with amusement. She couldn't stand the woman.

"I think on the morrow I'll go speak to him again," Graeme decided. "This time I'll make sure he has scrolls and ink to communicate, and will ask if he'd like to be outside fer a bit. Then I'll ask if he'd like me mother moved from his room to her own."

"What if he says aye, and yer mother is upset or offended?" Annella asked with interest.

"Too bad," Graeme said dryly.

"Ye've no problem banishing yer mother to another bedchamber?"

"Nay, no' if she's been passin' her days doing naught but makin' me father miserable," he assured her. "Hell, I'd happily banish her to a cottage outside the walls if she's been doin' that. Me da deserves better."

When Annella didn't comment, he asked, "Is she the reason ye're so eager to flee Gunn fer MacKay?"

"Aye," Annella said without even needing to think about it. Eschina Gunn had done her very best to make her miserable since her wedding. Or actually, really since the morning after her wedding when it was discovered William had left in the night like a thief. Rather than say that, Annella found herself admitting, "But also because I should like a proper marriage. One with a handful o' bairns, and a husband who is actually there."

"Ah. Aye, I'd like that meself."

"Ye'd like a husband?" she asked innocently.

Graeme looked startled, and said quickly, "Nay. I meant a wife and bairns, no'—" He paused, and shook his head when a soft laugh slipped from her. "Ye're teasin' me."

"Aye," Annella admitted, and they fell into a companionable silence for a minute before Graeme spoke again.

"Do ye think yer father will be able to arrange another marriage fer ye?"

Annella glanced at him sharply. "Aye, of course. Why would he no'?"

Graeme shrugged and caught her arm to steer her around a branch hanging in her path before saying gently, "Well, 'tis most like no' an issue, but I ken that yer dower was generous when ye married me brother."

"Aye," she agreed. Both her and Kenna's dowers were generous.

Graeme nodded. "But yer older now, lass. An even larger dower might be needed to lure a husband."

Annella stiffened and stopped walking at those words. That simply wasn't something she'd even contemplated. She'd passed twenty and two years. Nearly twenty and three. Many would consider her overripe and too old to marry. She was also a widow. They might worry over whether she could produce children for them since she'd been married six years without having a bairn. Not everyone knew of the humiliating circumstances of her marriage, and that her husband had fled almost as soon as the "I dos" were done. And those who didn't, would assume her husband had been plowing her fields these six years with no crop to show for it.

"And," Graeme continued, regaining her attention, "I would wonder that yer father would be willing to take from yer brother's inheritance to arrange another marriage fer ye."

Annella frowned at these words. Take from her brother's inheritance to get her another husband? She hadn't thought about it like that, but that was exactly what would have to happen. Even to her that didn't seem fair. She'd had her chance. It wasn't Payton's fault that she'd been so unappealing her husband had fled the marriage bed and run off on a "pilgrimage" with the village lightskirts. Besides, it wasn't only Payton who would be affected if her father did that. Having ruled Gunn these last six years, Annella knew what it took to run a castle and its clan. How having enough coin in the coffers could mean the difference between a clan surviving or not surviving either a drought or too much rain that affected the crops. Her desire to marry again and expecting her father to pay for it could leave the MacKay clan in a perilous position if he agreed.

"I'm sorry, did I upset ye, lass?" Graeme asked with sudden concern, drawing her to a halt. "Either ye've gone suddenly pale, or the light here's queer, cause right now yer face looks white as the moon this clear night. Here, sit yersel' down."

Annella found herself urged backward a step or two until she felt something against the back of her legs and then plopped down to sit on what she suspected was the stone half wall that separated the fruit trees from the garden where chestnut and hazel trees grew along with various flowers.

Graeme sat beside her, retrieved a skin from his belt, and uncapped and handed it to her. "Have a sip o' this. Ye'll feel better."

Annella accepted the skin, raised it to her lips and tipped it up to pour some liquid into her mouth. But she tipped it too far, and had to gulp quickly to keep from spilling it all over herself. She'd barely swallowed the last of what she'd taken in of the potent brew before she was gasping for air, sputtering and coughing.

"I said sip, lass. 'Tis uisge beatha." Graeme's voice was alarmed as he took the skin away with one hand, even as he began to pound on her back with the other. "Breathe, lass. 'Twill pass, jest breathe."

Easier said than done, Annella thought as she alternated gasping in long draughts of air and coughing. Good Lord, Gunn whiskey was strong. It took a few minutes for the coughing to stop and her breathing to ease, and then Annella shuddered and sagged where she sat. It took her another moment to realize that she was leaning up against Graeme's side while he now rubbed her back soothingly.

"There, that's better," he murmured. "All right now?"

Annella raised her head from his chest to answer him and then stilled. Their faces were now inches apart, so close she could feel his breath on her lips. She stared at him silently, taking in the lines of his face with interest, realizing only then that this was the first time she'd really looked at the man since the morning he'd arrived.

That first morning he'd been filthy from his travels, and his hair had been long and shaggy, as had the full facial hair he'd been sporting. Now his clean dark hair seemed a little shorter, though it still fell past his shoulders. He was also clean-shaven. Annella wasn't sure when he'd cleaned up. Had he still had the shaggy hair and beard when she'd approached her brother and him out in the courtyard that morning? She hadn't really got that close before her brother had left Graeme and come to greet her, and honestly, she hadn't paid the other man much notice. The same was true of that night at dinner. She'd been headed for the trestle tables, noted the presence of her brother and the other men, but then the blacksmith Silas's brother had arrived, babbling frantically that Silas was burning up and his wife, Mary, had sent him to beg her to come check on him and she'd rushed away.

Other than her examination of him on first meeting, Annella hadn't paid the man any more attention than she would a gnat. And now here they were out in the garden at night and she was paying attention. Fortunately, the moon was full with little in the way of clouds to obscure its light and she could make out all of his features pretty well. Not as well as she would have in daylight, but enough to verify that he was indeed a handsome man as she'd first thought. He looked absolutely nothing like her recollections of his brother William. Her husband had been twenty to her sixteen when they'd married. In her memory he'd been all long limbs and lean muscle, with sharp features and blond hair. She'd thought him handsome and felt lucky to marry him.

This man had dark hair, his features were blunter, and his body . . . Her gaze slid down to his shoulders and across what she could see of his wide, muscular chest. Unlike her husband, this man was more than twice as wide as her. It made her feel positively tiny . . . and safe.

She lifted her head to peer at his face again and decided that while her husband had been attractive in a youthful way, Graeme had a different appeal. He was all man, his features hardened by experience and the passage of years. His mouth didn't look hard though. It was lovely, with a full lower lip to balance out the thinner upper one, she thought and wondered what it would feel like if she ran her finger over that lower lip.

Annella drew in a surprised breath at her own thoughts, and noted that Graeme not only looked good, he smelled positively amazing. Why did he smell so good? she wondered a little fuzzily as she inhaled his scent again. She didn't remember thinking that about her husband. Although, to be fair, she might have been too terrified to smell anything on her wedding night.

"Lass?"

His voice was a deep rumble, and she almost felt the sound under her fingers where they'd somehow spread out over his chest. Annella lifted eyelids she hadn't realized she'd let drift to half-mast and met his gaze as she whispered, "Ye smell nice."

Graeme looked a little stunned at the words. Something she could completely understand, because Annella hadn't meant to say them, they'd just somehow slipped out. But she didn't take them back. She was feeling too relaxed at the moment. The whiskey seemed to have warmed her all the way to her toes, and eased the tension she usually carried around in her body to the point of languor.

"Ye smell good too," Graeme finally responded.

Annella smiled at the words and didn't resist when the hand rubbing her back urged her closer. She didn't even react when his lips brushed across hers. At least, not at first. She just enjoyed the way his warm lips moved over her mouth. It seemed natural and felt good and Annella didn't protest.

A little moan slid from her when he caught her lower lip between both of his and drew on it gently. She couldn't really say how that suddenly turned into a full-on devouring, with her lips parting under his and his tongue delving in to explore as his mouth ravished hers.

God in heaven, it was the most exquisite thing she'd ever experienced. Pleasure was suddenly filling her from every direction, flowing from her toes to the top of her head and back, rioting throughout her body. She found herself grasping at the front of his shirt and plaid, pressing herself more firmly against him, her body almost writhing in its desire to get closer as his hands moved over her back, molding her to him.

When his mouth left hers to travel down her throat, a small mewl of protest slipped from her lips and then her head fell back at the delirium his exploring mouth caused. One of his hands left her back and slid around to find and close over a breast through her gown. Annella gasped and cried out, her back instinctively arching to thrust herself into the caress as he kneaded and plucked at her through the cloth separating them.

Graeme immediately returned his mouth to hers, capturing the excited sounds she was eliciting as he toyed with her breast and the nipple that was quickly pebbling under his attention. So distracted was she by the passion he was drawing from her, that she didn't at first notice when he shifted her to sit across his lap. It wasn't until his mouth left hers to replace his hand at her breast that she noted their position and how improper it was. But when he then began to suckle and nip at her tender flesh through the quickly dampening material of her gown, she let the awareness slip away. At least she did until his now free hand began to glide under her skirts.

Some small part of her brain went quiet as his fingers slid up her calf and past her knee, but her body was still responding, shifting restlessly in his lap, her hands clutching at his shoulders now. And then his hand went still, and he lifted his head to claim her lips once more. This time though, his kiss was more soothing than exciting. There was still passion, but a gentler one, almost apologetic. His hand then retreated. Once it was out from under her skirt, he broke the kiss, wrapped her in his arms, and pressed her head to his chest to simply hold her while she caught her breath.

It took several moments for her body and her breathing to calm. Once both had, Annella remained still in his embrace, unsure what to do. Should she apologize? Slap him? Beg him to continue what he'd been doing? In truth she was torn between begging him to continue, and rushing away to the safety of her room to sort out what the hell had just happened. But Annella suspected she should probably be apologizing for being so wanton, and maybe giving him hell for being so free with her.

Except that he was the one who had ended it.

He released a sigh so deep she felt it through her body as if it had been her own, and then Graeme eased her away and brushed the hair gently back from her face. "I'm sorry, lass. That was no' well done o' me. I fear ye're just so lovely and sweet I could no' help meself, and once I tasted ye . . ." He simply shook his head, not finishing the thought. Instead, he urged her to her feet, promising, "I'll try to behave better around ye in future."

Annella again had no idea how to respond. She had no idea why he'd stopped what he was doing, and supposed she should say thank you, or something of that ilk. But really, she just wanted to stamp her feet in protest at his promise to behave better. She had enjoyed his kisses very much and, as shameful as it was to admit it, would have liked an opportunity to enjoy more of them.

In the end, she simply ducked her head and brushed imaginary wrinkles out of her gown until he took her arm and turned her to walk her back toward the castle, saying, "I'll see ye to yer chamber."

Chapter 4

ANNELLA WAS LYING ON HER SIDE, PEERING out the window of her bedchamber when she heard her door open. The sound made her immediately close her eyes to feign sleep. She wasn't yet ready to get up and face the day, and not just because she hadn't slept much in the night. She'd spent the better part of it reliving the walk from the blacksmith's back to the castle, the shared dinner on the steps, the walk through the gardens and the kisses with Graeme. She'd spent the other part with Graeme's words running through her head.

I would wonder that yer father would be willing to take from yer brother's inheritance to arrange another marriage fer ye.

Annella had never considered where the money for a new dower would have to come from. In truth, she hadn't even considered the matter of a dower. All she'd been thinking was that she would marry again, and this time to a man who would see her before signing the contracts, and therefore would most assuredly be willing to bed her and give her the children she'd always wanted. Otherwise, he wouldn't agree to marry her.

Graeme's words, however, had widened her focus to include how her father would manage to get her another husband. A dower, and no doubt a rather hefty one. Not only did most people not know that her husband had left in the night after marrying her, but absolutely no one except her knew that he hadn't even consummated the marriage.

A sigh almost slipped from Annella's lips before the rustle of movement as someone crossed the room reminded her that she wasn't alone. Opening her eyes little more than slits, she saw Florie reach the washstand and pick up the empty pitcher there. She quickly closed her eyes again as the maid started to turn back, then listened to her return to the door and pull it softly closed.

Heading down to fetch water for my ablutions, Annella thought as she opened her eyes once more. Her gaze returned to the window where sunlight was just starting to reveal the cloudy sky outside, but her mind immediately returned to what had been occupying it all night. In all good conscience, she couldn't expect her father to take from MacKay and its people to pay a second, hefty dower for her. It would be terribly selfish of her even to ask that . . . and Annella wasn't that selfish.

But where did that leave her? That was the question that she'd been pondering through the night. She'd only come up with two solutions. The first option was that she should confess that William had not consummated the marriage, but instead had cut his hand and spread the blood on the bed for proof of consummation before leaving their room. If she did this, her father could have the marriage annulled, and demand her dower back, allowing him to arrange another marriage for her using her original dower and without touching her brother's inheritance.

Of course, this would be a humiliating ordeal all the way around. Not only because the whole of Scotland would then know that William had found her so unattractive that he hadn't been able to bring himself to bed her even once before fleeing on his "pilgrimage," but also because she would have to be examined to prove her claim. Annella wasn't sure who would be appointed to the task, but the King's doctors were all men and she cringed at the thought of the lot of them kneeling between her naked thighs to poke and prod to find her maidenhead. Actually, the idea made her feel positively ill.

That left the second option, resigning herself to never having a proper husband or those children she'd always wanted, and instead, living out the rest of her days as a widow at MacKay. Annella had no doubt that her parents would welcome her back and allow her to remain. She was equally sure her brother, Payton, would let her remain after their father passed and he became laird. But if she chose this option, it would not only be a husband and children she would need to give up on but experiencing the passion and bedding that other wives and mothers enjoyed.

That was something Annella had never concerned herself with ere last night. But just the memory of those few heated moments with Graeme in the garden made her body tingle and shiver. It seemed terribly unfair that she would never experience those sensations again. What would have happened if he hadn't stopped? Where had the mounting passion been leading? Of course, Annella's mother had prepared her for the marriage bed, telling her what would happen. She knew the mechanics of it. But she wanted to experience the delirium and passionate explosions she'd heard about when she and her sister, Kenna, had listened in on the chatter between their cousin Jo and her friends some years ago. She'd thought it had all sounded silly and exaggerated at the time. Surely nothing could feel as good as they'd been waxing on about, she'd thought.

She'd been wrong, Annella acknowledged. She had been in something of a delirium last night, forgetting where and who she was and that this wasn't proper at all, just craving more. It seemed incredibly unfair to her that she'd been six years married and never experienced any of it. William hadn't even kissed her properly on their wedding night.

Sucking her lower lip into her mouth, Annella closed her eyes as she relived last evening's brief moments of passion.

Could just any man stir that passion in her, or was Graeme exceptionally skilled? She had no idea, but what if it was only Graeme who could make her tremble and moan? It meant that once she left here for MacKay, she'd never enjoy it again. The thought made her frown unhappily.

Perhaps she should try to get him to kiss her again . . . or even more. His touching her had been amazing and—Annella smiled crookedly at her thoughts, because the truth is she wanted to experience more . . . all of it. She wanted Graeme to bed her fully. That admission to herself was only a little shocking. After all, she was a married woman. Well, a widow now, she supposed. Whatever the case, no one thought she still had her maidenhead, so what matter was it if she lost it? Aye, she suspected she'd enjoy being bedded by Graeme, and at least then she would have memories to hold close over the next decades.

Of course, if it was as grand as she suspected it would be, Annella would rather experience those things more than once. But she vowed not to be greedy. Just once would have to be enough. Or mayhap two or more times depending on how long she remained here.

Now the issue became how to get Graeme to bed her. He'd certainly been very ardent in the garden. At first at least. But then he had brought an end to the kissing relatively quickly, and apologized. However, in his apologizing, he'd also claimed that once he'd tasted her, he hadn't been able to resist, or words to that effect. It was hard to recall his exact words. She'd been in something of a state at the time. No matter though, the point was this suggested that he'd only stopped because she was a lady, and that he *was* attracted to her.

Wasn't he? Annella bit her lip as she pondered the matter. Sadly, her husband's complete lack of interest in her on their wedding night had damaged her esteem terribly . . . and in a way that all her successes at running Gunn and its people could not mend. Which meant she had trouble believing that Graeme might find her attractive enough to bed.

Maybe he'd only been interested in her because it had been dark in the gardens, and he hadn't been able to see her properly. Would he still find her attractive in daylight? Or had he even really found her attractive last evening? Perhaps he had said what he had to be kind and he hadn't really enjoyed the kisses at all. Perhaps that was the real reason he'd stopped.

If that was the case, he'd hardly trouble himself to kiss her again, let alone bed her. Annella scowled at the possibility and briefly considered the merits of blackmailing him into bedding her. She could threaten to seek an annulment and demand her dower back if he didn't.

Having run the castle and worked the books these last six years, Annella knew that Gunn had been in a bad way when she'd married William. Her dower had brought some desperately needed coin to the clan. It turned out that Gaufrid Gunn, William's father, had not only not enjoyed being laird, he had, in fact, not been very good at it. Aside from some bad luck with inclement weather damaging the crops two years in a row, he'd also made some very poor decisions that had left the Gunn coffers seriously depleted. In fact, Annella's marriage to William when it happened, had basically saved the people of Gunn. That was part of the reason that Gaufrid had stepped down and let William take on the mantle of laird a week before the wedding. Everyone had felt sure the son would do a better job than the old man, including Gaufrid himself.

Of course, in the end, William hadn't been there to

do the job, and Annella had performed it in his stead. Fortunately, she'd been damned good at it. She'd managed to bring things around so that if she reclaimed her dower, it would not leave them in dire straits right away, but it would leave them in an uncomfortable situation that could easily become perilous if anything unexpected happened before they could build up coin again.

That being the case, blackmail might actually work, she considered. Or at least it might have if her conscience didn't immediately set up a squawking at the very idea of it. How could she even consider something so appalling? Did she really want to force a man to bed her? Where was her pride?

Sighing, Annella rolled onto her back and stared at the material over her bed. She was taken with the idea of Graeme bedding her. She really wanted more of those kisses. But blackmail did seem a step too far. She'd probably roast in hell did she dare it.

Perhaps rather than blackmail, she could seduce him. The thought was a tantalizing one. The only problem was she had no idea how to go about it. That wasn't something she'd ever even considered doing before. Heck, she hadn't even been kissed before last night.

A married woman six years, and only now that her husband was finally known to be dead had she been kissed. That just seemed to be her luck. Although that hadn't always been the case. She'd been very lucky growing up. She'd had wonderful, loving parents in a powerful and wealthy clan. Her childhood had been quite happy.

It was only once she'd come to Gunn that everything had gone to hell. Between her absent husband, her miserable mother-in-law and feeling so alone, life had been wretched here. At least at first. Over time, successfully carrying the burden as chatelaine, laird and healer had helped her grow confident and self-assured enough to be able to deal with it all, including her bitchy mother-in-law. The question was, would that confidence and self-assurance aid her in seducing Graeme? Because she really did want to experience more of the pleasure he'd shown her last night before she returned to the bosom of her family.

Aye, she would seduce him, Annella decided firmly and tossed the linens and furs aside to sit up on the edge of her bed. She was supposed to help Graeme take up his position as laird and make the transition smoother. It was why she couldn't leave right away. Annella had no idea how he expected her to do that, but supposed she would find out. Besides, she had to face him sometime, and it would be good to know how he reacted to her in daylight. She was afraid he wouldn't find her attractive at all, which would make her seducing him more difficult. Not impossible perhaps, but it might call for large quantities of uisge beatha and darkness to get the task done. Still, it was better to know so she could plan.

Nodding, she stood and walked to her chest to begin searching for a gown to wear.

"I THINK WE'LL STOP AND REST HERE A BIT."

Annella glanced around at Graeme's comment to see that they were in a pretty little clearing at the side of a river. A spot she'd never seen in the six years she'd lived at Gunn. She had no idea where it was, exactly. She'd been deep in thought since leaving the last villein's cottage, trying to sort out whether Graeme might be attracted to her or not. The aid he'd wished from her this morning had been to take him around and introduce him to the villagers and villeins on his land. Something Angus had done for her after she'd married William and he'd left. Actually, it was something Angus could have easily done for Graeme too, but she hadn't said as much and had simply gone along with the request.

They'd ridden out after breaking their fast to start the tour, and had been at it for hours. By her guess it was around the nooning now and she still had no idea whether Graeme found her attractive in daylight, or last evening in the gardens had just been a moonlight-induced aberration.

He'd barely looked at her and had been quiet at the table that morning, leaving his friends Teague and Symon along with her brother, Payton, to carry the conversation. They also hadn't talked much as they'd ridden out, and each time they'd stopped, he'd concentrated on the individuals she'd introduced him to, so it was hard to tell what he was thinking or feeling in regards to her.

"Lass?"

Pushing her thoughts away, she glanced around to see that Graeme had dismounted and was now beside her horse, holding his arms up to help her down.

Managing a smile, she released the reins of her mare and dismounted. He caught her as she dropped toward the ground, and eased her landing. Annella murmured a soft "Thank ye" for it, then reclaimed her mare's reins and followed him to a tree to affix them to a branch. Graeme did the same.

"I'm afraid lunch'll be a rehash o' yester eve's meal," Graeme said apologetically as he moved along his horse's side. "Cook did no' ha'e time to make aught ere we left. Except the bread. That's fresh made this morn. It was just finishin' when I collected the meal."

Annella's eyes widened as Graeme moved to retrieve a sac she hadn't noticed hanging from his saddle. She was a little vexed for not thinking of it herself. "Thank you fer thinkin' o' it. I myself did not even consider what we would do about the nooning meal ere we left."

Graeme waved her thanks away. "I expected as much."

Annella glanced at him sharply. "You did?"

"Aye," he said with amusement as he now retrieved a rolled fur and led her to the edge of the river. "I was told ye ha'e a tendency to ferget about things like the need to eat and sleep when yer about yer day."

Automatically taking the sac he handed her, Annella frowned with dissatisfaction at what felt like a criticism as she watched him lay out the fur for them. But when he gestured for her to sit on it, she dropped onto one side and asked a bit irritably, "Who said that?"

"Angus," Graeme answered promptly, taking up position across from her.

Annella scowled at the name. Angus was always acting an old woman around her. Fussing that she needed to eat and sleep more, that she'd make herself sick and so on. Or at least he had when he was her first. Now he was Graeme's first, she supposed . . . and telling tales on her like a child.

"And Tavis, Florie, Cook, Aiden, Brodie, Silas . . ."

Annella's mouth dropped open as he listed off name after name of the soldiers and servants who had carried tales about her. But once he reached Silas, the blacksmith, she sat up straight and asked, "You talked to Silas?"

"Aye. This morn. I went down to the loch to clean up ere breakin' me fast, and stopped in on the way back to check on him."

"How was he?" she asked at once.

"Good, I think," he said reassuringly. "He was awake and talkin'. Had some color in his cheeks, but no sign o' fever. His wife, Mary, said he was much improved and she's hopeful."

Annella nodded and relaxed a little. She'd meant to check on him this morn, but hadn't had the time. Graeme had told her of his plan to have her take him around and introduce him to the villeins and serfs at table, and he'd wanted to leave the moment she'd finished breaking her fast. She was glad to know the blacksmith was doing well. Still, she'd want to check on him for herself when they returned.

"Mary and Silas are both very grateful to ye, and wished me to tell ye so," Graeme added softly.

Annella waved that away with a touch of embarrassment. It was her place to see to their welfare. She was their laird. Or had been, she corrected herself with a sigh and then set down the sac he'd given her to hold.

They were both silent as they worked together to set out the fruit, chicken, cheese and bread. But when Graeme produced a skin, her eyes widened as she recalled the coughing fit she'd had the night before and what had followed.

"Mead," Graeme told her with a faint smile that softened as his eyes dropped to her lips and stayed there.

Annella swallowed. While his gaze was only on her lips, she was suddenly feeling overwarm and aware of every inch of skin on her body as it all seemed to prickle under his attention. Despite her decision to seduce him, that wasn't her intention when she suddenly licked her lips. It was purely because her mouth had suddenly gone dry.

In fact, she hadn't considered that the action would have any kind of effect on him until Graeme suddenly groaned and closed his eyes, saying, "Oh, lass, ye're killin' me here. 'Tis hard enough no' touchin' and kissin' on ye without ye—"

His words died abruptly when Annella leaned forward over the food between them to place her lips on his. She just couldn't help herself. His words proved he did want her in daylight too, and the memory of his kisses the night before, combined with that fact just unleashed her impulses. Sadly, though, she had no idea what to do next. How to kiss him as he'd kissed her.

For one moment, they were just frozen, her lips pressed to his mouth unmoving, but then he let his breath out, caught her by the upper arms and drew her to him across the food, even as he turned her so that he could press her down onto her back on the fur.

Annella went willingly, her arms slipping around his back when he released his hold on them to brace himself as he came down on top of her. Then he was kissing her as he had the night before, his mouth devouring hers, and tongue exploring. Annella moaned as the remembered pleasure from last evening roared through her body. It was as if it had just been waiting on the edges to make itself known. It was also overwhelming and so delicious she wanted it to never end.

Recalling how he'd stopped their kissing the night before, she clung to him now, her body arching up into his even as he pressed down into her. When she felt his knee nudge hers, she let her legs fall apart, and then gasped and writhed when he rested between her legs and pressed his hardness against her very core through their clothes. The excitement that sent charging through her was heady and she thrust back, thoughtlessly rubbing herself against that hardness.

Graeme broke their kiss to growl, "Lass," but that's as far as he got before she caught him by the ears and dragged his mouth back to hers. He resisted for a heartbeat, and then kissed her more passionately, almost violently, his body thrusting against hers, and one hand moving over her body. He found and caressed one breast through her gown, then released it to tug at the neckline of the dress until her laces gave way and her breasts were exposed. Annella felt the warm breeze brush over her hardening nipples, and then his hand was there, claiming first one and then the other.

Groaning, she wrapped her legs around his waist to pull his hips tighter against her as he caressed her bare flesh, then cried out when he broke their kiss to claim one erect nipple and draw it into his mouth. The sensation was so overwhelming that she almost missed his hand now dragging her skirts up, baring her legs then hips so that he could squeeze his hand between their bodies and find her center.

Annella froze then, gasping for air as he began to caress her core, his fingers moving cleverly over her wet warmth and drawing more moisture from her. It was as if her body was weeping for his attention, she thought—and then lost all ability to think when something began pushing into her.

This was it! Dear God! Her mother had told her what to expect from the bedding, and she knew this must be his manhood she was feeling. He was going to claim her as her mother had said would happen. Her mother, however, hadn't told her how good it would feel. In fact, she'd said it might hurt the first time, but there was no pain here, just pleasure. Graeme was still caressing her at the same time, and her body was responding as it wished, writhing and shuddering even as her warmth closed around his firm manhood, drawing him in and egging him on. Her hips were moving now too, thrusting into him, trying to urge him deeper, and then all of the passion and heat that had been building in her suddenly seemed to pull tight before exploding.

Crying out, Annella clutched at Graeme and nearly wept as pleasure poured over her. Almost mindless at that point, she was wholly unprepared when something much bigger than what she'd thought was his manhood suddenly thrust into her. Her cry then was one of shock and startled pain as he broke through her maidenhead.

Graeme froze at once, fully planted in her and panting. He raised himself up slightly to peer at her stunned face with concern. "Sorry, lass. I thought—I mean ye—William did no' e'en . . . ?"

Annella shuddered slightly and shook her head. Humiliation flowing through her that he knew her secret, she closed her eyes in shame.

Graeme pressed a kiss to first one eyelid and then the other, and when she reluctantly opened her eyes again to meet his gaze, he smiled crookedly and said, "Lucky me."

Annella was still blinking at that when he slid one hand between them again and resumed caressing her. Her eyes widened with surprise when the pleasure she'd thought killed by the brief pain of the breaching began to stir and stretch within her. When he kissed her again, she responded tentatively at first and then with growing need. Graeme remained still otherwise, and simply continued to kiss and caress her until she herself began to move, her hips shifting against him as her excitement returned to full force. Then he too resumed moving, sliding himself out and then thrusting back in as she lifted her hips in time with his. Soon, her humiliation of a marriage was forgotten and they were moving together, struggling toward the passionate explosion she now knew waited at the end of this growing need and tension.

Annella broke their kiss and screamed her pleasure when it happened, a sound that was quickly drowned out by his shout when he joined her a heartbeat later.

ANNELLA WAS WEAK, TREMBLING AND AS LIMP as a cloth doll when Graeme finally collapsed. Dropping onto his side next to her, he drew her with him as he rolled onto his back and arranged her so that her head rested on his chest and she lay half on top of him. He then wrapped one arm around her and kissed the top of her hair before letting his head fall to rest on the fur.

They lay in silence for a moment, each trying to regain their breath and then Graeme opened his eyes and peered at the sky overhead. It had been gray all morning, but was more so now with the clouds darkening and threatening rain. He was thinking they should probably head back to the keep, but wanted to sort things with Annella first. He hadn't planned to seduce her today. He'd hoped to woo her a bit, and mayhap even kiss and caress her some more too, but not to take her as he had.

Graeme supposed he should have known better than to think he could play with fire and not get burned. It had been hard as hell for him to stop their encounter the night before. He should have heeded that and kept his hands to himself today. Instead, he'd taken her on a fur in the woods . . . and he'd taken her maidenhead too. That had been something of a surprise, although considering what he knew of William, perhaps it shouldn't have been, he thought, and then moved on to thinking about the future instead of a past he didn't understand.

The future was that he and Annella would have to marry. He'd breached her maiden's veil and poured his seed into her. She could be with child even now.

Neither of them had a choice, which made him feel a touch guilty, because he was getting what he'd wanted. He wasn't sure how Annella felt on the topic. But Graeme knew she didn't like his mother and had been eager to escape to MacKay to find another husband. He may have just forced her into doing the very last thing she would have wanted. None of which mattered now, he told himself firmly. She could be carrying his son or daughter thanks to what they'd done.

That possibility in mind, he rubbed his hand over Annella's back and murmured, "We'll ha'e to marry, lass."

Annella stiffened on top of him and then pushed herself up to peer at him. "Nay."

The word surprised Graeme and he scowled at it. "Aye."

"Nay," she repeated insistently. "There's no need fer ye to marry me. I seduced ye."

A short huff of laughter slipped out that Graeme quickly cut off. He didn't want to upset or embarrass her, but found her claim ridiculous. The lass had proven to be as inexperienced as a babe, though her enthusiasm and responsiveness had made up for it. Still, he was the one who had done the seducing. "Lass, ye didna—"

"Aye, I did," she said firmly. "I kissed ye and seduced ye in the doin'"

Graeme peered at her with interest, as much for her accent as for the words. He'd noticed that her speech became more Scots than English when she was excited or distressed, so her slipping into Scots now told him how distressed she was. But that just made him smile. While it was true she'd pressed her mouth to his first, that was all she'd done. He was the one who had urged her lips open and turned it into a proper kiss, coaxing the passion to life in her. But before he could say as much, she spoke again.

"And then when ye tried to stop, I jest pulled yer head back and kissed ye again, stopping ye from stopping."

Graeme's smile widened at the claim. He supposed she meant when he'd stopped and growled "lass." It was true, he'd had a momentary twinge of guilt that had urged him to bring an end to what was happening, but . . .

"And the seducing was even planned ahead," she announced.

That caught his attention, and he eyed her sharply as she continued.

"I mean, I had no idea that we'd be here in the clearing today, so I suppose 'twas no' fully planned," she qualified. "But this morn as I lay abed, I did decide to seduce ye and get ye to bed me so I could experience a proper bedding before taking on me widow's weeds and living out me days at MacKay."

"Widow's weeds and livin' out yer days at MacKay?" he echoed with disbelief. "What happened to ye wantin' to marry again and ha'e bairns?"

Annella shrugged a shoulder carelessly. "As ye pointed out last night, I'm far too old to be desirable to wife. 'Twould take a lot o' coin to convince anyone to have me at this late stage, and that would be unfair to me brother. So, I've decided to tell me da I'm no' interested in marrying again and wish only to be allowed to live out me days in me childhood home in the bosom o' me family."

Graeme was sure his eyes nearly leaped out of his head at this news. Those comments hadn't been meant to convince her not to marry, but in the hopes that she might think her options were not as vast as she might hope and to look more favorably on him for husband. Obviously, that hadn't worked as he'd hoped.

"So ye see," she continued now, "this was all planned. I wanted ye to bed me, and there's no need fer ye to marry me. I'd no' make ye do that. In fact, I do no' e'en want it."

"What the devil diya mean ye do no' want it?" he barked with outrage.

Annella appeared taken aback at the way those words exploded out of him. She considered him warily for a minute before reasoning, "Well, ye do no' *really* want me, and I'd no' like to marry someone who was forced by circumstance to make the offer. Besides," she added quickly when he opened his mouth to argue, "I truly do no' like yer mother. And yer brother Dauid is quite annoyin' too." She shook her head. "I'd rather go home to MacKay, thank ye verra much."

Graeme scowled at her words. Truthfully, he also disliked his mother and found Dauid annoying. He considered saying so and offering to have both of them moved to a cottage outside the gate, but before he could, Annella shifted on him, tugged the neck of his shirt aside to reveal part of his chest, then bent her head to lick one of his nipples. The action, and the fact that it actually affected him, startled Graeme so much that the words got caught in his throat.

"Mmmm," she murmured watching his nipple pebble from the attention. "There's no reason we canno' enjoy our time ere I leave though, is there?"

Graeme actually found himself feeling offended and glowered at her for the suggestion. Did she seriously think she could just bed him and leave without consequence?

"Lass," he said firmly, catching her arms and holding her up and away when her tongue slid out and she would have licked him again. He then just held her like that, scowling as he noted that he hadn't even removed his clothes, or hers either for that matter. Her gown was gaping open on top leaving her breasts bare, and her skirts were presently caught around her waist and hips, but she still wore it. He'd tossed up her skirts in the woods and had at her like an animal.

Clucking with irritation, Graeme sat up, taking her with him before saying firmly, "We ha'e no choice, lass. Ye could be carryin' me bairn e'en as we speak."

When Annella's eyes widened at his words and her hand moved protectively to her stomach, he knew for certain that she had not even considered the possibility of getting with child when she'd plotted this seducing business. He, on the other hand, had. Though he'd hoped to convince her to marry him with his kisses, caresses and passion, and not have to resort to her possibly being pregnant to push the point.

She was silent so long that Graeme began to relax, thinking he'd won the argument. But when her gaze returned to his, Annella shook her head.

"Nay. There's no need to panic. 'Tis possible yer seed'll take, but it may no'." Urging him to lie back again, she sprawled on top of him once more and added huskily, "I suggest we just wait and see."

"Wait and see?" he asked with disbelief.

"Aye." She began to run her fingers lightly over his chest, exploring it with interest. "Ye wanted me to help ye take o'er as laird, and I agreed, so no one will think anything o' me staying two or three weeks until I ken fer sure." She paused and then lifted her head to peer at him solemnly. "Chances are I'm no' with child, and as I was the one doin' the seducin' I'll no' make ye marry me fer it."

"Ye would no' be makin' me, lass," he assured her, fighting not to laugh. The idea was amusing, especially since he too had been plotting to get her bedded. The only difference was he'd intended on it being followed by a wedding.

"I would," Annella argued, "and ye do no' ha'e to lie to spare me feelings. I ken I'm no' much o' a prize. Me own husband could no' be bothered to e'en consummate our marriage. I'll no' make ye—" Her words ended on a gasp as he suddenly sat up, forcing her up with him.

Graeme took a moment to shift her to sit in his lap, then tipped her head with a finger under her chin so that she met his gaze. "I do no' ken what happened that night, but I can tell ye truthfully that William found ye more than appealin' and wanted very much to bed ye on yer wedding night."

Annella's eyes narrowed with obvious doubt and she asked him, "Then why did he no' bed me? And why did he ride off with the village lightskirt?"

Chapter 5

ANNELLA WATCHED THE FROWN CROSS GRAEME'S face at her question. He seemed to think hard before speaking, but finally said, "The night o' yer wedding, after ye were taken above stairs by the women, William pulled me aside and asked what I thought o' ye. I was honest and said ye were a pretty lass and seemed smart and kind. I thought he was lucky in our parents' choice o' bride fer him."

Annella swallowed back the sudden lump in her throat at those words. She'd felt so unattractive and unlovable these last six years since her husband had abandoned her, that she was pathetically grateful for Graeme's kind words.

"William agreed with me," Graeme added and then caught her face when she started to turn her head away. Meeting her gaze, he said firmly, "He did. He thought ye beautiful, and said in the short time he'd been allowed to spend with ye the day before, that ye'd proven to be sweet and sharp-witted. He was actually lookin' forward to married life with ye, and that worried him."

Annella blinked, and straightened slightly. "What? Why?"

"We had a cousin, Ellie. She was tiny like you. She was married the year before, just a few weeks ere she would ha'e turned sixteen. Nine months later she died on the birthing bed along with the bairn she was strugglin' to bring into this world," he said solemnly. "William was worried fer ye. Ye too are small and slender like our Ellie was, and ye'd turned sixteen no' long ere the wedding. He was afraid o' the same thing happenin' to you. He was also concerned about how to ensure the first time was no' horrible fer ye. He wanted to cause ye as little pain as he could. So ye would no' loathe the marriage bed."

Sighing, Graeme lowered his head briefly, and then raised it again and admitted, "I suggested he go talk to the village lightskirt, Maisie."

"*What?*" she squawked with shock and a bit of anger.

Graeme nodded apologetically and explained. "I thought—and told him—that she should be able to give him advice on how to pleasure ye properly and ease yer first time. But I also thought—and told him—that on top o' that, she most like kenned ways to keep from gettin' with child. After all, she was a lightskirt, if she did no' ken how to avoid gettin' with child, she'd have had a dozen o' them hangin' off her skirt by that time. I suggested mayhap she could tell him those ways and he could tell ye so ye could avoid gettin' with child fer a year or so and ha'e a better chance o' survivin' the birthin' bed."

Annella slumped in his lap, all the starch going out

of her. Dear God, Graeme was the reason her husband had gone to the lightskirt he'd ended up running away with.

"I do no' believe he ran away with Maisie," Graeme said as if reading her mind. "He ne'er showed any interest in her ere I sent him to her. He ne'er partook o' her pleasures either, and I ken that fer a fact."

"How?" Annella asked at once.

"Because she told me so herself," he responded. "The night ere yer wedding she asked me did Will think he was too good fer her or something, because he ne'er came to see her. She said to tell him she'd happily service him and fer free that night as a weddin' gift."

When Annella's eyes narrowed on him, he said, "I did no' pass on that message."

"Nay. I'm sure she told him herself when he went to her for advice," Annella said dryly. "And at your suggestion."

Graeme reached out to brush a strand of hair back off her cheek. "I ken me brother. If he did leave on a pilgrimage, it was most like because he did no' like whatever method she used to prevent gettin' with child and would no' expect or want ye to do it. Mayhap he feared he'd no' be able to resist bedding ye, and thought to avoid ye fer six months to a year to let ye age a bit and give ye a better chance at survival."

"What mean you if he did leave on a pilgrimage?" she asked, eyes narrowing. "Payton said ye found his body just outside Jerusalem." He'd told her that just this morn while they were breaking their fast, along with several other little stories about the journey itself, most of them including Graeme and things he'd done or said. It had quickly become clear to Annella that her brother liked and respected the man she'd just given her virginity to.

"Aye, we did," Graeme admitted, and then shrugged helplessly and said, "But William was the newly sworn laird here. He took that seriously and was no' the type to shirk his responsibilities to run off on something as lengthy and useless as a pilgrimage."

They were both silent for a minute, considering that, and then he sighed and ran a hand through his hair, before saying, "But it seems he did, and the only reason I can think he did was fer you."

Annella lowered her head and pondered what he'd said. Graeme didn't think William had run off with Maisie. Yet Maisie had gone missing the same night her husband had left. Graeme also found it hard to believe William would abandon his responsibilities as new laird and ride off on a pilgrimage. Yet they'd found his body outside of Jerusalem. It was beginning to sound to her as if Graeme hadn't known his brother as well as he'd thought.

"The point is, lass," Graeme said, drawing her from her thoughts and urging her face up so that she met his gaze again. "You *are* a prize, a fine one indeed, that any man would be lucky to have." He brushed his thumb over her lips gently. "William thought so too, and did want to consummate with ye. As for me . . ." Leaning back a bit, he let his gaze slide down over her body where he'd set her.

Annella was suddenly aware that she was on her knees, her legs straddling his hips, her gown bunched up around hers, and the unlaced front of her gown gaping open so that her breasts were on view. Graeme's eyes almost seemed to catch fire as his gaze took all that in. Then he reached out to rub the knuckle of one finger over one nipple and smiled when it instantly hardened.

"Aye," he said, his voice a low growl. "Ye're no' *makin'* me do anything. I find ye more than desirable. I plan to wed ye as soon as I can and bed ye as often as I'm able."

The last word was a bare whisper against her lips before he claimed her mouth in a searing kiss that had her shifting eagerly against the hardness caught between them and wrapping her arms around him. But Graeme immediately urged her back a bit so that his hands could close over her breasts and caress and fondle them as he kissed her.

Annella responded eagerly, all thoughts of the past and her inadequacies pushed from her mind as he brought her passions to life. When his hands left her breasts for her hips and he lifted and shifted her until he could lower her onto his staff, Annella broke their kiss and threw her head back on a long moan of pleasure.

"Aye, love," Graeme groaned as she raised herself slightly and lowered herself again. "That's it. Ride me," he growled, then closed his mouth over one nipple. He suckled it briefly, then rasped his tongue over the hardening tip as one hand left her hips to slip between them to caress the center of her excitement. His other hand was still at her hip, urging her up and down, setting a tempo that soon had them both gasping and panting with need.

Annella was a second away from finding her pleasure, and completely taken by surprise when Graeme suddenly gave up caressing her, caught her at the waist and lifted her. Her gown slid away then, snaking down her body to pool on the ground just before he set her back down, this time on her knees facing away from him.

He'd shifted to his knees, Annella realized when she came to rest against his groin. He moved one hand between her legs and began to caress her while the fingers of his other hand wrapped around her thigh and urged her back until she felt his shaft press against her opening. When he slid into her again in this position, she gasped and reached back for him. Finding only his side, she gave that up and instead held on to his lower arms for balance as Graeme began to pump into her while his hands continued to touch, fondle and caress, one between her legs and one moving over her breasts.

Whimpering at the three-pronged assault, Annella twisted her head against his chest and then froze when he began to kiss and nip at her neck. Turning her face back and up to him, she was relieved when his lips covered hers and he thrust his tongue into her mouth. She sucked feverishly at his tongue until she couldn't control her actions anymore and then cried out as her passion overtook her. She was only vaguely aware that his voice quickly joined hers.

"WE SHOULD RETURN TO THE KEEP."

Annella opened sleepy eyes and gazed over what she could see of the clearing. She was lying on Graeme again and appeared to have dozed off. Her gaze slid skyward as she tried to determine how long she'd slept and she frowned when she saw that the clouds overhead were heavy with rain.

"We'll be lucky do we get back ere the rain comes down," Graeme said, following her gaze.

"Aye," she breathed and forced herself to move.

Annella was quick about dressing, but paused once her gown was on as she noticed the bits of food and fruit staining it. Her gaze shifted to the fur then and she briefly closed her eyes. They'd just set out the food when she'd kissed the man and set light to their mad passion. Unfortunately, in their feverish need for each other they'd forgotten all about the food, and it was now crushed and ground into the fur as well as their clothes.

A soft laugh by her ear was followed by Graeme pressing a kiss to her forehead. Then he gathered her up in his arms and turned toward the river.

"What are ye doin'?" Annella asked with alarm, catching at his shoulders.

"We need to clean up," he pointed out gently as they reached the water's edge. He began to wade in. "Do we return like this, all will ken what we've been up to."

"Aye, but—" Annella cut off the words and snapped her mouth closed as she felt the cold water reach her behind, and Graeme dropped to his haunches to submerge them both. The water only reached their necks when he stopped, which was a good thing because Annella was squealing at the shock of it and would have got a mouthful.

When she saw that Graeme was grinning at her caterwauling, Annella snapped her mouth closed again, scowled at him and then pressed his chest, demanding release. He let her go at once and she shifted away and stood. The water hadn't been quite to Graeme's waist before he'd squatted, but it was well past her own. Annella shuddered in response to the cold liquid, but didn't rush out. She was in it now and may as well clean her gown ere getting out. She was still scrubbing at it when Graeme waded out of the river. He was back a moment later though with the fur they'd been seated on.

With her gown as clean as she would be able to manage, Annella let it drop and then moved over to help Graeme with the fur. Already soaking wet, neither of them paid much attention when the rain started, they simply finished what needed doing, then made their way out of the water and over to the horses.

The beasts were cowering as close to the tree trunk as they could get to avoid as much of the rain as possible. Feeling bad for them, Annella gave both horses a soft word and pat before Graeme caught her by the waist and lifted her into the saddle.

"I'LL TALK TO YER BROTHER THE MINUTE WE GET back," Graeme said suddenly as he mounted his own horse. Once seated, he glanced her way and asked, "Do ye wish a big wedding with yer parents and—"

"Nay," Annella interrupted, frowning now. "I told ye. I'll no' make ye marry me."

"And I told *you* that ye're no' makin' me," he countered with irritation.

"Well, ye're no' makin' me either," she snapped.

Graeme scowled. "I took yer innocence, lass. Honor demands I marry ye."

Annella snorted at the claim. "You merely took what yer brother neglected to. Something everyone already believes he took." Noting the agitation this seemed to be causing him, she sighed and said more calmly, "I enjoyed what we did, but I'll no' make ye marry me o'er it and have ye come to resent me. Now, let's head back and get out o' this rain."

She didn't wait for a response, but put her heels to her mare and set her moving, leaving him to follow.

"I'M MARRYIN' YER SISTER."

Graeme was aware that Payton froze where he sat to the left of him at the high table, and then jerked around to gape at him. He was also aware that Symon and Teague, who sat on his right, were reacting in much the same way. He didn't look at any of them. Instead, his gaze was focused firmly on the mug of ale he was presently turning on the tabletop.

"Ye asked her?" Payton said finally.

"Aye."

"And she said aye?" Payton sounded surprised.

"Nay," Graeme admitted.

There was a pause and then Payton asked with confusion, "She said nay?"

"Aye."

Payton let out his breath. "So, ye're no' marryin' Nella?"

"Aye. I am marryin' her," Graeme assured him. "But I need yer help."

Turning to the other man, Graeme saw that the expression on Payton MacKay's face was one of bewilderment as he said, "But if she does no' want to marry ye, I can no'—"

"What will happen to her does she return to MacKay with ye?" Graeme asked, interrupting him.

"Well . . . I suppose me da will arrange another marriage fer her," he said slowly.

"She does no' want that," Graeme announced. "She has decided to don her widow's weeds and live out her days at MacKay."

Payton's eyes widened at that.

"Oh, ye poor bastard," Teague said, eyeing MacKay pityingly.

Annella's brother straightened at once and scowled. "Me sister is a perfectly lovely lass. She can live at MacKay as long as she wishes. E'en after me parents are passed and I'm laird. She's always welcome there."

"I somehow do no' think she'll only be livin' there though," Symon commented.

"Nay," Teague agreed.

"What mean ye by that?" Payton demanded, sounding a little concerned.

This time it was Graeme who answered. "They mean the lass has run Gunn for six years, inside and out. She's ruled the servants, the soldiers, the villeins, the serfs and just every livin' creature under Gunn clan protection." He paused and raised his eyebrows. "Do ye really think she'll be able to just stand by and abide, keeping her nose out o' matters at MacKay? Or anywhere else she resides fer that matter?"

Payton frowned. "Well, she only did that because William left, and yer father was injured. She had no choice. I'm sure she'll be happy to relax and allow others to take the lead now so that she can embroider or . . . do whatever women like to do."

"Ye think so, do ye?" Graeme asked with amusement, and when Payton nodded, he said, "Am I no' laird here now?"

"What?" He appeared bewildered by the question. "Aye. It was made official yestermorn. Yer people pledged their fealty to ye and everything."

"Aye." Graeme nodded, and then asked mildly, "Then why is yer sister o'er there bending me first's ear and—judgin' by his solemn face and the way he's noddin' his head—givin' him orders?"

Payton followed his gaze and stared in horror at where Annella did appear to be instructing the man on something.

"Does she do as she plans and stay at MacKay, she's yer problem," Graeme pointed out.

Payton hesitated, and then shook his head. "I'm sure Da will arrange a marriage fer her. She's too young to—"

"She does no' want to marry again. She does no' think 'tis fair to take from yer inheritance to make a second dower fer her."

"A second dower?" he asked with surprise. Payton obviously hadn't considered that his sister would be expected to have another dower should a marriage be arranged.

Before Graeme could respond, Teague leaned forward to eye the other man with amazement. "Ye think any laird worth their salt wid take the lass without a dower? Nay," he assured him. "She'll need a dower."

"A hefty one too," Symon said solemnly. "Pretty as she is, she's getting long in the tooth."

"Added to that, she was married for six years with no bairn to show fer it," Teague commented.

"Her husband has been away these six years," Payton snapped irritably.

"Aye, but how many men ken that?" Symon asked, and then pointed out, "Graeme did no' e'en ken about that, and her husband was his brother."

"'Tis a shame the consummation did no' get her with child," Teague said now. "Then any prospective husband wid at least ken she could produce them."

"There was no consummation," Graeme announced.

"What?" Payton gave a disbelieving laugh. "I was at the wedding, Gunn. The bloodied sheet was hung from the rail the next morning. It was consummated."

"William must ha'e cut his hand or cut himself elsewhere to produce the blood. Or mayhap yer sister did, but I assure ye, the marriage was no' consummated."

"How would you know?" Payton asked with obvious disbelief.

"Because she still had her maidenhead when I tupped her this morn."

"Oh." Payton frowned and then his eyes widened with shocked realization and he jumped to his feet. Scrabbling for his sword, he whirled on Graeme, roaring, *"What?"*

"And that's the other reason ye should help me get her to marry me," Graeme said mildly. "She could be carryin' me bairn e'en now."

Payton hesitated, apparently undecided whether to battle him for daring to tup his sister or not. Graeme's making it plain he wanted to make things right and marry her seemed to decide him and finally, he slid his sword back into its scabbard, growling, "Well, I'll get her to marry ye. I'll tell her she has to. She can no' just go around being tupped and no' marrying."

He turned, no doubt intending to march over and tell her right then, but Graeme caught his arm and jerked him back to sit at the table again. "Ye canno' order her to marry me."

"I can. I'm her brother and our da is no' here. That means she's in me charge. If I order it, she'll ha'e to—"

"I did no' mean ye *could* no' order it. As her brother ye ha'e the right," he said soothingly, though he suspected, right or not, Annella wouldn't obey the man. She had been too long making up her own mind on things to just bow to others now. Actually, Graeme suspected she was going to present something of a challenge as a wife. Oddly enough, he didn't mind the idea.

"Then what did ye mean?" Payton asked with irritation when he didn't go on.

Blinking his thoughts away, Graeme shifted his gaze back to the brother of the woman he hoped to marry. "I meant . . ." He hesitated, and then said, "Look, do ye go o'er there rantin' on how I tupped her this morn, and she must wed me to retain her honor, she'll ken I told ye."

"Aye, she would," Symon commented. "And I'm thinkin' that wid no' be a good thing."

"It'd mean a poor start fer the marriage," Teague agreed.

"Exactly," Graeme said grimly. "And I'd rather no' ha'e a poor start."

Payton relaxed a bit and nodded with understanding. "Then how can I help ye claim her to wife?"

"Ye need to catch us tuppin'," Graeme announced. "Then ye can act all outraged and say honor demands I marry her. I'll agree, and . . ." He shrugged.

Payton stared at him as if he were mad for a moment, and then said, "Ye're tellin' me ye're goin' to tup her again? And ye expect me to be all right with that?"

Graeme scowled. "Well, we'll no' be actually tuppin' when ye catch us. Ye need to interrupt ere that. But we needs be far enough along that the situation is obvious and ye can be outraged."

"And when is this to happen?" Payton asked with concern.

"I do no' ken," Graeme muttered, eyeing the woman across the hall who was now talking to his second. She appeared to be giving orders to him too, he noticed. Marriage to her was definitely going to be interesting. There would no doubt be many battles over power and struggles for control. Graeme liked challenges, battles and struggles. At least he'd never be bored.

"Well, how am I to interrupt if ye do no' ken when 'twill happen?" Payton asked with exasperation.

"Ye'll ha'e to follow us around, will ye no'?" Graeme said with some exasperation of his own. "But make sure ye're no' seen, or she'll no' allow tuppin' and the whole plan'll go to hell."

"How am I to do that?" Payton asked with disbelief.

"We can help," Teague offered.

Symon nodded. "Aye."

"How?" Payton asked at once, his expression dubious.

Graeme didn't care to hear how his friends thought they could help. Standing, he muttered, "I'm goin' to go invite her to walk in the gardens by moonlight. Slip through the kitchens and try to hide yerselves about out there so ye can interrupt when I start in seducin'. But no' too soon," he warned. "Kissin'll no' be enough to force her to wed. Ye'll ha'e to wait until I set in caressin' and such. Mayhap let me get her gown off her shoulder or something."

He waited until all three nodded in understanding, then headed over to where Annella was watching his second hurry out of the keep.

"IS ALL WELL?"

Annella turned at that question and smiled faintly when she saw Graeme approaching. The man had been avoiding her since their return just after noon that day. She knew he'd been annoyed with her over this marriage business. He obviously had a strong sense of honor, and she admired him for that, but marriage hadn't been part of her plan. She had absolutely no desire to marry Graeme and be stuck here with Eschina for another six or sixty years. The woman didn't bother her as much as she had when Annella had been younger, but she was still a thorn in her side. Besides, she suspected the woman would be furious if they married. It might make her redouble her efforts to make her life miserable. Annella just had no desire to have to deal with that.

Fortunately, it appeared he'd got over his hurt pride,

or the injury to his honor or however her rejection of marriage had affected him and was speaking to her again. It made her smile warmer than it perhaps should have been, as she answered him. "Aye. All is grand. I was just tending a matter or two."

Graeme nodded in understanding, and then said gently, "Ye do ken ye're no longer laird here, do ye no', lass?"

Annella blinked at the soft words, because in truth, she'd forgotten that. She was so used to running everything and ordering everybody about that she'd automatically questioned both Angus and Brodie. She'd wanted to make sure they'd checked that the men on the wall had all shown up for the shift change, that Brodie had remembered to arrange a hunt and chosen men for it for the next day to gain more meat for Cook to make their meals, and various other tasks. All of which were none of her business now, she supposed. She was no longer the acting laird here. Annella wasn't even sure if she was chatelaine anymore, although she'd continued to fulfill that role too since Graeme's return.

Much to her relief, he didn't belabor the issue, but changed the subject, asking, "Could I interest ye in a leisurely walk around the gardens to settle the sup?"

It wasn't just the words that caught her attention, but the way his fingers trailed down her arm and the heat that was pouring off his chest to warm her side. The man was standing extremely close, and he smelled delicious, she noted, licking suddenly dry lips.

"Oh, lass, do no' taunt me so," Graeme groaned.

"Would that I could kiss those sweet lips yer lickin', suck yer tongue into me mouth and—"

His words died on a surprised grunt when Annella caught his arm and started to pull him with her toward the keep doors. She couldn't help it. The man had stirred her blood and she needed his kisses and caresses again. It wasn't just his words that had affected her. He had continued to move his fingers up and down her arm, but shifted them around to the inside of her arm, so that the back of his knuckles had grazed her breast through her gown with each passing. Now her whole body was tingling, and it did seem to her that since he started it, he should be the one to fix it.

"Lass," Graeme said a moment later, sounding concerned when she tugged him out the doors, down the steps and headed across the bailey, "I thought a nice walk in the gardens wid—"

"I've a better idea," Annella assured him, continuing to pull him behind her as she crossed the courtyard at speed. He muttered something she didn't understand. She caught the words *no' to plan*, and thought he mentioned her brother, and the names of his two friends, but couldn't be sure. She didn't really care either. Her mind was focused on one thing. The pleasure she'd enjoyed that morning when she'd seduced him, and seducing him again to once more experience that pleasure.

Odd as it seemed to Annella, now that she'd tasted the bliss he'd shown her, she couldn't seem to get it out of her mind . . . and thinking about it just made her crave enjoying it again and again. She was like old Thome at MacKay and his desire for drink. The man hadn't been able to pass a moment without uisge beatha to warm his belly. She was feeling the same way about Graeme and his pillicock. Only it wasn't her belly he warmed with that.

"The stables?" Graeme sounded surprised as she dragged him inside and led him toward the back of the stall-lined building. "Would the gardens no' be— What are ye doin' now?"

Annella ignored the question. What she was doing should be obvious. She'd released him and was climbing the ladder to the loft. She hurried up the rungs quickly and moved away from the ladder to give him room to join her. The roof over the loft was low, making standing out of the question, so she remained on her knees and began to undo her lacings.

"Lass, I really think we should go to the gardens," Graeme argued, but his voice didn't sound like it was coming from behind her. More like below her.

Glancing around, Annella saw with a little exasperation that he hadn't climbed up to join her. His voice *was* coming from below. Huffing out a little breath of irritation, she crawled back to the ladder on her hands and knees, and leaned out to look down at him. "Are ye coming or no'?"

Graeme opened his mouth to respond as he tipped his head back to look at her, but no words came. Instead, his mouth just stayed agape and his eyes widened and then kind of glazed over as he reached blindly for the ladder without taking his gaze off of her. Actually, off of her chest, she realized. She'd got her lacings undone before crawling back to the ladder and her gown was now gaping open with her breasts spilling out.

Smiling, Annella backed away from the ladder, and then glanced around to see what was available. Not much, it seemed. Lots of straw, some hay too, but nothing else. She should have brought a fur or something, she thought and then glanced swiftly over her shoulder when Graeme's arms closed around her from behind.

Chapter 6

THEY WERE BOTH KNEELING IN THE STRAW, HIS legs on either side of hers, she realized, and then his hands found and closed over her breasts, even as his mouth claimed hers. Annella moaned as his tongue thrust in to explore and his fingers and palms worked over her breasts. The man had such talented hands, but honestly, she was sure his kisses were what had her writhing, gasping and reaching desperately for him.

Annella slid one hand up and back to caress his head, while her other dropped to cover his hands and press them tighter to her, urging him on. In the meantime, her bottom began to press back against the hardness poking at her through their clothes. When Graeme groaned in response, his fingers tightening around her breasts as he palmed them, she rotated her hips, rubbing eagerly against him, excited to feel him growing larger and harder under her efforts.

When he gave off caressing her and suddenly started tugging her gown off her shoulders, Annella helped, shrugging out of it and pushing it over her hips. She then twisted away from him to drop to sit on the straw and kicked and pushed the gown off her legs as well. She'd barely finished the task when Graeme was crawling up her body. He'd shed his plaid and shirt while she was undressing and was now completely naked.

It was the first time Annella had seen him without a shirt and plaid and she mourned the fact that it was by the weak lamplight that was barely making its way up to the loft from the stables below. Still, it was enough to see that he was beautiful to behold, all rippling muscle, wide shoulders, and narrow hips with arms and legs that were large and strong from years of wielding a sword and riding into battle on horseback. Sadly, she couldn't properly see his pillicock in this light and from this angle, but she didn't get long to fret over that. She'd barely reached out to run one hand over his chest before he was lowering himself and claiming her mouth.

Annella did love his kisses. The pandemonium they stirred in her was positively delicious and she immediately started to wrap her arms around him in response, but before she could, he broke the kiss and began to trail his lips down her throat, shifting his body down her body as he did, so that his shoulders were out of her reach. Annella plunged her fingers into his hair instead, running them across his scalp as he kissed his way to one breast and began to draw on the hardening nipple there.

Moaning, Annella twisted her head in the straw, her back arching to offer herself to him more fully as his clever fingers began to toy with her other breast.

As if that was a cue, however, Graeme let her nipple slip from his mouth and continued to trail his mouth downward, tickling over her stomach.

Gasping back a laugh, Annella tightened her fingers in his hair and tried to urge him back up, but he wouldn't be dissuaded from the path he'd taken. His lips continued to tease their way downward, gliding over one hip as his hands urged her legs apart. Confused now, Annella reluctantly let her legs open for him and then half sat up on a shocked cry when his head suddenly ducked between her thighs and he began to lick and suck at the folds guarding her center.

Her thighs immediately tried to close and she began to tug almost violently at his hair in protest, but then his tongue slid between her folds and lashed across her already excited flesh. The shock of pleasure that shot through her then had Annella falling to lie on the loft floor with a grunt and her hips now shifting and rising to meet his mouth as he worked. She thought she heard Graeme chuckle then, but it wasn't the sound so much as the vibration of his mouth against her suddenly frenzied skin that affected her. Hips bucking, she released his hair for fear of hurting him and reached out for something, anything to hold on to as his tongue then continued to flick over her.

Unfortunately, there was nothing around her but straw and she ended up just clutching handfuls of it and closing her eyes as her hips writhed under his attention. She was vaguely aware of Graeme holding her thighs open as his mouth worked over her flesh, only because it frustrated her need to move. He was in complete control, and driving her mad.

Her whole body was strung tight and trembling. One minute she wanted to plead with him to put an end to the chaos he was creating in her body, and the next she wanted to beg him never to stop. But she couldn't get either request out, Annella simply didn't have the capacity. Her heart was pounding, her breath coming in harsh gasps.

Just when she thought she couldn't bear it for another moment, the tension in Annella's body snapped and an overwhelming wave of pleasure washed through her. She began to convulse helplessly, her mouth opening on a scream that came out as little more than a choked cry.

Graeme immediately stopped what he was doing and shifted over her to thrust into her. Groaning, Annella wrapped her arms and legs around him, clinging to him as if he were the only thing that could keep her head above water in rough seas. When Graeme caught her hands and removed them from around his neck, she opened her eyes in confusion. Before she could protest, he had straightened, grabbed one of her ankles and pulled it over his shoulder while leaving the other on the floor. The move left her wide-open to him, and he took advantage, caressing her with his free hand as he continued to thrust.

Annella shattered with the second thrust, her body tightening and shuddering around his as he continued to touch and pump into her. That second wave of pleasure wasn't done before a third started, which was followed quickly by another and another. Annella didn't know where one orgasm ended and the next began.

She was nearly sobbing and delirious from the

overwhelming pleasure battering her mind and body before Graeme finally left off touching her. He immediately grasped her by both hips and thrust deep one last time. Stiffening then, he gave a short shout and gripped Annella's hips tightly as he poured himself into her.

GRAEME WOKE UP WITH A START AND WAS AT first confused as to where he was and what had roused him, but then he heard a soft nicker and the clop of hooves on hard-packed dirt as a horse or horses shifted and his memory returned in full. Sitting up abruptly, he glanced around the dark loft in search of Annella, but she wasn't there. Nor were her clothes. The damned woman had left him there asleep in the straw.

And that after ruining his plot to have her brother catch them at houghmagandie and demand a wedding.

Muttering under his breath, he quickly dressed, donning shirt and plaid, and then crawled to the edge of the loft to peer down. The stables seemed empty, so he swiftly descended the ladder and slipped from the building.

Graeme had no idea how long he'd slept, or even how long they'd been in the stables ere that, but was sure it had been a good hour or more all told. Positive that was long enough that Payton, Teague and Symon would have given up on catching them this night and left the gardens, he didn't bother going there, but instead headed into the keep.

The fact that the trestle tables were being broken down and set out of the way against the walls in

preparation for people to sleep told him that he had
indeed been long in the stables, so he wasn't surprised to see Payton, Teague and Symon at the still-
standing head table. He went there at once, ignoring
the odd looks he was getting from everyone he passed.
Graeme supposed they were worried that he and the
men would be up carousing well into the night, keeping everyone who slept in the great hall awake, but he
had no intention of doing that.

"Ye did no' come to the gardens" was Teague's
greeting.

"Nay," Graeme agreed grimly, snatching up his
friend's ale and gulping down half of it before slamming it down. "I invited her to walk in the gardens but
she had other ideas and instead dragged me to the—"

"Stables?" Symon finished for him.

Graeme glanced to him with surprise. "Aye. How
did ye ken?"

"Because straw and hay are all o'er yer plaid," Payton said dryly.

Glancing down sharply, Graeme saw that he was
right. It looked like he'd taken away more straw with
him than had been left behind in the loft, dammit. No
wonder everyone had been giving him odd looks.

"Ye tupped her again, didna ye?"

Graeme raised his head at Payton's resigned question and grimaced for answer. It really hadn't been
well done of him, and he *had* intended on dragging
her to the gardens. At least he had right up until she'd
leaned out of the loft to peer down at him with her
bosoms hanging out and taunting him. A man could
only take so much. Waving away Payton's question,

he asked, "Did ye see her? She was gone when I woke up and—"

"My sister came in some time ago and went straight above stairs," Payton told him grimly.

"Aye," Teague agreed and then grinned and said, "And she too looked like she'd been rollin' in the hay."

"Did anyone notice?" Graeme asked with concern.

"O' course," Symon said with amusement. "Although they probably did no' ken why she was covered with straw and such."

"At least, no' until ye entered in the same state," Teague said with a grin.

Cursing, Payton stood abruptly.

"Where are ye goin'?" Graeme asked, grabbing his arm as he started to move away from the table.

"To tell me sister she must marry ye," Payton said, as if that should be obvious. "Her state and yours on returnin' makes it obvious what ye've been up to. The whole castle kens. She'll ha'e to agree to marry ye now."

Graeme shook his head at once. "Yer sister's no' a fool, MacKay. She ran Gunn fer six years, and ran it well. She no doubt noticed the state o' her gown once in her room and has already come up with an explanation."

"What explanation could she possibly give to explain it?" Payton asked with disbelief.

Graeme felt his eyebrows rise at that. He could think of half a dozen possible explanations just off the top of his head, but before he could speak, Teague hissed, "Watch yer tongues, she's comin'."

Graeme glanced around to see her rushing toward them from the stairs, still in the same gown, but it had been denuded of the straw and hay that he'd been told had covered it earlier.

"Oh, good, you are back, m'laird," she said from far enough away that she had to speak loudly. A strategic action, Graeme realized, as most of the people in the great hall went silent and turned to hear what would follow.

"I realized when I got to me room that I had no' thanked ye fer what ye did ere rushin' off back to the keep," she continued apologetically, still speaking loudly.

"Thank him?" Payton asked with disbelief.

"Aye." Annella peered to her brother with surprise and explained, "The man saved me life."

Not even Graeme had expected that. None of the half a dozen possible explanations on the top of his head included lifesaving. So, he was listening with as much interest as everyone else when she continued.

"I noticed while we were out touring Gunn land this morning that me mare was favorin' a leg."

"Ye did, did ye?" Payton asked grimly.

"Aye. I meant to have a look, but the rain started and we had to race back to the keep. The wild ride back pushed it from my mind and I did no' recall it again until we were finishing the sup tonight." She clucked her tongue at her own lapse of memory, and then said, "Well, of course I thought I'd best have a look straightaway ere I forgot again."

"O' course ye did," Teague said with understanding when she paused.

Graeme glanced toward the other man, and almost could have believed he was taken in by this tale if it weren't for the twinkle in his eye. Shaking his head, he glanced back to Annella, thinking to himself that while her Scots came out when she was angry or excited, she sounded almost pure English when she was giving voice to bold-faced, obviously well-thought-out and preplanned lies. *Good to know*, he thought as Annella smiled at Teague and nodded.

"Aye," she said. "However, just as I was about to leave, Grae—Laird Gunn asked where I was headed and when I explained, he decided to accompany me." She turned to grace Graeme with a grateful smile now, and added, "He said 'twas not safe fer a lass to be stumbling about in the dark on her own. I thought that was silly. I'm perfectly safe here at Gunn."

Annella glanced around at the people in the hall who had drawn closer as she spoke. It was as if she was inviting opinion, and everyone down to a child now nodded in agreement. Aye. Their lady was safe in Gunn night and day. Beaming at them for the support, she turned back to face Graeme and Payton as she went on.

"But I was ever so grateful he did accompany me in the end. Not only did he help me examine my mare, he's actually the one who saw the small, sharp stone stuck in her hoof. I might have missed it otherwise," she added with amazingly believable self-recrimination.

Sighing, Annella shook her head in regret and continued, "But he did see it, and tried to hold the hoof still while I removed it. I did manage to get it out, but it must have been sore, because even as I did my mare jerked away and reared wildly."

Eyes widening dramatically, she told Payton, "Why, if Laird Gunn had not grabbed me and rolled us both across the straw floor out the way of my mare's slashin' hooves . . . well, I could have been killed."

Closing the few feet that separated them, she clasped Graeme's hands and looked up at him earnestly as she said, "Thank you, m'laird. I should have taken the time to say so ere rushing off. I was just so overset by all that had happened. But thank you for what you did in the stables."

Graeme felt a grin tugging at his lips and had to suppress it. No one would understand that response, because no one but he could see that her eyes were sparkling with wicked humor as she thanked him for what she "did in the stables." They also could not see the way she was brushing her fingers over the meat of his palm in a caressing motion that actually affected him.

"Oh dear, and you're covered with straw from it," Annella said now and began brushing him down. Her running her hand quickly down the front of his plaid had a definite effect on Graeme. His cock had already been yawning and stretching as her words brought the memory of what he'd really done in the stables to the forefront of his mind, but now it was jumping around under his great kilt like a child after too many sweet treats.

"I had a lot of straw on myself too when I got back but cleaned up when I saw it," Annella said as she shifted closer, her shoulder now brushing the front of his plaid as her hands moved to his side and then around to his arse, still brushing busily away.

Graeme almost groaned and closed his eyes when her shoulder nudged and then pressed against his growing erection, rubbing it as her body moved in concert with her hands. Catching back the sound and forcing his eyes to remain open, Graeme caught her hands.

"'Tis fine, do no' trouble yersel', Lady Annella. Wid ye care fer a drink?" he asked, urging her toward the table, but ensuring she was positioned to hide his body's response from everyone in the room except for Payton, Teague and Symon. There was nothing he could do about their seeing the state he was in, except hope none of them looked down.

"Oh, thank you, nay," Annella said, patting his shoulder once he was seated and the table could hide his erection. "Between the tour this morning and the stables this evening, I fear all the excitement today has quite worn me out."

"Minx," Graeme whispered under his breath as her gaze slid from his tenting plaid to his face and back.

Annella smiled widely and then swung away. "I'm to bed, m'lairds. Sleep well."

Graeme watched her go, his gaze on her skirts and the way her hips moved as she walked. He wished he could envision what they looked like under all that cloth, but he hadn't really seen her naked. Not in daylight. Well, he'd seen her breasts that morning but—

"Is that really how ye both got straw all o'er ye?"

Graeme blinked at that question from Payton MacKay and then turned to peer at him with disbelief. He was just thinking that the sister was smarter than the brother when he noted the half hopeful, half pleading expression on the man's face and understood that Payton wanted to believe Annella's story was true. Even if it wasn't true. Graeme considered that briefly. He'd never had a sister, but he supposed he wouldn't want to know she'd had her skirts tossed up in the stables like a—

"Damn," Graeme breathed as he realized he'd done it again, taking Annella in the basest way in a place where a lady of gentle breeding should not be exposed to such behavior.

"Well?" Payton asked.

"Aye," Graeme lied almost absently as he stood up. "The mare, the hoof, the rearing, the rolling . . . 'Tis all true." He didn't stay to hear Payton's response, but headed for the stairs and his bedchamber. He had some plotting to do. Not only on how to have Annella's brother catch them so that he could force his sister to marry him, but also some ways to handle and redirect Annella from the woods, the stables and anywhere else that wasn't the gardens where they would be interrupted before he forgot himself and had at her again. The next time he actually bedded the woman, it was going to be in a bed . . . as her husband.

Chapter 7

"ARE YE GOING TO TRY TO LURE ME SISTER TO the gardens again tonight?"

That question from Payton drew Graeme's gaze away from where Annella stood across the great hall. Two days had passed since his encounter in the stables with her, and two nights when she had missed dinner to tend to the injured or ailing. Much to his surprise, Graeme had actually found himself missing her presence at table, but he was also frustrated that her absence had forced him to temporarily shelve his attempts to make her his wife.

Tonight, Annella had actually joined them at sup. But she'd barely been at table long enough to eat before the stablemaster had approached with a blond soldier and requested a moment of her time. She'd agreed at once and followed the two men to where she presently stood. A long conversation had followed and was still happening.

"Well?" Payton asked impatiently.

Scowling, Graeme glanced to the man he hoped

to make his brother by marriage and nodded grimly before turning back to where Annella had apparently finished her talk with the stablemaster and was now talking to Angus. Again. The lass just couldn't seem to get it into her head that she was no longer laird here, and that dealing with Angus was now his job.

"Ye're sure ye can get her there this time?" Payton asked with narrowed eyes.

"Aye," he snapped, meeting the other man's gaze with firm determination. He would get Annella to the gardens tonight, or die trying, Graeme vowed to himself and then grimaced at how ridiculous that sounded in his own mind. All right, perhaps he wouldn't die trying, but—

"So, ye want us to go out ahead o' the two o' ye and hide in the gardens . . . again?" Payton asked dryly.

"Aye, I'll—Where the devil did she go?" he asked with surprise as his gaze slid back to where Annella had stood a moment ago, only to find the spot empty.

Payton, Teague and Symon all peered in the direction he was looking, but no one had an answer.

Frowning, Graeme scanned the room quickly, but Annella was nowhere to be seen. He considered the stairs, but she'd been close to the keep doors and couldn't have crossed the great hall and got up the stairs and out of sight in the short time he'd looked away. She could have got outside though.

Cursing, Graeme stood, but then paused to tell Payton, "Get to the garden. I'll bring Annella there." He then turned and hurried for the doors.

He spotted Annella the moment he stepped out of the keep and his eyes narrowed. She was entering the stables, but not alone. A tall, blond man he recognized as a Gunn soldier was holding the door for her, and once she'd entered, followed her in.

Graeme immediately felt jealous rage roar up within him. She wouldn't! Would she? Mouth tightening, he jogged down the steps and hurried to the stables. On first entering, he didn't see anyone, but then he followed the sound of voices to the back of the building. The stalls took up the better part of the stables, but ended five feet before the loft, and under the loft was a large area divided into three sections. On the left was a room where saddles and such were stored. On the right was a small chamber where the stablemaster slept. In the middle was an open area where a few things were stored, including several stacks of straw and hay at the front that blocked the view of at least half of the small area between the storage and sleeping chamber. In the half that was open to view, Graeme could see Annella kneeling, her body sideways to him.

His earlier jealous rage giving way to confusion, Graeme moved silently up the aisle between the stalls. He was three-quarters of the way to her when he realized she wasn't alone. In fact, there was a man with her. Presumably the blond man, though he couldn't be sure since all he could see was a man's limp cock hanging in front of her face. The rest of the owner of that appendage was out of view behind the stacked bales of straw and hay.

A bellow of rage pouring from his mouth, Graeme crossed the last ten feet or so in a heartbeat, and grabbed Annella by the arm. He jerked her to her feet even as she turned her head toward him with surprise.

"M'laird!" she squawked, yanking at her arm with irritation. "What the devil are ye doin'?"

"Me?" he asked, rounding on her with amazement. "What are ye doin'? Out here in the stables—"

"Examining a soldier with the clap," she snapped, cutting him off.

"So, I was right and 'tis the clap?"

Graeme blinked, his head swiveling to the man who had spoken. Hamish, the stablemaster, was standing next to the blond man, who still stood with his pillicock on display. His puss-filled pillicock, Graeme saw, despite the way the limp thing was hanging down as if in shame. His gaze shifted back to Hamish. He hadn't even noticed the stablemaster standing a step behind the blond man, but then he hadn't really taken note of much after spotting that cock in Annella's face.

When she tugged on her arm this time, Graeme let her go.

"Aye, 'tis, Hamish," Annella said on a sigh. "Ye ken what needs doin' to remove the worst o' the pus."

"Aye," Hamish assured her with something of a wince. Graeme couldn't blame him. With the clap, pus clogged and filled a man's pisser, making draining the dragon terrible painful. The best way to deal with it was to clap it hard between the hands, or between two hard surfaces, to force the pus out. It wasn't pleasant, and he didn't envy the stablemaster the job, let alone the soldier about to suffer it. He was, however, grateful that Annella would not be performing the task. It seemed the stablemaster had just wanted a consultation on the man's ailment, not for her to tend it.

Graeme didn't think she should even have had to

consult on the matter, but kept his mouth shut and simply waited as she gave the blond soldier instructions on what to do for his ailment after the stablemaster finished with him. It didn't take long, and then she turned to head for the stable doors.

Graeme immediately fell into step beside her, but was silent until they were outside again. Clearing his throat then, he asked, "Do ye often consult on such cases?"

"Often enough," Annella said solemnly. "But usually just to consult. The men are no' comfortable comin' to me on such matters and approach Hamish instead."

"Is he a healer?" he asked with interest.

Annella bobbed her head from one side to the other in a gesture he didn't understand until she said, "Of a sort. He kens a great deal about animal care. Horses in particular. Some o' that knowledge can be applied to men as well."

"Horses get the clap?" Graeme asked with something like horror.

"Nay," she said on a laugh. "Well, at least I've never heard of it happening," she corrected herself and added, "The men would just prefer the stablemaster treating them with one hard whack than myself. I'm not sure if 'tis they fear I'll not clap hard enough and have to do it several times, or because I'm a lady and they're embarrassed."

Annella shrugged. "Whichever it is matters little to me. I'm just glad Hamish handles it rather than me. 'Tis bad enough examining the men while they stand about blushing like bashful lads."

Graeme wouldn't have been blushing to have her face inches from *his* pillicock, and he doubted very much if it was bashfulness that had the men she examined doing it. More like it was embarrassment at having a diseased and oozing cock.

Glancing around, he noted that the bailey seemed empty. Everyone appeared to be inside. Other than the men on the wall, of course. But they were all looking outward, watching for anyone approaching the castle. Shifting his gaze back to Annella, he recalled that he was supposed to lure her to the gardens and suggested, "Would ye care to take a walk about the gardens ere bed?"

ANNELLA CONSIDERED THE SUGGESTION BRIEFLY, but frankly the idea wasn't an appetizing one. It had been a long day for her and she was tired, so she shook her head at the offer. "Nay, I fear I—"

Her words died on a startled gasp as Graeme suddenly caught her arm, whirled her toward him and planted a kiss on her that had her toes curling. It wasn't until he broke the kiss and pulled back to look down at her that she recalled where they were and that the men on the wall, or anyone in the bailey even, might have witnessed his kissing her. But then she glanced around and noted that there didn't appear to be anyone else in the bailey, and the men on the wall were just dark silhouettes against a slightly lighter sky, indistinguishable from one another. Which she supposed meant that none of the men on the wall would recognize them either, if they could even see them.

"Come to the gardens, lass," Graeme murmured,

his lips trailing to her ear and nibbling there before moving down her neck.

Annella almost folded at the lovely sensations he was causing in her, but then he reached around to cup her behind and she winced as she was poked in the bottom by what she suspected was a bit of straw. She must have picked up a few stalks while kneeling in the stables. Hopefully that was all, Annella thought with vexation. She'd found it in places straw had no business being the night she'd had her tryst with Graeme in the stables.

"Come with me to the gardens," Graeme repeated, his hands rising to close over her breasts through her gown as he nuzzled her neck.

"Nay," she moaned, but her body was arching, pushing her breasts into his caressing hands, and her head was tilting to allow his mouth better access to her neck. Whatever weariness had been claiming her was now being pushed out of her body by the hunger and need pooling low in her stomach and making its way further south. Still, she didn't want to return to her room later with bits of straw, or grass and leaves in places it wasn't meant to be. When Graeme stiffened and started to pull back, she added, "I should like to try a bed fer a change."

Graeme's eyebrows jerked upward at her words. "A bed?"

"Aye." Smiling, Annella leaned back in his arms, deliberately pushing her hips against his, and said, "A bed would be lovely, do ye no' think?"

He seemed to debate the matter briefly, but when she rubbed herself from side to side against the growing hardness under his plaid, he nodded. "Aye. That could work."

Annella raised her eyebrows at that, but before she could say anything, he brought her around to his side again and almost jogged her the last twenty feet to the keep stairs.

Once there, he pressed a quick kiss to her lips, then urged her up onto the first step, saying, "Ye go ahead. I'll wait a moment so as no' to draw attention, and then come to yer chamber."

"Oh, nay," Annella protested at once, whirling back to face him. "Ye can no' come to my room. Florie will be there. She sleeps on a palette in my chamber."

"Oh." Graeme frowned. "That's a problem."

"Aye. So, I shall come to yer room instead."

Annella didn't give him a chance to respond, but simply turned and hurried up the stairs to the keep doors.

Graeme watched until she'd slid inside and then turned to rush along the keep, headed for the gardens in back. He had to find Payton, Symon and Teague. The plans had changed, and this was even better. The men could wait in the room across the hall from his, crack the door to watch for Annella to slip from her chamber and scurry to his, wait a few minutes, and then burst in to catch them. Aye, this was much better. He'd have the lass married by midday on the morrow, Graeme thought with satisfaction.

He found the men easily enough. He just walked through the vegetable and fruit gardens to the back gardens and said, "She's no' comin.'"

Payton, Teague and Symon immediately appeared

out of the surrounding shrubbery and trees to approach him.

Graeme waited until they were close enough he could speak quietly, before explaining that she would be coming to his chamber instead, and telling them of his revised plan to catch Annella, this time in his bed.

Payton appeared both annoyed and impatient as he listened. It seemed apparent that he was eager to have this business done. Teague and Symon, on the other hand, were acting as if it were a lark. Graeme supposed the escapades were staving off the boredom he felt sure must be descending on them. After all, they were used to constant travel and battle, both of which tended to rouse the blood. Actually, so was he, he realized. Though, he wasn't feeling the least bit bored.

Deciding he'd leave that to ponder later, he finished explaining what they should do and then led them back into the keep and above stairs. He watched them slip into the room across the hall from his to watch for Annella's arrival, and then entered his own chamber and closed the door.

Graeme was peering around the room trying to decide what, if anything, he should do to prepare for Annella's arrival when a very slight grinding sound caught his ear. He turned toward the sound just in time to see the passage door open wide enough for Annella to slip through.

Graeme's eyes widened incredulously. She was wearing a white cotton sleeping gown. It was floor length, with long sleeves, but the sweetheart neckline left a lot of her upper chest on display and the material was thin from age and use. Very thin. The material of most of her gowns was thin from use too, he thought now. It was as if she hadn't had a new gown in the six years she'd been here.

The faint grinding sound coming again drew his attention to the fact that she had slid the passage door closed.

"How did ye ken about the secret passages?" Graeme asked with amazement as she turned back to face him. Truly, he'd almost forgotten the damned thing was there, and certainly hadn't considered she might use it.

"William used the passage in our room to leave the keep the night o' our wedding," Annella explained quietly as she crossed the room. "I saw how he opened the passage door and later tried it for meself and then went exploring to find where the passage went and found the other entrances to and from the other chambers."

"Oh," Graeme said weakly and glanced toward the door, trying to think how to let the men across the hall know she was here.

Soft pressure on his chest drew his gaze down. Annella had reached him and placed her hand there. She was now gazing at his wide chest with an interest that roused his interest. When she started to move her hand, following the curve of muscle through his shirt, he caught it at once. But it helped little, she simply leaned up on tiptoe and pressed her lips to his. This time she didn't just place her mouth on his and stay still. Annella had learned a bit during their previous encounters. She brushed her lips over his lightly, then paused to nip at his upper lip, then offered his lower lip the same treatment before sucking it into her mouth.

Graeme had managed to remain completely still up until that point, but finally, he broke. Clasping her face and tilting it to the angle he desired, he thrust his tongue past her lips and set about devouring her. She responded in kind. There were soft moans, tangling tongues and mounting passion, and then Graeme's hands moved of their own volition and began to travel her body as he backed her toward the bed.

Annella's sleeping gown hit the floor first, but was quickly followed by his plaid and shirt.

Her brother and his friends could wait, Graeme decided as he bore her down to the bed. He'd sort out how to draw their attention later.

IT WAS POUNDING ON HIS DOOR THAT WOKE Graeme. A yawn claimed him at once as he blinked open sleepy eyes, but it gave way to a scowl as the pounding came again. Muttering under his breath, he tossed aside the linen and furs covering him and stood to cross to the door, uncaring that he was naked. He always slept nude, and anyone who decided to interrupt his sleep could damned well deal with it.

Graeme interrupted a third knock by pulling the door open. Payton paused with his fist still raised in the act of knocking, and then blinked as he took him in.

"Ye went to bed?" Teague asked with exasperation. "Ye could no' come let us ken that—"

"Ne'er mind that now," Payton interrupted impatiently, apparently startled out of surprise by the man's words. "Annella's missing."

"Missing?" Graeme echoed with alarm.

"Aye. My soldiers finally arrived with the wagon carrying William's bones, but Dauid was in the cart with them rather than on horseback. He's apparently badly wounded. I sent one of the lads up to fetch Annella while we carried Dauid in, but he returned to say her maid answered the door and me sister was no' in her bed. She's missing. We must start a search. She—"

The rustling of material behind him had Graeme glancing over his shoulder even as Payton did. Annella was out of bed and just finishing pulling her sleeping gown back on. They were just in time to catch a tantalizing glimpse of shapely calves and ankles before the thin cloth finished dropping into place.

"Annella?" Payton choked out his sister's name, but when Graeme turned back, the man was glaring at him.

Graeme couldn't blame him. It really hadn't been well done of him to bed Annella. Again. He should have resisted his baser urges and found some way to make a noise to alert the men waiting across the hall of her presence.

"You—" Payton began in accusation. Fortunately, that was as far as he got before Annella interrupted him, because Graeme was quite sure whatever he had intended to say would have given away their plans to force her into marriage to him.

"This is no time for discussions about what I'm doing here," Annella snapped as she snatched Graeme's shirt and plaid, then crossed the room. "Dauid is hurt and needs aid."

Graeme took the clothing she shoved at him, but then handed his plaid to Payton to hold so that he could quickly shrug into his shirt. He would have donned his plaid next, but even as he grabbed the heavy material from Payton, Annella was pushing past her brother and out into the hall, asking, "Where is he?"

"Annella," Payton barked in alarm, and hurried after her, reaching out as he did as if to stop her. He needn't have bothered. His sister had already stopped dead just a couple of steps past the door.

Frowning, Graeme stepped out into the hall to see what had brought her to such an abrupt halt. His own feet froze though when he saw the men filling the hallway. Teague and Symon were there, but so were another twenty men, a mix of Gunn and MacKay soldiers.

"I'm marryin' her," Graeme snapped as twenty-three pairs of eyes slid from Annella to him.

Annella's shoulders briefly slumped in defeat, but just as quickly popped up and back again. Her chin lifted as well, and she started moving forward through the quickly parting men. "I assume this means ye brought Dauid up to his chamber?"

Graeme felt pride bloom in his chest. The lass had bigger ballocks than—His thoughts scattered and a scowl creased his face again as he noted that her gown was so thin it was near see-through in places, most noticeably to him at that moment was the area around her derriere.

Opening the plaid he hadn't yet donned, Graeme pushed past Payton and quickly wrapped the heavy material around her shoulders.

"What are ye doin'?" Annella asked with exasperation when he then tried to close and tie the top corners of it in front to wholly cover her. It was an awkward maneuver that had him pressed against her back, his arms around her and hands working under her chin as they walked.

"Aye. What are ye doin', Gunn?" Payton snapped, grabbing his arm to stop him.

"I'm trying to cover up me bride," Graeme snapped with irritation. He'd think the man would want his sister more modestly covered.

"Well now ye ha'e," Payton said grimly. "So mayhap ye could go get another plaid fer yerself and stop swingin' yer pillicock about."

Graeme glanced down at himself to see that he was wearing one of his shorter shirts, and his pillicock was indeed swinging about beneath the hem. Cursing, he turned abruptly and rushed back to his room to quickly grab a fresh plaid from his chest, then simply wrapped it around his waist as he rushed back out into the hall. He was just in time to see Annella disappearing into a room up the hall. Dauid's bedchamber, he realized, and followed.

"Oh thank God. I feared I'd die ere they found ye, Nellie," Dauid said weakly when she reached the bedside.

Annella's mouth tightened at the nickname he'd plagued her with for years. It didn't matter how many times she asked him not to call her that, he just kept doing it because he "liked it." Apparently, it didn't matter what she did or didn't like.

Pushing her irritation to the side for now, she ran her gaze over him, noting that his color was fine, he wasn't breathing faster than normal, he wasn't sweating overmuch, and when she pressed the back of her hand to his forehead, he didn't feel cool. He was displaying none of the signs she saw when someone had taken a bad wound and lost a lot of blood. On top of that, there wasn't blood anywhere except on the filthy bit of cloth she could see between the fingers pressing it tightly to his lower side. In fact, if he weren't clutching that to the area just above his empty scabbard, she wouldn't have thought him injured at all.

"Move yer hands, Dauid. Let me see yer wound," she said finally, bending to nudge them away even as she said it. But his moving his hands and the dirty cloth with blood staining it, didn't help. Annella couldn't get a good view of the wound through the hole in the cloth of his shirt. She had to tug his shirt out of the waist of his plaid to get a proper look. Her eyebrows drew together as she examined him. The wound was a slice in his side just above where his scabbard rested.

Straightening, she glanced around until her gaze landed on her brother. "I need my medicinals. Go to my room and have Florie fetch them to you fer me."

The moment Payton headed out of the room, Annella turned her attention back to Dauid and pressed the bloodstained cloth against his injury again, as she asked, "What happened?"

"We stopped to . . . walk in the woods," he finished, looking embarrassed.

Drain the dragon, Annella translated in her head.

"And while I was distracted, someone came up behind me and—" He gestured to his injured side.

"Did ye see who 'twas, brother?" Graeme asked grimly.

Irritation flickered in Dauid's gaze as he glanced to his brother, but disappeared as he turned back to Annella and said, "I only caught a glimpse as I fell, but 'tis sure I am that 'twas a Morgan."

Fortunately, Payton returned then with her medicinals and Annella had an excuse to turn away, hiding her expression. Her gaze slid over the people in the room as she took her bag. There had been a lot of people in the hall, soldiers mostly, but there were nearly as many in the room itself. Annella took that to mean that Dauid had been making a fuss and insisting he was at death's door since gaining the injury. She wouldn't put it past him. The last six years, Dauid had either been whining and complaining and demanding attention, or arrogant and annoying and insisting he deserved her attention. She always found it hard to believe he was only a year younger than her. The man acted like a child most of the time.

Clicking her tongue with irritation, she set the bag on the bed and started sorting through the various ingredients and salves inside as she said, "He's fine. 'Tis little more than a scratch. There's no need fer a death watch. Clear out."

There was an immediate mass exodus from the room, including her brother and Graeme. Annella scowled as she watched the pair of them put their heads together and start talking in low voices as the door was pulled closed behind them. She didn't have a single doubt that they were even now plotting how to force her in front of the priest. She wasn't pleased with the idea. A man wasn't forced to marry if he indulged in a little houghmagandie. Why should a woman be?

Well, okay, sometimes men too were forced to marry. It depended on who they were dallying with and—

"Are you all right, Nellie?"

"Hmm?" She glanced at Dauid with confusion.

"Ye were frownin' after me brother as ye watched him leave the room," he explained. "Has he been annoyin' ye since his arrival? I ken his rough, vulgar ways must be a trial, but once I take on the position o' laird, I'm sure he'll head back to his mercenary pursuits and leave us be." Smiling, he reached out to place his hand on hers and added, "If he does no', I promise I'll tell him to go. I'll no' let him bother me sweet Nellie."

"Ye ken I hate it when ye call me Nellie," Annella snapped impatiently, tugging her hand from under his. Turning her attention to quickly collecting what she needed to clean his wound, she added, "And what do ye mean when you take on the position o' laird? Graeme is—"

"I ken he's the second son and next in line," Dauid interrupted. "But he'll pass it up and 'twill come down to me. He's no' interested."

"He's no'?" Annella asked, not hiding her surprise. It didn't seem to her that Graeme had been reluctant to take on the task. He was laird by the nooning on the day after his return.

"Nay," Dauid assured her. "Graeme prefers the excitement o' battle to the more boring chores o' sitting about doing sums, listening to the complaints o' our villeins and judging their disputes. He's always said so."

Annella merely grunted at that, then set down the

various items she'd collected and moved around the bed toward the door.

"Where are ye goin'?" Dauid asked at once.

"To find a servant to fetch some ale to mix the tonic in," she explained, and opened the door to find Florie there, jug and mug in one hand and the other raised to knock.

"I thought ye'd need this." Florie handed over the empty mug and the jug full of what smelled like ale, and then added in a whisper, "I ken ye usually ha'e to dose him so ye can work in peace."

"Aye. Thank ye, Florie," Annella said sincerely and turned to head back to the bed as the maid closed the door for her.

"Is that ale?" Dauid asked with interest, his nostrils flaring.

"Aye." Annella poured some in the mug, then grabbed one of the tinctures she'd taken from her bag of medicaments and dumped some of that in as well.

"Yer givin' me a sleepin' potion?" Dauid said with accusation.

Stirring the concoction, Annella said mildly, "I have to sew yer side."

"Nay. I'm sure 'twill be fine without sewin'." He sounded alarmed now.

"It needs sewing," Annella said firmly, and turned to him with raised eyebrows. "The question is do ye want to take this and sleep through it? Or shall I call the men back to hold ye down while I stitch ye?"

"Fine," Dauid grumbled in resignation. He took the mug from her, scowled down at the contents, then raised his gaze to her and said, "But once I'm laird—"

"For heaven's sake, Dauid, drink it," she growled impatiently as she moved away to gather the items she'd need to clean his wound. "I do no' want to be at this all night. I'd like to get some sleep."

Annella briefly considered telling him that Graeme hadn't turned down the position and was laird now, but then decided that could be someone else's problem. Between his determination to call her Nellie, his smarmy smiles and his tendency to constantly touch her hands or arms at every opportunity . . . Well, frankly, she just couldn't be arsed to put up with the temper tantrum that would no doubt follow if he'd had his hopes pinned on being laird.

Chapter 8

"Nay."

"Aye."

"Nay," Annella repeated grimly, and turned from her bedchamber window to glare at her brother. He'd followed her to her room after they'd broken their fast that morning. She hadn't been surprised. Nor had she been surprised when Payton closed the door behind him and announced that she would marry Graeme . . . as if he had a right to order it.

Annella hadn't been impressed. She'd had little sleep last night thanks to the Gunn men. First Graeme had kept her awake with his bedding skills, then she'd had to tend Dauid. Although, it really hadn't taken all that long for her to take care of her young brother-in-law, she acknowledged. At least not once the tincture had done its work and put him to sleep. After that though, sleep had eluded her. She had known her brother would demand she marry Graeme come morning, and she'd spent the better part of the night fretting over that and what she should do.

The truth was, Annella didn't dislike Graeme. She certainly enjoyed the bedding with him. A lot. But that didn't mean they would do well being married, and that was her worry. They hadn't talked much since his arrival other than the night he'd walked her back to the keep from the blacksmith's cottage, and the little they'd talked while touring Gunn land to introduce him to the villeins who farmed it.

Annella supposed that didn't really signify much since she'd passed even fewer words with William before they'd married. As she presumed happened with most new brides, she'd arrived the day before the wedding, been too shy to say much to William during the sup that night and had married the next day. Which was all well and fine, but that was then and this was now. Annella was no longer a new bride, young and malleable. She'd run Gunn on her own for six years and was used to her independence. What if Graeme expected her to be a submissive, dutiful wife? Annella wasn't sure she could manage that, and really, from what she'd seen so far, she was worried that might be the case. Not because of anything he'd done, but because of what he hadn't done.

The idea behind her staying here rather than returning home to MacKay right away had been to help Graeme take on the mantle of laird so the transition went smoothly. But other than that tour that had ended with him taking her maidenhead on top of their picnic in the clearing, he hadn't approached her for anything to do with the castle and its people. In fact, he was usually up and out of the keep before she reached the table to break her fast, no matter how early she woke.

The only time she saw him was at the sup and after when they just seemed to end up getting caught up in passion. At least they had on two of the last four nights since the picnic in the clearing, and it no doubt would have been four out of four had she not been called away to tend a birthing mother in the village one night, and an injured soldier the next.

That was another problem, of course. She was playing with fire letting him bed her repeatedly. She'd started taking bird's nest after their first time. Also known as wild carrot, it was supposed to help prevent getting with child. At least that's what her cousin, Jo, had told her. Of course, if it didn't work and she got with child, she'd have to marry him. But until then—

"I will no' marry Graeme," she said firmly.

"Ye will," Payton insisted. "Ye have to. I order it, and as yer brother I have—"

"Nothing," Annella interrupted grimly. "Ye have nothing . . . no right nor power o'er me. That all ended when I married William and became a Gunn."

"What?" he asked with shocked disbelief, and then his eyes narrowed. "Well then, ye'll no' mind if I send a messenger to Da about this, will ye?"

Annella's shoulders sagged with defeat. She would not defy her father, and she knew very well that he would insist on marriage once he knew the situation. She was neatly trapped.

THE WEDDING WAS HELD LATE THAT AFTER-noon, just before the sup and directly after the ceremony to inter William's bones in the family crypt in the chapel. It had seemed a good idea to bury her previous husband before marrying her next.

Graeme had wanted both ceremonies to be held in the late hours of the morning with a feast at the nooning and the consummation to follow. Annella had been shocked at the suggestion. Consummating in daylight? According to the church, that was a sin, one their priest would surely protest. Besides, she'd pointed out, it would be impossible for Cook to prepare a proper feast by the nooning.

Fortunately, before Graeme could point out that they'd done more than a little consummating in the clearing in broad daylight their first time, Teague, Symon and her brother, Payton, had voiced their agreement and had taken on the chore of convincing him. Leaving them to it, she'd gone to talk to Cook about a feast for that night, then had gone on her daily rounds. She had two lassies in the village with child and two who'd just had their bairns over the last week that she'd wanted to check on. Then she'd looked in on the blacksmith, relieved to see that the infection hadn't returned and while his healing would be slow, he *was* healing. She'd then gone to check in on Raynard too. He was recovering from his wound more quickly than the blacksmith. Unfortunately, that meant he was beginning to whine about wanting a drink. Annella had told him no, and insisted he couldn't get out of bed yet. She'd ordered that one of the men should continue to watch him to ensure he didn't, and to be sure he didn't drink either. It truly was too soon for him to be up and about, but she was also hoping that if he was away from drink long enough, he might not have such a yen for it.

By the time she'd seen to everyone, it had actually been midafternoon. Annella had returned to the keep, intending to have a late nooning meal, only to have Florie rush her the moment she entered the great hall. Grabbing her arm, the maid had hurried her to and up the stairs, ignoring her protests and insisting she needed to prepare for the wedding.

Annella had managed to break away from her briefly at the top of the steps, telling her she must check on Dauid. He, however, had been sleeping peacefully, leaving her little excuse to avoid preparing for the ceremony. She'd left his room and given herself up to her maid.

What had followed was torture to Annella's mind. Bathing in midafternoon to wash her body and hair, followed by sitting forever while Florie brushed her long tresses dry and then put them up in some sort of painful mass that involved at least a dozen different braids all over, pulled so tightly into a crowning glory on the top and back of her head that she quickly had a headache.

Annella had scowled at her maid the whole time, sure she had no idea what she was doing. After all, before Florie had become her lady's maid six years earlier, the lass had been a scullery maid with no experience, and there had certainly never been an occasion before this for her to dress her hair.

Still, Annella had maintained her patience and suffered through it in silence . . . until it came time to choose a gown for her to wear. That had been a truly depressing endeavor indeed as Florie had pulled out every single dress in the chests and discarded each as either too frayed, too damaged, or worn too thin to do for her wedding. Annella hadn't even been able to argue over it. Every gown she possessed had come with her when she'd traveled here to be married six years earlier. They were all in a shameful state. But new gowns meant an afternoon with a traveling cloth merchant, selecting fabrics and then haggling over prices, followed by debating which style of gown was to be made. Then there would be fittings. All of which added up to a lot of time she hadn't had to put toward something as frivolous as a pretty gown.

In the end, she'd had to make do with a pretty but frayed gown of pale blue as the best of the lot. Florie had not been pleased. She'd muttered endlessly about how shameful it was for her lady having to present herself in such poor attire and reminded her that she'd repeatedly pointed out that Annella should make the time and have new gowns made.

Annella had actually been relieved when Payton had knocked on the door asking if she was ready . . . until she recalled that her brother was there to escort her to marry Graeme. She'd begun to drag her feet then. Not that it had made much difference, Payton had simply taken her hand over his arm and pulled her cheerfully along with him.

The wedding had taken place on the chapel steps with damned near every Gunn in the clan there to witness and then pledge their fealty to her as lady . . . again.

Annella had been grim-faced throughout the ceremony and feast. This marriage wasn't what she'd wanted. However, she had no one to blame for its necessity but herself, and knew it. She never should have allowed herself to fall asleep in Graeme's bedchamber, let alone his bed.

Annella had tried to delay the inevitable by saying her parents should be there, and that they should also wait for Dauid to heal and be able to attend, but neither her brother nor Graeme had thought that was necessary. Both had said since there had been several men in the hall to witness when she'd left Graeme's room the night before, they should marry at once. She had given in a little less than gracefully, but neither her brother nor Graeme seemed to notice.

Despite the dearth of time, Cook had done a fine job preparing the feast to follow and Annella made sure to compliment her for it once she finished her meal. Then Graeme had stood, taken her arm and bid everyone "good eve" before walking her to the stairs and up them.

Truly, Annella had experienced as much discomfort in that moment as she had on her first wedding night with William. Not because of what was coming, as had been the case back then; she'd had sex now and had nothing to fear in that regard. Her discomfort this time was because every single person in the great hall knew what they were heading to their chamber to do. It had made her self-conscious and embarrassed, right up until Graeme had closed the door, stepped up behind her to wrap his arms around her and began nuzzling her neck. Annella quickly forgot everyone and everything then, and gave herself up to the pleasure he brought to life in her.

Really, that was the only part of the day that Annella enjoyed. As annoyed as she'd been about the need to marry, she could hardly blame Graeme for it. Actually, she supposed she should be grateful that he wasn't annoyed at "having" to marry *her*. At least he hadn't seemed to be. They'd enjoyed hour after hour of pleasure in a comfortable bed without the need to be rushed and he'd shown her many new and diverse ways to find that pleasure. He'd spent the better part of the night on that tutelage.

Which is why she was so late waking up this morning, Annella supposed as she rolled over in bed and glanced out the window to see the sun high in the sky. By her guess it was only an hour or two before the nooning. A shameful hour to be still abed, she thought, but merely smiled and stretched luxuriously as memories of the night before slid through her mind. If she had that to look forward to, she would definitely enjoy this marriage more than her first, Annella acknowledged and was grinning as she tossed aside the furs and bed linens covering her.

She was quick about her ablutions and dressing and was heading for the door when it opened to allow Florie to poke her head in.

"Oh! Ye're awake," the maid said, pushing the door further open to enter. "The laird said to let ye sleep, but I've been checkin' on ye regular like to see were ye up. Actually, I was startin' to fret a bit. Ye rarely sleep this late."

When Annella merely mumbled something of an

agreement and continued toward the door, eager to get out and go below to break her fast, Florie grinned slightly, and added, "But then ye're no' the only one who slept late this morn. Most o' the castle did, though they're all up and about now . . . except yer brother. Now yer up, I think he's the only one still abed, but then yer husband's friends kept challengin' Laird Payton to drinkin' contests last night after ye and the laird retired. In the end, he was so fou' they had to carry him up to his bed."

Annella's eyebrows rose at that as she passed the maid and led the way out into the hall. "Still abed, ye say?"

"Aye."

"Mayhap I should check on him then," Annella decided, a devilish smile claiming her lips as she started up the hall to the chamber her brother had been put in. No doubt he'd have a sore head this morning, she was thinking, and would not be pleased should she make a lot of racket to wake him up. Which, of course, she fully intended to do.

It would serve him right for his high-handed nonsense, Annella thought as she opened his door and sailed in without bothering to knock. Much to her disappointment, however, her brother was not snoring away in his bed. Instead, Payton was at the small table by the window, bent over the basin that rested there and scooping water out of it with both hands cupped together, which he then splashed over his face.

Disappointment flowing through her that she couldn't wake him up as she'd planned, Annella crossed the room to stand beside him. Payton was pale, with misery racking his face that told her he was indeed suffering this morning. Unfortunately, he looked so pitiable that she no longer felt like tormenting him.

"Do ye want a tonic fer yer head?" she asked solemnly.

"Oh, dear God, do no' bellow at me this morn, Nella. I can no' take it," Payton groaned, closing his eyes and covering his face.

Annella's eyebrows rose at the complaint, because she hadn't bellowed at all. In fact, she'd spoken more softly than normal out of sympathy. Shaking her head, she turned to glance at Florie, who stood waiting in the open door. Rather than speak, she merely mouthed, "Medicinals." The girl understood at once and hurried back into the hall and out of sight.

Annella turned back to her brother, intending to suggest he return to his bed, but was forestalled when the sound of a commotion made its way to them through the open window. Frowning, she stepped to it and leaned out to peer into the bailey below. Her eyes widened in shock when she saw the large contingent of warriors heading for the drawbridge at a fast trot. Graeme was at the front, with Teague and Symon on either side and at least a hundred Gunn men following. Every man bristled with weapons: swords hanging from the waist, maces, war hammers or crossbows strapped to their backs and daggers strapped to their arms and sticking out of their boot tops.

"What the . . ." she murmured with shock and worry.

Payton stepped up to her side to peer out and cursed

under his breath. Whirling to hurry toward the door, he muttered, "He must have got his answer from Morgan. Dammit! He should have sent fer me. I told him I would stand with him."

Annella turned in time to see him rush out through the open door. He didn't close it. She paused to peer out the window again, a frown tugging at her lips. Stand with him for what? Answer from Morgan about what? She wondered over the words with confusion, and then recalled Dauid saying that he was sure it was a Morgan who had attacked him when he'd arrived wounded.

Cursing now herself, Annella spun away from the window and rushed after her brother.

"THERE THEY ARE."

Graeme peered at the army on the hill opposite the one they were on and nodded grimly at Teague's words, then glanced around with surprise when a fourth horse rode up and squeezed its way between his mount and Symon's. His eyebrows rose when he recognized his brother-in-law, Payton. The man hadn't been around when he'd gathered the others to ride out, and he hadn't gone looking for him. On purpose.

"So ye thought to ride out without me and hog all the fun fer yerselves, did ye?" Payton asked with a grin that didn't cover the signs that he was not presently feeling all that well.

"'Tis no' yer fight," Graeme said solemnly. "And I do no' think yer sister wid be pleased with me do I get ye killed."

"She's already displeased with ye fer ridin' off

to battle the day after the two o' ye wed," Payton told him with amusement, and then grimaced and added, "But then she's no' pleased with me either at the moment."

"Why?" Graeme asked with interest.

"I ordered the stablemaster no' to saddle her mount and to keep her there when she followed me to the stables intending to ride after you."

"I ken the lass has run the keep these six years, but surely she did no' think to ride into battle with us?" Symon asked with disbelief.

"Nay. I'd say she thinks to ride into battle on her own," Teague said dryly, and when the men all looked to him with surprise, he nodded to the valley below.

Graeme turned to peer where his friend directed to see Annella coming from the woods to the right side of the valley. She was riding her mare astride and bareback. It seemed the stablemaster had refused to saddle the horse to dissuade her following them, but that hadn't stopped her. She was galloping up the opposite hill now, her hair and skirt whipping out behind her. Fortunately, the daft woman had worn braies, and wasn't baring her naked ankles, calves or thighs to the men now spread out along both sides of the valley, he noted.

For one moment, Graeme's heart stopped beating and his body went cold, then he ordered the others to remain where they were and urged his own mount down the hill. Like her, he rode more quickly than he should have. The hill on this side was steep and rocky enough to be a danger. Graeme was lucky his mount didn't lose its footing and tumble, crushing and smashing him against the boulders and rocks that made up the trail he took. But he was desperate to get to Annella before she got herself killed.

Despite his recklessness, Annella had reached the other army before he had even reached the valley floor. Heart in his throat, Graeme watched his wife ride straight up to whom he presumed was the Morgan laird. Much to his relief, no one attacked her or dragged her from her mount as he had feared would happen. Instead, much to his surprise, after a brief discourse, the man he thought was Morgan detached himself from the group and accompanied Annella down the opposite hill to the valley floor and halfway across to await him.

Graeme's relief did not make him slow his mount. By then he'd reached the valley floor and was racing toward the pair. He began to slow as he drew nearer, confused by what he was seeing. Despite the fact that he'd been ready to go to battle over the attack on his brother, the Morgan and Annella were both smiling and chatting like old friends. They were even chuckling about something.

Their chuckles faded to faint smiles as he reached them, and Annella nodded mildly at Graeme and said, "'Tis fine, m'laird. I explained to Laird Morgan about Dauid, and that having been away so long, ye could no' ken what sort o' man yer brother was. And that this is surely all my fault fer no' explaining things to ye as I should have."

Before Graeme could ask what she meant by his not knowing what sort of man his brother was, she exclaimed, "Oh! Pray forgive me, m'lairds. I should introduce ye to each other. Laird Graeme Gunn, this is Laird Colban Morgan, a neighbor and dear *ally*."

Graeme grunted what could have been taken for a greeting, unsurprised when the Morgan gave a similar response. The smile the Morgan had been beaming at Annella had shriveled noticeably when he'd turned to Graeme. It seemed obvious that the only reason the men lined up on either side of the valley weren't shedding blood that very minute was because of his wee wife explaining matters Graeme still didn't understand and soothing the Morgan.

"Thank ye, Colban, fer being so understanding and remaining the friend and ally ye've always been to Gunn," Annella said now, smiling widely at the man. "Ye must come fer a meal soon. 'Tis been near a month since yer last visit."

Graeme was scowling over that, when the Morgan had the temerity to claim her hand and press a kiss to the back of her fingers. Still bent over her hand, he then peered up at her through heated eyes and said, "'Twill be me pleasure, whether before or after yer visit home to yer parents at MacKay. Whichever is most convenient to ye."

Graeme's eyes sharpened as they moved between the man and Annella. He knew they hadn't been lovers these six years since he'd taken her maidenhead himself barely a week ago. But he didn't like the way the man was rubbing his fingers over hers, or the calf eyes he was giving her. And what was this nonsense about her going to her parents' home to visit? She was his wife. She would stay here with him. As a wife should. Dammit.

Graeme was so annoyed at the possibility that she planned to leave him and return to MacKay despite their being married now, that he almost missed the nod the Morgan gave him before he turned his horse to head back up the hill to his men.

The moment his back was turned, Annella's smile died and she scowled at Graeme as she urged her mare to close the short distance between them.

"Ye—" Graeme began, intending to ask what the devil was going on between her and the Morgan, and inform her that she would not be leaving him to go home to MacKay, but she held up a hand to silence him. Graeme was so startled by the commanding gesture that he obeyed it.

Stopping her horse next to his so that they were side by side but facing opposite directions, Annella said grimly, "The Morgans did no' attack Dauid."

Graeme blinked as his mind quickly had to shift with the topic change. "Then who—?"

"No one," she snapped, interrupting him again. "Yer brother is a clumsy oaf. He's always hurtin' hisself. Judgin' by the wound and where it was, I can guarantee ye that he was tryin' to put his sword back in his scabbard, missed and accidentally sliced himself." Mouth tightening with vexation, she added, "It's no' e'en the first time he's done it either."

Graeme gave a start at that announcement. "He's had a similar wound before?"

"Three times in the six years I've kenned him," she said grimly. "And each time he's claimed 'twas a Morgan to blame, when all ken 'tis him."

He pondered that briefly, but then recalled the

Morgan's expression and the way his voice had dropped intimately as he'd spoken to her, and he frowned and asked, "Yer sure 'twasn't the Mor—?"

"Where did yer ship land?" Annella interrupted impatiently.

When he blinked in surprise and didn't respond right away, she said, "I'm guessin' Inverness or Aberdeen?"

"Nay," he said at once. "We'd have had to wait a month or better to take a boat landin' in either place. We thought it best to take one that was immediately available and setting out fer Dundee. Landin' there and ridin' the rest o' the way wid be faster than waitin' on one o' the scheduled boats landin' further north."

Annella nodded. "So, you and the party Dauid traveled with did come up through the south, approaching Gunn through Sutherland?"

"Aye," he agreed.

"Well, I ken ye've been away a long time, husband, but Morgan resides to the Northwest o' us," she reminded him. "And the Morgans are no' allies with the Sutherlands."

"They're no'?" he asked with surprise. "They used to be when I was young."

"Aye, well, they are no' anymore. They had a fallin'-out three years ago. They'd as soon kill as look at each other now. So, I promise ye, 'tis no' verra likely that a Morgan would be on Sutherland soil." She paused for a moment to let that sink in, and then added, "Aside from that, how would Dauid have e'en kenned it was a Morgan? It's no' like they're foolish enough to wear bands on their arms, or certain colors to identify themselves. So, he would no' ken. He would ha'e had to recognize them, which he did no' claim." She shook her head with exasperation. "Nay. Dauid was no' attacked. He did it to himself by accident and blamed a Morgan because he was embarrassed and detests Colban."

Graeme stiffened at her familiar use of the Morgan's first name, but simply asked, "Why?"

Annella appeared irritated by the question, but then reluctantly admitted, "He thinks the Morgan is too familiar with me and does no' show me the proper respect due a married lady."

Well, Graeme could hardly argue with that. He hadn't liked the way the man had kissed and caressed her fingers, or the hungry look in his eyes as they'd devoured her.

"Ye nearly started a war with our neighbor and ally o'er nothing," she reprimanded him grimly.

"I thought Dauid had been attacked." He excused himself with a frown.

"Something ye would ha'e kenned was no' true had ye just talked to someone who kenned him," she growled.

"Aye," Graeme conceded and ran a hand through his hair. "I should ha'e talked to Angus ere rushin' off like I did after receiving Morgan's response to me message." His mouth thinned again as he recalled the missive he'd received after sending his challenge to the Morgan for the assault on his brother. The man had said he'd nothing to apologize for. None of his men had attacked Dauid, but if 'twas battle he wished, he'd happily oblige.

Sighing now, Graeme admitted, "Angus did seem to want to tell me something this morn ere we rode out, but me blood was up and I just . . ." His words trailed off. Annella wasn't listening anymore. She was riding off, head high, back straight and rage pouring off her body in waves that were almost visible.

"She does no' seem pleased," Teague commented, bringing Graeme's attention to the fact that Teague, Symon, Payton and Angus had made their way down the hill to his side. They must have started the dangerous trek the moment the Morgan had ridden off, taking his soldiers with him.

Graeme eyed Angus. "What were ye tryin' to tell me ere we rode out?"

"That 'twas most like no' a Morgan who injured yer brother," he admitted solemnly.

"And what do ye think happened to him?" Graeme asked.

Angus grimaced, but said, "He's careless and impatient. The combination often leads to incidences where he is harmed."

"Ye think he accidentally cut himself while trying to sheathe his sword and lied to cover his embarrassment," Graeme said plainly.

"Aye," Angus confessed.

"Where is Lady Annella goin'?" Symon asked suddenly, watching her disappear into the trees that edged one end of the valley.

"There's a path o' sorts through the woods," Angus explained. "'Tis shorter and avoids the rocky inclines."

"That's how she got here so quickly." Payton

sounded a little irritated. Apparently, he'd been fretting over the fact that she'd arrived basically on his heels when he'd left ahead of her and on a strong stallion versus her wee mare.

Recalling what had been said between Annella and Morgan, specifically the bit about his coming for a meal before she left, Graeme scowled at his brother-in-law and asked, "What is this nonsense about yer sister planning to go to MacKay?"

Payton's eyes widened with surprise and he immediately shook his head. "I've no idea. She has no' mentioned anything to me about traveling home to MacKay."

"Well, she can no'. We're married now. She can no' just go haring off as she likes anymore."

Payton grunted in agreement and then complained, "I do no' ken what happened to her here at Gunn. She was ne'er this stubborn and cantankerous growing up at MacKay."

"Do no' look at me," Graeme said at once when Payton cast an accusing eye his way. "I was no' e'en here."

Payton scowled with displeasure, and then said, "She fought marryin' ye. I had to threaten her with Da to get her to agree. And that after two or three dozen men saw her comin' from yer room too," he exclaimed, shaking his head with disbelief.

"I'm surprised she had to be made to do it at all," Teague said, meeting Graeme's gaze with a question in his own. "After all, ye're laird now, with wealth and power, and she certainly does no' seem to find bedding with ye repulsive."

Graeme merely shook his head at the words. He too
didn't understand why Annella had been so reluctant
to marry him. Truth to tell, he was actually a little offended by the fact that threats had had to be used to
get her to say I do. To his mind, they were perfect for
each other. She was strong and passionate and—

"I'd guess it's Lady Eschina that made her reluctant
to marry ye and ha'e to stay at Gunn," Angus said
suddenly.

Graeme's head whipped around and he speared the
man with his eyes. "Me mother?"

"Aye. The morning after yer tour o' Gunn to meet
the villeins, Lady Annella assigned old Bea to stay
in yer parents' bedchamber and help with yer father.
Yer lady mother protested that 'twas no' necessary,
but Annella insisted. Ever since then, Lady Eschina
has been comin' below to break her fast. She ne'er ar-
rives ere ye've left, and then she sits about in the great
hall fer the better part o' the day makin' a nuisance
o' herself until just ere ye return fer the sup. She then
returns to the chamber she shares with yer father."

Graeme felt a little bit guilty at this news. During his conversation with Annella when he'd learned
that his father was supposed to have a scroll, ink and
quill next to him to make his wishes known, and that
it was something that had been missing when he'd
visited, he'd said he'd talk with his father and have
his mother removed from the room if necessary. But
he hadn't. He'd been too busy trying to sort out how
to get Annella to marry him. She'd had to take care
of the matter herself. Not by removing his mother,
of course, but by setting another maid in the room to

ensure his father suffered no abuse from his own wife
and her maid.

Sighing, he shifted a little impatiently and asked
Angus, "What do ye mean when ye say me mother is
makin' a nuisance o' herself?"

"Makin' comments and criticisms, snide remarks
that I ken get under Lady Annella's skin," Angus answered, and then added, "Like she used to do when
Lady Annella first came. Only then the comments
were about how she was ugly and such a poor wife
to William that her son had run away rather than live
with her and such."

"What?" Payton asked with dismay.

"Aye." Angus nodded. "That went on fer a good
year or two after William's leaving. At first, Lady
Annella was obviously distressed and upset by the
words, which just made Lady Eschina's attacks
worse and more frequent. But as Lady Annella
gained confidence in running this whole damned
place by herself, she reacted less and less to Lady Eschina's words until she was simply ignoring her as if
she couldn't hear what she was saying, or didn't care.
Not getting any reaction, Lady Eschina appeared to
grow weary o' the game and started spendin' more
and more time in the chamber she shares with the old
laird. She rarely came below the last year ere this."

"But now she's comin' below again," Graeme muttered to himself, annoyed that he hadn't been aware
of any of this. He was usually up at the crack of dawn
and off to the loch to swim and clean himself. Then
he spent the rest of the day handling his new duties as
laird, only returning to the castle to eat his sup. He'd

never even seen his mother below stairs, let alone witnessed these verbal attacks on Annella.

"Aye," Angus told him. "Like before, she's criticizin' everything Lady Annella does, commentin' that useless as ye are, yer probably a better laird than she ever was, and blamin' her fer William's death, sayin' that were she a better wife, he'd have stayed and yet live."

Graeme's mouth tightened at this news. It was no wonder the woman hadn't wanted to marry him and remain here. Who would, with his harpy mother chasing them around making their life miserable? It was time to deal with his mother, he thought grimly.

Chapter 9

"*A*RE YE SURE WE NEED TO PACK ALL THIS?*"* Florie asked unhappily as she peered over the stack of dresses piled up next to the chests.

"Those are not the gowns I'm taking with me," Annella admitted solemnly. "That pile is the gowns that are too frayed or worn to take to MacKay."

Florie's eyebrows rose, and then her gaze slid to the one dress lying by itself. "Ye're no' thinkin' to take the blue one with ye, are ye? 'Tis stained."

Annella rolled her eyes at the reminder. As if she could forget that. The sky-blue gown had been her favorite of all the new gowns she'd brought with her to her wedding and new life. But the first time she'd worn it, Lady Eschina had "accidentally" knocked over a goblet and spilled wine all over her. Sitting back on her heels now, Annella frowned and admitted, "I was going to try again to get the stain out."

"I've tried, ye've tried, and even old Maggie tried to remove the wine stain directly after it happened," Florie reminded her gently. "'Twill no' come out."

"Right," Annella muttered with defeat, and then shook her head unhappily. "None o' me gowns is suitable fer wearin' in company."

"Nay," Florie agreed, and couldn't resist adding, "As I've told ye repeatedly, ye need to ha'e new gowns made."

"Aye," Annella agreed miserably. That would mean a delay to her being able to visit her family, but she simply couldn't arrive at MacKay with naught but rags on her back.

"Are ye sayin' ye're willin' to ha'e new gowns made?" Florie asked carefully, obviously having trouble believing it. Annella could hardly blame her. The maid had been trying to convince her to get new gowns made for at least the last three years of her six-year marriage without result.

Annella's gaze slid over the old, worn gowns in a pile and she sighed dejectedly. She didn't want to show up to her childhood home looking like a beggar. Her parents would be outraged and blame Eschina and Gaufrid, and while neither of them had been particularly welcoming since William's leaving—all right, Eschina had been positively awful—the point was, they were not at fault for the state of her wardrobe. At least not directly. She had been in charge of the coffers and their contents these last six years. She could have spent the coin and made the time to repair her wardrobe with a dress here or there. But she hadn't, and now it was a problem. Annella wanted to visit her mother for advice, but would be ashamed to arrive in any of the gowns she owned. She needed gowns befitting a lady before she would go.

"Aye," Annella said finally, and Florie fairly leaped to her feet, suddenly buzzing with excitement.

"This is wondrous!" her lady's maid exclaimed, hurrying for the door. "News came yesterday that the travelin' cloth merchant was at Sutherland. I'll send a lad with a message to him, requestin' he stop here fer some trade. Oh, this is grand!"

Annella watched her go with some amusement. The maid was so excited you'd think she was the one getting new gowns. Her gaze moved to the stack of old gowns again and she grimaced slightly. She really had let her wardrobe go these last years. But she simply hadn't had time to bother about new gowns. Now, she supposed she did. In fact, she had become so efficient at running things when she'd been burdened down with the chores of chatelaine, laird and healer, that now that the tasks of the laird had been taken off her hands, Annella found herself with a little too much time. Not a lot, but enough that she didn't need to rush about so much and had a moment here and there to herself. But time to herself meant time for unwanted thoughts to creep in. Like worries about her new marriage, new husband and the new feelings he inspired in her.

Unfortunately, those feelings were lust and fury. The lust she didn't mind so much. Passion was about the only thing she was enjoying about marriage. The fury though . . . Annella stood to move to the window.

Leaning against the deep ledge, she closed her eyes and tipped her face up to let that day's breeze brush over her cheeks. It cooled her skin. Unfortunately, it did not do much for the sudden fit of temper she was suffering. Her husband was a dolt. She had run Gunn for six years and had done it so successfully that she'd earned the respect of her new people. Unfortunately, her husband couldn't show her the same respect. Two days later she was still fuming over the fact that when she'd pointed out to Graeme that he should have spoken to someone before simply believing Dauid and going after the Morgans, he'd agreed and said, Aye, he should have spoken to Angus. Angus! Not her, but her previous, and now his, first.

She'd wanted to throttle him. Instead, she'd turned her horse and ridden away for fear of doing him some injury in front of their men.

Sighing, Annella turned her head so that her cheek rested against the cool stone framing the window. She had decided at the feast following their wedding that she should travel home to visit her family. She missed them and had only realized how much when she'd thought she would soon be home with them. But now she had a secondary reason for the trip. Annella needed advice from her mother on how to deal with a husband who obviously didn't respect her intelligence or abilities. Her mother, Annabel MacKay, was the smartest woman she knew. She also managed Annella's big, strong, terse father with a deft hand. The two never argued that she saw, yet her mother always seemed to get her way. Annella wanted her to teach her how she did it. She wanted a marriage as happy and satisfying as the one her parents shared.

"HAVE YE SPOKEN TO NELLA ABOUT HER planned visit to MacKay?"

Graeme scowled at that question from his brother-in-law, mostly because he had *not* had the conversation. It had been four days since the interaction with Morgan where he'd learned that she planned on traveling home to MacKay for a visit. He had intended to confront her on the matter, but somehow, every time he got around his wife, every thought in his head tumbled out, and he found himself doing his best to get them both out of their clothes for a different tumbling. The damned woman had bewitched him or something. That was the only explanation he could see for why he found himself following his cock whenever near her.

Rather than admit any of that, Graeme growled, "Why are ye still here, Payton? I thought by now ye'd ha'e headed home to give yer parents the news o' me brother's death, and yer sister marryin' me."

Payton shrugged that away without concern. "I gave one o' the men who traveled from MacKay with me a message while we were on the ship to Dundee and ordered him to carry it to MacKay once we landed. He was one of the first to disembark when we came ashore. No doubt he reached MacKay around the same time as we reached Gunn."

Pursing his lips he added, "O' course, that message only said that William was dead. I did no' ken ye'd be marrying Annella at the time. Still, by now, my parents have probably packed up half the castle and are traveling here to tend to Annella." Eyeing him sideways he continued, "No doubt they expect to carry her away with them. I'm no' sure what they'll think when I tell them that ye compromised Nella and I had to force the two o' ye to wed."

"Ye did no' ha'e to force me to do aught," Graeme snapped. "It was yer sister ye had to order to it."

"I still can no' believe she fought marryin' ye like she did," Teague commented, sounding more amused than disbelieving.

Graeme scowled at the taunt. It was a bit of a sore spot for him. He'd wanted the lass on first seeing her, or perhaps it was fairer to say, on first hearing her bellowing at Raynard. 'Twas of no consequence, he thought. The point was, he'd decided pretty quickly he wanted her to wife. She, on the other hand, had had to be dragged to the altar kicking and screaming. Not literally, of course. She'd walked there silent and grim on her brother's arm. But it had been more than obvious to one and all that she wasn't overjoyed to be marrying him. It was then he'd determined to woo her.

The fact that he had the horse behind the cart on this didn't bother Graeme. Most men barely met their future wives before the wedding and had to do their wooing after the ceremony if they wanted a happy, cooperative wife. So, woo her he would. The problem was, he had no better idea how to do that with Annella than he would with more delicate and fragile women. How did most husbands woo their wives?

Sadly, none of the three men around him could answer that question. None of them were married. Mayhap he should have a chat with his father, Graeme considered, but then shook his head. His father had obviously done a piss-poor job of the matter himself after marrying Graeme's mother. At least, that was his guess based on the fact that his mother had loathed his father as far back as he could recall. Although, honestly, it did seem a mutual feeling. His father had never seemed to much like his wife either.

"Aye," Symon said suddenly, interrupting his thoughts. "After years o' watchin' women throw themselves at yer feet at every turn, Lady Annella's reticence was somewhat o' a surprise."

"Women did no' throw themselves at me feet," Graeme growled with irritation. "At least no more than they did fer you two, and that was jest because they kenned we were successful and had the coin to pay them."

"Ah," Symon cried out, clutching his chest. "Stop! Ye wound me with yer words. I *believed* all those lasses with their claims o' undyin' devotion and love."

Graeme snorted at the words and opened his mouth to give a sharp retort, but paused as he spotted the wagon being led into the bailey. "Is that the cloth merchant?"

The other three men turned to look where his attention was fixed.

"Looks like it," Teague said with a shrug.

"Aye. The bolts o' fabric sticking out the back rather give it away," Payton said dryly.

"Aye," Graeme agreed, thoughtfully.

"What are ye thinkin'?" Symon asked, amusement tinging his voice. "Ye got that *'I've a fine idea'* look to yer face."

"I'm thinkin' I should buy Annella some cloth," he admitted, and then added, "As lady, she should be dressed in the finest raiment, yet every gown she wears appears to be fit fer nothin' but the rag pile."

"I had noticed," Payton said solemnly.

"Hmm," Teague murmured, and then said, "However, I think yer wife beat ye to it. I was in the great hall a couple o' days ago when yer lady wife's maid came down to send one o' the lads to Sutherland to ask the cloth merchant to stop in once done his commerce there."

Graeme stiffened at the words and then straightened his shoulders and thrust his chest out. "Well, she'll no' be buyin' anything. I shall do it fer her. In fact, I'll buy e'ery last bit o' cloth the man has. She'll ne'er again wear frayed or worn gowns. That should please her."

Positive he'd found a way to woo his new bride, Graeme headed for the merchant.

"'Twas verra kind o' yer husband to buy ye all this cloth," Florie said tentatively. "I'm sure he was tryin' to be thoughtful."

Annella merely grunted at Florie's comment, afraid to open her mouth lest she reveal her true opinion of her idiot husband and the asinine idea he'd had the day before of buying every stitch of cloth the cloth merchant possessed. Every time she looked at the stacks of cloth he'd had the men pile up in their bedchamber, Annella wanted to gnash her teeth. In her mind, all she saw was the coin they must have cost. Coin she and the people of Gunn had worked tirelessly to build up over the last six years. Coin wasted, since she couldn't use half of the cloth purchased. Not just because there was so much of it, but because half of the fabrics were not colors she would ever wear. Some because, with her complexion, they would make her look sallow and sickly, and others because they were just plain ugly.

"It was kind," Florie insisted, apparently unhappy with her lack of enthusiasm.

Mouth tightening, Annella set her sewing aside and stood to cross the room and open the shutters of a window to let some fresh air in. She didn't know if it was the cloth or the room itself, but something smelled displeasing to her.

Probably the rush mats, she decided as she inhaled the fresh air now pouring into the room. It had been a while since she'd had the rush mats removed and fresh ones made to replace them, Annella realized as she moved to open the second window. She supposed she'd have to see to that soon, she thought as she pulled the shutters open on this window. Annella froze with the shutter not quite fully open when something large flashed past outside. She blinked, both surprised and bewildered, but then the sounds of shouts and screams had her leaning to peer out the window.

Annella's eyes widened incredulously as she took in the scene below. Her husband and brother were lying just inches from a large stone that hadn't been in the bailey the last time she'd looked, and everyone else in the courtyard appeared to be rushing toward them with concern. Biting her lip, Annella peered over the two men, but when they began to move and she was assured they were fine, she turned her attention back to the stone. It was the size of a small cow, but probably weighed twice what a cow would. Recalling that something large had flown past the window as she'd opened the shutters, she decided it must be a merlon from the battlements and leaned out to peer upward.

Her eyes widened incredulously as she spotted someone hanging from the wall where the merlon used to be. It took a moment before she recognized that it was Dauid dangling there, legs kicking, hollering his head off. Cursing, Annella withdrew from the window even as the people below began to exclaim with alarm at the precarious position her brother-in-law was in.

Ignoring Florie's questions as to what was happening, Annella pushed away from the ledge and rushed from the bedchamber.

The stairs at the end of the hall led up to the battlements, and she hurried to them. Annella had no idea what she would do once on the wall. She knew there was no way she would be able to pull Dauid back up onto the battlements by herself, so was relieved when she pushed through the door at the top of the stairs and saw that two soldiers had already reached him and were pulling him back up onto the parapet.

Sighing with relief, she crossed to the men as they set Dauid on his feet, holding him by each arm to be sure he was steady and wouldn't tumble off the battlements again.

"Oh, Nellie," Dauid cried on spotting her. "Thank goodness ye're here. I nearly fell to me death. 'Twas awful."

"Aye, I saw," Annella said quietly, her gaze sliding over his flushed face and then taking in the fact that he appeared a little shaky on his feet. Not a surprise after the shock he'd had, she supposed. "What are ye doin' out here, Dauid? And what happened?"

"Oh." He sighed the word miserably. "I woke up feelin' a bit better this afternoon and thought some fresh air might speed me healin' along, so came up to walk the wall. But I guess I overestimated me strength. I'd no' gone far when a dizzy spell came o'er me. I leaned against the wall to steady meself, but then it suddenly was just no' there and I was tumblin'. Fortunately, I managed to catch hold o' the edge and hang on until help came." He smiled with gratitude at the two soldiers still on either side of him, and then frowned slightly and said, "I hope no one was hurt by the fallin' bit o' wall."

Annella almost snorted at that description. The boulder that had fallen had been more than a "bit o' wall." But before she could respond, Ludan, the man on Dauid's left, said, "Nay. Laird Graeme would ha'e been. Fortunately, Payton MacKay saw the boulder falling and managed to push our laird out o' the way."

"Aye," Johnne, the soldier on Dauid's right, agreed. "Yer brother saved yer husband's life and that's certain, m'lady."

Annella's eyes widened at this news. While she'd seen the two men lying on the ground close to the boulder, she hadn't really put together what that meant. Especially once she'd spotted Dauid hanging from the wall and in immediate peril. She was now a little confused at the sudden cacophony of emotions rioting within her at the realization that her dolt of a husband had nearly been killed.

"Husband?"

Annella forced her emotions aside at that weakly spoken word from Dauid and glanced to him. Seeing the wounded expression in his eyes, she sighed inwardly. She'd known the lad had feelings for her. He'd pretty much followed her around like a puppy for the last six years. He'd even professed his love a time or two until she'd told him it was improper. She was a married woman. His sister-in-law. It was a sin for him to say such things to her, to even think them, and he should never mention such again. That had prevented his repeating the words, but hadn't stopped his calf eyes following her all the damned time. She'd begun finding tasks and chores for him to perform just to get him out from under her feet.

Now, she eyed the younger man and thought a bit resentfully that this news was something her husband should have imparted to his brother. And why hadn't he? she wondered with irritation. It had been near a week since they'd wed. Just as Annella thought that, Graeme's voice sounded behind her.

"We married four days ago, Dauid. I meant to tell ye, and jest forgot."

"We married five days ago," Annella corrected a bit sharply, not even bothering to look at the man. Forcing a smile for Dauid's benefit, she added, "The day after ye arrived home."

She stepped around Dauid then to move over to the spot where the section of wall had fallen away, and frowned as she took it in. The missing portion of wall was huge. It was hard to believe the mere weight of a man leaning against it could dislodge such a large chunk of the merlon, until she noticed the grooves in the mortar where the stone had rested. The merlon hadn't just loosened on its own over time; someone had helped it along.

"How the devil did this happen?" Graeme asked suddenly, stepping up beside her and taking her arm as if afraid she might tumble out through the opening and fall to her death. Before Annella could respond, Johnne said, "Yer brother said he came out fer air, overexerted himself, leaned against the wall to rest and it suddenly just gave way."

In the next moment, Graeme urged her back a step or two and then released her and bent to examine the grooves she'd noticed.

"He's lucky we got to him quick as we did, m'laird. God's truth he was hangin' on by the tips o' his fingers and those were slippin' when we grabbed him."

Grunting, Graeme stood and glanced around, then shifted his gaze to Johnne in question. The other soldier and Dauid were now gone.

"Ludan thought he'd best see yer brother back to his room ere he fainted," Johnne explained. "The lad was shaken up and swayin' on his feet."

The word *brother* made Annella wonder where hers was. He'd been with Graeme below, and knowing him, she would have expected him to accompany her husband up to see what had happened. The fact that he hadn't had her suddenly worrying. "Where's Payton?"

"Probably on his bed by now," Graeme said with a faint amusement she only understood when he added, "Last I saw, Teague was carryin' him there while Symon went in search o' you."

"Carrying him?" Annella asked with alarm. "What—?"

"He's fine. He just twisted his ankle, or set it wrong as he propelled us both out o' the way o' the boulder.

He could no' set weight on it when we went to get up. But—"

Annella didn't hear anything else. She was already hurrying for the door back into the keep to find her brother.

"LEG UP," ANNELLA SAID FIRMLY AS SHE RE-turned to the solar where Florie and her brother were. They'd all three been in there since the accident that had injured her brother's ankle just after the nooning. Keeping Payton from trying to join the other men outside was hard enough, but keeping him in a chair with his leg resting on the small table she'd put in front of him was even worse. However, he'd done some serious damage to his ankle. It was presently twice the size it normally was and obviously pained him.

"The edge o' the table's cutting into the back o' me leg," Payton complained with irritation, though he did set his leg back on the table.

Changing direction, Annella moved to the rolls of material that had been stacked against the wall. She picked one that was yellow and purple that she found particularly ugly and quickly unrolled a good bit of it. She cut off the long length of cloth, then folded it over and over and set it under her brother's leg for him. "Better?"

"Aye," he grumbled reluctantly, and then frowned at her and said, "Yer face looked like a dog's arse when ye came in. Is there a problem?"

Annella's mouth immediately tightened with the same agitation she'd been feeling since visiting her father-in-law's room and finding poor Bea tending to her father-in-law. Alone. It seemed that Graeme had carried through with his threat to remove his mother from the castle. Lady Eschina and her maid, Agnes, had been moved to a cottage in the village.

Unfortunately, her husband hadn't fully considered the effects of such a move. Lady Eschina and Agnes had done more than just torture the poor man. They'd also tended to everything from feeding to bathing him, including seeing to his privy needs. Mind you, they'd used those tasks as other ways to torture the man, by withholding food when annoyed with him, or refusing to let him use the glazed earthenware bedpan Annella had had made for him until it was extremely uncomfortable for him and so on. At least they had before she'd assigned Bea to stay in the chamber with them to help. They'd known the maid would report their misdeeds to her should they pull anything like that in her presence, so had tempered such behaviors. At least when Bea was there.

Annella had used the excuse that she worried that they must be exhausted and would welcome aid in helping to tend to her father-in-law to account for Bea's presence. But she could hardly order Bea or any other maid to remain in the bedchamber at night with the couple. What need was there for a third pair of hands when the couple was sleeping?

Speaking of Bea, as Graeme had removed his mother and her maid from the chamber, he'd ordered Bea to continue tending to his father's needs. Unfortunately, he hadn't thought to arrange for more than the one maid. One woman could not do it all on her own.

Even Eschina and Agnes had frequently needed aid; another maid to run the meals, medicinals and other items up for the three of them, as well as strong older lads to help get him from the bed to the bath while they changed the bedding. Even turning him onto one side or the other to help prevent bedsores was almost impossible for one person to accomplish on their own. But Bea wasn't in a position to ask for help from the other servants. She'd been trying to do everything by herself, poor thing.

Annella had felt horrible when she realized the situation and had immediately arranged for a second maid to join her, and two more to replace them in the evenings. She'd also given them permission to send for a couple of men to help when there was actual lifting and moving needed.

Annella was still annoyed that Graeme hadn't thought of that, or at least spoken to her so that she could think of it for him. The man just stomped about doing one thing after another without considering the consequences, or finding out what was needed by those who did know. She supposed that was a warrior's trait: riding into battle and cutting down one enemy after another with little concern or thought. He appeared to handle the things that came up at Gunn in the same way, which was damned annoying when it caused issues.

"Is there?" Payton asked.

When Annella pulled herself from her thoughts and turned a blank expression his way, her brother repeated his earlier question.

"Is there a problem to explain your sour mood?"

Sighing, she forced the memory and her angry thoughts away and simply said, "Nay."

It was a bald-faced lie, and she knew her brother would recognize that, but he didn't push the matter and simply shifted restlessly in his seat as he asked, "How long am I goin' to have to rest me ankle?"

"Until the swelling goes down and ye can put weight on it without it paining ye," Annella said mildly as she reclaimed her seat.

"Well, how long will that be?" Payton asked impatiently.

Annella shrugged and picked up her sewing. "Two or three days or more."

She tried to hide her amusement when the answer made her brother curse. Honestly, men were the worst when it came to any kind of ailment or injury. Half the time they acted like wee bairns, and the other half they were impatient to be up and about and prolonging their issues. She'd take a sick woman over a sick man any day.

"Is it no' nearly time fer the sup?" Payton asked irritably.

"Nearly," she agreed, and then glanced at him and raised her eyebrows. "Would ye rather we bring food up to ye, or for one o' the men to carry ye below?"

"He'll be carried and like it."

Annella glanced around sharply at those words to see her husband crossing the room with purposeful strides. He didn't even slow, but walked straight to her brother and scooped him up as if he weighed nothing.

"Shut it," he said sharply when Payton began to squawk in protest. "Ye hurt yerself savin' me life. 'Tis only fair I be yer legs til yer back on yer own."

When Payton reluctantly fell silent, Annella stood and hurried to the door to open it. Graeme hadn't closed it, but he'd opened it with enough energy that it had hit the wall and then bounced back so that it was only ajar a few inches. Annella pulled it wide for her husband to carry her brother through and then gestured for Florie to follow and the two of them trailed after her husband to the stairs and down them.

One glance at the great hall told Annella that she'd misjudged the hour when she'd said it was nearly time for the sup. It was obviously past time for the meal. Teague, Symon, Angus and Dauid were already at the high table. It seemed her brother-in-law was feeling better after his near fall, Annella thought, as she let her gaze slide over the other tables in the large room. Every single one appeared full. Thinking Florie would have some trouble finding space to sit for the meal, she slowed and glanced back to cast the maid an apologetic look.

Florie merely smiled and waved away her concern. "Ne'er fear, m'lady, I'll squeeze in somewhere."

Relaxing a little, Annella nodded and continued down the stairs. Graeme was moving quickly though, and the brief delay had her arriving at the table after he'd already settled her brother and taken his own seat. Despite the irritation that claimed her on seeing Dauid there, Annella managed a smile of greeting for her brother-in-law as she took up position between him and her husband, but her gaze was moving along the table in search of Florie. When she saw that the maid had found a spot to squeeze into between two of her friends, she relaxed a little and finally addressed Dauid.

"'Tis good ye feel well enough to join us at table," she murmured, not adding that it wasn't a surprise. His wound was healing nicely with a scab already formed. Although, she supposed he wasn't fully healed if weakness had claimed him on the battlements. That thought brought concern to her face and she commented, "I hope ye had a servant walk ye below, Dauid. It would no' be good did ye grow weak or dizzy on the stairs and take a tumble."

Annella didn't really hear his response. She'd picked up her goblet as she spoke and brought it to her lips, but the scent of it made her pause and raise it to her nose instead to inhale more deeply. The moment she did, she felt her blood run cold.

"This ale tastes off."

Graeme's words had her head turning sharply and then she snatched his mug from him and lifted it to her nose. Cursing, she set both drinks on the table and barked, "Poison," as she launched to her feet and turned on him.

Graeme's eyes widened in shock, though she suspected more from the way she suddenly caught his head, tipped it back and began to try to push her fingers to the back of his tongue.

"Wife, what the hell," he muttered, catching her by the wrists to move her hands away from his face.

"Ye must purge," Annella said, not bothering to hide her panic. "Our drinks were poisoned. We must make ye toss up what ye drank or it'll kill ye."

Graeme met her gaze briefly, and then cursed, released her and turned away to stick his own fingers down his throat.

Chapter 10

GRAEME STEPPED SILENTLY INTO THE BEDCHAMber he now shared with Annella, and then quietly closed the door. Despite his best efforts, there was still a soft click as it closed. Wincing, he glanced quickly to the bed where his wife slept. Fortunately, while she stirred and turned on her side in her sleep, she didn't wake up.

Relieved, Graeme relaxed and silently crossed the room, removing his belt and sheathed sword as he went. He managed to set them on the chest at the foot of the bed without causing a clatter, then straightened, his gaze moving over his sleeping wife. Even in the dim, dancing light cast by the fire, she was beautiful. But it was a different beauty than when she was awake. During the day, Annella was a beautiful Valkyrie, proud, strong and commanding. In sleep her beauty was softer, almost innocent. The difference fascinated him and he wondered which better represented her true nature. Perhaps both did, he thought now. His wife was a study in contrasts, and so far, he liked every facet she'd revealed to him.

Annella stirred sleepily and rolled onto her back, the fur shifting downward as she went so that more than her personality was revealed to him. The woman might be wearing a sleeping gown, but it—like every other scrap of clothing she owned—was worn and frayed. The difference was the sleeping gown, thin to begin with, had become damned near see-through after years of wear. He could see her nipples clearly through the nearly transparent cloth, and the sight made Graeme freeze. He then closed his eyes and barely restrained the groan that wanted to leave him.

He'd stayed up late talking to the men about the attempt to poison him and Annella that evening at sup. They'd tried to puzzle out who could be behind it while Annella had still been there, but had failed miserably. She had suggested that perhaps his mother was angry about his removing her from the castle. However, Graeme had found it hard to believe that was likely, as had the other men. In the end, even Annella had admitted that murdering them seemed a strong response to the action.

Unfortunately, not one of them had been able to come up with an alternate possibility by the end of the meal. Annella had given up then and retired, but Graeme had remained at the table to talk to the men. Not about who might be behind the attempt to poison them, but what should be done about it.

They had all quickly agreed that two trusted soldiers should be set to guard the buttery at all times. It would be taken in three shifts so that all beverages were guarded day and night. These guards would oversee the servant presently in charge of the buttery and the distribution of the beverages stored within. They would make sure that nothing was done to the drinks, and that Graeme and Annella's beverages were always served from fresh barrels or butts. The servant would then test each drink himself, tasting it to be sure it was not poisoned, before personally delivering it to Annella and Graeme. He and the drinks would be escorted to the table by one of the two soldiers on duty to ensure that nothing was done to the drinks before they reached Graeme and Annella. All of them had agreed that this was the best way to ensure that another attempt to poison them could not take place.

When Dauid had then suggested that a similar system should be made for the food they ate as well, Graeme had agreed. He'd also been rather annoyed that he hadn't thought of it himself.

After assigning Angus the chore of picking the soldiers he considered the most reliable for the task, Graeme had announced that he wanted to set some men to guard his wife as well until the matter of who had poisoned them was resolved. No one had argued this plan of action. The problem had come because Teague, Symon, Payton and even Angus all seemed to think that he should have a guard as well. Graeme hadn't thought it necessary and they'd argued the point for quite a while.

It was Payton who had pointed out that Teague and Symon were usually with him anyway. They should just be sure to always be with him while he was up and about, then Annella's guards could stand watch outside their chamber at night.

"Unless Teague and Symon plan on leaving Gunn

soon?" Payton had added, glancing to the two men in question.

Graeme had been startled and even a little alarmed at the suggestion. He'd met the pair on the first job he'd taken as a mercenary on leaving Gunn. The job was to stand with the MacIntoshes against the neighboring clan, the Robertsons, whom they'd been battling with over land, or perhaps the hand of one clan's daughter. Graeme couldn't remember now. At any rate, he'd encountered Teague on the journey there, and once they realized they were both heading to the same place and for the same reason, they'd joined up for the tail end of their travels.

They'd reached MacIntosh just ere darkness fell and after talking to the MacIntosh laird's man, had set up camp together on the edge of where the other mercenaries were already settled. They'd worked together, building a fire and making oatcakes to eat and then had rolled up in their plaids to sleep on either side of the fire. The next morning they'd woken up to find a third man asleep at the far end of their dead fire. That had been Symon. He'd arrived a couple of hours after dark and the MacIntosh laird's man had apparently directed him to bed down with Graeme and Teague, who had been the last to arrive before him.

Thus had begun a friendship that had only strengthened and grown with the passage of time. The three had continued to camp together, keeping an eye out for their comrades' possessions along with their own, guarded each other's backs in battle and traveled together to each new job, their number making them safer than a man traveling alone would have been.

When Dauid had arrived at their last job at Mac-Kinnon and babbled his tale of a missing William and the search for him before falling into exhausted sleep, Graeme had talked over the situation with Teague and Symon. They'd previously planned to travel south to the Fergusons, who were looking for warriors to join them against the Douglases. But both of his friends had said family was more important than coin, and if he wished to join the search for his brother, they'd be happy to accompany him and lend their aid. Graeme was grateful for the offer, but all he'd said was that he'd decide after questioning Dauid in the morning. The three of them had then rolled up in their plaids to sleep.

Graeme had never got the opportunity to ask more questions of Dauid in the morning. He was the first to wake the next day, had considered waking the others, but a serious need to relieve himself had sent him into the woods instead. Graeme had returned just moments later to watch Payton MacKay riding into camp with two dozen soldiers at his back.

"That's Nellie's brother," Dauid said, waking up quickly at the arrival of so many men and horses in the small clearing.

Ignoring him, Graeme had given Payton a long once-over. Deciding he looked like he could handle himself, he'd said, "MacKay?"

"Aye" had been the spare answer.

"Ye're headin' out to look fer me brother William?" Graeme had asked.

"Aye," Payton had repeated, this time adding, "Will ye join us?"

Graeme had glanced to Teague and Symon, and when each gave an almost imperceptible nod, he answered for all of them. "Aye. We'll join yer party. Just let us saddle up."

And so, the three of them had headed off with Dauid, Payton and the MacKay soldiers he'd brought with him to look for Graeme's brother William, a journey that had ended up taking them nearly all the way to Jerusalem. The excursion had lasted just a few days more than six months by the time they'd reached Gunn, yet Graeme hadn't even considered that his friends might move on now that he was laird. Now he admitted to himself that they would eventually move on. The idea saddened him, but he knew it was inevitable. Still, he was grateful for their loyalty and friendship when— after exchanging a glance with Symon—Teague had said, "We'll stay here at Gunn until these troubles are resolved at least."

"There ye are then," Payton had said with satisfaction. "They can continue to watch yer back while ye're up and about. Then Annella's guards will take over standing watch at the door o' yer bedchamber at night." He didn't give anyone a chance to protest, but had then turned to Angus to ask, "How soon can ye set up a guard fer Annella?"

Angus had hesitated and frowned. "That depends on which ye think is more important. I've two men right now I could post to guard the buttery or Lady Annella, but the rest o' the men I'm thinking about are either manning the wall or sleeping after a long shift. It'll take a bit o' time to find replacements for the men on the wall, and to rouse—"

"I do no' want men who are like to fall asleep on the job," Graeme had said firmly. "Put the two men available at the moment on the task o' guarding the buttery. Tomorrow morning is early enough to assign guards to Annella. She's already safely abed, and I'm heading up meself now, so . . ." He'd shrugged. "We should be safe enough this night."

When the men all murmured in agreement, Graeme downed the last of his mug of ale and stood to leave the table with a murmured, "Good sleep."

He had to take a somewhat circuitous route to the stairs. All but the high table had been taken apart, the pieces stacked against the wall to make room, and the great hall floor was already half covered with people settling in to sleep. But there were still a lot of people milling about talking to others, or looking for family members or friends they usually slept near. Graeme had to move cautiously to avoid stepping on anyone, but was grateful to leave that behind and start up the stairs.

He knew it had been a while since Annella had gone up to the chamber they shared and hadn't expected her to still be awake. Even so, if he was being honest with himself, he'd been disappointed when he'd entered the room to find her sound asleep. As usual his body had started to perk up at the very idea of joining her in bed, and didn't seem to care the least little bit that she was not awake. Her well-worn to the point of being see-through sleeping gown was not helping with that, and for one moment, Graeme actually considered kissing her awake, stripping away the sleeping gown she wore and sinking himself into her moist heat. But then his better, less selfish side spoke up, telling him that he should let her rest.

Graeme's head heard and agreed with the suggestion. From what he understood, his wife had suffered more than enough disturbed nights in the six years she'd been at Gunn, thanks to her skills as healer. In fact, she was still suffering them. Annella had been woken up a few times since their wedding. Graeme had accompanied her each time she was called away to tend to someone. Twice it had been children with the ague and fever. The third time had been a woman in labor. Annella had sent him out of the cottage for that one, but he'd waited outside for her to finish and then had walked her back to the castle and their chamber. That being the case, he would not disturb her sleep, Graeme told himself firmly.

Sadly, his cock didn't have ears and couldn't read his mind. That or it simply did not care how he felt on the subject. Whichever the case, it was up and ready to go. Since scowling down at the tent it was making under his plaid did not help, Graeme decided a quick dip in a cold loch was in order. He considered going back out through the door, but that would mean creeping through the people spread out on the great hall floor. Not to mention that if Payton and the others were still below at the table, they might decide he shouldn't go alone. Frankly, he wasn't in the mood for company, or to be more precise, he wasn't in the mood for the comments and taunts his tented plaid would bring about.

That thought in mind, Graeme crossed the room and silently opened the entrance to the secret passage. While there were several exits to the passages, the furthest one actually opened up into an area not far from the clearing where he'd first made love to Annella. The water in the river that rushed by there came down from the mountains and was always ice-cold. A dip in that should definitely take care of his overeager erection. In fact, as he stepped into the passage, Graeme fancied that it was shrinking a little just at the thought of what was awaiting it at the end of this walk. Distracted as he was with these thoughts, he never saw the person lurking in the darkness, but as he turned back to pull the panel closed, agony suddenly exploded in his head.

AT FIRST, ANNELLA WASN'T SURE WHAT HAD stirred her from sleep. A sound maybe? Aye, there it was, a soft rustling as material moved, and then . . . Was Graeme dragging something across the floor? Confusion roused her a bit more from the deep sleep she'd been in before being stirred awake, and then the sound of liquid splashing on the wooden floorboards caught her ear just before the scent of uisge beatha reached her nose.

Nose twitching, Annella finally opened her eyes. She barely caught a glimpse of the dark figure standing next to the bed before fire exploded all around her, seeming to engulf the figure.

Sitting up abruptly, Annella stared with confusion at her bedchamber. At first, she thought the entire room was afire. The flames certainly seemed to be everywhere. Certainly, it was in front of, and on both sides of, the bed. For one moment she sat still, unsure what to do, and then she managed to shake herself out of her paralysis and began to move. She had to get out of there. Somehow. She had to figure out a way through the fire. How far did it stretch beyond the bed?

That question poking at her mind, Annella shifted the furs and linens aside and stood up on the bed to try to get a better idea of what she was dealing with. Was it just a ring of fire around the bed? Or was the whole room aflame? Unfortunately, smoke rises and standing up put her firmly in the cloud of smoke gathering above her. She managed to get a quick glimpse of the situation, but then was claimed by a coughing fit. It was as she lowered her face to cover her mouth that she spotted the body on the floor next to the bed.

Annella immediately dropped to her knees on the bed. The air was better here, but she had to wait for her hacking coughs to stop before she could crawl to the edge of the bed. Despite the thick smoke, she could see the body on the floor, and with her face just inches from his, she immediately recognized her husband. He was being roasted alive by the fire surrounding them. As was she.

Reaching down, Annella shook Graeme's shoulder, hoping to wake him. All that did was make his head move a bit from side to side until it fell all the way to the right. It was then she saw the wound on his left temple. Graeme had taken a terrible blow to the head and was unlikely to wake up. It was on her to get them both out. The question was how?

Annella took a quick look around to see what she had to work with. Not much. Both bedside tables were empty, and the bed itself held only furs and linens.

Cursing, she slid off the bed, dragging the furs with her. Holding them close to keep them as far from the fire as she could, Annella eyed the area nearest her and then shifted her gaze to Graeme. Did she throw the furs on the fire and hope it covered them without bursting into flame? At least long enough that she could run across without getting burned and perhaps get to the water pitcher and basin by the windows and—And what? There wasn't enough water there to put out the fire. It would also leave her on one side of the flames and her husband on the other.

Okay, Annella reasoned, then maybe she threw the furs down and dragged Graeme across it to the other side of the fire. From what she'd seen when standing, the flames did not fill the whole room. Yet. At the moment, it was perhaps a foot-deep band around the bed. If Graeme were conscious, they probably would have just jumped off the bed and through it, praying the whole while that their clothes did not catch fire. Sadly, he was not conscious.

"All right," she muttered determinedly and stepped over Graeme so that she was between him and the fire. Annella then took a deep breath that she hoped would get her through what was coming, tossed the fur over the flames in front of her, then quickly turned and bent to grab her husband's hands. Straightening her legs then, she attempted to drag him swiftly across the fur to the area of flooring not yet on fire.

Graeme moved with surprising ease. As large and heavy with muscle as he was, she'd expected it to be a struggle. Instead, his oiled plaid allowed him to glide across the wooden floor with more speed and much less effort than she'd expected. He didn't, however, slide over the fur, instead the pelt was caught up around his head and shoulders and moved with them. Annella almost stopped when she noted that was happening, but then saw that the flames had been smothered where the fur had lain and she was dragging Graeme across lightly charred floorboards, not fire.

Desperate to get them both away from the flames as quickly as possible, she tried to move more swiftly, and didn't stop moving backward until her behind bumped up against something. Raising her head then, she took in the situation at a glance. What she'd bumped into was the wall. They were outside the ring of fire, although Graeme's booted feet were closer to the flames than she was happy with. However, from this side, she could better see that it wasn't the floor so much as the rush mats on the floor that were on fire, and judging by the light scorching where the pelt had smothered the flames, the fire hadn't yet got a proper hold on the wood under the mats.

Dropping Graeme's hands, she tugged the fur out from under his head and shook it out. Blackened rushes fell around her. The fire that had been eating them had been doused and pulled away from the others by the fur. If she was quick enough, she might be able to smother the rest of the flames and completely put out the fire before it spread or did too much damage to the room.

Annella had barely had the thought when a coughing fit claimed her. Knowing time was of the essence, she ignored it, stumbled around Graeme and cast the fur over the section of flames between the wall and the spot she'd dragged her husband through. Annella then stomped on the fur for good measure before lifting it from the floor. Relieved to see that it had worked, she moved back the way she'd come and threw it down again over another area of flames, and then another.

By the time she reached the bottom of the bed, Annella had dropped to her knees to take advantage of the better air there as she repeated that task over and over. She was working her way around the end of the bed, gasping for a breath that wouldn't choke her, when she was suddenly grabbed by the shoulders and dragged to her feet.

Glancing around with confusion, she recognized Payton, and then he scooped her up. Annella tried to tell him to get Graeme, but a paroxysm of coughing made that impossible. When it finally stopped, she leaned weakly against her brother's shoulder and peered behind him, relieved to see Teague following them out of the bedchamber with Graeme in his arms. Past them, Symon was leading a group of men with buckets into the burning room. The fire would be out in no time, Annella thought with relief, and sagged in her brother's arms, then frowned as she noted his hobbling gait.

"Yer ankle," she cried, but her voice came out a husky rasp rather than the sharp protest she'd intended.

"Me ankle is fine," Payton assured her grimly. "How are you? Were ye burned?"

Even as Annella opened her mouth to answer, her brother said, "Ne'er mind. I'll see fer meself shortly, and I'd rather ye no' talk. The smoke obviously affected yer throat. I think it best ye do no' use it until we get some liquid in ye that can soothe it."

"I'll find a maid to fetch her some honey mead."

Annella's eyes had started to droop closed, but blinked open at that and she saw that Dauid was keeping pace with her brother. When he saw that her eyes were open, he smiled reassuringly. "'Tis glad I am that ye're alive and well, Nellie. When we saw the smoke seepin' out from under yer bedchamber door and the light of flames showing through the cracks, we feared what we would find inside."

"Fetch enough honey mead fer Graeme too, Dauid," Teague said sharply. "I'm sure he'll need it as well."

Annella saw fury flash briefly on Dauid's face at the order, but it was quickly gone as he turned to move out of sight. Presumably, to fetch the mead, or order a maid to do it. She wasn't really sure which, but was just glad he was gone. It saved her from snapping at him about calling her Nellie and perhaps doing her throat damage.

"Can ye tell us what happened?"

Annella shifted her gaze to her brother, but before she could speak, he again said, "Ne'er mind. Ye should no' talk yet."

She managed not to roll her eyes at this, but then glanced around with curiosity when he carried her into a room. His room, she realized.

"Payton can take my room, and I'll bunk with Symon until yer room is fit fer use again," Teague announced when her expression showed her confusion.

Annella just managed to offer him a smile before Payton was suddenly turning toward the bed to set her down. Her bottom had barely hit the fur-covered surface when Teague was laying Graeme down on the other side of the bed. She immediately moved to try to check on his head wound, but Payton caught her by the shoulders and pulled her back around to sit facing him. He'd settled on the side of the bed, no doubt to give his injured ankle some respite, and was now examining her hands.

A scowl immediately claimed his expression. "Ye burned yerself."

Annella frowned at his choice of words. He made it sound like she was responsible for it, instead of the person who'd set the damned fire. Then she realized what he'd said and snatched her hands from his hold to examine them herself. Much to her relief, while she'd sustained a few burns, probably while trying to put the fire out, they weren't that bad. Some were blistering, but most were just red spots where she'd got lightly scorched.

"Do ye ha'e a salve to put on yer wounds?" Payton asked, and then immediately said, "Do no' answer that. Ye should no' be talkin' just now. I'll find Florie. She'll ken where yer medicinals are." Standing up, Payton then started to hobble away muttering, "I hope they were no' destroyed in the fire."

"I'll go find out where Dauid got to with that mead else we'll ne'er hear how the fire started," Angus announced, and Annella glanced with surprise to where the old soldier stood beside Teague. She hadn't realized he was there too, but supposed she shouldn't be surprised. The man had been sitting with her husband and the others when she'd left the table.

She was watching the soldier leave, when Teague asked, "Was the fire an accident?" Before she could try to speak, he added, "Nod yes, or shake yer head fer no."

Annella shook her head for answer, then rose up onto her knees so that she could shift on the bed to face Graeme and look him over. He was lying with his right side to her, so she couldn't see his head wound until she caught his chin and turned his face.

"Then I gather that was no accident either?" Teague asked.

Knowing he was talking about the head wound, Annella hesitated the briefest moment, but then shook her head again. She hadn't seen how her husband had taken the injury, but she *had* seen a dark figure before the rush mats had burst into flame and briefly blinded her. It seemed likely that the intruder was responsible for both the fire and Graeme's wound.

Wanting to wipe away some of the blood from his wound to get a better look at the damage done, Annella glanced around for a clean bit of cloth to dab at it with. Unfortunately, unless she wanted to start ripping up the bed linens, there was nothing she could use. She'd have to wait for Payton to return with her bag.

Sighing, Annella shifted her gaze over the rest of him then. Unlike her, his hands seemed fine and there didn't appear to be any other burns on his person. But recalling his booted feet lying close to the fire, she shifted down the bed, taking a quick glance at his legs as she went to be sure there were no burns or other wounds there. A quick perusal didn't reveal any, so Annella shifted her attention to his boots. They seemed fine, which she supposed wasn't surprising. Leather tended to stand up well under fire in her experience. That didn't mean his feet were fine inside them though. Leather might resist melting or igniting when fire was near, but that didn't mean it didn't grow hot. Worried about his feet, she reached for the nearer boot and started to try to remove it, only to stop on a cry of pain. Actually, Annella didn't cry out. She meant to, but the sound that came out was more along the lines of a pained croak.

"Yer damaging yer already damaged hands," Teague said with reproach. "Just sit still. I'll remove his boots fer ye if ye think 'tis necessary."

Annella nodded to assure him that it was indeed necessary, and then waited impatiently as he walked to the foot of the bed and set to the task. He had both boots off faster than she would have managed one, and then stepped back to allow her to examine Graeme's feet. Annella didn't touch them. She didn't need to. Besides, her fingers were still throbbing from her attempt to remove his boot. The activity had burst a couple of the blisters on her fingers, and she knew that—aside from hurting like a bugger—it increased the risk of infection. She couldn't touch anything until the burns on her hands and fingers had been cleaned, salve applied and fresh linens wrapped around them.

Sighing, Annella sank back on her heels and glanced impatiently toward the door. But the sight of her brother returning with her bag of medicinals in hand, and Florie trailing him with two pitchers, two mugs and a concerned expression on her face, had her perking up at once.

Chapter 11

"ARE YER HANDS TROUBLIN' YE? SHOULD I put some fresh salve on?"

Annella glanced up with surprise at that question from Florie, and then looked down to see that she was rubbing one cloth-covered hand over the other. Her expression became something of a grimace as she peered at the white clubs her hands now resembled. Her brother's skill at binding a wound left much to be desired. Unfortunately, Florie had taken one look at the bloody wound on Graeme's head and had nearly dropped the pitchers and mugs she carried on the bed-side table, before fleeing the room making heaving sounds. She really had a problem with blood.

Sadly, the maid's defection had left Teague and her brother to tend to their wounds. Teague had actually done a fine job of cleaning Graeme's head wound, applying salve and wrapping linen around his head. He'd obviously tended to such tasks before. Annella supposed she shouldn't have been surprised. Working as mercenaries, the men must have encountered and even received a lot of different wounds. She guessed it would have been more surprising had they not gained any skills in that area after ten years at war.

Payton, however, had never worked as a mercenary. He had spent the last several years laboring next to their father at MacKay, learning all he would need to know to run the castle and clan when their father retired or died and he took on the job. All of which meant that her brother had absolutely no skill in the healing arts. Hence, why her hands looked like they belonged on one of those fabled mummies they supposedly had in the far-off land of Egypt.

Sighing, she let her hands drop back to her lap and said, "Nay. 'Tis fine, thank ye, Florie."

When the maid nodded and returned her attention to the cloth she was sewing, Annella glanced at her brother. A smile began to tug at her lips as she took in the expression of deep concentration on his face as he cut the cloth Florie had given him to work on. Honestly, he looked like a lad learning his numbers and—The thought died, her mouth suddenly turning down into a scowl as she noticed that he had lowered his injured leg so that his foot rested on the floor. Again.

"Leg up," she ordered sharply. Thanks to his carrying her around and having to put weight on his sore ankle, Payton's injury was as bad as it had been directly after he was hurt. He needed to keep it elevated.

Grumbling under his breath about bossy sisters and other things she didn't catch, Payton raised his leg and again rested his foot on the small table she'd had Florie set before him to use to keep his leg elevated.

Sighing, Annella glanced around the solar. Her

gaze skated over the bolts of cloth stacked against the
far wall. Not for the first time, she thought how for-
tunate it was that Graeme had ordered them removed
to the solar. He'd set men to the task the afternoon of
the fire. He'd said it was because he thought the light
was better in the solar for them to work on her gowns.
The truth, however, was that he'd grown tired of tripping over the bolts of cloth stacked all around their
bedchamber. Annella hadn't cared why he'd given the
order, she'd just been glad to get them out, especially
after the fire. As annoyed as she was with her husband
for spending so much coin on the cloth, she would
have been ready to kill someone had the expensive
cloth gone up in flames.

Shifting abruptly in her seat, Annella peered down
at her hands again. They were useless stumps at the
moment. She couldn't even cut cloth like Payton, let
alone sew. And she had no idea how she was meant to
eat, something that was presently on her mind because
she'd had naught but a couple of sips of honey mead
that morning when she'd gone below to break her fast.
Not because she hadn't been hungry, but because Annella simply hadn't known how she could possibly eat
the bread and cheese that had been on offer. Picking
up her mug had been hard enough. Food had seemed
impossible. She'd have to sort it out at the nooning,
however, because her stomach was aching in a most
unpleasant manner to let her know it was empty and
unhappy with that state.

Deciding she needed to do something to distract
herself from her hunger, Annella stood abruptly and
headed for the solar door.

"Where are ye going?"

Pausing halfway across the room, Annella turned back, noting that while it had been sheer boredom that had driven him to offer to help with cutting out panels for the dress Florie was working on, he appeared to be doing a fine job of it. The realization made her smile as she answered his question.

"I was just going to check on Gaufrid," Annella explained, mentioning Graeme's father. Although the truth was that she really wanted to check on the women she'd set to the task of tending him and make sure all was well and that they didn't need anything.

"I'll go with ye," Payton said eagerly, setting aside the cloth he'd been working on.

"There's no need to trouble yerself," Annella said with a frown of concern as he reached for the staff with a cross piece at the top that she had given him to assist in getting around.

"Aye, there is," Payton insisted, using the crutch to help him get to his feet and then shifting it under his right arm to aid him in walking. "Someone tried to poison you and yer husband last night, Nella. Then set yer bedchamber on fire with you in it. Ye're no' to be without someone to watch over ye until we sort out who is behind these attacks."

"Never mind," Annella said with irritation as she moved away from the door. She wouldn't go if he insisted on accompanying her. He really needed to stay off the leg for it to heal.

"Are ye sure?" Payton definitely sounded disappointed. Apparently, she wasn't the only one slowly going crazy being stuck in this room.

"Aye. I'll check later," Annella said at once, moving back to her seat.

"No' alone. Ye can no' be alone until this is resolved," he reminded her solemnly.

As if she'd forget that, Annella thought with annoyance as she sat down. After a moment of just sitting there bored, she decided to go through the events of the night before. Perhaps something would stand out to her that would help them solve this issue. What seemed to strike her most clearly was how lucky they'd been. Of course, having someone who wanted you dead and was actively trying to bring about that result was not good luck, but everything else had been, to her mind. First, she'd recognized the smell of the poison among the sweeter notes of her beverage and had not drunk it. Second, while Graeme had taken a gulp, he'd managed to bring it back up.

Of course, Annella hadn't been sure whether they'd been quick enough at the time, and had spent the rest of the meal eyeing him warily and asking how he felt. Not that they'd gone ahead to eat right away after that. First, Graeme had had her check the beverages of the other men at the high table to be sure their drinks had not also been dosed with the poison. Once assured that the drinks of the others appeared fine, he'd turned his attention to questions about who had brought or been near his ale and her mead. When no one seemed to recall seeing anyone near their drinks ere they'd joined everyone at table, Cook had been brought out and questioned. Unfortunately, she'd not been able to shed any light on the situation either. She'd been busy with meal preparations and knew nothing of the beverages. Neither had the servant in charge of the buttery.

Finding no satisfaction, Graeme and the men had begun to discuss who might wish her and him dead. When they hadn't managed to sort that out, they'd moved on to discussing what should be done in light of this attempt. Having retired, Annella had missed that part of the conversation, but the end result was apparently that Payton was to keep her close, while Teague and Symon would trail Graeme around. The attempt to burn them alive had not changed that decision.

Of course, Payton wasn't the only one guarding her. There were presently two soldiers standing guard outside the door to the solar who also would have followed her to Laird Gaufrid's room, had she gone.

Sighing, Annella shifted in her chair. She was restless now and also worried. She had no more idea who could have put the poison in their drinks than the men did, but whoever it was had either been unskilled or so serious in their determination to see them dead that they'd taken the risk of the scent giving away the attempt. Had they used a lesser amount of the poison, she never would have smelled it. But the larger the dose the quicker the reaction, and the more likely the result would be death. That was another bit of luck for them. Neither of them had suffered for it. At least she hadn't, and Graeme had claimed that he was fine.

Then there was the fire. They'd been very lucky to escape it with the few injuries they had. Despite how annoying she found the state of her hands and the wrapping on them, Annella knew it could have been so much worse. Aye, so far, they'd survived two murder attempts with little issue. That didn't mean they would next time though . . . if another attempt was made.

Scowling, Annella stood and paced to the window. After years of rushing about running everything at Gunn, sitting about doing nothing was grating on her. Added to that, she was extremely annoyed that she couldn't continue working on the gowns she'd planned to make. She needed several new gowns if she was to visit her family, and Florie working alone with the little help Payton could offer meant it would take forever.

Perhaps she should set several servants to the task to help Florie, Annella considered. Or even hire some villagers to the task. The thought made her scowl as she realized she'd have to ask Graeme for the coin to do that. Something else that made her want to grind her teeth. Annella was the one who had been in charge of the coin prior to this. Now Graeme held the purse strings, and she had to ask him ere spending a single coin.

Her gaze narrowed suddenly as it caught on a soldier riding slowly across the bailey toward the front gate with a sac hanging from his saddle. It looked like—

"Is that Raynard?" Florie asked, making her aware that the maid had joined her at the window.

"It looks like it," Annella acknowledged, her gaze narrowing on the man. He shouldn't really be riding. He was well enough now that he could be up and about so long as he didn't overdo it, but she had continued to order him to stay abed and told Angus to keep one man with him at all times to ensure he did as ordered and didn't drink. While some walking and movement would have been fine, bouncing around on horseback was not. Even the slow walk would need him to use stomach muscles better not tested until he was completely healed. However, a trot, canter or gallop could cause serious damage at this point.

"I wonder where he's goin'," Florie murmured with curiosity, and then asked, "Should he be ridin' yet?"

"Nay," Annella growled and whirled to head for the door. This time she didn't bother to answer her brother when he asked where she was going. Leaving him scrambling for his crutch, she stormed out of the room. The two men set to guard her immediately straightened from where they'd leaned against the wall on either side of the door and rushed to follow on her heels as she hurried for the stairs. Annella ignored them. Her mind was flying this way and that as she tried to sort out where the devil Raynard was going and why.

"Mayhap we've been lookin' at this the wrong way."

Graeme tore his gaze away from the men battling in the practice field and glanced at Symon at that comment. Arching one eyebrow in question, he asked, "What mean ye by that?"

"Well, instead o' tryin' to figure out who might *want* ye dead, mayhap we should be lookin' into who would *benefit* if ye and yer lady wife were to die," he suggested.

Graeme considered that as he turned his attention back to the men. He'd been overseeing the men at battle-practice since becoming laird. He needed to know what skills there were among his men to use them effectively. While he'd started out just watching them practice attacking each other with whatever weapons they chose, more than a week ago he'd begun having them use different weapons each day to see which they were best at. First, he'd had them all battle with swords, then the mace, then the battle axe, followed by a day each for the spear, lance, crossbow, longbow and, today, daggers.

Today, however, he was having difficulty keeping his attention on the men. Instead, his mind was taken up with the murder attempts on him and Annella. He knew it was on Teague's and Symon's minds as well. They'd been talking about who would have gotten away with dosing their drinks at the table, or setting already dosed drinks there. A servant had been the only answer, but what servant would want him and Annella dead? Now Symon was approaching the problem from a different direction . . . and a good one too, he thought, and murmured, "Aye."

All three men nodded and considered the matter, and then Teague pointed out, "Dauid would become laird did ye die."

"Aye, but he's sweet on Lady Annella," Symon argued. "He'd ne'er poison her."

"Nay, ye're right," Teague agreed with a disappointed sigh.

Graeme glanced at his friends sharply. "Me brother is sweet on me wife?"

Symon raised his eyebrows in surprise and then glanced to Teague, before saying, "Did ye no' notice how he went on about how brave and brilliant she was when we sat around the fire of a night on the journey to find William?"

Teague nodded. "All he seemed able to talk about was Payton's sister."

"Aye, but that's because Payton was asking after her," Graeme said with a small frown. In his mind he remembered Payton asking questions about his sister and then Dauid answering. Graeme had usually lost interest in the conversation rather quickly after that and let it fade from his awareness as he sharpened his sword, cleaned and oiled his saddle or carried on various other necessary tasks of a night.

"Aye, Payton would ask a question about her," Teague agreed. "But usually just the one, and that was enough to have Dauid going on fer hours about how smart, strong and beautiful she was."

"Aye," Symon agreed. "'Twas obvious he more than admired her."

"Actually, I'm surprised he did no' kick up a fuss when he learned ye married her while he was abed," Teague commented. "And if the poison had been in only yer drink, I'd ha'e bet on it being Dauid behind it. But since 'twas in both beverages, it can no' be him."

Graeme was scowling at this when a shout drew his gaze toward the stables. For one moment, he was confused at what he was seeing. Two soldiers were running toward a rider even now exiting the stables at a trot that quickly became a canter as horse and rider passed the two almost panicked men, headed for the drawbridge. The guards immediately gave up the chase and rushed into the stables, shouting for horses to follow their "Lady."

Cursing, Graeme headed for the stables at a run.

Much to Annella's relief, Raynard was keeping his mount to a trot and not a canter or gallop . . . either of which could have done his injury serious damage. Unfortunately, a trot was not much better for his wound, and she'd been determined to get to him and stop his ridiculous ride as quickly as she could. However, while Annella had been quick about making her way out of the keep and across the bailey to the stables, talking her guards into helping her onto her mare's back and then tying her reins around her bandaged hands for her so they could ride out after Raynard had taken much longer. The two men hadn't felt it was safe for her to ride her horse, let alone be outside the walls. They'd argued long and hard against both before giving in to her demands. Too long. Aware that every moment could be doing more damage to Raynard, Annella hadn't had the patience to then wait for the men. The moment they'd started away to collect and ready their own mounts, she'd ridden out of the stables, headed for the gate.

Annella felt somewhat bad about that, but knew the men would catch up quickly. She was more concerned with Raynard and his health. He had almost reached the far end of the large cleared area between the castle's outer walls and the woods by the time she caught up to him.

"Where are we going?" Annella asked pleasantly once her horse was next to his.

Raynard glanced to her with a start. While he must

have heard her galloping up to him, he obviously hadn't expected whoever was approaching to be Annella. He gave her a fierce scowl for her trouble, and then turned to face forward, saying nothing.

"Ye would no' be ignorin' yer lady, would ye, Raynard?" she asked, still keeping her tone deceptively pleasant.

"Ye're no' me lady anymore, m'lady. Yer husband, the laird, cast me out."

Annella was so stunned at this news that she unintentionally jerked on her reins. They immediately tightened painfully around her bandaged hands. Though, judging by the mare's sound of protest, and the way she stiffened and jerked her head up and back, Annella's hands weren't the only thing to suffer discomfort from the abrupt action. Recalled to the situation, she quickly leaned forward and murmured soothingly as she ran one bandaged hand down the mare's neck to calm her. Then she had to urge her to move more quickly to catch up to Raynard again.

"Why did he cast ye out?" Annella asked the moment she was beside him once more.

"Said ye do no' need a useless drunkard at Gunn," he growled.

Her mouth tightened. "Were ye drinkin' again?"

"No' since ye sewed me up," he said almost resentfully.

Annella sighed unhappily. Her husband was the most infuriating—

"Wife!"

She glanced around with amazement, thinking it was as if her thoughts had brought him to her.

Graeme was still a good twenty feet back, but closing the distance quickly, with four men not far behind. Squinting, she managed to recognize her two guards and Teague and Symon, Graeme's friends, but also—whether he liked it or not—his guards until they sorted out the business of who had tried to poison them.

Mouth compressed, she waited for Graeme to reach them and then demanded, "Tell Raynard to get back to the castle." Her husband first looked surprised and then glowered at her for the order. "Nay. He's a drunkard and a—"

"And ye're a new laird who has been away fer a decade, kens not what goes on here and does no' have the sense in his head to ask," she snapped.

"The devil I ha'e!" he barked in surprise at the attack.

Annella clucked with irritation and pointed out, "Ye damned near started a war with our allies because ye could no' be bothered to ask questions."

Discomfort crossed Graeme's face and he muttered, "I ha'e admitted that was a mistake and I should ha'e talked to Angus to—"

Furious that he still thought he should talk to Angus and not her, Annella continued over him, "Ye removed yer mother and her maid from yer father's chamber—"

"O' course I did! She was makin' ye and me da miserable," Graeme protested, outraged.

"Aye, she was, and surely yer father and I would have been grateful that ye had her removed, except that ye did no' then have the wit to replace her and her maid properly to tend to yer da."

"Bea was already there to tend him," Graeme countered quickly. "She was there ere I sent me mother and her maid to the cottage, and has been there every time I've visited me da since."

"Aye. Bea. A lone woman. On her own. With no right or way to send fer strong men to help when she needed it," Annella pointed out with exasperation. "Were ye expecting her to stay in his chamber day and night, hefting yer father o'er her shoulder to carry him to the tub to bathe? Or to a chair whilst she changed his bedding? Or to get him on the bedpan?"

"Er . . ." Realization battled with dismay on Graeme's face, but Annella wasn't done.

"And do no' let us forget the ridiculous amount o' coin ye wasted buying every last strip o' blasted cloth the cloth merchant had in his wagon."

"I thought to please ye," he growled quietly. "Ye need new gowns."

"Aye. I do. But I do no' need a whole wagon full o' cloth to do it." Annella shook her head with disgust. "Did ye e'en look at the cloth ere ye purchased it? Half is so ugly I would no' make an enemy wear it." Renewed fury flowing through her now, she bellowed, "Do ye ken how long it took me to build up the coins in Gunn's coffers to a point that we would no' starve should drought hit us? And then ye just throw it about like yer father did ere ye, depleting our coffers for naught."

She saw the shock on his face, but was on a roll. "And now ye've seen fit to cast Raynard out? Without kenning a thing about him, or the circumstances behind—" Annella's words ended on a gasp as he

suddenly leaned over to tug the tied reigns from her
bandaged hands, then pulled her from her horse to his.

"Escort Raynard back to the castle!" Graeme
barked and then set his horse to gallop for the trees.

Annella looked over her husband's shoulder as he
carried her off, not surprised to see that the men were
surrounding Raynard, but just sitting arguing as they
watched Graeme ride off with her. She had no doubt
they were disagreeing with leaving them unguarded
and debating whether to obey his order or follow
them. When the men finally turned toward the castle,
she shook her head and thought, so much for their being guarded. Apparently, it was only her they thought
needed protection and so long as Graeme was with
her, they would let her be. Although, if she was to be
honest, she didn't really mind. It was a relief to be free
of being trailed about for a bit.

Sighing, she sagged in Graeme's lap and glanced
with curiosity in the direction they were going. They
were almost breaking through to the clearing where
they'd had their first picnic before Annella recognized
where he was taking her. She stilled at once in his
arms, confusion rife within her. Her body was recalling the pleasure he'd given her on that picnic when
he'd taken her maidenhead. She nearly melted into
him then, but her mind was still angry as hell at the
man for making decisions and giving orders without
first looking into matters.

She was still trying to sort out how to react when
he bent to ease her to the ground, then followed her
down. Annella stood where he'd set her and watched
silently as he tied his mount to the same branch of the

same tree they'd tied the reins of their horses to on their first visit here. She then eyed him warily when he turned and walked back to her.

When Graeme took her arm gently and walked her down to the river's side, Annella went reluctantly, and just as reluctantly settled on the large boulder there that he urged her onto. She watched warily as he shifted to stand directly in front of her, but then he spoke.

"It was a mistake fer me to wage war against the Morgans. Ye're right, I should ha'e asked around and found out more ere challengin' them to battle."

Annella swallowed, but didn't comment.

"And I can see now that while me intention was good in removin' me ma from the castle, me execution o' that left much to be desired. As soon as we get back, I shall ensure Bea has the help she needs."

"I already did," she said, her voice a little sharp.

"Thank ye." Graeme's voice was solemn.

Annella shifted a bit impatiently, but otherwise didn't react.

"Now," he went on, "I'll admit that in me eagerness to please ye, I may ha'e gone a bit o'erboard in purchasin' everything the cloth merchant had. Howbeit, I promise I will find a use fer every scrap o' cloth ye do no' care to use."

Annella stared at him wide-eyed, not because of his vow to use every scrap of cloth she didn't use, but because of his claim that he'd done it in an eagerness to please her. That was really rather sweet.

Unaware of what she was thinking, Graeme said, "But I'd appreciate it did ye explain this business about me da throwin' coins about, and our starvin' in a drought."

Annella closed her eyes briefly, and then opened them and explained, "From what I have been told, yer da did no' just give up running Gunn to William on a whim. He hated the business o' managing and taking care o' everyone, and he was horrid at it." She hesitated, but then simply said, "The Gunn coffers were completely empty when I took over."

"When I returned home to Gunn fer the wedding, I suspected that things here were no' as well as they should ha'e been, but I had no' realized it was so bad," Graeme murmured, with a small frown, but then said, "Even so, I'm sure William told me back then that ye had a large dower. He thought that was why our da was pushin' fer the weddin' to happen sooner rather than later when yer parents wanted to wait another year. William felt sure our da wanted the coin to replenish the coffers."

"Aye. I'm sure that is why yer da was pushing to get the wedding done," Annella agreed. "Gunn needed the coin. But the coffers must have been light or even empty fer a while. There was much that needed repair here when I took over the task o' laird. The drawbridge had several areas where the wood was rotting, the curtain wall had holes, and loose stones, the keep roof had a leak, as did the chapel, and . . ." She waved one bandaged hand unhappily, not even wanting to think about everything she'd tended to. "By the first year's end, the coffers were near empty again, and I've spent the last five years since then slowly building them back up so that we would have enough coin to feed our people should drought or root rot hit and affect our crops."

"I see," he said solemnly. "I did no' ken."

"Nay, ye did no' ken. Even worse, ye did no' *ask*," she snapped. "Ye have no asked me aught since taking over. Ye've just stomped about—"

"I used me own coin to pay fer the cloth, no' coin from Gunn's coffers," he interrupted her.

"Yer own coins?" Annella repeated with confusion.

"I've been a mercenary fer ten years, wife," he pointed out gently. "I've made a lot o' coin o'er the years. I also had little to spend it on since me life was made up o' riding from battle to battle, sleepin' on the ground wrapped up in me plaid and eating the gruel and oat cakes whichever laird we were battling for supplied us." He paused to let that sink in and then added, "I saved a lot of coin."

"A lot?" she asked weakly.

"Aye," he assured her. "Now tell me about Raynard."

Annella blinked, her brain struggling with the subject change. She wanted to ask him how much a lot of coin was, but Raynard was important too, so she let go of her questions and said, "He may be a drunk now, but Raynard was once one o' the finest soldiers at Gunn. And not that long ago either."

Graeme's eyebrows went up. "Really?"

"Aye," she assured him. "Raynard was yer da's second when I arrived. He was then mine fer the last six years until this past winter. He was strong, brave, honorable and reliable. There was no' a man among the soldiers he did no' ken everything about, from their family to their skills in battle. And there was no question he did no' ken the answer to, or could no' find the answer to if he did no' ken right off."

"What happened this past winter?" Graeme asked solemnly, when she paused for breath.

Annella felt her throat tighten and tears sting the back of her eyes. She had to stop and force herself to swallow to clear the way to get the words out. "His wife, Ella . . . She was me friend," she admitted, blinking her eyes rapidly to keep the tears at bay. Glancing away, Annella cleared her throat and said quickly, "Their cottage caught on fire in the night. Ella and their newborn bairn died while Raynard was patrolling the wall in the place o' one o' the other men who was feeling poorly. He's felt guilty e'er since. Thinking if he'd set someone else to the task and been there, he might have saved them or . . ." Sighing, she shook her head.

"He started drinkin' to drown his guilt and sorrow," Graeme said solemnly.

"Aye, but I'm hoping with a little more time . . ." She paused and shook her head, acknowledging if only to herself that she was beginning to lose that hope. Pushing her thoughts aside, she continued quickly, "It's only been nine months. I'm sure he'll soon—"

She stopped babbling when he suddenly tugged her up off the boulder and against his chest. Her husband then closed his arms around her and simply held on. Annella closed her eyes, realizing only then that the tears she'd been trying to banish had spilled over. Her cheeks were wet.

Graeme held her in silence for a long time, and continued to hold her when he finally said, "Ye're right.

I've been marchin' about makin' quick decisions and tossin' out orders without first findin' out how things are usually done, who were allies, or anything else."

"'Tis what warriors do," Annella excused him. She was warm in his embrace, her nose twitching as she inhaled his lovely scent. "There's no time to second-guess or ask advice in battle and ye've been knee-deep in battle fer a decade, so 'tis habit fer ye to make quick decisions with what little information ye ha'e."

A soft rumble of laughter had his chest vibrating against her. "It sounds to me like yer makin' excuses fer me, wife."

Annella blinked her eyes open with surprise. She *was* making excuses for him. Good Lord, a minute ago she'd wanted nothing more than to rake him over the coals for stupidly neglecting to simply ask questions, and now she was making up excuses for him?

"But I promise ye, I'll no' be so free with coin in the future, and will ask Angus ere makin' any decisions until I better ken—Oomph!" he gasped out when she suddenly pulled back and kicked him in the leg.

Grabbing his shin, he gaped at her with amazement. "What the devil was that for?"

"For saying ye'd talk to Angus ere making decisions," Annella growled, furious all over again.

"Well, who else should I ask?" he snapped, surprise giving way to anger.

"Me, ye daft bastard! Ye should talk to me! I was laird here fer six years ere you, and I was damned good at it," she informed him proudly.

"Aye. Angus said ye were as fine a laird as could be," Graeme admitted, his anger quickly fading.

"Then why would ye no' come to me?" Annella asked with frustration. "I mean that was the plan, was it no'? I was to stay to help ye take up the position o' laird so the transition would be smooth as possible. Yet, ye've no' only no' come to me with questions, ye say ye should have talked to Angus. Ye ken *he* worked fer *me*, do ye no'?"

Heaving out a sigh, Graeme straightened and pulled her against his chest again. Holding her there, he said, "When I arrived ye'd been carrying the weight o' three different positions here at Gunn. Ye hadn't slept more than an hour or two in as many nights and that was apparently a common occurrence. Yer people were so worried, they slipped a tincture into yer drink to make ye sleep and refused to allow anyone to wake ye."

Annella jerked back in his arms, her eyes wide. "I kenned it," she said with disgust. "Who was it? I'll ha'e 'em flogged."

"Nay. Ye'll no'," he said with amusement, tugging her back against his chest. "'Cause ye ken they did it out o' love and respect and worry o'er yer well-being." When Annella didn't argue and relaxed against him, Graeme continued. "Besides, I was grateful to them. Ye were so eager to leave Gunn, I suspect ye would ha'e left that day had they no' ensured ye slept through it."

Annella merely shrugged in his arms, because honestly, had she not slept through it, she probably *would* have left that day.

"I'm aware me family has failed ye something awful these last six years. Ye were an innocent and eager young bride when ye arrived, and a day later ye were suddenly responsible for everything and every livin' soul here at Gunn. Ye took on those tasks without complaint, workin' yerself to exhaustion, and yer reward, I've been told, was to be barraged with insults and accusations from me mother."

Annella nodded solemnly. She didn't know what any of this had to do with his not coming to her with questions or for aid in his taking over as laird, but Eschina had been brutal with her insults. Constantly reminding her that William had found her so lacking, he'd ridden off with the village lightskirt. A frown started to tug at her lips as she recalled something that had been tickling at her mind since Graeme had told her he didn't believe his brother had run off with Maisie. Tilting her head back, she asked, "Did they find Maisie's body with William's?"

Graeme's eyes widened slightly at the question, but then he shook his head slowly, his expression suddenly thoughtful. "Nay. In fact, from what we learned, he was actually traveling with two other men."

"Men?" Annella asked with surprise. As far as she knew no other men had left Gunn the night her husband had supposedly ridden off with Maisie.

"Aye. We stopped at every village, cottage or shack we encountered on the way to Jerusalem to ask after William. We followed several leads that led nowhere. 'Tis why it took us so long to return," he explained, before continuing, "But we were a half day's journey from Jerusalem and beginning to think we would have to return to Gunn empty-handed when we reached a village where we were told three Scots had arrived there some years ago. All three were so ill they had trouble remainin' in the saddle. They stopped there in search o' a healer to help them, but they had camp fever—typhoid," he added the proper term. "The village elders could do little. All three died and were buried together."

Graeme smiled crookedly, and then admitted, "We were lookin' for a man and a woman, so nearly did no' trouble ourselves to dig these men up to check to be sure one o' them was no' William. But Dauid insisted we should, pointing out that William may ha'e joined the two other men fer safety on the journey."

He shrugged. "In the end, he was right. They were buried almost on top o' each other. Teague, Symon, yer brother and I were removing the first two skeletons, when Dauid suddenly cried out, jumped into the grave we'd uncovered and took a ring off o' the third skeleton. 'Twas William's signet ring, given to him when he became laird."

Annella took a moment to digest that and then frowned. "I wonder what happened to Maisie?"

Graeme shook his head slowly. "She may no' ha'e left with him that night. I've asked around about it since ye told me that, and from what I can tell no one recalls who claims to ha'e seen them leave together. I suspect 'twas just a rumor started because they both went missin' the same night. She may ha'e just left on her own," he suggested. "Or mayhap she did ride out with him, but simply to catch a ride to Aberdeenshire or one o' the other port cities."

"Or mayhap she was traveling with them but died and was buried along the trail ere they reached the village where the rest o' them died," Annella murmured.

"Mayhap," Graeme acknowledged reluctantly, but then shook his head, his expression troubled. "I still find it hard to believe William ran off with her. It was no' in his nature to dally with lightskirts."

Annella smiled crookedly and then just shrugged. It no longer mattered to her what William had done or not done. While his defection had shattered her childish dreams of a fairy-tale marriage and hopes of a love match like her parents enjoyed, the truth was she hadn't known her first husband. The only thing he'd really hurt was her pride.

Her thoughts scattered when Graeme suddenly drew his arms from around her to clasp her face in his hands. Tipping her head up, he pressed a kiss to her forehead, then her nose before straightening and saying solemnly, "I will ne'er leave ye and run off with a lightskirt, or any other woman, lass. I'm happy to be wedded to ye, and willin' to do what I can to make this union a good one."

Annella felt herself melt under the words and his solemn expression, and a small smile tilted her lips before they were covered by his mouth claiming hers.

Chapter 12

GRAEME PUT ALL THE PASSION HE POSSESSED into kissing Annella. Not just because she inspired that burning need and desire in him, one he'd never experienced to this level before in his life. He also did it because he didn't have the words to tell her how he felt about her. He wanted to tell her that he respected and admired her for her strength and wit. He honestly did not know and could not imagine any other woman in Scotland standing up to him the way she had over Raynard and all of his other missteps since becoming laird in his brother's, and therefore her, place.

Most women found him intimidating. They bowed their heads and peered up shyly through their eyelashes at him and spoke in soft whispers. Not his Annella, she was proud, commanding, walked with her head up and had absolutely no problem bellowing at him like he was a clumsy new recruit among her soldiers. He didn't even mind that she'd called him an idiot earlier in front of others. It had surprised him, but his ego wasn't so weak that her words hurt him.

Besides, once she'd begun to list her complaints with his decisions, Graeme realized that he had indeed been an idiot in those situations. A war with the Morgans would have not only ended their being allies with the neighboring clan, it would have meant injuries and deaths on both sides. Fathers, sons and brothers gone . . . because he hadn't stopped to question what his brother said.

Annella was also absolutely right about his removing his mother to the village with her maid, Agnes. He hadn't thought of the repercussions and the fact that the maid, Bea, would need aid tending his father. Graeme had been in a lot of battles and seen a lot of different injuries. He'd even helped the healers on the battlefield, holding a man down while the injured were sewn up, or limbs were amputated. He'd also carried the injured and dead to tents or whatever wagon waited to carry them away. He had not, however, been there to witness how they got on once healed. He'd had no idea that his father had to be shifted to one side or the other to prevent bedsores, and he hadn't considered that paralyzed as he was from the waist down, he could not get himself to the garderobe or in and out of a bath.

As for the wagonload of cloth he'd purchased, he hadn't even considered the number of coins he was throwing into that effort to please his wife, or that she'd worked hard to put coin away for their people. True, the coins he'd used had been his own from his years of mercenary work. Still, while he'd known or guessed that all was not well when he attended the wedding, he hadn't realized Gunn had been in such a bad way and in dire need of her dower when William had married her. He now wondered if it had been so as far back as when he'd left a decade ago. How long had Gunn been limping along, his father praying they were not beset by a crop failure or plague until Annella's dower could be claimed to act as a cushion?

Now there was Raynard. Unlike Annella, he didn't think Raynard would be able to shake the crutch drink had become for him. At least, not as long as he was here at Gunn, where memories of a lost bairn and wife he'd apparently loved would be everywhere he looked, taunting and torturing him with his loss. But the man might, were he to go somewhere else. Someplace where those memories had a chance to fade. Knowing that this behavior was new and the result of a great loss, Graeme no longer intended to cast him out though. Another plan had come to him.

One he didn't care to think of at that moment as his wife moaned and responded to his kiss, her body pressing and writhing against his as her bandaged hands slid up around his neck. She was fire in his arms, uninhibited and demanding. Unashamed of her need. Graeme had to admit that was one of the things he liked best about his wife. Not the sex, although he was grateful and did love that, but more important to him was her honesty. She did not play games. He never doubted where he stood with her. He knew when she was angry, happy, sad, and when she wanted him. He appreciated that and decided to show her how much.

ANNELLA MOANED IN PROTEST WHEN GRAEME broke their kiss to trail his mouth down her throat, but then gasped when his tongue dipped into the hollow between her breasts as he began to tug at the neckline of her gown. Panting with the sudden increase of excitement within her, Annella withdrew her arms from around his neck to reach for her lacings and help him bare her breasts, only to pause when her bandaged hands came into view, reminding her of how useless they were at the moment.

Chuckling, Graeme caught her wrists and moved her arms out to the side, then bent to the task of undoing the laces himself. He didn't undo them all the way, push her gown off her shoulders and remove it as expected. Instead, he simply undid the lacings enough to tug the neckline down below her breasts, baring them to his eager mouth.

Annella groaned, her head tipping back and her bandaged hands moving to rest on his shoulders as he found and began to nip and then suckle at first one nipple and then the other. It was wonderful and frustrating as hell at the same time. She wanted to touch him, run her hands through his hair and clasp his head to her breast. But all she could do was arch into his caresses and murmur her pleasure as his mouth made a meal of her breasts and his hands cupped and squeezed the cheeks of her bottom.

"Husband," she moaned, her tone pleading for more, and Graeme immediately let the nipple he was suckling slip from his mouth so that he could lift his head and kiss her.

Annella kissed him eagerly back, gasping when his hands tightened on her bottom and he lifted her off the ground to press her firmly against his groin so that she could feel his excitement. Annella immediately tried to wrap her legs around his hips, but he released her behind to force her legs back down, then lowered her until her feet were on the ground once more and he broke their kiss.

When she moaned in protest and opened her eyes, Graeme smiled. Leaning back slightly, he lifted one hand to her breast and began to palm and knead it. "What do ye want?"

Annella blinked in confusion at the question. "I . . ."

"What do ye want, love," he repeated when she hesitated, now rolling her nipple between finger and thumb.

"You," Annella groaned, and at first thought it had been the wrong answer when he suddenly gave off playing with her breast and stepped back. Blinking, she opened her mouth to beg him not to stop, then stilled, her eyes going wide when he suddenly dropped to his knees, lifted her skirt and ducked under it.

Mouth open in surprise, she gaped down at the Graeme-shaped lump under her skirt, and then a startled squeak slipped from her and she reached for that lump when he grasped her ankles and urged them further apart. Balancing herself with one bandaged hand on top of his skirt-covered head, she swallowed and then started to breathe in shallow pants as he began to trail kisses up the inside of one leg. His lips and tongue moved from her knee up toward the apex of her need and nearly reached it before he suddenly backtracked to do the same up her other leg. This time he didn't stop, however, but drew that leg over his shoulder and buried his face between her thighs.

Annella cried out and then moaned as his lips, tongue and even his teeth scraped over sensitive flesh. The excitement and need that brought to life in her left her gasping desperately for air, and her legs were suddenly so weak they could no longer even hold her up. Fortunately, her husband was prepared for that, or at least did not seem surprised by it and braced her with a hand on the hip of the one leg she was standing on, so that it and his shoulder under the other leg kept her upright. Annella almost wished he'd let her fall to the ground. She had a desperate need to thrash and arch under his ministrations. Instead, she could only curve over him and groan and mewl under the pleasure he was giving her as he made love to her with his mouth.

Her excitement was such that Annella lost all awareness of her surroundings. Her world narrowed to that space between her legs as he worked. Eagerly sucking one of the folds that protected the core of her into his mouth, and then releasing it to lick and lave the pearl of her excitement with his tongue instead. Annella's body couldn't take such extreme pleasure for long, and then she threw her head back and screamed out with rapture as her body began to convulse with her release.

Consumed by the sensations that had taken over her body, Annella was completely unaware of her husband or anything else until he was suddenly thrusting into her. Opening her eyes, she saw that she was now on her back on the ground. Her skirts were up around her waist, and Graeme was between her open legs, holding her hips off the ground so he could more easily plunge into her.

When her gaze slid to his face and she saw the tightness in his jaw, and the need in his eyes, Annella reached for his chest, wanting to caress the hard muscles there only to once again be hampered by her bandaged hands. Cursing the burns and blisters that had made them necessary, she let them drop to rest on her chest and instead did the only thing she could, and drew her feet up closer to her behind, then lifted herself into his thrusts, urging him to go harder and deeper.

Growling, Graeme met her gaze. He then removed one hand from her hips, leaving the other only to direct her movements as he reached down to where they were joined and began to caress her as he plunged into her with the violence and depth she demanded.

"Aye!" Annella cried, thrusting up into him one more time before her thought processes were stolen by the explosion suddenly consuming her body. Fortunately, her muscles twitching and convulsing around his hard member brought her husband to release a heartbeat later and he joined her in mindless pleasure.

"Do ye forgive me fer me idiot mistakes?"

Annella stiffened where she lay curled into Graeme's side, her head on his chest. She must have fallen asleep after the loving, because she'd opened drowsy eyes just moments ago to find herself in this position rather than flat on her back as she'd been during her last moment of consciousness. Opening her eyes, she considered his question and then grimaced and said, "They were no' idiot mistakes, husband."

"Verra well, do ye forgive me me no' idiot mistakes?" he asked.

Annella couldn't hold back the chuckle his words brought. Raising her head, she smiled at him and said, "Only if ye forgive me temper, and fer callin' ye names ye did no' deserve."

Graeme smiled briefly, then grasped her by the waist and lifted her to lie on top of him, then drew her head down and kissed her.

Annella moaned and writhed against him as the fire he'd just sated sprang immediately back to life within her. Her skirt had still been caught around her stomach when he'd shifted her. It hadn't dropped lower with the movement, so that her naked flesh was making direct contact with his as she moved against him. Sucking on his tongue with demand, Annella let her legs spread and allowed her knees to drop to rest on either side of his hips. She then ground herself against the growing hardness pressing against her, before breaking their kiss and pressing her bandaged hands to his chest to push herself to sit up on him. The action caused a little pain in her fingers, but not enough to dampen the excitement building within her.

Once upright, her gown immediately dropped to rest on him, covering her bottom and legs. Her breasts were still on display, however, and Graeme's gaze moved over them hungrily, before he grinned and asked, "Now what are ye goin' to do, wife?"

"I'm no' sure," she admitted, and then slid herself experimentally over him so that her wet heat rubbed along his hard shaft. Her eyes immediately widened at the sensations that sent through her. Then she smiled wickedly and did it again and again, until Graeme groaned and reached for her hips. Annella immediately knocked his hands away with her bandaged hands. "I'm in charge this time."

He didn't argue. He simply reached for her breasts instead.

"Oh, aye," Annella breathed, shifting over him again and arching into his touch as his hands closed over the full globes. Pressing her hands against the backs of his for encouragement, she began to slide back and forth over him more quickly, pleasuring herself on his shaft until they were both taut with excitement and breathing hard. When she could not take it anymore, Annella lifted and shifted her hips until his erection popped up to press against her opening. She then carefully lowered herself onto his shaft, moaning as he filled her.

Annella almost stopped then, unsure of herself, but she wasn't one to shrink from a task. Biting her lip, she leaned into his hands that she still covered with her own, and used her leg muscles to lift and lower herself. She wasn't sure she liked it all that much. It definitely felt better when he was controlling this, but Annella didn't give up and continued to lift and lower herself, leaning further into his hands as she did. Ah. That made all the difference. This angle had the apex of her excitement rubbing against his body as she moved, reigniting the fire that had been waning.

Realizing she'd closed her eyes, Annella opened them, intending to look down and see if this position was as good for him, and then screamed and threw herself to the side when she saw the bow and arrow visible through the trees directly ahead of her.

She wasn't quick enough. The archer must have released the arrow even as she started to move. Annella felt it like a punch when it struck her in the right shoulder and she grunted at the pain, just before crashing to the ground on her left side.

Annella's left leg still rested along her husband's hip from the knee down, while her right leg lay across his groin. Not for long, however. While Graeme had obviously been taken by surprise, he was moving no more than a heartbeat after she threw herself off of him. He immediately rolled out from under her leg and to his feet in one smooth move, scooped her up and took the few steps necessary to reach the large boulder she'd been sitting on earlier. He then dropped to his knees and eased her to the ground to examine her wound.

"'Tis buried deep," he muttered with concern.

"Aye," Annella said shakily. She was not happy with the knowledge since her mind had already moved on to consider what would need to be done to remove it.

"'Twill ha'e to be pushed out rather than pulled," he said apologetically. "Pulling could cause more damage than has already been done."

"Aye," Annella agreed, somewhat surprised at his knowledge. But then she acknowledged that Teague was not the only one who had worked as a mercenary for the last ten years. Her husband too had no doubt seen a variety of wounds. He may even have received such a one himself. He did have a scar on his shoulder, but there wasn't one on his back in the same place and she'd thought it looked more like a knife wound than an arrow. But the two were similar enough that it was hard to tell.

"'Twill ha'e to wait until I've dealt with whoever shot ye and get ye back to the keep," Graeme muttered, and then met her gaze. "Did ye see who 'twas who shot ye?"

Annella shook her head. "All I saw was the arrow and part o' a bow sticking out o' the bushes across from us."

Graeme grunted at this news, kissed her forehead, then raised himself up slightly to peer over the boulder in the direction the arrow had come from.

When Annella then saw his head turn toward where his plaid and—most importantly—his sword, lay some feet from the safety the boulder offered them, she bumped his arm with one bandaged hand and hissed, "Nay."

Graeme met her gaze and smiled reassuringly as he patted her arm. "Do no' worry, wife. I was just taking in our options. A sword would do little against someone standing twenty feet away with a bow and arrow anyway."

Annella relaxed a little at his words and then glanced around. They were on the river side of the boulder and, unlike Graeme, she couldn't see over the large mass of stone. All she could see was the narrow strip of grass on this side of the boulder and the water rushing by beside them.

"Ye may as well come out! Ye're just delaying the inevitable!"

Annella's gaze shot to Graeme with shock as she heard that shout and recognized the voice.

Meeting her gaze, he said, "I'm gettin' the strong impression that me mother's no' happy about bein' moved out o' the castle."

Managing to bite back the small bark of laughter that his words inspired, she shook her head and asked, "Ye think?"

"I do," he said solemnly. "I really do."

Annella couldn't stop her laugh that time. It was the way his eyes were twinkling even as he said the words so seriously.

"Oh, aye, laugh away, you two, but I've more than a dozen arrows and all the time in the world."

Annella's mouth tightened at those words, her earlier urge to laugh dying an abrupt death.

Graeme offered her a reassuring smile, then shifted to his haunches and popped his head up, presumably to see where his mother was. He was just as quick at pulling it back down below the cover the boulder offered, but almost wasn't quick enough. Annella sucked in a horrified breath as an arrow whistled past, the light breeze of its passing stirring the hair on the top of his head before it was low enough to be safe.

Graeme reached up to feel his head as he settled beside her, then noted her expression and offered, "Me mother is a fine bow woman. She taught me and me brothers archery as lads."

"Great," Annella muttered and then scowled at him and added, "And if that's you tryin' to reassure me all will be well, ye failed miserably."

This time it was Graeme who let a startled laugh slip out.

"Aye. Keep laughin'." His mother sounded irritated now. Apparently, she didn't feel they were taking her seriously, because she added, "But I'll be the one laughin' in the end. O'er yer graves."

Graeme's laughter died and he glanced sharply to the end of the boulder.

Annella didn't have to ask why. Eschina's voice had come from closer than the twenty or so feet that had divided them the first time. She was only mayhap ten or fifteen feet away now. But her voice also sounded as if it was coming more to the right, rather directly in front of them too. She was making her way to the right and forward, hoping to get around the boulder and shoot them from the side.

Annella tapped Graeme's arm to get his attention. When he glanced her way, she ground her teeth together against the pain she was about to cause herself, and began to ease herself back along the side of the boulder toward the other end, using her good arm and both legs to sort of scoot along. Her thinking was that, if necessary, they could duck around the end of the boulder if Eschina came around the other side.

She thought it was a grand idea. While Eschina could certainly then maneuver her way back around front and approach the opposite side of the boulder, they could then just scoot back behind the boulder and around the other side, remaining under cover. His mother couldn't shoot them through the boulder, so as long as they kept it between them and her, they were safe.

If they were lucky, after a bit of time doing that, Eschina would get frustrated and try something stupid, like climbing up onto the boulder so that they would have no escape. But that would put her within grabbing distance, and Graeme would no doubt take her out then. Annella thought it was a brilliant plan, so was more than a little upset when Graeme's gaze shifted from watching her scoot backward to focusing hard on her wounded shoulder.

When she saw him shake his head and glance around, then pick up a rock that was about half the size of her fist, Annella knew he planned to stand and hurl the rock at his mother. She decided right then that she would need to have a talk with Father Gillepatric about some of those stories he told them from the Bible at mass. Her husband obviously thought his mother was Goliath and he her David. But there had been no mention of Goliath having a bow and arrow that she recalled. And Annella was sure that Eschina already had her bow up, arrow nocked, ready to let fly, and would let go the moment he came into view. Her husband would most like be dead before the rock left his hand.

Unless she aided him by distracting the old woman. The sudden thought had Annella quickly shifting to crouch on the balls of her feet and waddling back to his side. She managed the chore without raising any part of her body above the cover of their boulder, but the effort cost her. While she was only using her feet to move, she must have automatically clenched the muscles in her upper body as she went, because her shoulder wound screamed its protest at her for the movement.

"What are ye doin', lass?" Graeme growl-whispered.

"I'm goin' to distract her so that ye can hit her with yer rock," she gasped, and then took a deep breath to try to ease the pain roaring through her before giving it up and calling out, "I ken ye're angry at Graeme fer tossin' ye out o' the castle, but why shoot arrows at me?"

"I hate ye," Lady Eschina snapped. "Ye were such a poor wife ye sent me son runnin' off to his death. I'll ne'er forgive ye fer that."

Annella rolled her eyes. She hadn't been a wife to William at all. She hadn't been given the chance to be one. The moment their family and friends had left the chamber after seeing them both abed, William had kissed her forehead, said it had been a long day, she should rest, and then had cut his hand with his knife. Once the blood bubbled to the surface, he'd pulled back the furs on the bed, wiped the blood on the bed linen, and then had dressed quickly and slipped out through the secret panel in their room . . . never to return. All told, they couldn't have been alone in the room for more than five minutes before he'd left, and it had only been that long because he'd had trouble finding where the men had tossed one of his boots as they'd disrobed him.

She didn't bother explaining that to Eschina. Annella had already told the woman that at least a dozen times in the days after the wedding and William's defection. Then Eschina had changed her insults, declaring she'd been too ugly for him to be able to bear her in his bed so he had fled. She'd realized then that there was no winning with the woman. Lady Eschina would forever blame her for William's leaving. Realizing that, Annella had done the only thing she could: she'd ignored the old woman's barbs and insults and simply smiled and gone about her business, acting as if they didn't trouble her. The truth was though that every barb had found its mark, and she had been relieved when the verbal assaults stopped.

"Is that why ye poisoned both our drinks?" Annella called out, purely because she wanted to know for sure it had been her.

"Oh, I did no' do that," Eschina said with amusement.

Annella could sense Graeme's gaze moving to her with uncertainty, and then his mother finished, "Me maid, Agnes, did. I surely would ha'e drawn attention in the great hall after me own son so publicly cast me out and sent me down to live in a cottage like a peasant," she said bitterly. "But I knew that as a servant, Agnes would not draw attention. And I was right. Agnes was able to fetch the ale and mead, dose them and set them on the table without anyone even noticing."

Annella's mouth tightened at this happy claim, but simply called out, "And the fire in our bedchamber? Was that Agnes too?"

"Oh, nay. That was me," Eschina assured her with pleasure. "I did no' need Agnes fer that. I simply used the secret tunnels to get to yer room. I intended to wait there in the passage until ye were both asleep and then slip in, pour the uisge beatha on the bed and set ye both alight." Her voice sounded positively dreamy as she admitted that, but it quickly turned annoyed as she added, "But rather than retire as I'd expected, Graeme headed for the secret passage where I was waitin' in the dark."

Bitterness lacing her voice, Eschina told her, "He always was a difficult boy. Verra contrary. Tell him to do somethin' and it would never get done. Tell him he couldn't accomplish somethin', and he'd work like a demon to prove ye wrong."

Eschina made a sound of disgust. "Instead o' settin' ye alight in the bed ye shared, I had to knock him out when he stepped into the passage and drag him back into the room. O' course, there was no way I could heft him up onto the bed on me own. So, in the end I had to leave him on the floor next to the bed. That's why I started a fire around the bed rather than on it. I was afraid yer screams as ye burned would wake him, givin' him the chance to escape. With the fire encirclin' the two o' ye except where the wall was, I was sure ye'd both die. But nay, ye woke up and managed to get half the fire put out ere the men came to help ye."

She clucked her tongue with irritation. "Ye're provin' to be just as difficult as me son."

Her mother-in-law obviously meant that as an insult. But Annella didn't see it that way. She liked, admired and respected Graeme, and was proud to be considered like him.

"What about the merlon?" he called now, and Annella glanced at him with surprise. When she hadn't heard him make mention of the grooves in the mortar showing that someone had loosened the stone that had nearly seen both brothers dead, she'd begun to think she'd misunderstood what she'd seen. That the grooves were some naturally occur—

"What about the merlon?" There was no doubting

the confusion in Eschina's voice as she echoed his question.

"There were signs someone had chiseled away at the mortar, loosening the merlon to make it fall," Graeme said tightly.

"Really?" She sounded amused now. "Well, that's naught to do with me. I've been nowhere near the battlements in years." She paused briefly and then said, "I had Agnes poison yer drinks tryin' to kill ye, I set yer room ablaze in an effort to see ye dead, and now I'm just goin' to shoot ye. They say third time's the charm. Let us hope that old sayin' is true."

Eschina added the last line in a grim undertone Annella wasn't sure they were supposed to hear. But she was more concerned with the woman's claim that she hadn't been responsible for the merlon falling and nearly crushing Graeme. Frowning, she glanced toward her husband just in time to see his muscles bunch as he started to straighten, rock in hand. Cursing under her breath, she quickly pushed up with her legs, popping into view even as Graeme did.

Annella wasn't surprised that the abrupt movement caused pain to radiate through her shoulder, but she had little time to worry over that. As she'd expected, Eschina had her arrow nocked and ready. However, she had been waiting with it aimed at a spot that was presently between where she and Graeme stood. But Eschina didn't hesitate more than a heartbeat before making her decision and turning the arrow on Annella.

Apparently, her mother-in-law hated her more than Graeme, Annella thought and knew her husband could

not possibly throw his rock before Eschina loosed her
arrow. Realizing it was up to her to save herself, Annella did the first thing she thought of and simply
dropped to sit on her butt behind the cover of the boulder. She hit the ground hard and fast, sending a jolt
through her body that immediately had agony roaring
through her shoulder and radiating outward.

Annella gasped at the pain, the hand of her uninjured arm instinctively reaching up toward the arrow.
Fortunately, she caught herself before the bandaged
paw touched it and caused her more pain. Forcing her
hand down, she glanced worriedly to her husband, but
stilled with concern when she saw that Graeme was
frozen, the hand holding the rock only half raised.
Worried, she immediately shifted her gaze to his
chest, afraid she would find an arrow protruding from
him, but there wasn't.

"Thank ye."

Those words from Graeme had her lifting her gaze
back to his face. He wasn't talking to her. He was
looking beyond the boulder. Moving carefully, Annella shifted her legs beneath herself again and lifted
herself enough to poke her head above the boulder.
Her eyes widened when she didn't see Lady Eschina.
Instead, Dauid was crossing the clearing. When he
stopped and knelt out of sight in the spot where Eschina had been standing earlier, Annella struggled to
her feet.

Once fully upright, she was able to see Eschina
lying on her side on the ground, bow still in hand,
though the arrow was nowhere to be seen. There was,
however, another weapon visible, a knife that was

presently hilt deep in one side of her neck, with the tip protruding out the other.

"Who—?" she began with confusion. Sure Dauid couldn't be the owner of the knife, she glanced around the clearing in search of Symon or Teague or even her brother, because Annella was positive there was no way someone as clumsy as her brother-in-law could—

"Mother taught us all how to throw knives too," Graeme told her. "Dauid was always verra good with a knife."

Annella's eyebrows rose slightly, and she shifted her gaze back to her mother-in-law just in time to see Dauid pull the knife from her neck. The woman didn't moan or move. Annella was pretty sure she was dead, but started to move around her husband, intending to go check on her. Graeme's hand on her arm stopped her.

"Ye're swayin' on yer feet, love," he said with concern.

Surprised by the words, she started to shake her head, but paused at once when the movement made her a little dizzy. In the next moment, Graeme had scooped her into his arms and was walking around the boulder, heading for his horse.

"Is Nellie all right?"

Dauid's voice pierced through the faint fog that had descended over her mind, and Annella scowled. She hated that nickname.

"There's an arrow in her shoulder!" Dauid exclaimed with alarm. "We should pull it out."

"No' till we get her back to the castle," Graeme said at once.

"But—"

"She could die if we try it here. We need to get her back to the keep. Symon is handy with wounds. Now here, take her and lift her up to me once I'm on me mount."

That made Annella's eyes open and she saw with surprise that they'd already crossed the clearing and reached his horse. Her gaze shifted to Dauid as Graeme set her in his brother's arms, but for once, Dauid wasn't looking at her. At least not her face; his gaze was on her breasts, which were still on full display above her gaping gown. She wasn't the only one to notice.

Cursing, Graeme tugged up her neckline and quickly pulled her lacings tight and then tied them for her. Annella was grateful. Tying them herself would have been impossible with the state of her bandaged hands.

"Pass her up to me."

Annella opened eyes she hadn't realized she'd closed to see that Graeme was mounted now. *When had he done that?* She wondered over it as she was lifted, and Graeme bent in the saddle to slip his arms under her and haul her the rest of the way up and onto his lap. He moved slowly and most carefully, and still the small jostling that couldn't be helped made her moan in pain.

"Sorry, love," Graeme said, sounding almost as if her pain pained him.

"Wait, I'll fetch yer plaid and sword fer ye," Dauid said, and she heard a rustling that suggested he'd hurried away.

"Nay, bring them back yerself, along with Mother," Graeme ordered as he arranged Annella more securely in his lap and reached for the reins of his mount.

"Nay. Ye'll need yer sword to defend Nellie should bandits attack ye on yer way back to the castle," Dauid argued firmly, his voice drawing nearer. She guessed that meant he was already returning with the items. That being the case, Annella wasn't surprised when she felt movement as Graeme apparently took the plaid and sword from his brother. She heard the soft hiss of his sword being sheathed, and then felt the weight of his plaid covering her legs and stomach. He didn't try to cover her any higher than that, probably to avoid the possibility of unintentionally nudging the arrow in her shoulder, she supposed.

"I'll find Mother's horse and then bring her and her mare back to the castle."

Dauid's voice pushed away some of the sleepiness that had been creeping over her, and Annella opened her eyes with alarm. "Is she no' dead?"

"Aye, she's dead, love. Ye're safe now," Graeme assured her solemnly, and then shifted his gaze away from her to what she assumed was Dauid, though she couldn't presently see him. She was facing the opposite direction in Graeme's arms, with her back to where Dauid would be standing. Still, it must have been the younger man, she concluded when Graeme said, "Thank ye fer that, brother. I owe ye me life."

"She was goin' to shoot Nellie with her bow. I could no' allow that."

She really hated the name Nellie, Annella thought with irritation, and then Graeme urged his horse to move out of the clearing. She bit back a moan and stiffened in pain at the jostling it caused. But there was worse to come when they reached the path. Eager to get her back to the castle and the help that awaited them there, Graeme immediately spurred his mount to a faster pace, first a trot, then a canter, and finally a gallop that caused enough agony that she quickly sank into unconsciousness to escape it.

Chapter 13

ANNELLA OPENED HER EYES, BLINKED, AND then gaped briefly at the woman who was leaning over her, before saying, "Mother?"

Well, that's what she tried to say. But what came out was a croaking sound similar to the one she'd made after the fire. Alarm immediately raced through Annella, but her mother didn't seem surprised or overly concerned. She simply patted her arm soothingly and turned to pick up a mug from the bedside table, then slid an arm under her upper back to raise her enough to drink from it.

Annella almost whimpered with relief when the cool liquid slid past her dry and cracked lips and over her tongue to fill her parched mouth. She didn't swallow right away. Instead, she used her tongue to swish the refreshing liquid around, trying to let the fluid reach every nook and cranny of arid flesh before finally allowing the sweet nectar to slide down her throat.

"More?" her mother asked, and moved the mug back to her lips again when she gave a weak nod.

Annella wanted to gulp the beverage thirstily down, but knew that wouldn't be a good thing and might result in her simply bringing the liquid back up. With that worry in mind, she forced herself to simply take in a mouthful of the liquid, pause to move it around before swallowing, and then do it again. Annella managed four such swallows before her stomach warned her that was enough for now.

When she paused, she whispered, "Thank ye." Her mother immediately took it away to set the mug on the bedside table again. She didn't lay Annella back down right away, but instead took a moment to quickly stack pillows behind her back with her free hand, to help her remain upright. Only then did she ease her back against the pillows.

"There," Annabel MacKay breathed out with satisfaction as she quickly tucked the linens and furs around her daughter. "How do you feel?"

Annella rather felt like hell, but didn't think her mother would appreciate her saying so. As a healer herself, and one trained by the woman asking that question, she knew what she really wanted to know. "I feel as dry as bone. Me head hurts. Me shoulder's painin' me, and . . ." She hesitated, and then gave up her recitation of her symptoms and asked, "What happened? When did ye get here to Gunn? Is this Gunn? Or am I at MacKay? Where's me husband?"

Her gaze quickly flickered over what she could see of the room around them. Annella relaxed a little when she saw they were in her bedchamber at Gunn. No signs of damage remained though. It looked as fine as it had before the fire. Although, there hadn't really been much damage to begin with other than the rush mats being destroyed, a bit of scorching of the floorboards and some smoke stains on the walls, bed drapes and bedding. The fresh rush mats could be covering the scorching if they hadn't been able to remove the marks with a plane and scraper. But any smoke damage had been washed from the walls, and the bed drapes and bed linens had obviously been cleaned.

That look around also gave her an idea of the time. She could see it was late night from the darkness that the lit candles on the bedside table and the fire in the fireplace were struggling together to push into the corners of the room.

"Annella."

Hearing the sharp note of concern in her mother's voice, she turned to her in question. Worry was etching furrows into her mother's still beautiful face.

Ignoring all of the other questions Annella had asked, her mother focused on her first one, and asked tensely, "Do you not recall what happened to you?"

Annella opened her mouth to say no, but then paused to consider. She'd obviously been ill for some time. What was she not remembering? After a moment of searching her mind for her last memory, Annella found several nuggets that she was sure brought color to her face: Graeme disappearing under her skirt, his talented tongue moving over her heated flesh, her straddling his hips, taking him inside her and then riding him.

The next memory that flashed across her mind was much less pleasant as she recalled spotting the bow and arrow protruding from the bushes directly in front of her across the clearing. The rest of the memories then crashed over her in one large wave.

Eschina had tried to kill them.

Frowning, Annella shifted her head and tucked her chin down close to her neck to try to look at her right upper chest just below the shoulder. There was nothing to see. The wound she'd taken was covered by a nightgown, and probably linen binding under it, she supposed.

"Someone named Symon removed the arrow and tended your wound," her mother told her, actually sounding relieved. No doubt because Annella's attempt to look for the wound had made it obvious that her memories were intact.

Picking up the mug of mead again, her mother urged her to drink more as she told her, "Graeme said this Symon person had to push it through and out yer back. He said you *did no' like that*."

Annella nearly laughed at her mother's dry tone and bad accent as she imitated Graeme, but that was impossible with a mouthful of mead. In the next moment, the desire to laugh died, and she swallowed hard as a brief memory flashed through her mind. It was of her waking up to find herself in terrible pain and surrounded by several men. She recalled Graeme, Payton, Teague and even Angus trying to hold her down and Graeme bellowing "finish it" as she screamed and thrashed in agony. She must have fainted then, because no other memories were coming to her.

"How long was I asleep?" Annella asked finally when continued poking and prodding didn't reveal any more memories.

"I understand 'twas near to a week," her mother told her quietly, turning to set the mug back on the bedside table when Annella pushed it away. "Yer husband said they did their best to clean the wound ere binding you, but you came down with a fever anyway. It kept you under these last six days."

"Oh," Annella breathed, but thought, well, that explained why she was so parched on awaking.

"To answer your earlier questions, aye, you are at Gunn. Your father, your sister, myself and our traveling party arrived three days ago. As for where your husband is, it took me more than two of the three days we have been here, but I finally convinced him to go below for the sup tonight, and then find his way to a bed. From what your brother said, Graeme has not slept since you were injured other than dozing off here and there while watching over you. I do know that other than occasionally dozing off sitting up in a chair, he did not sleep in all the time that I sat here with him. It took two full days of harassing him and a promise to fetch him the moment you woke before he agreed to sleep, and he only did so then because your fever had broken and you were out of danger."

"I'm awake, but ye have no' woken him," Annella pointed out with a faint smile.

"I lied," her mother said with a slight shrug. "I have no intention of waking him until I know if you are happy, or wish us to take you away. So"—she arched an eyebrow in question—"are you happy, sweetling? Or did your brother force you into marriage with a brute you cannot bear to share a bed with?"

Annella's lips compressed at the question. Graeme

definitely wasn't a brute, and she had absolutely no problem sharing a bed with him. If anything, she enjoyed it too much. Certainly, if Father Gillepatric knew how much she enjoyed her wifely duties, he'd be demanding the Gunn coffers' entire contents of coin to pay her indulgences. He'd probably also have her on her knees begging God's forgiveness for the rest of her days.

She definitely didn't think she wanted her parents to take her away. Annella hadn't been planning on running away to MacKay, she'd been thinking to visit. She missed her family. But they were here now. They could visit, and then next spring or maybe even sooner, perhaps she and Graeme could go visit her family at MacKay in return. As for whether she was happy . . .

"He does no' talk to me," she blurted, some of her frustration leaking into her voice.

Her mother blinked, tilted her head slightly to contemplate her, and then asked, "At all?"

"At all," Annella assured her, and then sighed and said reluctantly, "Well, he . . . did talk to me one time. I was tending the blacksmith—he took a terrible burn," she explained. "It got infected, and I went down to get out as much of the infection as I could. When I finished and came out of the blacksmith's cottage, Graeme was waiting with a sack of food since I'd missed the sup. We walked back, ate on the steps o' the keep and then talked some while we walked in the gardens."

Annella was smiling at the memory, but then her smile faded and she sighed. "But he has no' talked to me like that again. No' even to ask me questions about

Gunn that he needs to ken the answers to so that he can rule efficiently."

Irritated now, she turned her gaze to her mother. "Did Payton tell ye that me husband nearly caused a war with our neighbors and allies, the Morgans? And all because he did no' ken what was going on and did no' bother to ask?"

Annabel opened her mouth to respond, but Annella wasn't finished.

"Or, did he tell ye that me husband moved his mother and her maid out o' his father's chamber—which was a fine thing because she was apparently tormenting him," she assured her. "But when he removed his mother and her maid, he left poor old Bea to tend to him. Alone. How was she to properly tend to him on her own, I ask you? She could no' move the poor man around by herself. But me husband did no' think o' that and did no' talk to me so that I might point it out."

Annella nodded firmly to emphasize his lapse, before continuing, "And then there is the matter o' the wagon o' cloth he wasted coin on purchasing from the cloth merchant. A *wagonload*!"

"I am sure—" her mother began.

"And he tried to cast Raynard out fer drinking too much," Annella growled, her irritation mounting again with each example of how her husband's lack of communication with her had caused problems. "Raynard is a good man, who never drank until just recently when he lost his wife and wee bairn to a fire. He needs time to heal. And Graeme would ken that if he had troubled himself to simply talk to me."

"Aye, well," her mother started soothingly, but Annella interrupted her again.

"How do ye make Father listen to ye?"

Lady Annabel hesitated, and then, rather than answer that, asked, "Do you spend any time alone with him?"

"Aye. Nay." Annella shifted impatiently in the bed. "He's always gone when I wake up. I usually do no' see him until the sup, and then he's usually talking to Payton and the other men. After that we retire to our bedchamber."

"And what happens then?"

Annella felt her face flush with embarrassment as some very carnal memories came to mind of what usually happened when her husband joined her in bed.

Apparently, her expression and blush were answer enough for her mother. A gentle smile of amusement claiming her lips, she said, "I see . . . and do you enjoy that portion of your marriage?"

Annella huffed out a breath of air and said honestly, "Too much. Several nights, I have been determined to talk to him when he reached our chamber, but all he need do is look at me that way he has, and every thought o' talking falls out o' me head." She sighed, smiled crookedly and admitted, "The bedding really is all that cousin Jo and her friends claimed it was when we visited Sinclair."

Her smile faded then and she told her, "And I'm very annoyed at William for making me miss out on those pleasures for six whole years while he was off traveling about and getting himself killed."

"Did William looking at you make you feel the

way your husband does?" her mother asked with interest.

Annella was surprised at the question, and actually had to think back to try to recall. All she really remembered about her wedding day and night, as well as the night before it—which was all the time she'd had with William—was being nervous and anxious. Scared, really, like the untried young bride she had been.

When she admitted as much to her mother, Lady Annabel asked gently, "Yet you did not feel that way with Graeme?"

"Nay, but 'twas an entirely different circumstance, Mother," she argued with a small frown.

"And an entirely different man," her mother pointed out. When Annella simply stared at her with uncertainty, she explained, "Not every man will affect you as your husband obviously does. And the bedding with William may not have been as . . . pleasurable for you."

"Really?" she asked, sitting up a bit in her surprise. "I just assumed all men . . ."

When Annella hesitated, her mother said, "Our old cook, Angus, made pasties much better than the cook who replaced him when he passed, do you not think?"

"Ayyyye." Annella drew out the word, unsure why her mother had changed the topic so abruptly. When the older woman than raised her eyebrows and waited, as if expecting her to say something, Annella said the only thing she could think of. "Millie, the cook here at Gunn, makes fine pasties, but they are still no' as good as the ones old Angus made at home."

"This is your home now, dear," her mother reminded her gently, and then said, "But, my point is, when it comes to pasties, the cook makes all the difference. A different cook means different recipes and different skills." After a brief pause, she added, "And 'tis the same with husbands and the bedding."

Annella leaned back against the pillows as she considered that. It had never occurred to her that men were like cooks and pasties. Actually, that was rather concerning, she thought, and asked her mother to clarify. "Does that mean if William had no' left and then died, that I might have been stuck with bad pasties in the bedchamber for all the days o' me life?"

"'Tis possible," her mother said with a shrug. "But he also might have talked to you more."

She went stiff at that. "So, I must choose between good pasties in the bedchamber, or a husband who would speak to me?" Annella started shaking her head before she even finished the last word. Not leaving time for her mother to respond, she protested, "That does no' seem fair."

"Life is not always fair, daughter," Annabel MacKay said gently.

Annella scowled at the comment, but then her eyes widened as another thought occurred to her. Pity entering her expression, she patted her mother's hand. "I'm sorry, Mother."

"For what?" she asked with confusion.

"For yer having suffered a lifetime o' bad pasties being married to Father."

Now it was Lady Annabel who was sitting up straight. "I have not suffered anything. Your father has given me wonderful pasties from the first time we enjoyed pasties."

"But he talks to ye. I have seen it," Annella pointed out, frowning now as well. "And ye just said—"

"I know what I said," her mother interrupted impatiently. "But I just meant . . ." She paused briefly and then explained, "Some women have husbands who speak to them, but perhaps are not as good at pasties in the bedchamber. While other wives have husbands who give them good pasties, but perhaps have difficulties speaking to them as much. However, there are also some wives, *like myself*," she added firmly, apparently not wanting Annella to think poorly of her father, "who are lucky enough to have husbands who speak to us *and* give us amazing pasties in the bedchamber. Do you see?"

Annella slumped unhappily back against the pillows. "Aye, I see. I should resign meself to a husband that gives me amazing pasties, but will no' talk to me."

"Not necessarily," her mother said at once. "Making pasties is a skill. If our old cook had passed on the recipe and his steps in making them, I'm sure any future cook could learn to make them just as well."

Annella narrowed her eyes and tried to follow along with what her mother was saying. She seemed to be suggesting that a husband could be taught to be better at the bedding? But by whom? She couldn't have done the training. Aside from having had no experience or skill in that area herself before Graeme, she couldn't even call the bedding *the bedding* while talking to her mother, but was using *pasties* instead. How could she have possibly done the teaching? Not that it really mattered anyway, she supposed. He was amazing at tupping, and certainly needed no training in it. Getting him to talk to her was the problem.

As if Annella had spoken her thoughts aloud, her mother said, "In the same way, I am sure a husband can learn and be convinced to talk more to his wife."

"Oh," Annella said simply. She lowered her gaze briefly as she considered that and then shifted her eyes back to her mother and asked, "How?"

After a hesitation, Lady Annabel confessed, "I am not sure. Your father did not have to be taught or convinced to talk to me. I was actually the quiet one. We were not encouraged to speak at the abbey where I was raised. We actually had periods where we were not supposed to talk at all." She grimaced at the memory and then added, "Aside from that, I had not even spoken to a man other than the priest since being sent to the abbey as a young child. Yer father was the one who had to coax *me* into conversation."

"Well, how did he do it?" Annella asked.

Her mother considered the question briefly, and then said, "By asking questions. He asked me about my parents and my life first at Waverly and then the abbey, and . . ." She shrugged. "He just kept asking questions until I was comfortable enough to talk without needing questions to prod me."

"Hmm." Annella frowned over that and then asked, "But what if Graeme does no' wish to talk to me?"

"Oh, I do not think that is very likely," her mother assured her with a faint smile.

"Well, he has no' shown any great desire to talk to me up to now," Annella pointed out dryly.

"That is odd, because all he did the two days we sat watch over you together was talk."

Annella blinked in surprise. "About what?"

"You," her mother said softly. "About how fine a job you had done at running Gunn and taking care of its people since coming here. He admired ye for that and complimented your father and I for raising such a fine, capable lass."

She snorted at that. "He was no' even here to know if that's true or no'."

"Aye, but he said his clan members told him and he could see the results of your leadership in how well-fed, rosy-cheeked and happy his people are. He said 'twas obvious they all love and respect you." Her mother smiled faintly when Annella blushed and glanced away, and then continued, "He also informed me you are beautiful, kind and intelligent, and he considers himself lucky to have you to wife."

When Annella turned wide eyes back to her, Lady Annabel grinned and added, "Graeme said that the first time he saw you bellowing at Raynard, then slamming a pot over his head to shut him up while you tended his wound, he knew you were the woman for him."

Groaning, Annella covered her face with her left hand. She hadn't realized her brother, Graeme and the other men had been there for that. For some reason she'd just assumed they'd arrived later, while she was bandaging up Raynard or something. Actually, the truth was she'd rather hoped that was the case so she didn't have to feel bad or embarrassed at her less than ladylike performance that night. It seemed she hadn't been that lucky.

"I think Graeme loves you, sweetling," her mother said gently, and when Annella glanced up with amazement, and then shook her head in denial, Lady Annabel nodded firmly. "And I do not think you will have to find a way to make him talk with you. He did tell me that just before the attack in the clearing, you had complained about his not bringing issues to you that he might have with taking on the position of laird. And he had meant to address the matter and speak to you on it, but then his mother shot you with her bow and he never got the chance. He regretted that mightily."

Annella bit her lip and avoided her mother's gaze now. It hadn't exactly been just before the attack. There had been some houghmagandie between the two.

"So, you see? I think all will be well," she assured her. "While Graeme has been away in battle these last ten years and may not be used to or comfortable with talking to ladies, he wants to talk to you. And I think if you ask him a question or two to help him along, all will be well."

Annella nodded with a sigh, and then said wryly, "And if no', at least I am no' suffering with bad pasties."

"What's this about bad pasties?" Ross MacKay asked, stepping into the chamber.

"Husband." Annella's mother stood and went to the tall, strong man, then braced her hands on his chest and leaned up on tiptoe to kiss his cheek in greeting. "What are you doing up? I thought you would have gone to bed hours ago."

"I missed me wife and worried fer me daughter

so thought I'd come to check on ye both." He kissed his petite, blonde wife on the forehead, slipped his arm around her waist and ushered her back to the bedside. Releasing her there, the MacKay bent to give Annella a cautious hug and peck on her forehead as well.

"'Tis good to see ye awake and recoverin', daughter," her father said as he straightened. "Ye near to ga'e yer mother and I fits when we arrived to learn ye'd taken an arrow in the chest, gone down with a fever, had been fightin' it fer days and had no' regained yer senses at all yet."

Annella smiled crookedly, unsure if she should apologize or not. She didn't get the chance to decide before her father continued, "And then we found out that while we'd traveled here to rescue ye from this place and take ye home now that ye were a widow, ye'd gone and married another damned Gunn."

"Husband," Lady Annabel said in a warning tone.

"Well, she did," Ross said with irritation. "We sent Payton and the boys on the search to hopefully find proof that her neglectful bastard o' a husband was dead so she could be free o' the Gunns, specifically that nasty old bitch mother o' her husband's. They did find her husband's body, and I thought her misery here was finally done, then she went and married the other brother and nearly got herself killed by the old bitch who birthed him."

"Husband!" Lady Annabel barked in shock.

"Payton made me!" Annella said quickly in self-defense. "I wanted to come home. But first they said I should help Graeme take up his position as laird to smooth the transition for our people, and then Payton made us marry."

"He did, did he?" her father asked with interest. "And why would he do that?"

Annella opened her mouth, closed it and then leaned back against the pillows. "I think I'm growing weary. Goodness, wounds and fevers take the strength right out o' a body."

"Hmm." Her father sank to sit on the edge of the bed next to her, caught her chin and turned her face toward his. "We can ha'e the marriage annulled and take ye home with us, do ye wish it."

"Nay," Annella said quickly. Swallowing, she said more calmly, "We are wedded and bedded. 'Tis done."

"But are ye happy?" her father asked solemnly.

Annella hesitated, unsure how to answer that. She had moments of pleasure in her marriage, and moments of pure frustration and fury. She wasn't sure she could claim happiness though. In the end, she said carefully, "I am no' unhappy."

Her father raised an eyebrow. Not satisfied.

"He treats me verra well," she tried again.

His second eyebrow rose.

Scowling resentfully at her father, she snapped, "I want to stay."

A slow smile curved her father's lips. Letting his finger drop from her chin, he glanced over his shoulder at his wife. "Payton is right. Our sweet, shy daughter has grown a backbone o' steel."

"I somehow doubt he put it that way," Annella scoffed, recalling his complaining that she'd grown stubborn and difficult.

Her father didn't deny it, he merely kissed her forehead again and then stood to turn to her mother. "Come, wife. Ye've no' had sleep these two nights. Our daughter's awake now. Ye can rest."

"Oh, but I was going to wake Graeme as I promised and then go see if Cook left broth for Annella," her mother protested as Ross MacKay took her arm to lead her to the bedchamber door.

"''Tis all taken care o'," he assured her soothingly. "When I arrived and heard yer voices from the hall, I sent one o' the soldiers guardin' her door to wake the lad. Told him to go see about findin' her some broth after that. Annella will be fine. Her husband'll see to her now he's had some rest."

Her father prevented any further protest by ushering his wife from the room.

Annella let her head fall back on the pillows and closed her eyes. She didn't know if she had a steel backbone, but she *had* changed since coming to Gunn six years ago. She wasn't sure if the change was for the better or not, but she was glad not to be crying herself to sleep every night as she'd done during her first year here. That year had been the hardest of her life so far; married, yet abandoned by her husband. A lady and chatelaine, yet struggling to carry the weight of her husband's duties as laird as well. All without the love and support of her family, and instead the recipient of Eschina's vile insults and curses.

An image of Eschina lying in the clearing, a knife through her throat, rose up in her mind and Annella frowned as she recalled her father's words. *I sent one o' the soldiers guardin' her door* . . . Why were soldiers still guarding her door? Eschina was dead. Wasn't she? The possibility that she might not be was a rather distressing one. The woman had made it obvious she would not rest until she saw both her and Graeme in the ground. Dear God, she hoped the woman was dead.

Chapter 14

THE LOW MURMUR OF VOICES CAUGHT HER ear, and Annella blinked her eyes open to see Graeme entering with a wooden bowl in one hand and a trencher in the other. Behind him, a soldier leaned in, nodded at her and then pulled the door closed as Graeme carried his treasures to the bedside table and set them down.

The moment that was accomplished, he turned to peer at Annella and then dropped to sit in the chair her mother had been occupying moments ago. He took her hand in his.

Annella stared at their entwined fingers, only to blink in surprise when she realized the linen wrappings were gone. Her hands and fingers were naked and nearly back to normal. The burnt and blistered skin must have healed while she lay unconscious in the bed, Annella realized. How had she not noticed that while her mother was here?

"How are ye feelin'?"

Annella glanced up at her husband, surprised to see

the concern that had been heavy in his voice also re-flected on his face. She frowned slightly as she took in the dark shadows under his eyes and the exhaustion still hanging over him. "Me mother told me ye had no slept since the clearing until she convinced ye to lay down after the sup tonight?"

"No' much," he admitted with a crooked smile that quickly faded. His expression was incredibly solemn when he said, "Ye were verra ill, wife. Payton and I mostly sat about watchin' o'er ye, dribblin' broth down yer throat, placin' cold cloths on yer forehead and prayin' fer yer fever to break. I e'en had to carry ye down through the passages to the river a time or two fer a cold dunkin' when yer fever was burnin' ye up and we feared it boilin' yer brain."

For some reason this news made her eyes tear up. Annella had no idea why. While it was sweet that her brother and husband had worked so hard to see her well, it was hardly something to weep over. But she'd been a healer for a long time and had witnessed others having exaggerated emotional responses in such situations, so didn't fret over it too much. Fortunately, her husband didn't appear to notice her weepy state and continued.

"Payton only left when yer parents arrived. Yer mother and father came up to see ye the minute they learned ye'd been injured. They sat with us fer a bit, and then yer father insisted Payton go below with him to give an account o' what has happened since he left MacKay. Yer mother took his seat when he left, and then she and I continued to watch o'er ye until the fever broke just ere the sup tonight. Yer mother said while ye were on the mend, ye'd sleep fer a while yet, and insisted I should go below and eat somethin', then bathe and get some sleep so I could be awake, rested and no' stink when ye woke."

Annella smiled faintly, but asked, "Did ye sleep?" because, honestly, he didn't look like he had.

"Aye." When her expression revealed her doubt about the veracity of his words, he admitted, "It took a while fer me to fall asleep, but I did rest fer a bit."

Annella squeezed his fingers sympathetically. Despite having slept for six days and not having been awake for long, she was growing weary again. But the murmur of voices from the hall had her glancing toward the door.

"'Tis most like fresh men replacing the soldiers in the hall," Graeme said reassuringly.

Annella swung her gaze back to him and asked, "Why are there guards on our door? I thought—Is yer mother no—?"

"She's dead," Graeme said baldly.

Annella relaxed a bit, relieved to know she hadn't been wrong. She distinctly recalled Eschina lying in the clearing, the knife through her neck. She did peer at him with concern though, wondering how he was taking it. As awful as the woman had been at the task, Eschina *had* been his mother. She had also planned to kill him. Annella supposed that would be enough to leave him feeling conflicted. Hoping to take his mind off of whatever emotion the woman's death caused in him, she asked, "And her maid? Agnes?"

"Gone," he said, anger thick in his voice. "I should ha'e sent men out to fetch her back to the castle the moment I returned with ye, but we were all busy tending to yer wound. By the time I thought to send soldiers to Mother's cottage, Agnes had fled. No doubt she heard ye'd returned with an arrow through the chest but we were both alive, and then when Dauid followed with Mother's body, the news o' that too would ha'e spread fast. She would ha'e kenned she might be in peril too if Mother had talked ere dying. She probably thought it prudent to leave rather than wait around to find out."

"No doubt," Annella agreed, and then shook her head. "A woman on her own . . . she'll no' survive long on the run."

"Nay, she will no'," Graeme agreed solemnly. "Still, I sent a couple soldiers out to track her. If she's dead when they find her, at least her family will ken."

"And if she is alive?" Annella asked with curiosity.

"She tried to murder her laird and lady," Graeme said solemnly. "She would be taken to the king's court to be judged and punished."

Annella nodded solemnly, but thought the woman would be luckier to be killed while on the run. At least that would most like be done quickly. Being caught and dragged to court for judgment and punishment would be a long drawn-out hell with a grim ending. The king was not known to be lenient to murderers, especially commoners trying to kill nobles.

"Do ye want more to drink?"

Annella considered it briefly, but while she was thirsty still, she'd rather wait a little longer to be sure her stomach did not cast out the liquid she'd already taken in, so she shook her head.

"I'd rather rest a bit," Annella confessed, unsurprised that she was weary already. It would take time for her to build her strength back up. Her gaze slid over her husband, and she frowned and added, "You should too. Ye need yer rest or ye'll fall sick yerself."

Graeme hesitated, his gaze sliding away to a spot on the floor, and then said, "I would no' want to unintentionally jostle ye and cause yer wound to pain ye. I've a pallet next to the bed. I'll sleep there."

"I'd rather ye join me," Annella said quietly. She didn't have to ask twice. This time, Graeme didn't hesitate, but stood and walked around the bed. He removed his plaid, but left his shirt on, then lifted the blanket and climbed into bed next to her. But he left a good foot of space between them despite the fact that he was on her uninjured side . . . which was an oddity for her. Graeme had always taken the side closest to the door prior to this, leaving Annella to sleep on the side he was presently on. Annella supposed her spot in the bed now was because he'd carried her straight in and set her on the closest side for them to work on.

Whatever the case, she was grateful for the switch because it allowed her to roll on her uninjured left side and curl up against him. Graeme stiffened at first, but then shifted his arm so that she could nestle her head on his chest. Once she was comfortable, he let his arm rest curled around her so that his hand was on her hip, as far from her shoulder as he could place it without detaching his arm from his body.

Annella closed her eyes then and tried to sleep, but her mind was on Agnes and what would become of the old maid, so that it was a while before sleep finally came to claim her. Her breathing had deepened and she was just dozing off when she heard Graeme whisper, "Thank ye, God, fer no' takin' her from me."

For some reason his words made her want to cry again, but sleep claimed her before the feeling could bring on tears.

THE SUN WAS SHINING IN THROUGH THE WINDOW when Annella next awoke. Graeme was still abed with her, which was unusual. He was generally up and out of the castle by the time she woke and went down to break her fast. But that wasn't the case this morning. He was still on his back next to her and she was still cuddled up with her head on his chest. It seemed neither of them had moved while they'd slept. Annella could only think exhaustion was the reason behind that.

"Are ye hungry, love?"

Annella stilled briefly in surprise as she realized her husband was awake, and then eased away to lie on her back next to him so that he could move if he wished. "How long have ye been awake?"

"No' long," he answered easily and rolled onto his side, then shifted up onto his elbow so that he could see her face. "How are ye feelin' this day? Does yer shoulder hurt?"

Annella smiled faintly. "No' much at all. Which probably should no' surprise me since I've had the wound a week now."

"Aye. Ye slept through the worst o' the pain o' healin'," he agreed, and then commented, "Ye must be thirsty and hungry."

"Aye," Annella admitted, which rather surprised

her. While her thirst was to be expected, the hunger gnawing at her stomach wasn't. She hadn't been the least bit hungry last night, but perhaps the small amount of liquid she'd had before falling asleep had worked through her system, waking up her wants.

Graeme got out of bed and stripped off the shirt he'd slept in as he crossed the room to begin searching one of his chests for a fresh one. Annella found her eyes sliding over him with interest, taking in the way his muscles shifted under his skin as he moved. This was the first time she'd got to have such a long look at him; usually when he was naked, she was too and they were doing things that didn't allow for long inspections of his body.

Her husband was strong, wide and muscular in form with scars to tell of his years of working as a warrior. None of them detracted from the fact that he had a beautiful body.

Realizing she was licking her lips with an interest she probably didn't have the strength to satisfy at the moment, Annella forced her gaze away and then managed to sit up. It took a little more effort than she would have expected and left her breathing heavily, but she managed it. Irritated by a weakness she wasn't used to, she determinedly pushed the linens and furs off herself and shifted to sit with her feet on the floor, then paused to catch her breath and rest a moment before trying to rise.

"Oy!" That barked exclamation had her glancing wide-eyed to Graeme as he strode toward her, a shirt in hand. "What are ye doin'?"

"I thought to go below to break me fast," she explained, her gaze dropping to his swinging member as he crossed to stand in front of her. This was definitely the first time she'd got a look at that part of him, and she couldn't seem to stop staring at it. It wasn't the first time Annella had seen a man's cock. She was a healer after all. She'd examined probably a dozen over the years for the clap or other ailments, and had even had to stitch up two others. One from an injury gained at practice, and another given to an unfaithful husband by his less than pleased wife when she caught him with another woman. The husband had nearly lost his manhood that day, and while Annella had done her best to sew him back together, she knew it wasn't working as well as it had ere the incident.

"Love, ye ha'e to stop lookin' at me like that," Graeme said, his voice a little husky. "Ye're in no shape fer the things yer puttin' in me head with the way ye're starin' at me cock and lickin' yer luscious lips."

Annella froze, tongue still out and halfway across her upper lip, then pulled it quickly back into her mouth. She couldn't stop staring, however, because Graeme's member had started to grow and harden. It was much more impressive that way, and grew more so by the second as she watched it stretch and stand up.

Cursing, Graeme whirled away and crossed back to the chest, tugging his shirt on as he went. Sadly, it was one of his longer shirts and dropped below his bottom by several inches, hiding that from view too. He did have a nice rounded bottom, but she'd known that from grabbing and holding on to it on more than one occasion as he'd tupped her.

"Ye're no' goin' below, so get that out o' yer head," Graeme said firmly as he set to the task of donning his plaid. "I'll send one o' the guards to arrange fer water to be heated and a bath brought up. He can fetch back food and drink fer us to break our fast with too."

"Ye'll eat up here, with me?" Annella asked, surprised. He hadn't once broken his fast with her since arriving. In fact, she rarely even saw him during the day. Although that was partially her own fault. She knew he did sometimes take the nooning meal in the keep each day; it just happened that it had always occurred when she was off tending someone who was ill, or tending to one of the tasks that took her down to the village, such as market day.

"Aye. I'll break me fast with ye. But then I must go see what's occurred while I was up here with ye this past week. Let us hope the place has no' gone to hell while we were both indisposed." Finished donning his plaid, he turned and walked back with a wry smile, then bent to kiss her forehead, before scooping her into his arms to turn and lay her on the bed again.

"Stay," he ordered as he covered her again. Graeme then walked to the door and opened it to speak to the men outside.

Annella took that opportunity to give herself a quick sniff and grimaced when she did. A week of fever and no bathing had left her a little more than odiferous. Honestly, she wasn't sure how he'd managed to sleep in the same bed as her, which made her think—

"Have them tell Florie that the bed will need stripping and new linens put on," she called out.

Graeme glanced back to give her a nod and then finished giving his orders.

"I can at least sit at the table by the fire to break me fast," Annella said as he started back toward the bed.

Graeme glanced toward the small table by the fire and the two chairs at it and then nodded. Tossing aside the linen and furs he'd just covered her with, he scooped her into his arms and headed for the table with her.

"'Tis all right to hold yer breath do ye wish," she whispered. "I'll no' be offended. I ken I smell poorly."

"Aye, ye do," he agreed with amusement. "And I've ne'er seen yer hair so limp and greasy."

Annella was flushing with embarrassment when Graeme added, "Yet ye've never smelled as good, or looked so lovely to me as ye do now ye're awake and I ken ye'll live."

Eyes widening, she glanced to him sharply, but they'd reached the table and he quickly set her in one of the chairs and then walked back to grab up one of the furs from the bed. Graeme brought it back and tucked it around her lap solicitously.

"Rest a bit while we wait," he ordered before returning to the bed and stripping away the rest of the furs. He folded and set those on one of the chests, then removed the bed linens from the bed in swift, economical motions. Graeme had barely rolled the linens up and dropped them on top of another chest when a knock sounded at the door.

The moment he opened it, a passel of maids filed in carting the tub, food and fresh linens.

"We were told last night that yer fever had broken and ye'd most like wake by mornin', so Millie started water heating fer ye at the crack o' dawn so ye can bathe," Florie announced, looking her over with eyes filled with a combination of relief and happiness as she set down the tray of food she'd carried in and began to pour her what appeared to be watered-down cider. "It should be along soon."

"Thank ye," Annella murmured, accepting the mug she handed her. Despite Eschina being behind the poison attempt, and being dead, she still took a cautious sniff of the cider, smelling for any trace of a scent that didn't belong.

"There are still guards on the buttery. A fresh cask o' cider was brought up and opened, and one o' the guards walked us up to be sure no one fiddled with ye or the laird's drinks," Florie told her reassuringly.

Annella smiled at her, and then sipped from her mug, sighing as the cool liquid satisfied her immediate thirst.

"Cook also made fresh pasties fer ye if ye think yer stomach can manage it. She, like the rest o' us, was e'er so happy to hear ye were finally recovering," she added softly, pausing to squeeze Annella's shoulder gently before continuing. "But she sent bread and cheese in case ye were no' up to pasties yet, and a bowl o' broth in case ye were no' sure ye could manage that," Florie announced as she began setting the food out.

"Ye must thank her fer me," Annella murmured before taking another drink of the cider.

"I'll ha'e one o' the other maids pass along yer thanks," Florie assured her. "I'm remakin' the bed while ye eat and then will help ye with yer bath."

Annella nodded and thanked her, then smiled at Graeme as he settled in the seat across from her.

"Are those pasties?" Graeme asked with interest as he surveyed the feast set out for them.

"Aye. I'm no' sure what kind though," Annella admitted. Normally, pasties were filled with a seasoned meat and vegetables. But old Angus back at MacKay had also made sweeter pasties filled with fruit. Millie, the cook here at Gunn, had started making those as well after Annella had told her about it. Both were tasty and popular with the people of Gunn, and Florie hadn't mentioned what kind these ones were.

"Beef and veg," Graeme announced with satisfaction as he broke one in half. "No doubt she thought that'd be better to build yer strength, and easier on yer stomach than fruit just yet."

"Aye," Annella agreed, but shook her head when he offered her half. She hadn't eaten in a week other than dribs and drabs of broth and any other liquids they had managed to get down her while she was unconscious. As much as she would have liked the delicious-smelling pasties, she felt it was better to at least start with broth. If that went down well, she might try a bite or two of one of the pasties after that to finish off.

Graeme hesitated at her refusal, and then set the half he'd offered her next to the wooden bowl of broth Florie had set before her. "Ye should at least attempt to ha'e a bite or two, love. 'Twill help ye gain yer strength back more quickly."

"Aye," Annella agreed, a smile curving her lips. He'd called her love. It wasn't the first time. She was sure he'd called her that a time or two already since she'd woken the night before, and she did remember him calling her that in the clearing after she'd been wounded as well. It was nice. It made her feel all warm and squishy inside.

Telling herself that she was being silly, and that calling her that didn't mean he felt the emotion behind the word, she turned her attention to the broth, pleased to find that it was very nice and full of flavor. Millie had obviously cooked it down so that the flavor was more concentrated for her. An effort to help build up her strength, she knew. She also knew no one else would be enjoying the broth. The cook had probably made a small batch for her alone.

Annella's stomach felt full when she finished the broth, but not uncomfortably so. Not feeling there was any danger of it coming back up, she eyed the half pasty lying next to her bowl and then gave in and picked it up. She could manage a bite or two and it would help with her recovery.

"Mmmm," she moaned as the flavor exploded on her tongue with the first bite.

"Aye. Good, eh?" Graeme said with amusement, watching her face as she enjoyed the pasty.

"Mmm-hmm," Annella murmured as she chewed and swallowed the bit of delicious pasty. Had she thought Millie's pasties weren't quite as good as old Angus's at MacKay? Impossible, she decided as she took a second bite. That or Millie had somehow improved her pasties since the last time she'd made them.

A knock at the door caught her ear, and Annella glanced around to see Florie toss the last fur on the freshly made bed before she rushed to answer it. Another parade of maids entered with buckets of steaming water in hand this time, and Florie oversaw the bath, testing for temperature as each pail of water was poured in, deciding when enough water had been added. Her lady's maid then saw the other women out and closed the door.

Annella half expected the maid to harass her into getting into the bath at once, so was surprised when she instead went to sort through one of Annella's chests. Choosing what she should wear after, she supposed.

"All done?" Graeme asked when Annella reluctantly offered him the rest of her half pasty after managing three bites.

"Aye. I would no' make meself sick, so 'tis better to stop."

"Aye," Graeme agreed solemnly, popped the remains of her pasty into his mouth and quickly chewed and swallowed as she chuckled at him. He grinned in response, swallowed down a bit of cider, then stood and scooped her out of her chair.

"I can walk," she protested when he carried her to the tub.

"Love, ye were pantin' and swayin' like a reed in the wind after just sitting up in bed. I'd no' trust ye to walk anywhere," he announced. Setting her on her feet next to the steaming tub, he held her steady with a hand on her arm, and then tipped her face up with a finger under her chin and ordered solemnly, "Florie is to call me when ye're done with yer bath and I'll return to lift ye out and set ye on the bed again. Understood?"

When she nodded, his stern expression softened and he kissed her.

Annella kissed him back, sighing into his mouth when he deepened it and thrust his tongue past her lips. She did love his kisses, and felt her toes curl at the effect he had on her. When his hands moved over her, she moaned and then gasped as he broke their kiss to tug her gown up and off, forcing her arms up over her head to manage the task.

"Husband," she protested breathlessly as she leaned into him. "Florie is here."

"Aye. Well, she has to be to help ye with yer bath, does she no'?" he asked with amusement.

Graeme was scooping her up again even as he spoke. A moment later she found herself set into the warm water.

"Too hot?" he asked when she gasped as he set her to sit in the steaming liquid.

"Nay. 'Tis good. I like it warm," she assured him a little breathlessly. It always felt just that touch too warm at first, but she quickly adjusted.

"Good," Graeme murmured, sounding a tad distracted.

Pulling back slightly, Annella saw that his gaze had caught on her breasts. The hunger of his expression made her suddenly feel beautiful and powerful. Without even thinking about it, she arched her back slightly, thrusting her breasts forward and up a bit, then ran one hand from his shoulder to the back of his neck and slid her fingers into his hair, scraping her nails over his scalp in a way that she'd noticed he seemed to like.

He responded as she'd hoped, claiming her mouth and kissing her almost roughly as his knuckles brushed over one taut nipple. But he broke the kiss just as quickly and straightened to stride away across the room.

"Call me when ye're ready fer me to remove her from the bath, Florie," he ordered gruffly.

"Aye, m'laird," the maid murmured as the door closed behind him. Florie then turned a grin her way as she crossed to the tub, and teased, "Fer a minute there, I thought he'd be joinin' ye in the tub and I should just slip out o' the room fer a bit."

Annella grinned in return, despite the heat rising to flush her face. "I would no' have complained."

"I could tell," Florie assured her with a laugh that died suddenly as her gaze shifted to Annella's covered wound. The arrow had entered in her upper right chest, just below her shoulder and gone out her back at around the same spot. All of which meant that a lot of linen wrappings had been needed to cover the entrance and exit both. Concern claiming her features, she asked, "Do we need to change yer wrappings, and add salve or anything?"

She peered down at the linen covering and shook her head. "Nay. It looks like Mother must have changed them recently. I'll check with her first."

Florie nodded, and then clucked her tongue. "Oh, Lord, that must ha'e hurt like the devil, m'lady. No wonder ye were screamin' as ye were."

Annella glanced at her with alarm. "Was I loud?"

"They could hear ye from the bailey and the cottages.

Some e'en claimed they heard ye in the village, though I'm thinkin' that's a bit o' exaggeration."

The maid shifted to peer at Annella's back as well, and she sighed. "Aye. They said the arrow had to be pushed through, but I did no' believe it. That seemed a stupid move to me. Why would they cause ye more pain and damage like that?"

"It had gone most o' the way through already. At that point, pulling the arrow back out the way it went in can cause more damage if ye accidentally turn it even the least little bit. Ye could nick a vein missed on the way in during the effort," Annella murmured, glancing at the linen wrapping covering the wound and wondering what it looked like. She doubted it was too bad. At least it shouldn't be huge, just the width of the arrow. She supposed she'd see soon enough.

"Well, we'd best get to bathing ye ere the water cools," Florie said with feigned good cheer, and then frowned and asked, "Do I need take care no' to get yer bandages wet?"

Annella hesitated, considering her wound, and then sighed unhappily. She knew she was about to make this bath harder. "Aye. We should probably no' get it wet yet."

Florie nodded slowly and then straightened her shoulders determinedly. "Verra well, we can manage it. I'll just call up one o' the young maids to help us."

Annella didn't protest. She knew they would need the assistance if she wished her hair washed, and she did. It was lank and nasty, definitely in need of washing after a week of fevers. While she could hold a folded piece of linen over the bandage on the front to prevent it getting wet, she couldn't do anything about the one on her back while water was poured over her hair and splashed about. Assistance would be useful.

Sighing, she leaned back in the tub to wait while Florie slipped from the room.

Chapter 15

ANNELLA SIGHED HEAVILY AND SHIFTED IN the bed. When that got no reaction, she scowled at Florie, and then her mother, and finally her younger sister, Kenna. Not one of them noticed. All three were sitting in chairs around her bed, their heads bent to the sewing they were working on in an effort to help make her new gowns.

At first, Florie had been the only one sewing while Lady Annabel and Kenna had tried to distract Annella, but when her mother had asked Florie what she was making and the maid had explained and then wittered on about the state of Annella's wardrobe, or lack thereof, her mother and sister had immediately insisted on helping. They'd settled in to cutting and sewing, leaving her to sit bored and fretting. She hadn't been allowed a task herself, for fear of ripping the stitches below her shoulder.

She truly did appreciate their efforts. Unfortunately, she was also embarrassed that there was a need for it. More than that though, Annella was embarrassed that her mother and sister not only knew of the need, but knew that that need was purely her own fault, thanks to Florie's big mouth. The thought made her glare at the maid again, which she no more noticed than the scowl.

Muttering under her breath, Annella shifted her gaze to the window and the sunny sky beyond. It was a beautiful day. She should be out there enjoying some fresh air. But was she? Nay. She was stuck inside. Not just inside, but in her bedchamber and this was her third day there since she'd woken up. She was not even allowed to go below to the great hall. Everyone insisted she must stay abed and allow her body to heal.

Annella wouldn't mind so much was her husband not avoiding her. She hadn't seen him once since he'd left her to her bath three days ago. He hadn't even returned to lift her out of the bath when Florie had gone below to tell him that she was done as he'd insisted the maid do. Instead, Florie had returned with Kenna and their mother to assist her out of the bath. She'd been told Graeme had received a message from Morgan and that he, her father, her brother, Teague and Symon had immediately ridden out to meet with their neighbor and ally.

Even with the three women working together, getting her out of the tub had been an effort. Which is why Annella decided right then that she would start walking and lifting things to try to build up her strength more quickly. She'd known everyone would protest and insist she wait and take things slowly, so she'd decided she'd start these small efforts only when she was alone.

Her mother, sister and Florie had sat with her through the morning that day as they'd awaited news of what happened at Morgan. The other three women took turns at looking out her window whenever there was a clatter in the bailey that might be the men returning. They were all curious about what Morgan's message had been about, and worried over what might come of it.

It was well after the nooning meal when the men returned. Annella, her mother and sister had taken their meal in her chamber, and were still there when the men on the wall began calling to each other that "the laird is back." Her mother had gone below to find out what had happened, leaving Kenna and Florie with Annella to wait. All three of them had been bursting with curiosity and worry by the time her mother had returned. Annella had been more than relieved to be told that Morgan had written because there had been a sighting of a woman fitting Agnes's description on Morgan land. Unbeknownst to Annella, Graeme had sent messengers to all their surrounding allies describing Agnes and asking them to keep an eye out and inform them if she was seen.

Unfortunately, Agnes had disappeared by the time Morgan had led Graeme and the others to where her small camp had been. A search was performed without success, and Morgan had then invited them to enjoy the nooning meal before leaving. Over the meal, Graeme had explained what Agnes was wanted for. Morgan had immediately promised to have his men take her into possession should she be spotted again.

This was all well and grand. Annella was certainly

relieved that Morgan appeared to have gotten over the
near war that Graeme had almost caused on first taking
up the mantle of laird. From what her father later told
her when he'd come up to sit briefly with the women, it
even seemed that Graeme and Colban Morgan had got
along well and were becoming friends. Always good
for allies. However, Annella would have been happier
if her husband had come up to share this news with her
himself. When she'd said as much, her mother and father had pointed out that he'd taken a week away from
his duties to care for her and had much to do now. She
would no doubt see him at the sup.

But Annella hadn't seen her husband at the sup.
Her sister had arrived with the servants following behind with food and drink. As they'd set it all out for
them, Kenna had announced that Graeme was still out
working and had not come in at all for the meal so she
thought she'd dine with her that evening in his place.

Their mother had joined them after the sup, and the
women had sat with her, continuing on with their sewing until Annella had begun to nod off. They'd then
insisted she sleep and left her alone.

Tired as she had been, Annella had taken that opportunity to try to walk a short distance. It had indeed
been short. She'd managed less than a half a dozen
steps that first try before collapsing back onto the bed,
dragging herself under the linens and furs and quickly
falling into an exhausted sleep. Graeme had come to
bed at some point after that. He'd also been gone before she woke in the morning. Annella only knew he'd
been there at all because his side of the bed had been
disturbed and the shirt he'd been wearing the day be-

fore was lying over a chest for Florie to take away for washing.

The second day had been a repeat of the first, only without the business with Morgan as part of it. Instead, her husband had apparently just been kept busy taking care of neglected business around the keep. Too busy to join her for a single meal, and again sneaking into the chamber after she was asleep and leaving ere she woke in the morning. Annella had tried to remain awake to speak to him that night. But her efforts to walk and rebuild her strength had left her too exhausted to be able to keep her eyes open. She was annoyed with herself over that, but not too annoyed. Annella knew her body needed that rest to heal.

However, this was the third day. It was past the nooning and, again, she hadn't so much as seen her husband. She'd been told the men had gone on a hunt to fetch back meat for Cook, something that had been neglected while everyone waited to see if she would survive. Her mother had explained that to her, which was good since her husband couldn't be bothered to tell her himself.

Annella was beginning to think her husband had lost interest in her and decided she was a troublesome wench he regretted marrying. Would he set her aside? Would she have to return to MacKay after all? Or did he just intend to ignore her for the rest of her days?

Well, bugger that! Now that she had experienced the bedding, she had absolutely no intention of doing without it. And she wanted children, dammit! Graeme would see to his husbandly duties, or she would ... Well, she'd complain to Father Gillepatric, Annella thought grimly. Or the king even. As her husband, Graeme was expected to bed her and get her with child, and she would see him do it. She would *not* have another marriage like the one she'd had with William. She would not be abandoned alone and childless while he was off doing as he wished, even if it was right here at Gunn rather than off in some foreign land. And she would not spend another moment stuck in this chamber where he could easily avoid her.

Grinding her teeth with determination, Annella tossed the furs and linens aside and slid out of bed.

"Annella! What are you doing?" her mother asked with alarm. Setting aside her sewing, she stood quickly and rushed around to catch Annella's arm as she made her teetering way to the nearer of the chests holding her gowns. "Get back in bed, sweetling. You are not strong enough for this yet."

"And I will no' be until I use me arms and legs and build up me strength again, Mother," she said grimly in response, refusing to be urged back to the bed. "Ye ken that."

"Aye, but you have been terribly ill. We nearly lost you. Another day or two of rest, at least, would—"

"Another day or two o' rest and I shall surely start pulling me hair out," Annella growled, shaking off her mother's hand and dropping to her knees before the chest.

Her efforts to walk each day to build her health had helped a great deal, but she suspected actually eating again had helped too. It appeared some of her lack of strength after waking had been because she'd lain on her back for a week, with naught but drips of broth and other liquids to sustain her. Her second day of trying to walk had seen a vast improvement over the first, and she suspected it would be the same again today. She could walk down to the great hall, she told herself firmly.

"Annella, why do we not get you back into bed, child? 'Twould be—"

"Why is my husband avoiding me?" Annella interrupted her mother to ask.

Lady Annabel straightened from trying to grasp her arm to urge her up. "I am sure he is not avoiding you."

Her mother couldn't even meet her gaze as she spoke the lie. Annella turned back to the chest as she felt tears swell to fill her eyes. Mouth set, she opened the lid of the trunk and began sorting through her gowns in search of one that was wearable.

"I'm nearly done the neckline on this gown," Kenna said suddenly into the silence. "And I think Florie is almost ready to sew the hem o' the surcoat, then 'twill be ready to wear too. I think we can get it done by the sup. Can we no' Florie?" she asked hopefully.

"Aye," Florie agreed quickly.

Annella turned to look as Kenna stood and shook out the ivory-colored gown she was working on. Florie followed suit with the dark surcoat for her to see. It was the first gown, started even before her being wounded and her family arriving. They'd begun with it because it was as simple to make as it was lovely. It consisted of a plain white gown that would be worn beneath a dark blue surcoat, or any other color of surcoat really. This one was dark blue though, with flared sleeves, and the lacing crisscrossing over the front from the neckline down to nearly waist level.

The white gown had intricate embroidery along the neckline, which was what Kenna was working on. It was more than three-quarters finished and beautifully done. Kenna had always done fine embroidery. As for the surcoat, it had fine silver embroidery along the trim and around the arms just before the flaring of the sleeve started. Annella could see that Florie was just finishing with the lacing, but then the hem would be all that needed doing to make it wearable. Her gaze slid from one item to the other and she could envision how it would look when worn together. It would be lovely, she knew.

"This is a good plan," her mother said suddenly. "You girls continue working, and I'll go call for a bath to be sent up."

"A bath?" Annella asked with surprise. She'd had a bath on first awaking and hadn't done much since then but lie about in bed being bored.

"Aye, a bath," her mother said firmly. "A nice relaxing soak, and then I shall change your bandages, followed by drying your hair before the fire and dressing it nicely for you so that you look pretty in your new gown for the sup . . . and for your husband."

Annella held back any further protest at that and nodded reluctantly. It couldn't hurt to look as nice as she could for her husband. Maybe it would encourage him to stop ignoring her, she thought hopefully.

"OH," KENNA BREATHED. "YE LOOK LOVELY, SISTER."

Annella gave a little nervous laugh. "Ye've seen me in naught but me sleeping gown fer days, and that after arriving to find me on death's door and debating whether to stay or go. I'm sure me being up and about in anything would look lovely to ye at this point."

"No doubt," Kenna agreed with a grin before her expression became solemn again and she added, "But no' as lovely as ye look in this gown and surcoat. Blue has always looked more than fine on ye. Whether a fine sky blue or a dark blue like this surcoat. It brings out the color o' yer eyes, and the style is very flattering."

"And yer hair looks lovely too, m'lady," Florie told her with some wonder, and then added, "Ne'er fear, I paid attention to what yer mother was doin' and can do it meself fer ye next time."

Annella smiled faintly and touched her hair. Her mother had created several loose braids along the front of her head, loose enough that she would not suffer a headache. She'd also left several wispy tendrils of hair to frame her face before drawing the smaller braids back and down into larger loose braids on either side of her head that lay over her shoulders and down her chest. Her mother had then hurried to her room and returned with a diamond-and-sapphire-studded circlet for her to wear as well. Annella felt beautiful. In fact, she hadn't felt this beautiful since she'd left MacKay. It was a nice feeling.

"Are the men back yet?" she asked, lifting her head to glance at the women facing her. She knew from her mother's expression that they were not.

"Nay," her mother admitted, "but—" She paused and whirled to the door when a knock sounded, "Oh, that will be our new man."

Annella glanced to Kenna in question. "New man?"

"Aye." She smiled. "We're taking a Gunn soldier back to MacKay with us when we go. Father and yer husband have already arranged it between them."

Annella's eyebrows rose slightly at this news and she glanced to the door with curiosity as her mother opened it. She heard her say, "Aye. She is ready. In fact, your timing is perfect. Pray, come in—"

"Raynard," Annella gasped as she recognized the soldier entering the chamber.

"M'lady," he said politely, closing the door and following her mother across the room.

"Ye're no'—Ye—" Annella broke off and turned on her mother. "Kenna said ye're taking him to MacKay?"

"Aye. But right now he is here to carry you below. Your father, brother and husband are not yet returned, and I do not trust you can manage the stairs alone. So, let us go. We can be seated at table and enjoy a mead or cider while we wait for the men to arrive."

Annella opened her mouth to protest that Raynard wasn't going anywhere. The words never left her lips, however. Instead, a surprised gasp slid out as Raynard—responding to a gesture from her mother—scooped her off her feet and turned toward the door with her in his arms.

Annella remained silent as Raynard carried her out of the room and along the hall. Not by choice. Unfortunately, caught by surprise as she'd been, she'd instinctively reached toward him to hold on . . . with her right hand. The action had caused sharp pain in her shoulder as the muscles that had been damaged there by the arrow protested the unexpected movement. It took her until they reached the stairs for the pain to ease enough for her to speak.

"Ye do no' have to go, Raynard," she assured him solemnly as he started down the stairs with her. "I shall talk to me husband, and—"

"I want to go."

Annella frowned. His words had been solemn and sad, but firm. "Why? Is it me husband? Me? Have I been too hard on ye about yer drinking?"

A short laugh slipped from his lips. He shook his head. "Nay. Me goin' to MacKay has naught to do with anyone but me." He hesitated briefly and then said, "There are too many memories here fer me, m'lady. Wonderful memories o' me Ella and our wee bairn, Colleen," he added unhappily. "They tear at me e'ery minute o' the day and I can no' bear it."

He paused to clear his throat as if something blocked it, and then said, "I can start afresh at MacKay. Those memories will no' follow me there and torment me. Or, at least, do they follow me, they'll fade sooner away from here."

Annella swallowed back a thickness in her own throat as she took in his words and had to fight not to give in to the sudden urge to cry. She missed Ella. She missed the old Raynard too. The pair had always been smiling and laughing and had made her laugh too. Raynard had changed since the death of his wife and child, but he was still her last connection to her dear friend. It felt like she was losing Ella all over again in a way, or at least the last connection she had with her, and she wanted to weep.

"Ye'd best no' cry, m'lady," Raynard said quietly as they reached the bottom of the stairs. He started across the hall toward the high table. "Ye'll make yer eyes and nose all red and spoil the pretty picture ye make just now fer yer husband."

His words surprised a snort from Annella. "I fear me husband would no' even notice."

"Aye, he would," Raynard assured her, and then slowed as he dropped his gaze to meet hers. "Ha'e ye no' yet realized our laird loves ye?"

Annella peered at him with disbelief. "Nay."

"Aye," he assured her. "He's as besotted with ye as I was fer me Ella."

"But he's been avoiding me," she protested. "I have no' seen him in almost three days. No' since the morning after I woke."

"Aye," he agreed, and then said dryly, "And he's been rushin' about Gunn like a boar with a sore hoof e'er since."

When Annella glanced at him with surprise, he nodded solemnly. "Reminds me o' meself after Ella finished birthin' our Colleen. She was torn up pretty bad in the birthin' if ye'll recall?"

"Aye," Annella agreed, unsure why he was bringing that up.

"Afterward, ye said as how she could no' indulge in . . . wifely duties," he finished, a blush rising up his neck to his cheeks that suggested he was embarrassed to be talking about it with her. But he struggled on. "At least, no until she was healed all proper."

"Aye," she repeated, more to fill the brief silence that followed than for any other reason.

Heaving out a sigh, Raynard said, "Well, I loved me Ella, and I always wanted her somethin' fierce. E'en when I kenned I should no' trouble her. So, I began to avoid her rather than risk somethin' I kenned she also wanted but should no' indulge in. I started takin' extra shifts, and fillin' in fer some o' the men when they were under the weather, or just lazy. It gave me an excuse to avoid her and the temptation to love her."

"The night o' the fire," Annella began, but he silenced her with a look.

"Aye. I took the watch to avoid temptation again," he admitted. "But that's no' the point I'm tryin' to make, Nella."

Annella swallowed at the nickname her family had given her as a child. She'd shared it with Ella, and she and Raynard had taken to using it as well. Only ever when they were away from others. Raynard hadn't used it at all since Ella's passing though. Until now.

"The point," Raynard continued, "is that avoidin' each other, e'en fer the good o' her health, made us both miserable. She got snappy, and I was stompin' about much like the laird is now."

He stopped at the high table and looked down at her, then shifted his gaze to her shoulder, where her injury was hidden by the gown and surcoat. "He loves ye, Nella. E'ery man, woman and child here at Gunn kens it. He was beside himself when he arrived back at the keep with ye after his ma shot ye, and he did no' leave yer side fer a minute from that moment until yer fever broke. The truth is, he only left then because yer mother threatened to ha'e yer father and brother drag him away and tie him to a bed did he no' go willingly to bathe, eat and sleep."

Annella's eyebrows flew up at that, but she wasn't really surprised. Her mother could be quite stubborn and determined when it came to someone's health and care. From everything she'd heard, Graeme had gone far too long without sleep and caring for himself by the time her mother had sent him away.

"He loves ye," Raynard repeated firmly. "I'd bet me life on it. On that and the fact that he's avoidin' ye now to avoid temptation and the possibility o' unintentionally hurtin' ye while ye're still healin'."

Turning toward the table, he finally set her down, gave her a sad smile and nod, then walked away.

"He's a good man," her mother said as she settled next to her.

Annella swallowed and nodded, then blinked rapidly to dispel the fine glaze of tears coating her eyes. It was the first time she'd seen the old Raynard, her friend, since Ella's death . . . and everything he'd said had pretty much broken her heart. She'd known he blamed himself for being away from Ella and their daughter when the fire broke out. She hadn't realized why he'd taken on that late shift on the wall rather than send for another soldier though. He'd done it for Ella, and in doing so had lost both her and their child. Annella wanted to weep and scream at the same time. Sometimes life was just so damned unfair.

"He will do well at MacKay, child," her mother assured her. "We will help him grieve and heal away from the memories haunting him here."

Annella glanced at her with surprise, briefly distracted by the sight of the soldiers that had been standing guard at her door, now standing behind them. They'd followed them below. Managing not to scowl at them for it, she shifted her attention to her mother. "Ye ken about—?"

Pausing, she eyed her mother briefly, as understanding rolled over her.

"Ye heard," she said, realizing her mother had been right behind them all the way from the bedchamber and had no doubt heard every word that had passed between her and Raynard.

"I did hear," Annabel MacKay admitted. "But I also already knew about his wife and child dying in a fire. Graeme said that he was your second until shortly before he returned and took up the title as laird. That he was a fine, dependable soldier with a sharp mind, and that his wife was a friend to you?"

"Aye." Annella sighed the word. "Ella and Raynard were both dear friends to me. They aided me greatly as I tried to find me footing here."

"Then your father and I owe him a great debt, and will be even more pleased to help him," Lady Annabel reassured her.

Annella nodded and glanced along the table until she spotted where Raynard now sat at the quickly filling tables. He was solemn faced as usual, but there already seemed to be a difference about him. She suspected it was hope starting to crawl out of the scorched earth of his heart. That he was seeing a possible future where his pain might ease a bit. She hoped MacKay was good for him. She would rather see him there and even just content, than here and as miserable as he had been since the fire.

The sound of the keep doors crashing open and the shouts of men caught Annella's attention and drew her gaze toward the entrance where men were rushing in, clearing the way for the people following. Frowning, she sat up in her seat, craning her neck to try to see what was happening through the people still milling around the tables in search of seats. Although most had stopped moving now to stare as chaos exploded. Dauid and Symon were holding the doors open, while Teague and Angus rushed ahead, barking at people to stand aside, aiding those slower to move with a shove here and there. Her father came in next, moving sideways as he hovered over Graeme, who was a step behind carrying—

"Payton," her mother gasped. She had stood up the moment the chaos started and now rushed away to hurry toward her son and the son-in-law who was carrying him toward the stairs.

Annella frowned after her, then glanced to Kenna as she stood to try to get a better look at what was happening. Annella tried to look herself, but nearly everyone in the hall had stood now and she couldn't see a thing through the wall of people. Sadly, short as she was, standing would not help. "Is Payton badly hurt?"

"I am no' sure," her little sister admitted with worry as she rose up on her tiptoes in an effort to see what was happening. Giving up that pose after a moment, she dropped to stand flat on the floor again, bit her lip, and then glanced to Annella uncertainly and asked, "Can I go see? Are ye all right here by yerself?"

"Aye, aye, go," Annella said, waving her away. She then sighed as she watched her sister disappear into the crowd. She wanted to go herself to see what had happened, but knew she was better off remaining where she sat. While her strength improved daily, she didn't trust being able to maneuver herself through the jostling crowd. It did seem smarter to wait for someone to bring her news. Annella had to fight the urge to make the attempt though.

"Oh, m'lady!" Florie pushed through the people blocking her way as she rushed to reach her.

"What's happened, Florie?" Annella asked with concern, catching the maid's hand as she stopped beside her. "Is Payton all right? Mother seemed concerned about him when she rushed off."

"There was an accident during the hunt," Florie explained. "Yer brother took an arrow."

"What?" Annella gasped with alarm and stood up.

"But 'tis fine," the maid said swiftly. "I was right beside yer mother when she reached the men and checked yer brother's wound. She said he got lucky in that it did no' hit anythin' vital. Then she told yer husband to carry him up to his room and she'd fetch her medicinals and follow. She then took a moment to send yer sister to the kitchens to ha'e boiling water and ale sent up to his room, told me to come reassure ye all would be well because she kenned ye'd be worryin', and then yer mother followed the men," Florie added.

Annella let out a slow, shaky breath at this news and settled back in her seat, but her mind was racing. "How did he end up getting shot with an arrow?"

"I do no' ken," Florie admitted unhappily, her gaze moving toward the stairs.

Following her gaze, Annella spotted her husband already stepping off the top of the stairs onto the landing, Payton still in his arms, and her father hard on his heels. Her mother was only halfway up the stairs herself, but easily moving as quickly as the men. Stopping to give orders to Kenna and Florie obviously hadn't delayed her too long.

"Mayhap I should go help," Annella said fretfully.

"Nay. Lady Annabel said ye were to wait here. She said as how she was going to be sending yer da down once the arrow was removed and ye were to keep him sat at the table and calm. She said the last thing she needed was him hoverin' behind her like a mother hen while she tended yer brother."

Despite the situation, Annella's lips quirked up at the words. It would not be the first time her mother had sent her father from the room while she tended to one of his sick or injured children. Her father had never handled such occurrences well. She suspected it was the helplessness. While his wife was a skilled healer and went to work attending to what needed doing, he could only stand helplessly by and watch as she worked. For a man used to being in charge of everything, events like this must be hell for him.

Sighing, Annella glanced to her maid and suggested, "Mayhap ye should go see that some uisge beatha is brought out fer me husband and father so that 'tis waiting when they come below. And fer Teague, Angus, Symon and Dauid too!" she called out as an afterthought as the maid rushed away.

Florie waved to let her know she'd heard her, but didn't even slow her steps.

Annella turned back to face the table, and then paused and raised her eyebrows when she saw that Raynard had come to stand next to her.

"I thought I'd best check and see if ye wished to go back above stairs?" he explained. "Either to yer brother's chamber, or yer own?"

"Nay. Thank ye, Raynard. Me mother wants me here to soothe me da's nerves when she sends him down." When he nodded and started to turn away, she said, "But, ye could go above stairs yerself and see if they need help holding Payton down while they remove the arrow. I know Teague, Symon, Graeme and me da are there now to do it, but there were four men holding me down and struggling with it when they removed the arrow from me. Payton is bigger and stronger. Yer help may be not only appreciated, but needed."

"Right away," Raynard murmured and hurried off as Florie rushed back.

"One o' the buttery guards is bringing the uisge beatha," she assured her. "But Cook's wantin' to ken if she should start sending out the sup, or wait?"

Annella opened her mouth to answer, and then paused, her eyes shooting to the top of the stairs and the landing when Payton's screams exploded from above. It seemed that the removal of the arrow had commenced.

Chapter 16

"I'M SURE 'TWAS AN ACCIDENT," GRAEME said with a frown as he approached the trestle table with his father-in-law, Ross MacKay.

Lady MacKay had ordered all of the men out of Payton's bedchamber the moment she'd finished removing the arrow from her son. That order had included her own husband. Laird MacKay had tried to insist that he would stay in case she needed assistance, but she'd pointed out that their daughter Kenna was there to help her. When the MacKay had still argued for staying, the determined woman had offered him two options, that she'd leave him to tend their son alone, or he'd leave so that she could get on with it. In the end, Annella's father had given in and stomped from the room with the other men.

The man had been completely silent as they'd descended the stairs, and then as they'd reached the last step, the MacKay had suddenly announced that he thought the arrow Payton had taken had been meant for Graeme. The possibility hadn't shocked Graeme, and he seriously considered it as they crossed the great hall. Once they'd reached high table and he'd dropped into his seat beside Annella, Graeme finally shook his head. "It would no' be the first time a hunter was hit by a stray arrow in a hunt, and there were a lot o' arrows flyin' when the boar—"

"There were a lot o' arrows shot *down* at the boar, no' *up* at the men on horseback," Annella's father said firmly as he took his own seat on Annella's other side. "I'm tellin' ye, I saw the whole thing as we caught up to ye. Ye were trying to keep the boar in place with yer boar spear and struggling to keep yer arse in the saddle at the same time. Payton was just ahead o' me. He grabbed up his own boar spear and started to ride around ye, no doubt hopin' to get on the beast's other side to help ye keep it in place. He was movin' quick, and just as he got behind ye the arrow struck him. If he had no' suddenly moved behind ye, the arrow would ha'e gone through *your* back and straight through yer heart. It was no' an accident. I'd bet coin on it."

"Are ye saying that the arrow Payton took was meant fer me husband?" Annella asked her father with concern.

Graeme glanced to her and opened his mouth to assure her everything was fine, but then paused when he actually took a look at her. His wife looked absolutely beautiful. Her hair and dress were perfection . . . and even with her concern, there was color in her cheeks he hadn't seen since she'd taken her own arrow more than a week ago.

"Aye," Laird MacKay said firmly, pushing Graeme out of his silence.

"I'm sure 'twas just an accident. No one wants to hurt anyone now me mother is dead," he said firmly. Although, in truth, he was starting to doubt that himself. He didn't want Annella to worry though. She was still recovering from her own wound. He didn't want worry or anything else to hamper her healing.

"Then why do ye still ha'e men guardin' me daughter?" Laird MacKay demanded.

"Aye," Annella said, turning on him now. "Why are there still guards at the bedchamber door and following me?"

"'Tis just a precaution until me mother's maid, Agnes, is found and either buried if she is dead, or brought to justice if she yet lives," Graeme said quietly, and then reluctantly explained, "There's a verra slight concern that she may seek vengeance fer me mother's death. The pair were two peas in a pod."

"Aye, and they are similar in looks too," Dauid said as he, Teague, Symon and Angus joined them at table. "I suspect Agnes was one o' me grandfather's by-blows, a half sister to our mother. 'Twould explain how unnatural close they were."

Graeme scowled at his brother for that bit of speculation. While he'd wondered that a time or two himself, it wasn't something one brought up in company. Especially in front of his wife's family. That thought had him glancing to his wife to see her shaking her head at his brother as she spoke.

"But if Agnes were seeking vengeance for Lady Eschina's death, she would be going after you, Dauid, no' Graeme. Ye were the one who killed Eschina," she pointed out.

Dauid shrugged with unconcern. "I doubt Agnes kens I killed Mother. No doubt she believes Graeme did it."

"But if she *does* ken 'twas you, and she *is* the one who shot the arrow, mayhap she was aiming fer you," Annella pointed out. "Where were you when Payton got shot? Were ye close enough it might ha'e been meant fer ye?"

"Nay," Teague said, joining the conversation from Dauid's other side. "He was ridin' with Angus at the back o' our group, behind Symon and me."

"Aye. He was behind me. Nowhere near the laird," Angus agreed.

"See," Dauid said, his tone reassuring. "I was no' the target. In truth, I'm sure no one was and 'twas all just an accident."

"And was the merlon fallin' also an accident?" Annella's father asked grimly.

Graeme glanced at him sharply. "What about the merlon?"

"I went up to the battlements to ha'e a look at where the merlon was after ye told us all that has gone on here o' late," he informed him grimly. "There were grooves in the remainin' mortar. The merlon did no' just loosen on its own. Someone loosened it a'purpose."

Graeme's gaze shot to Annella. She didn't appear surprised at this news. But then he realized she must have noticed it herself. She had, after all, examined the spot even before he had while they were on the battlements. She'd also asked his mother if she'd been behind the large merlon falling when Eschina was trying to kill them in the clearing, so knew it hadn't loosened naturally.

"Ye mean Mother loosened the merlon in a deliberate attempt to murder me?" Dauid squawked with dismay. "What did I e'er do to her? I mean, I understand her wantin' to kill you, Graeme, ye havin' cast her from the castle and sent her to live in a tiny cottage and all, but I did nothin' to deserve her wrath." He hesitated, and then added reluctantly, "Well, at least no' until I killed her anyway. And that was purely to save you, sweet Nellie." He made calf eyes at Graeme's wife, and then glanced his way and added as an afterthought, "And o' course ye too, brother."

"Thank ye," Graeme said dryly, but having noticed Annella's reaction to the name Dauid persistently called her, he added, "But do no' call me wife *Nellie*, brother. She dislikes it."

Dauid scowled slightly, but ignored him and said, "First, Mother tried to kill me, then she went after Graeme and Annella." He shook his head. "Our mother was obviously mad."

"Yer mother said she had naught to do with the merlon falling," Annella told him.

Dauid shrugged. "She was mad. Who can say what she did or did no' do? Besides, kennin' our mother wanted us dead, Agnes could ha'e done it fer her. But then did no' tell her she had, when her efforts failed and I survived."

Graeme scowled at his brother. Even as a young lad Dauid had always had to be the center of attention, but this was a bit ridiculous. "Are ye suggestin' that Agnes loosened the mortar in the hopes that someday you and no one else would go up on the battlements, lean against it and nearly fall to yer death when the stone slid away?"

"'Tis possible," Dauid insisted. "I ha'e always enjoyed walkin' on the battlements o' a night to take in some fresh air ere bed."

"And do ye always stop to rest and lean against that specific merlon?" Graeme asked dryly.

Dauid scowled at him. "As a matter o' fact, I often do."

Graeme just shook his head and took a drink from his mug, his temper oddly cooled by the heat of the uisge beatha sliding down his throat and into his stomach.

"Whether ye agree with me or no' that the arrow was meant fer ye, and a deliberate attempt to see ye dead, ye should increase yer security," Laird MacKay told him firmly. "And no' just on me daughter. Ye should ha'e a guard too. And mayhap e'en yer brother."

"It could no' hurt," Teague pointed out when Graeme didn't respond right away.

Shoulders slumping in defeat, Graeme nodded assent and glanced to his wife. Concern claimed him when he was just in time to see her cover her mouth to hide a weary yawn.

"Ha'e ye eaten?" he asked abruptly.

Annella shook her head. "I was waiting fer you and Da. Mother wanted me to . . . sit with Father until she had finished with Payton."

Ross MacKay didn't miss her hesitation and gave a snort at the words his daughter chose. "She wanted ye to distract and keep me calm so I'd no' go back up and get in the way while she tends yer brother."

Apparently unwilling to lie and deny it, Annella merely shrugged in response, and then winced as the action obviously caused pain in her injured shoulder.

Deciding he needed to see her fed and put to bed, Graeme glanced around in search of a maid to fetch their meal. He knew Annella would not leave until her mother released her from her charge to keep her father below, but he could at least see her fed while she waited. Perhaps he could even convince her to let him take over her duty while she retired and got the rest she needed.

Unable to see anyone he could wave over and order to fetch food, Graeme decided to go to the kitchens himself. He stood, then paused and glanced down when Annella caught his hand.

"Where are ye going?" she asked with concern.

"To tell Millie to send food out fer us now we're all at table," he explained, and then couldn't resist bending to kiss her. Graeme had meant it to be a quick peck, but the moment his lips met hers, he forgot himself and ended up deepening the kiss. It wasn't until Annella moaned that he remembered where they were and who sat next to them.

Breaking their kiss, he straightened abruptly. Managing a smile for her, Graeme turned to head for the door to the kitchens. He wasn't overly surprised when his father-in-law stood to join him.

"Ye're no' a stupid lad," the older man started.

"Thank ye," Graeme said dryly.

"So why are ye bein' so pigheaded about the arrow being meant fer you?" the MacKay growled.

"I'm no'," he growled back.

"No' what?" his father-in-law demanded.

Sighing, Graeme paused and turned to face his father-in-law. "I will concede that the merlon's fallin' was no' wholly an accident. Someone did work hard at loosening the stone, as ye said. Although," he added, "I doubt whoever left those marks in the mortar intended for it to fall when it did. There was no one on the battlements but the lookouts and me brother, who damned near fell to his death when it went over."

The MacKay grunted and nodded at that.

"And, o' course, I ha'e considered that there is a chance the arrow that hit Payton was meant fer me. He cried out into me ear as he was struck, and nearly fell across me horse. So, aye, I acknowledge that there still may be a threat out there. 'Tis why I ha'e guards on Annella still, and why Teague and Symon are still stickin' close to me."

"Well then, why the devil did ye—"

"I would rather no' trouble Annella with this. She was sorely wounded and is still recoverin'."

"Ah." His father-in-law nodded with understanding. "Ye're tryin' to protect her. Keep her from bein' anxious or scared."

"Aye," Graeme admitted and was surprised to see the older man immediately start to shake his head.

"Well, stop it. She *should* be anxious and scared," the MacKay said grimly. "Someone may yet be out there tryin' to kill her. She should be lookin' out fer that. No' wanderin' around all unknowin'."

"Ne'er fear, Nellie. I'll make sure nothin' happens to ye. Ye can always count on me."

Annella tore her gaze from her father and husband and turned to see that Dauid had taken over Graeme's seat now that it was empty. Rather than respond to what he'd said, she chose to ignore it and instead asked, "How is yer side healing? Has me mother seen to it while I was unwell?"

"Yer mother did tend to it fer me," Dauid assured her. "'Tis fine. She suggested I still keep the bindings on, but only to ensure me belt does no' rub on it and chafe the scab off before 'tis fully healed."

Nodding, Annella turned to glance over her shoulder to where her father and husband had finished speaking and were continuing on to the kitchen. That meant they would soon be eating.

"I meant what I said, Nellie," Dauid insisted. "I'll always protect ye, and ye must ken 'tis true. I killed me own mother to save ye."

"Aye," Annella murmured, turning back to offer him an only slightly annoyed smile for calling her Nellie again. She did owe the man her life, so said, "I'm sorry ye had to do that, Dauid, but appreciate that ye did. Thank ye fer savin' us."

Dauid waved her thanks away. "I'd do it again in a heartbeat," he assured her. "And I want ye to ken, if the worst occurred, and something were to happen to Graeme, leaving me stuck ha'ing to run this place with ye . . . Well, ye'd no' have to kick me in the shin like Graeme. I'm no idiot. I'd be consultin' ye on everythin' and anythin' o' import. I vow it."

"I'm sure ye would," Annella said and picked up her mug to down some of the mead in it. She was just too tired and worried about everything in her life to deal with Dauid. The man was an irritating little—

"The food shall be right out!"

Swinging around, Annella managed a smile for her husband as he stopped behind them, vaguely aware that Dauid was moving back to his own seat. Her father was with him, and both men quickly sat down on either side of her again.

"Ye have to stay cautious and on yer toes, but all will be well, daughter," her father murmured, patting her hand.

"Aye, be cautious," Graeme agreed, kissing her forehead. Pulling back then, he smiled and assured her, "But we'll keep ye safe."

"We will," her father concurred.

Good Lord, Annella thought. Everyone was vowing to keep her safe. For some reason, that just made her worry.

"THANK YE."

Annella opened her eyes drowsily and glanced around to see that they'd reached the bedchamber and one of her guards had rushed ahead to open the door for her husband.

They'd long eaten and Annella had been falling asleep at the table when Kenna had finally come below to tell them that Mother had done all she could for Payton. Their father could go above stairs to sit with their mother if he'd like. Her father had stood at once, of course, but he hadn't been alone; Graeme too had risen. He'd then scooped Annella up into his arms with a murmured, "Time fer bed, love."

Annella had smiled at the words and relaxed in his arms, trusting him to get her to their room. *And, of course, he had*, she thought as Graeme carried her into their bedchamber. Glancing over his shoulder, she offered the soldier a grateful smile as he pulled the door closed behind them. She expected her husband to set her down now they were in the room, but instead, he carried her around to her usual side of the bed and bent to place her on it.

It was as Graeme made to move away that they ran into problems. When he started to straighten, her surcoat tried to follow. His plaid, it seemed, had somehow become attached to her new garment. Her husband immediately paused, still bent over her, his face inches from hers.

Wide-eyed, Annella peered up at him, then down to where they seemed to be stuck together.

"Damn, me plaid pin is caught up on yer surcoat," Graeme muttered, sliding his hands between them to try to free them both.

"Do no' damage it," Annella said anxiously. She then stiffened and sucked in a little breath when his knuckles unintentionally nudged her breast as he worked, scraping over her nipple through the cloth.

Hearing the little gasp of sound, her husband glanced to her face in question. Graeme seemed to freeze when he saw her facial expression. Annella wasn't sure what it was, but knew that the faint, accidental caress—even through the cloth of both her surcoat and gown—had affected her. She didn't have to look to know that her nipple was pebbling under the clothing, eager for more attention. She could feel the little frissons of excitement shooting away from the spot and through her body.

"Sorry," Annella breathed to try to break the tense moment. Graeme stared for several seconds and then lowered his head and started to work again to free his pin. His knuckles again brushed across her nipple almost at once, but this time he realized what had happened and paused abruptly.

"I did no' mean . . ." he growled apologetically.

"I ken," Annella assured him, reaching up with her left hand to clasp his shoulder. She told herself it was to help her maintain her position and not unintentionally tug at the material. But the truth was, she just wanted to touch him. As he worked, she turned her head until her nose brushed his neck, then inhaled deeply, taking in his scent. He smelled so good to her.

"Lass," Graeme growled in warning.

Annella didn't respond. She'd missed him these last days. She just wanted . . . Well, the truth was she wanted him, and didn't give a damn if it might hurt her wound. Turning her head again, she let her lips brush across his cheek to his mouth and slid her tongue out to run it over his lower lip.

Groaning, Graeme caught her by the neck and shifted her head slightly, then gave her the kiss she was wanting. It started soft and gentle, and then just exploded into the deeper, more demanding kind she loved.

Annella immediately wrapped her good arm around his neck and pulled, arching upward at the same time in an effort to get closer. She only knew he'd managed to untangle where they were caught together when his plaid suddenly slithered away and down his body until it was caught by his belt. She immediately reached for his belt then and, even with only one hand to work with, managed to quickly undo it. The belt hit the floor in a tangle of plaid, and Annella slid a hand under the hem of his shirt, searching for him.

Graeme froze and groaned when her hand brushed his already hard shaft. He then went a little crazy when her fingers closed around it. Growling deep in his throat, he thrust his tongue into her mouth almost violently and quickly untied her lacings. He tugged impatiently to loosen them, and as soon as they gave a bit, began to shove her surcoat off her shoulders.

Annella instinctively started to try to help shrug the garment off, but pain immediately shot out from her wound, rending an agonized cry from her.

Graeme froze at once and pulled back. "Are ye all right, love? What—?"

He didn't need to finish the question. The moment he'd made space between them, Annella had reached up with her good hand to try to further loosen the lacings of her surcoat.

Cursing, he tried to help, damned near ripping the lacings out of their eyelets to get her free. Straightening then, he peered at her, his breath a little rapid, but finally his shoulders slumped. "Ye'd best get out o' that. I'll fetch ye a sleepin' gown."

He didn't wait for a response, but immediately turned to walk around the bed to go to her chests.

Biting her lip, Annella stood and carefully removed the beautiful surcoat. She laid it over the foot of the bed and then set to work removing the white gown and her chemise as well. It was a more difficult task, just as donning them had been. She couldn't raise the arm on her injured side without causing herself pain, so had to get her left arm out first, tug that side of both gowns over her head and then let the material slide down the arm on her injured side to remove them. It was a bit of a pain when she had help, but on her own it was worse. Still, she managed it. But when she tugged the cloth off her head, she found Graeme had returned and was standing before her, a sleeping gown held tight in his hands and his eyes eating her up.

Annella let her gown and chemise drop to the floor and stepped toward him, then blinked in surprise when he suddenly tossed the sleeping gown at her and spun away.

Annella caught the gown with her left hand, and gaped at Graeme as he hurried to the fireplace. Snatching one of the torches out of the nearest holder, he quickly shoved it into the fire Florie had built to light it. "Husband? What—?"

"Get yerself to bed, wife," he said tightly as he straightened, torch in hand, and began pushing the collection of stones needed to release the secret panel. "Ye need yer sleep to heal."

"But where are ye going?" she asked with confusion.

"For a nice dip in the river," he said a little snappishly as he pulled the panel open.

"But—"

"I'll no' be long." He stepped into the passage.

"But—"

Graeme turned back to pull the panel closed, but paused when he caught sight of her still standing there completely nude. His gaze slid over her from top to bottom, then back up to rove over her once more before he spoke again.

"On second thought, I may be a while," he muttered, then slammed the panel closed.

Chapter 17

ANNELLA STOOD IN THE SILENCE THAT FELL over the room once Graeme pulled the panel shut, a little bewildered at why he'd gone from passionate to surly so quickly. But then she was distracted by the sound of his footsteps moving away. She shouldn't hear that. Frowning, she donned her sleeping gown as quickly as she could. She stepped into it and dragged it up over her hips, then stopped to slide the hand on her injured side into the sleeve. Annella then gently tugged the gown up into place on that side, before working her other arm into its sleeve as well.

Donning it like this was much easier than it would have been trying to pull it on over her head, and she was rather impressed with herself for thinking of it. Of course, Annella couldn't tie the drawstring around the collar easily with only one hand, but she did her best as she crossed to the entrance to the secret passage.

She wasn't surprised to find that the panel was cracked open. Annella had expected as much when she was able to hear Graeme moving away. In fact, she could still hear his footsteps in the distance. She glanced around briefly as she debated whether to close it properly or just leave it ajar for his return, but then paused as her gaze landed on her husband's plaid lying in a heap next to the bed where it had fallen.

Clucking her tongue in exasperation, Annella hurried back to the bed and snatched up the plaid. Graeme's belt and sheathed sword hit the floor with a jangle and thud as she straightened with the cloth in hand. She stared at them with amazement. The daft man had gone out without—not only his plaid, but—his bloody sword!

Muttering under her breath about the idiocy of men, Annella quickly hung his plaid around her neck to free the hand on her good side and then picked up belt and sword. It was a bit tricky with one hand, and she had to be careful that the sheath didn't slide off the belt as she did, but she managed it. Still muttering under her breath, she hurried to the panel. Annella slid through the opening and peered along the passage just in time to see Graeme turn and start down the stairs at the end, moving out of sight. She instinctively opened her mouth to call out after him that he'd forgotten his plaid and sword, but then stopped herself. The sound of footsteps would not be heard in the rooms along the passage, but she wasn't sure if a shout might be.

After the briefest debate with herself, she eased the panel shut and started toward the light still visible at the end of the passage from his torch.

Annella had only taken two or three steps when a crack of light appeared at the far end of the passage nearer the stairs, then spread as another panel swung open into a room. She saw a figure briefly silhouetted in the opening, and then they stepped out with their back to her and pulled their panel closed. Whoever the person was, they were not carrying a torch of their own but seemed to be counting on the remnants of Graeme's torch to light their way. However, Graeme had got far enough ahead that the light that remained was dim and growing dimmer by the moment. The person now following her husband was little more than a silhouette to her, but it was enough to know that it was definitely a male.

Biting her lip, Annella hesitated, unsure what to do. She had intended to hurry after Graeme to give him his plaid and sword, but the presence of the third person had her dithering long enough that her companion in that darkness reached the end of the passage before she had decided. As he turned into the stairwell and started down, she caught the briefest glimpse of the man in the last of the dim light that remained. Recognition had her nose wrinkling with distaste, and she turned to hurry back the way she'd come.

Graeme would survive without his plaid and sword, she decided as she slid back into their bedchamber and eased the entrance closed. Besides, he was the one who had left them there, and while he'd left in a rush, surely he'd noticed by now that he'd left them behind? If not, it was his problem. As was Dauid, who was the figure that had stepped out to follow her husband.

Annella avoided her young brother-in-law as much as possible for a reason. She was not going to risk Dauid hearing her behind him and stopping to see who it was and then insisting on accompanying her. She'd be stuck with his calling her Nellie, casting calf eyes at her, and making his ridiculous vows to take care of her, keep her safe and never make her kick him in the shin. She loved her husband, but that didn't mean she would—

Annella paused. She loved him? No, she couldn't, she assured herself. How could she? They'd hardly spoken.

Although, she thought, her mother had once told her years ago that to know a body you must watch what they do rather than listen to their words. She'd said 'twas easy to speak lies, whereas actions were more honest. Annella supposed if she were to judge her husband that way, then he had done much to make her want to wring his neck. Honestly, she'd never met anyone as frustrating as he was with his resistance to talking to her.

On the other hand, her mind argued, he'd brought her food when she'd missed the sup to tend to the blacksmith, which showed he was considerate. He'd also bought a wagonload of cloth just to please her, and with his own coin, she reminded herself as the annoyance she'd felt at the time tried to lay claim to her again. Whatever the case, Annella thought that action must prove he was generous. He'd stood and nearly got himself killed trying to protect her from Eschina with naught but a bloody stone, and that not long after she'd called Graeme an idiot and kicked him in the shin too, so he was obviously forgiving and brave. He'd also stayed by her side and tended to her for days when she was struck down by the arrow, which was surely kind and caring. He made the most amazing "pasties in the bedchamber," proving he was passionate and giving. Finally, he was presently on his way down to take a cold swim in the ice-cold waters of the river to cool his ardor rather than risk hurting her by doing what they both wanted and—

Wait, she'd called Graeme an idiot and kicked him in the shin.

Silence closed in on Annella's brain following that thought, and then was shattered when Dauid's voice sounded in her head: *"I want ye to ken, if the worst occurred, and something were to happen to Graeme, leaving me stuck ha'ing to run this place with ye . . . Well, ye'd no' have to kick me in the shin like Graeme. I'm no' idiot. I'd be consultin' ye on everythin' and anythin' o' import. I vow it."*

She'd called Graeme an idiot and kicked him in the shin in the clearing. Before they'd made love. Before Eschina had shot her, and before Dauid had appeared and killed his own mother. How could Dauid know about that? She'd never told him, and was quite sure Graeme wouldn't. How had Dauid known?

The answer seemed simple. He must have been there. But that meant he'd watched them fight, watched them make love and had watched as his mother threatened to kill them. He'd only made his presence known and intervened when the old woman had actually aimed her arrow at Annella.

Oh, now she was angry. She'd never liked Dauid, but this was just—*He'd watched them make love in the clearing!* Knowing that made her feel dirty.

Muttering under her breath about how her brother-in-law was a fustilugs and a dalcop who hid in bushes watching private moments, she dropped the plaid on the bed. Annella then set to work donning Graeme's belt with the sheathed sword without hurting herself more than she had to.

First, Annella laid the belt and sword along the edge of the bed. Then, she bent slightly to take the end with the buckle in her right hand, straightened, turned slightly and reached behind with her left hand to grab the other end off the bed. She drew that end around, slid it through the buckle, pulled it tight and tied it off. Unfortunately, she did have to move her right hand some to manage the last bit, which pulled at the muscles along that side and hurt like the devil. But she just gritted her teeth and bore it.

Breathing out with relief once she'd finished, and pleased with her own ingenuity, Annella picked up Graeme's plaid. She slung that around her neck, then pulled on the end until both sides hung down her chest in almost equal lengths. Sadly, the plaid was long enough it would drag on the ground and possibly trip her up, so she caught the ends and tucked them into the belt. Satisfied she'd done her best, she returned to the mantel and pushed the stones to open the panel. Annella was taking Graeme his plaid and sword so that he could kill his disgusting, repulsive, immoral little brother. Or at least beat him senseless.

"DID YE COME HERE TO KILL ME, OR HIDE IN THE bushes all night?" Graeme asked as he finished rinsing himself off in the river and began to wade out. His gaze slid around the clearing as he moved. Between the light of the full moon bouncing off the water and the torch he'd stuck into the dirt next to the large boulder on the left of the clearing, the area was well lit up. Still, he hadn't yet spotted where his brother was. When he reached shore with no response to his question, he said, "I ken ye're there, Dauid."

The silence continued for a moment, and then there was a rustling to his left. Looking that way, he spotted the leaves of a bush moving. It wasn't far from the boulder where he'd set the torch. A moment later, Dauid pushed his way out, stopped next to the large boulder and quickly brushed himself down. He then straightened and met his gaze. "How did ye ken I was here?"

"Because ye followed me out o' the passages," Graeme said easily.

"Ye knew I was followin' ye that far back?" he asked with dismay.

"I first heard ye behind me on the stairs. I could no' be sure it was you then, but knew I was bein' followed."

Dauid's mouth tightened, his expression becoming resentful. "Ye should ha'e stayed where ye were, being a mercenary and fightin' battles. Ye ne'er wanted to be laird. Why the devil did ye take the title? 'Twas mine! I was meant to be laird."

Graeme considered him solemnly, then said, "So this is no' about Annella?"

"O' course it's about Nellie!" he roared furiously. "I have loved her since the first time I saw her the day she arrived here. She was beautiful and sweet and good, and she was so kind to me." His expression had softened as he said that, but it twisted with bitterness now. "William did no' deserve her. He did no' e'en consummate their marriage. All he did was say she must be tired, kiss her forehead, cut his hand and rub it on the bed linens so everyone would *think* he'd done his duty."

"Ye were watchin' them from the passage," Graeme guessed. That was the only way Dauid could know what had happened in the bedchamber that night.

"Aye. I could hardly believe it when he hopped out of bed and started gatherin' the clothes we'd stripped from him during the bedding ceremony. But once he'd collected them all and began to dress, I kenned he was leavin' the room, and would ha'e to do it usin' the passages. He could no' go back down to the feast. Da would ha'e sent him right back to his wife," Dauid pointed out. "His only option was the passages. So, I hurried back to me room, slipped inside and kept the entrance cracked to watch fer him. Then I followed him, as I did you tonight."

Graeme's eyes narrowed, but he didn't speak for fear of bringing an end to his brother's words.

"Do ye ken what the bastard did? He went straight to that whore, Maisie!" Dauid told him with fury. "He had a goddess in his bed, and he abandoned her to run to that puterelle." His brother shook his head with disgust. "I could no' let that insult stand. Nellie deserves better." Sliding his dagger from his belt, he added, "She deserves better than you too."

"I'm sure she does," Graeme said mildly, and then

just as calmly added, "It was no' William's body we found outside the village near Jerusalem?"

Dauid shook his head. "Nay. I brought the ring with me and just pretended to find it in that grave."

"I'm guessin' he did no' just gi'e ye the laird's ring," Graeme said, still keeping his voice mild and unaffected.

"Nay. I killed him outside Maisie's cottage when he came out." Holding the dagger in his right hand, Dauid rested the tip of it on the pad of the forefinger of his left, and said conversationally, "I only meant to kill *him*. But Maisie heard him fall and came out to see what had happened, so I had to kill her too."

"Where are their bodies?" Graeme asked, watching him twirl the knife against his finger.

"Buried no' too far from here," Dauid admitted. "I used the passages to bring William out. I had to carry him over me shoulder from her cottage to the passage entrance at the wall. Then I stripped his surcoat off to switch fer me own, fetched a horse to her cottage, dragged Maisie up before me and rode out with her."

"Startin' the rumors that William rode off with her," Graeme said on a sigh. Annella had been crushed to think that her husband had run off with the lightskirt, and all because of Dauid.

"Aye." Dauid smiled at his own cleverness, and then shrugged. "Really, though, I needed the horse to carry William through the last o' the passages and out to where I could bury him and Maisie. It would ha'e been difficult havin' to cart them both out through the tunnels o'er me shoulder and on foot one after the other."

"Aye," Graeme agreed grimly, and then asked,

"When did ye write the message supposedly from William, claimin' he was headin' off on pilgrimage?"

"After I'd buried them and cleaned up in the river here," he responded.

"Ye would ha'e done better to bury only Maisie and try to make William's death look like an accident so his body could be found and his death known," Graeme pointed out in uncaring tones as he walked to a tree on his right, where he'd hung his shirt over a branch to keep it off the ground.

"Aye," Dauid agreed, his tone wary as he watched him.

Facing him with the shirt in hand, Graeme noted that he was grasping the knife in a throwing grip now. Acting as if he hadn't noticed, he pushed first one arm and then the other through the bottom of the shirt and into the sleeves, and then quickly tugged it on over his head. Even as he did, Graeme heard Dauid move. He reacted instinctively, stepping swiftly to his left and turning sideways to his brother. He quickly tugged his shirt down into place even as he heard the dagger strike the tree trunk behind him. Graeme cast the blade a quick glance before turning to face his brother again. He didn't comment on the dagger, but was thinking to himself that he now had a weapon at least, if only a dagger. "It must ha'e driven ye mad to have everyone thinkin' William was alive and well and just off on pilgrimage. It meant Annella was still married rather than widowed."

"She was always patient with me. I knew she loved me, but she would never show me so long as she thought herself still married." His teeth ground together. "But I did no' ken how to reveal that William was dead without revealin' I killed him." The frustration he'd suffered those six years between William's death and the search showed in his voice. "Sadly fer Da I was no' as patient back then."

Graeme stiffened. "Da?"

"Aye. Three weeks after the weddin' I went to him, insistin' we should raise a search party to find William. I said I was sure he'd no' leave on his weddin' night. We should look fer him." Dauid's mouth flattened out. "He said it was too soon fer a search party. William would show up, he said, and turned to start down the stairs. I grabbed his arm to stop him, to continue to try to convince him, but he turned to snap at me to leave off and jerked his arm away. Then he began to lecture me on stayin' away from Nellie. He said he'd noticed me trailin' her around all the time and I was to leave her alone or he'd send me away to train to become a priest. Well, there was no way I was becomin' a priest," he said with disgust. "I was to be laird, and marry Nellie. So, I pushed him off the landing."

"And he fell down the stairs, ending up paralyzed and mute." Graeme's voice was calm, but fury was writhing inside him for what his brother had done to their father.

Dauid nodded, his tone conversational as he said, "While the great hall was unusually empty when we were arguin' at the top o' the stairs, the clatter he made tumblin' down the stairs drew servants from the kitchen. I hurried quickly away before I could be seen, sure he was dead. But nay. The tough old bastard survived."

"But he did no' remember arguing with you before the fall," Graeme said, recalling Annella mentioning that his father had sustained damage that left him unable to speak, and with no memory of the time from the wedding and up to his fall.

"Aye." Dauid grimaced. "That was lucky and unlucky fer me."

When Graeme raised an eyebrow in question, he explained, "Well, Nellie was acting as laird, but she would no' send out a search party either. I think his abandonin' her on their weddin' night hurt her pride."

Graeme cocked an eyebrow at the words. William hadn't abandoned his wife, Dauid had killed him. He was pretty sure that William had gone to Maisie for help and advice as suggested and William was intending to return to his bedchamber when Dauid killed him.

"Despite me best efforts to convince her to raise a search fer him, Nellie refused. She said William would return when he was ready." He sighed unhappily at the memory. "Unfortunately, the only person who could override her decision would ha'e been Father, but I was afraid to broach the subject with him, lest he get his memories back."

"And recall ye pushed him down the stairs, causing the state he's now in," Graeme said grimly.

"Aye."

Graeme stared at his brother. He'd suspected he was trying to kill him, but he'd never imagined Dauid had killed their brother, William, and pushed their father down the stairs too. Hell, with his mother thrown in, Dauid had killed two out of the four members of his family and incapacitated a third. Graeme himself was the last member of Dauid's family standing, and he was also trying to kill him. There was something wrong with the man, and he was, frankly, growing sick of having to look at him.

"So, when ye managed to fool us into believin' we'd found William's body outside that village near Jerusalem, ye thought we'd ride back, and ye'd become laird and claim Nellie. But instead, I became laird and married her, so ye tried to drop a merlon on me." He paused briefly, but when Dauid didn't deny it, he added, "Only, as Annella says, ye're a clumsy oaf, and ye managed to somehow tumble off the battlements right behind the merlon and would ha'e fallen to yer death had ye no' managed to grab onto the ledge and hold on until the men could pull ye up."

"I'm no' a clumsy oaf!" Dauid snapped. "I'd loosened the merlon, but not as well as I'd thought. I had to put me whole weight behind it to push it off. It did no' seem to be workin', and then it suddenly gave way and I could no' stop meself from going over with it. But I did manage to grab onto the ledge with one hand as I went, then got me other up on it too. So, I'm no' a clumsy oaf. And I do no' believe Nellie would call me one."

Graeme didn't argue with him, but moved on. "And ye were the one to loose the arrow that hit Payton, though ye were aimin' fer me and he just got in the way."

"Aye." Dauid looked unhappy. "Ye got damned lucky there."

He nodded in agreement. He'd got very lucky. Payton, however? Not as lucky. Though, like his sister, he'd been hit in the upper right area below the shoulder.

Only on him the arrow had gone back to front rather than front to back as it had been for Annella. If he didn't suffer fever, Payton would heal quickly, and Graeme suspected he wouldn't dare get fever with his mother tending him.

"How did ye ken?"

Graeme glanced to him in question.

"How did ye ken I was comin' to kill ye? How did ye ken I pushed the merlon off and shot the arrow at ye? How did ye ken?"

"Afraid someone else may sort it out?" Graeme taunted and was gratified to see anxiety cross Dauid's face. He'd suffered enough of that himself when he'd realized he was being followed and had fled the bedchamber weaponless and in naught but his shirt. Every moment on the walk he'd expected to be attacked from behind. He'd spent the walk trying to mentally prepare himself as he'd listened for any telltale sound that would give away that the attack was happening. Graeme had been confident that even unarmed he could win against a man armed with a knife. He'd thought he might even be able to disarm and win in a sword fight. An arrow through the back, however, would have been another thing. The only way to combat that was to avoid getting shot. So he'd moved quickly, weaving between trees so that his back was rarely open to attack.

"How did ye ken?" Dauid repeated angrily.

"What ye should be askin' is how should ye explain to Annella that ye allowed her to be shot by our mother ere botherin' to rescue her."

"I was no' here when that happened," Dauid said quickly. "I came later."

"Aye. Ye were here. Ye were here when we were talkin', ye watched us tuppin', saw her get shot—"

"Nay!" Dauid snapped.

"I heard that nonsense ye were spewin' at her as I returned to the table tonight, Dauid," he said patiently. "About protectin' her, and how if anythin' happened to me, and ye became laird, ye'd protect her and talk to her and no' be an idiot she needs to kick in the shin or some such rot."

"So?" Dauid said defensively.

"So, how did ye ken I kicked him in the shin and called him an idiot if ye were no' there?"

Graeme stiffened at those words and jerked his head around to stare with horror as his wife stepped out of the woods behind him. Real fear claiming him for the first time since he'd realized he was being followed and was unarmed, Graeme growled, "Wife, get back to the safety o' the keep."

Annella snorted at the suggestion, and then pulled a sword from her waist as she continued forward to his side.

His sword, he realized. And was that his plaid around her neck . . . and tucked into his belt?

"'Tis very heavy, husband," Annella said pointedly.

Graeme dropped his gaze just in time to see her let the sword lower so that she was holding it pointing down, but with its tip stuck into the ground taking most of the weight. The sight nearly made him groan. That was no way to treat a fine weapon like his sword. Biting back his outrage, he took the sword from her and even managed a "Thank ye."

"Me pleasure," she murmured and then turned her

attention to Dauid again and tilted her head slightly. "Ye do no' look pleased to see me, Dauid."

Actually, Graeme thought, it was not so much that Dauid looked displeased to see her, it was more as if he was as horrified to see her as he himself was. But for different reasons, he was sure. Graeme was horrified because he wanted her away from here and safe. He was quite sure that Dauid was horrified because he couldn't kill Graeme with her there, didn't know how much she'd heard and knew, and really didn't want her to know anything. Graeme wasn't at all sure how Dauid would react to her knowing either. It made the man unpredictable and a possible danger to his wife.

Deciding to get his brother's attention back on himself, Graeme shifted his grip on his sword to be better prepared and said, "I imagine the reason ye did no' kill Mother the moment she made it apparent she intended to kill us was because ye hoped she'd do yer dirty work fer ye, and kill me. Then ye could kill her, savin' Annella and, hopefully, gaining her gratitude."

Dauid peered from him to Annella and back, then just drew his sword and rushed him. Normally, Graeme allowed combatants to come to him. It never hurt to let them use up energy while you conserved your own. But this time he was desperate to keep the other man away from his wife. So, raising his sword, he strode swiftly forward to meet his brother.

BITING HER LIP, ANNELLA MOVED SEVERAL STEPS back to keep out of the way. She then leaned against a tree trunk to rest while she waited. The walk out had been a lot for her. She'd intended to lag behind Dauid a ways to avoid his detecting her presence behind him. In the end though she'd actually fallen further behind than she'd intended from sheer exhaustion. It had been a relief when she'd heard the men's voices ahead and had been able to follow the sound. When she'd spotted Dauid's silhouette ahead, outlined by the torchlight ahead of him, she'd silently moved around the clearing to come up behind Graeme.

Now she watched and silently hoped her husband wouldn't dally about this. She had absolutely no doubt that he would win this battle. All Graeme had done for the last ten years was fight for one laird or another, whereas Dauid had not. She'd seen the younger brother practice a time or two in the courtyard with the other men, but he wasn't especially good at it. He was also clumsy as hell, tripping over his own feet and whatnot.

Truthfully, to her this seemed like Dauid taking his own life by pretty much throwing himself on Graeme's sword. But she supposed there were worse ways for him to die. Facing the king's court and justice was one that would be worse. Not so much because of the method of execution—at least, hanging did not seem that bad to her—but it was the long, drawn-out wait to be hanged that seemed like torture to her.

She watched the men hammering at each other with their great swords and could tell Dauid was already tiring, while Graeme appeared fine. She suspected her husband could have killed his brother at any time, but the fact that he was battling his own brother was making him hold back and—Oh! Nay, she thought, eyes widening as her husband drove his sword through Dauid's chest. Not holding back then, or at least not holding back anymore if he had been. The two men remained frozen for one moment, gazes meeting over the sword, and then Graeme pulled his blade out and watched his brother drop.

"Is he dead?" Annella asked as Graeme wiped the blood off his sword on his brother's tunic.

He finished what he was doing and then turned away from his brother and walked toward her.

"Aye," he finally answered, his tone somber.

"I'm sorry," she said when he paused before her.

Graeme shook his head on a slight shrug. "There was somethin' wrong with him. He was no' right in the head. He killed William, pushed me da down the stairs and killed Mother. Although that last bit was justified," he added grimly.

"Aye, it was," Annella agreed.

Sighing, he ran a hand through his hair and said, "I'm sorry, love."

"For what?" she asked uncertainly.

"It seems ye've married into a half-mad family."

Annella smiled faintly and shook her head. "Nay. You, William and yer father seem sound. As fer yer mother, I suspect she was no' mad so much as bitter and angry that ye forced her out o' the castle. She could no' play lady o' the castle and torture anyone from a cottage," Annella pointed out.

"Ye do no' think her tormentin' me father as she did was mad?" he asked dubiously.

Annella smiled faintly. "Nay. Just nasty. I suspect she saw it as paying him back for her having to marry him and so made his life as miserable as she could."

"True," Graeme agreed, and then slid his arm

around her waist and turned her toward the edge of the clearing where the path was that would take them back to the entrance to the passages.

"Ye may be right about Dauid though," she commented, as they moved slowly across the clearing. "He had to have been mad to think I'd ever want to be with him. Especially when I have a husband as good, kind, generous and strong as you."

Graeme stopped abruptly, drawing her to a halt too and then turned her so that they faced each other.

When he used a finger to tip her face up to his, Annella smiled and said, "I love you," even as he said it. They both chuckled at that, and then Graeme's face grew somber.

"I'm a lucky man to have ye to wife, Annella Gunn. And I intend to spend the rest o' me days provin' that I love ye." Lowering his head, he pressed a gentle kiss to her lips, and then whispered, "And makin' up fer the hell me family's put ye through."

"I'll hold ye to that, husband," Annella warned in a soft murmur.

Graeme grinned. "I'm no' afraid o' ye, wife. So long as ye do no' ha'e a pot in yer hand to hit me in the head with, I'll ne'er be afraid o' ye."

Annella laughed and then glanced back to where Dauid lay unmoving in the grass. The torch was nearly burned down, the circle of light it was giving off, dimming and shrinking. "Are we taking him with us?"

Graeme glanced over to his brother. "Nay. I'll send men back fer him."

"Good," Annella breathed and turned with him to start along the path back toward the entrance to the passage. They hadn't gone more than ten feet or so when Graeme suddenly stopped again. Glancing to him, she went still when he grabbed the belt around her waist. At first, she thought he meant to remove it, but he just turned it until he found his sword's sheath and slid it home. Graeme then scooped her into his arms and started walking again.

Annella didn't protest being carried. The truth was she'd used up nearly every last bit of strength she'd had walking out here to bring Graeme his sword and plaid.

"Wife?"

Annella opened eyes that had just drooped closed. "Aye?"

"Thank ye." His voice was somber, as was his expression.

"For bringing you your sword and plaid?" she asked.

"Nay. I mean, aye, thank ye fer that too, but I was referrin' to all ye've done here at Gunn these last six years. I ken it was a lot o' work, but 'tis now a fine castle any laird would be proud to call home. Ye're a fine wife."

A smile of pleasure blooming on her face, Annella murmured "Thank you," but he wasn't done.

"And I ha'e to tell ye . . ." He paused briefly, and then said, "I mentioned before to ye that when I arrived back at Gunn I noted ye were exhausted and suffocatin' under the weight o' all the responsibilities that had been piled on ye after William's leave-taking. What I did no' get to explain then, because we got distracted with other issues, is that I wanted to ease the burdens ye carried. *That* is why I did no' approach ye with any issues and problems I encountered as the new laird. It's no' that I was no' talkin' to ye because I did no' think ye could help, or understand. I avoided bringin' issues to ye, because I wanted to relieve ye o' the burdens ye'd been carryin' alone fer so long. I hoped it would give ye more time to yerself, and may-hap make ye happier to stay here."

A smile began to pull at Annella's lips and she leaned back slightly in his arms to peer at him. "Truly?"

"Truly," Graeme assured her. "Ye're beautiful, smart and did wonders with Gunn when ye ran it, love. Angus has told me how bad things were here ere ye took over. By all accounts ye're a fine leader with a sharp mind. I admire and respect ye, and I'd be happy to take advice from ye, so long as it does no' place too much weight on *yer* shoulders."

"Thank ye, husband," Annella whispered, thinking he'd just given her the finest compliment she'd ever heard. She had the best husband she could ask for. It was funny sometimes how life turned out. The truth was, while she'd been crushed by William leaving on their wedding night and all that had followed, and was sorry William's life had been cut short by Dauid, if all of that had not happened, she would not now be with Graeme. Annella could foresee a fine, bright, happy future with her husband. One she may not have had with William.

Epilogue

"They're here!" Florie squealed from the door.

Annella straightened from placing the pillows on the bed and peered around the new bedchamber, looking for anything missing or out of place. Everything looked good to her though.

"'Tis perfect," her maid assured her with a smile. "The old laird will love it."

"I hope so," Annella said, rubbing her belly soothingly.

"Is the bairn kickin' ye?" Florie asked with concern as Annella walked over to join her by the door.

"The lad's just a little active today," she told her as she turned to survey the bedchamber one last time.

"Are ye callin' me daughter a lad again?" Graeme demanded, stepping up behind them and peering over their heads at the room beyond.

"'Tis a boy," Annella assured him. "A rambunctious little lad who will grow up to look just like his big, handsome da."

"Nay. 'Tis a little baby girl with a temper and beauty to match her mother's," he countered.

They grinned at each other, neither serious about the argument. They would be happy with whatever God chose to grace them with, whether a boy or girl.

Graeme kissed her forehead and then peered past her at the room again. "Father will like it." Smiling wryly, he added, "He'll especially like that he'll no' ha'e to be carried down from above stairs if he wishes to join us fer sup, or just fer company."

"Aye," Annella murmured with a faint smile. This room had been her mother's idea. Annabel MacKay had been quite fascinated by Gaufrid Gunn's issues with talking since his fall. While she'd agreed there was nothing to do about his being paralyzed, she had thought they might help him regain his speech. Her mother had begun to work with him while they were visiting, a visit that had lasted longer than intended while they'd waited for Payton to heal from his wound. Lady Annabel had made Annella's father-in-law perform strange exercises in the effort, such as blowing a horn, wagging his tongue up and down and biting into an apple or pear over and over again.

Annella had watched her mother working with him one day and hadn't understood why she was having him do these things. She certainly hadn't considered that they might do anything to help him. But by the time her parents were ready to leave, Gaufrid was able to make sounds that weren't quite speech, but close to it. That had been encouraging, and Annella knew her husband and his father had been grateful when her mother had invited Gaufrid to travel to

MacKay with them for a couple of months to continue working with her on his speech. The old man had been happy to go.

It was as they were breaking their fast on the morning they were leaving that her mother had leaned toward Annella and said, "Do you not think that corner there would make a fine bedchamber?"

Annella had peered at the spot, and then looked at her with bewilderment. "A bedchamber? In the great hall?"

"Aye." Her mother had smiled. "Think on it. 'Twould only take two walls and a ceiling to create a room in that corner. Then Gaufrid would not have to be carried below if he wished to join the table for sup or play chess by the fire. He would feel less of a burden and perhaps leave his room more, which would surely make his life so much better."

Annella had glanced at the corner and imagined a room built there, with a ceiling, a door, a bed . . .

"And perhaps you could have a special hand cart made," her mother suggested.

"A hand cart?" she'd asked uncertainly.

"Aye. One with a high back, lower sides and a short bottom, so that Gaufrid can sit in it and have his back supported by the high back of the wagon. Then a servant could simply lift him into the hand cart and wheel him out of his room to wherever he wished to be rather than have to carry him around like a child."

"Oh," Annella had breathed, imagining it.

"You could even put pillows and such in it to make him more comfortable," she'd suggested.

Annella had approached Graeme about her mother's ideas that night. He'd thought they were brilliant, and was sure they would help his father. He'd set men on both tasks in the months since their parents had left for MacKay. But Gaufrid's two or three months over the end of summer and the beginning of fall had been prolonged through the winter. Now it was almost the middle of spring and he was finally returning to them, accompanied by not just a company of soldiers for protection, but her mother and sister, who were coming for a visit. According to the message from her mother that had arrived weeks ahead of them, Gaufrid was talking again. She warned that his speech was slow and a little awkward yet, but would improve with time.

"I came to tell ye they were passin' o'er the drawbridge and we should go wait on the front steps fer them," Graeme said now.

"Aye." Annella smiled and allowed him to take her arm to escort her out into the great hall. She couldn't wait to see Gaufrid talking again. She knew the man had been miserable since his accident. Which hadn't been an accident at all, she recalled grimly. It was a secret she and Graeme had thought to keep from his father. Unfortunately, they'd had to tell him that Dauid was dead, and that he'd been killed in battle after he'd attacked Graeme. For some reason, that had released the memories trapped in Gaufrid's head, and he'd recalled Dauid pushing him down the stairs. Memories of the wedding and the weeks after that had followed quite quickly.

"Love? Is all well?"

Annella had stopped walking and now stood

completely still with her head bowed. Shock had brought her to a pause when she'd felt liquid rushing down her legs. Taking a breath, she waited another moment for the contraction that had preceded her water breaking to stop, and then said, "The bairn's decided he wants to meet his grandfather."

"Well, and sure enough he will now the old laird's back," Florie said with a faint smile. "He'll be here when ye birth the bairn."

"Aye. Well, he's arrived right in time then," Annella said dryly. "When I said he's decided to meet his grandfather, I meant he's decided to meet him *now*."

"What?" Florie and Graeme squawked together.

"Me water just broke," Annella said patiently.

Graeme and Florie immediately looked down, as did Annella. There was nothing to see until she noticed the dark line growing at the hem of her skirts. The material was soaking up the water puddling under her.

"Oh Lord!" Florie jerked up her skirt in an attempt to keep it from getting any wetter, and then Graeme scooped her up and carried her into his father's new chamber.

"What are ye doing?" Annella asked with dismay.

"Puttin' ye in a bed," he said as if that should be obvious. "Ye're havin' our bairn."

"Aye, but no' yer da's bed," Annella protested.

"Actually, I think that is perfect. That way he can meet your child ere you and the bairn are both moved above stairs," Annabel MacKay said lightly, bustling into the room. Glancing over her shoulder, she added,

"Inan, wheel Gaufrid over to the table. He shall have to wait to see his room properly."

"Nay!" Annella squawked, climbing off the bed the moment her husband set her down. "He should see it now. We have been waitin' forever to show him. Hello, father Gunn," she called happily.

Determined to greet him properly, Annella started forward, only to stop after one step when the next contraction hit. Gasping, she whirled away and bent to brace herself on the bed, hands clenching on the furs there as she waited out the pain. She could feel the concern pouring off of Graeme as he immediately stepped to her side. Grasping her arm with one hand, he began to rub her back with the other.

"How long ago was the last pain?" her mother asked, rushing across the room to join them.

It was Graeme who answered. "As long ago as it took me to carry her in here."

"Aye. No' long at all," Florie added with worry.

Lady MacKay turned to Annella again. "How long have you been having the pains?"

"Since last night," she gasped.

"What?" Graeme squawked by her ear. "Why did ye no' wake me?"

"Because there was no use the two o' us being awakened every hour, then half hour, when the pains came," she growled with irritation. "They were far enough apart, I kenned it would be at least morning ere the bairn came."

"'Tis nearly the sup, no' morning," Graeme pointed out, sounding more worried.

"Nay! Really?" Annella snapped sarcastically.

"Would you like to get up on the bed now, dear?" her mother asked.

Annella glanced around in time to see her mother patting Graeme's arm soothingly. Presumably to make up for her being short with her husband. For some reason that annoyed her.

"Nella?" her mother prodded. "Shall we get up on the bed now?"

"Nay," Annella growled. "*We* shall not. I like it right here."

"Should ye no'—What are ye doin'?" Graeme interrupted himself to ask, his voice about as shocked as Annella had ever heard it.

"I am squatting, husband," she snarled. "Me body wants to squat."

"Well, yer body can squat on the bed," Graeme insisted testily, trying to urge her upright. "Ye're no' relievin' yerself in the woods, ye're having our bairn, and ye'll drop her on the rush mats do ye no'—Lady Annabel! What the devil are ye doin'?"

Annella glanced around at that question to see her mother on her knees beside her, trying to look under her skirts.

"I am trying to see how far along she is," Lady MacKay explained.

"Do ye no' think it would be better did we get her abed first?" he demanded, beginning to sound more than a little stressed. Turning to Annella he said, "Ye really would feel better abed, wife. Just let me—"

"Touch me and I shall twist yer ballocks and squeeze verra hard, husband," Annella snarled.

"She does not mean that, Graeme. She is simply in a lot of pain at the moment."

Her mother's voice sounded odd and Annella gave up glowering at her husband to look around for her. The woman had given up kneeling beside her in favor of lying on her back and shimmying between her legs under her gown to get the view needed to assess the situation. Fortunately, while Annella was trying to squat quite fully, her husband's hold on her arm was keeping her up far enough that there was room for her mother to slip beneath her.

"Oh dear" was her assessment.

"What does 'oh dear' mean?" Graeme asked with alarm as Lady Annabel slid back out from under Annella and got to her feet.

"Oh, 'tis nothing to worry about," Lady Annabel said, managing to sound anxious, excited and soothing all at once as she grabbed a fur off the bed and set it on the floor just behind Annella. "'Tis fine. You should probably go fetch some uisge beatha to toast the baby's arrival with yer father. And quickly."

"I am no' going anywhere until I get me wife in the bed," he growled with frustration.

When he reached for her then, Annella barked, "Touch me and I'll hurt ye, husband."

"She does no' mean that," Lady Annabel assured him.

"Aye, she does," Graeme said dryly, and then shook his head and actually smiled at Annella as he knelt next to her and added, "And 'tis one o' the reasons that I love her."

Annella's glare died at that, her expression briefly softening.

Graeme started to lean in to kiss her then, but that's when her next contraction decided to strike. Distracted as she'd briefly been, Annella was caught by surprise and couldn't stop the scream the shock and pain brought from deep in her lungs. Her husband jerked back at once, fear and horror fighting on his face, but she didn't care.

"Pick her up and set her on the fur, Graeme, so I have room to work and the bairn has a soft landing if I do no' catch him."

"Catch her?" Graeme snapped with outrage. "'Tis our bairn, no' a ball. She needs to be abed!"

"Move her! Now!" Lady Annabel roared.

If it weren't for the fact that she was in a great deal of pain, Annella would have laughed at her husband's shock and the speed with which he obeyed the order. It was always amusing to see men brought to heel by her petite mother.

Graeme not only gave up trying to get her on the bed and moved her backward onto the fur, he also set her down with her side to the bed so that her mother had room to kneel in front of her. He then squatted behind Annella, his knees on either side of her. Annella grabbed at them to maintain her balance as she felt another contraction coming on.

"Thank you, son," her mother said almost apologetically as she knelt before Annella. "Now, if you will just help by holding her skirts up for me—Oh my," her mother breathed when Graeme did as requested, allowing her to take in the situation.

"Oh my what?" Graeme asked with concern.

"Nothing. All is well," she assured him soothingly,

and then told Annella, "I want you to push with the next contraction, dear. As hard as you can, I think—"

Annella wasn't sure if her mother said anything else or not. If she did, Annella couldn't hear it over her own scream as the next contraction hit. The strength and pain level of the contractions had grown with every passing hour, and the last had been bad, but none could compare to this one. This time the pain was excruciating. It felt like she was being torn apart and seemed to go on forever. Despite that, or perhaps because of it, Annella bore down and pushed as hard as she could. Just when she began to feel she couldn't bear it another moment, the pain abruptly ended, or at least was reduced to a mild throbbing in comparison. She only understood the sudden reduction in pain was because she'd managed to push out the bairn when her mother cried happily, "'Tis a boy!"

Breathing out with relief, Annella sagged back against her husband.

"'Tis a boy," Graeme said with wonder as her mother finished cutting the cord connecting the bairn to her and held him up for them to see.

Annella opened eyes she hadn't realized she'd let close and smiled faintly at the angry, red squalling infant her mother was even now wrapping clean linen around. Feeling oddly elated . . . and exhausted all at the same time, she said lightly, "I told ye it would be."

"Aye, ye did," he agreed. "Ye were right."

"I'm always right, husband, and ye would do well to remember that," she teased.

"As if ye'd let me," Graeme said with amusement, and then his expression turning solemn, he murmured,

"Thank ye for me son, and thank ye fer bein' me wife. I love ye, Annella."

"I love you too," she assured him just as solemnly.

He leaned down to kiss her gently, and then pulled back to whisper, "Now can I put ye on the bed?"

Annella raised her eyebrows. "And then what? Shall I sleep down here with yer da from now on, or were ye plannin' on all three o' us sharing his new bed?"

"Take her up to your room, Graeme," her mother suggested with amusement before he could respond. "I shall clean up my new grandbaby and take him out for your father to see, then follow you up to tend to Annella."

Relaxing, Graeme nodded, then shifted out from behind Annella, stood and scooped her up into his arms. Carrying her toward the door, he commented, "Have I mentioned ye're a sassy, bossy wench?"

"Aye, and ye love it," she answered around a yawn.

"Aye. I do," Graeme agreed as they reached the door. Pausing then, he kissed her gently on the forehead and said, "'Tis why I was hopin' fer a little girl just as beautiful and bossy as her mother. We shall jest ha'e to hope that next time the bairn is—"

"Next time!" Annella squawked with horror. "If ye think I'm lettin' ye anywhere near me after what I jest went through, ye ha'e another think comin', husband."

"She does not mean that, Graeme," Lady Annabel called out lightly.

"Aye, I do," Annella insisted on a growl.

"Nay, ye do no'," Graeme said solemnly and kissed her softly on the lips. It was gentle and so full of love that Annella felt her heart flutter.

When he ended the kiss and lifted his head, she smiled, and marveled at how her life had changed. Graeme's arrival had, for Annella, changed Gunn from a lonely, miserable prison to a happy home full of joy and hope for the future. Thank God her highlander had returned.

EXPLORE MORE TITLES IN
THE HIGHLAND BRIDES SERIES

DISCOVER THE ARGENEAU SERIES
BY LYNSAY SANDS

A Quick Bite

Love Bites

Single White Vampire

Tall, Dark & Hungry

A Bite to Remember

Bite Me If You Can

The Accidental Vampire

Vampires Are Forever

Vampire, Interrupted

The Rogue Hunter

The Immortal Hunter

The Renegade Hunter

Born to Bite

Hungry for You

The Reluctant Vampire

Under a Vampire Moon

The Lady Is a Vamp

Immortal Ever After

One Lucky Vampire

Vampire Most Wanted

The Immortal Who Loved Me

About a Vampire

Runaway Vampire

Immortal Nights

Immortal Unchained

Immortally Yours

Twice Bitten

Vampires Like It Hot

The Trouble with Vampires

Immortal Born

Immortal Angel

Meant to Be Immortal

Mile High with a Vampire

Immortal Rising

After the Bite

Bad Luck Vampire